Andrew Hammond began his working life in a cheap suit, sitting in the bowels of York Magistrates' Court, interviewing repeat offenders who always said they 'didn't do it'. After three years in the legal profession, Andrew re-trained as an English teacher. CRYPT is Andrew's first fictional series but he has written over forty English textbooks for schools and he can spot the difference between an adjectival and adverbial phrase at fifty paces (if only someone would ask him to). He now splits his time between writing and educational consultancy, and lives in Suffolk with his wife Andie and their four angels – Henry, Eleanor, Edward and Katherine – none of whom are old enough yet to read 'Daddy's scary books'. But one day . . .

CRYPT
COVERT RESPONSE YOUTH PARANORMAL TEAM

THE GALLOWS CURSE

ANDREW HAMMOND

headline

First published in 2011 by
HEADLINE PUBLISHING GROUP

9

Cataloguing in Publication Data is available from the British Library

ISBN 0 978 7553 7821 0

Typeset in Goudy Old Style by Avon DataSet Ltd,
Bidford-on-Avon, Warwickshire

Printed and bound in Great Britain by
Clays Ltd, St Ives plc

HEADLINE PUBLISHING GROUP
An Hachette UK Company
338 Euston Road
London NW1 3BH

www.headline.co.uk
www.hachette.co.uk

For the Muffintops of 8S (you know who you are)
and for Andie – my rock.

GHOSTS ARE THE STUFF OF FICTION, RIGHT?

WRONG.

THE GOVERNMENT JUST DOESN'T WANT YOU TO KNOW ABOUT THEM...

THIS IS THE TOP SECRET CLASSIFIED HISTORY OF CRYPT.

In 2007, American billionaire and IT guru Jason Goode bought himself an English castle; it's what every rich man needs. He commissioned a new skyscraper too, to be built right in the heart of London. A futuristic cone-shaped building with thirty-eight floors and a revolving penthouse, it would be the new headquarters for his global enterprise, Goode Technology PLC.

He and his wife Tara were looking forward to their first Christmas at the castle with Jamie, their thirteen-year-old son, home from boarding school. It all seemed so perfect.

Six weeks later Goode returned home one night to find a horror scene: the castle lit up with blue flashing lights, police everywhere.

His wife was dead. His staff were out for the night; his son was the only suspect.

Jamie was taken into custody and eventually found guilty of killing his mother. They said he'd pushed her from the battlements during a heated argument. He was sent away to a young offenders' institution.

But throughout the trial, his claims about what really happened never changed:

'The ghosts did it, Dad.'

His father had to believe him. From that day on, Jason Goode vowed to prove the existence of ghosts and clear his son's name.

They said Goode was mad – driven to obsession by the grief of losing his family. Plans for the new London headquarters were put on hold. He lost interest in work. People said he'd given up on life.

But one man stood by him – lifelong friend and eminent scientist Professor Giles Bonati. Friends since their student days at Cambridge, Bonati knew Goode hadn't lost his mind. They began researching the science of disembodied spirits.

Not only did they prove scientifically how ghosts can access our world, they uncovered a startling truth too: that some teenagers have stronger connections to ghosts than any other age group. They have high extrasensory perception (ESP), which means they can see ghosts where others can't.

So was Jamie telling the truth after all?

Goode and Bonati set up the Paranormal Investigation Team (PIT), based in the cellars of Goode's private castle. It was a small experimental project at first, but it grew. Requests came in for its teenage agents to visit hauntings across the region.

But fear of the paranormal was building thanks to the PIT. Hoax calls were coming in whenever people heard a creak in the attic. Amateur ghost hunters began to follow the teenagers and interfere with their work. But it didn't stop there. Goode and Bonati quickly discovered a further truth – something which even they had not bargained for. As more and more people pitched up at hauntings to watch the agents in action, so the ghosts became stronger. It seemed as though the greater the panic and hysteria at a scene, the more powerful the paranormal activity became. There was no denying it: the ghosts fed off human fear.

So where would this lead?

To prevent the situation from escalating out of control, Goode was ordered to disband the PIT and stop frightening people. Reporters tried to expose the team as a fraud. People could rest easy in their beds – there was no such thing as ghosts. Goode had to face the awful truth that his son was a liar – and a murderer. The alternative was too frightening for the public to accept.

So that's what they were told.

But in private, things were quite different. Goode had been approached by MI5.

The British security services had been secretly investigating paranormal incidents for years. When crimes are reported without any rational human explanation, MI5 must explore all other possibilities, including the paranormal. But funding was tight and results were limited.

Maybe teenagers were the answer.

So they proposed a deal. Goode could continue his paranormal investigations, but to prevent more hoax calls and widespread panic, he had to do so under the cover and protection of MI5.

They suggested the perfect venue for this joint operation – Goode's London headquarters. The skyscraper was not yet finished. There was still time. A subterranean suite of hi-tech laboratories could be built in the foundations. A new, covert organisation could be established – bigger and better than before, a joint enterprise between Goode Technology and the British security services.

But before Jason Goode agreed to the plan, he made a special request of his own. He would finish the building, convert the underground car park into a suite of laboratories and living accommodation, allow MI5 to control operations, help them recruit the best teenage investigators they could find and finance any future plans they had for the organisation – all in return for one thing.

He wanted his son back.

After weeks of intense secret negotiations, the security services finally managed to broker the deal: provided he was monitored closely by the Covert Policing Command at Scotland Yard, and, for his own protection, was given a new identity, Jamie could be released. For now.

The deal was sealed. The Goode Tower was finished – a landmark piece of modern architecture, soaring above the Thames. And buried discreetly beneath its thirty-eight floors was the Covert Response Youth Paranormal Team.

The CRYPT. Its motto: *EXSPECTA INEXSPECTATA*. Expect the unexpected.

Jamie Goode was released from custody and is now the CRYPT's most respected agent.

And his new identity?

Meet Jud Lester, paranormal investigator.

CHAPTER 1

MONDAY: 5.35 P.M.

CENTRAL LINE

In the darkness of the underground, among the bats and the spiders and the rats, another train thundered down a neighbouring tunnel.

People read their newspapers. Some tried the crossword. Two kids argued over who was having the last Haribo. A woman shuffled in her seat and dropped her folder of papers. They splayed out over the floor. Letters from clients. Telephone messages. Conference notes. Doodles on a pad. A day's work.

A speaker in the corner broke the silence. 'Ladies and gentlemen. The delay we're experiencing is due to a broken-down train up ahead at Holborn station. We apologise for any inconvenience caused.'

Passengers kept on reading. Delays like this were common on the Central Line.

The lights of the carriage flickered again. There was an electrical kind of buzz, more flickering, causing shadows to chase around the carriage, and then . . .

Darkness.

The woman on the floor kept scrabbling around, trying to collect up her work. Blindly her hands swept over the dirty floor, fishing for bits of paper. She was grabbing anything now and stuffing it into her briefcase. She felt nervous; she hated being trapped in between stations. And now in darkness too.

'It's so annoying!' someone said.

'We'll be off soon, don't worry about it,' said another.

Then silence.

Another announcement. 'Ladies and gentlemen. I'm sorry to have to inform you that we're experiencing an electrical fault. I'm sure we'll be able to fix it and will be on our way again soon. In the meantime, let me—'

The speaker clicked, buzzed and then fell silent.

Nothing. No light. No sound. No help.

People started chatting to one another quietly, trying to ease the tension.

'Always happens on the way home, doesn't it? Never on the way to work!'

'Typical!'

'You're right. We'll be off soon, though.'

'Yeah, don't worry about it, luv.'

'I never said I was worried. Just bored.'

Anonymous conversations in the dark.

One solitary emergency light above an exit door flickered on. Like a candle flame it brought a momentary comfort to the people around it.

One by one, other emergency lights blinked wearily into action, offering just enough brightness to read by. The conversations became unnecessary and passengers settled back into their private worlds of books and papers.

And then it happened.

One person saw it first.

She screamed – a piercing, chilling scream that ran right through everyone like a burst of cold air. People leapt up.

'What?'

'What's wrong?'

Confusion began to sweep through the packed train.

'What the hell was that for?'

'THERE!' she yelled. 'Out there! At the window! Look!'

Everyone turned their heads in the direction she was pointing.

There was a face.

In the tunnel outside, appearing through the shadows.

A lank, pale face, its cheek pressed up against the glass. Distorted and dribbling. Rings of swirling gases circled its head.

Screams spread through the carriage.

The hideous face peeled itself off the window, leaving a foul trail of cloudy dribble on the glass, like green and yellow algae. The glowing plasma that encircled it intensified as it contorted and puckered up to break into a gruesome smile. The sickly grin exposed brown, rotting teeth. Its cracked and bloodied lips widened. And kept widening. Soon they revealed a gaping hole in the centre of the face, towards which the dark, lifeless eyes now seemed to sink downwards. Features blending like smoky images.

On and on the mouth widened, jaw dislocating, eye sockets sinking yet further down into the black. Then, when the mouth could extend no more, and the void seemed vast, it spewed out a rank mixture of maggots and cockroaches. They hurtled at the window, some sticking to the mucousy dribble, others rattling against the glass like hailstones and scurrying in every direction, intent on finding a way in.

The rattling rose to a deafening din and the window finally gave way. Lethal shards of jagged glass launched in every direction. Flesh was pierced. Blood was pouring. The plague of beetles and lava began to gnaw away at passengers' faces. Like piranhas they worked, as their startled victims struggled frantically to brush them off, screaming and crying.

The thing at the window was now inside.

It scoured the seats. A mottled and congealed face. A mouth

now shrivelled, black and pursed. A body engulfed in a dark, swirling cloak that crawled with beetles. A dirty white shirt, open at the neck, revealing skin that peeled from the bone, like an old carcass for dogs. And a strange gaseous plasma that encircled it, merging the edges of its body with the rank air around it.

Suddenly, out of the black folds of dirty cloth, a grey, skeletal hand appeared. The fingers seemed dislocated and worn. Stippled bones, stripped of flesh. They clutched something tightly.

Polished wood. Metal fixings. Shiny barrel.

It couldn't be.

It was.

A seventeenth-century duelling pistol.

There was a deafening crack, which echoed around the carriage. The thunderous shot had been released in the direction of a businessman, cowering in the corner. He'd taken the bullet clean through the neck. His suited body slumped to the floor, spurting blood across the faces of the petrified onlookers. The ghostly apparition let forth a blood-curdling laugh of victory and reached down to the body. With a gruesome snap it broke the man's ring finger and pulled it clean from its socket. Right off. The ghost pocketed the bloodied finger, with its shiny gold wedding ring still attached. Turning to face the terrified passengers, now frozen with fear, it raised a hand and began lashing out.

There was an agonising shriek. The ghost had gouged out the eyes of a woman watching, mouth open, her body stiff with fear. She grabbed her face, collapsed to the floor and passed out. Fodder for the beetles.

Pandemonium broke loose. Deafening screams, frantic pushing and shoving. Panic blew through the train like icy wind in a tunnel.

'Get it OUT! Get it away from me!'

'Somebody! For God's sake.'

'Help me!'

Passengers clambered over one another, desperate to get to the doors. Some tried to prise them open with their fingers, their skin pressed white against hard metal rims – but they stayed shut. No way out. The ghost trudged on, deeper into the carriage of hell, firing off shots and spewing foul insects over everyone.

As it swept past, those who survived could see through their tears that it was, or had once been, a man, with a ring of rotting red flesh around his neck – a souvenir from the gallows, where the hangman's noose had wrung him dead.

Desperation grew further as people tried to escape through the broken window, or slammed their shoes frantically against other windows. In the rush of bodies, all anxious to get through the connecting doors into the next carriage, a woman fell to the floor and was trampled over. She pleaded for people to stop crushing her, but soon her voice fell silent. Her begging ceased. She lay squashed in the aisle, her neck broken.

Another loud crack from the pistol. The ghost forced its way through the mass of terrified passengers at the door and entered the next carriage along. More yells for mercy. He grabbed the first woman he found. He lifted her up and pressed her face close to his. She gagged on the smell of maggot-infested flesh. His stagnant breath gushed from the black hole in his face. She retched again. She stared into the black, eyeless sockets in front of her. Into nothingness.

He parted his lips, grinned, and through the sickly dribble, in a harsh, guttural voice, he whispered to her:

'Good day, madam. Your money or your life.'

CHAPTER 2

MONDAY: 5.53 P.M.

BATTERSEA HELIPORT

The rotary blades had already begun spinning and Jud's black, tousled hair rasped across his face. Dressed in the usual black leathers – ready for his bike ride across the city – he would be hot and sweaty in the helicopter, but at least it was only a short flight to London, and after spending a miserable summer break at home in Buckinghamshire, he just wanted to get up into the air and away.

Things were so different without Mum.

And after all they'd been through, he couldn't wait to get back.

The helicopter rose steadily and soon the castle grounds were shrinking beneath him.

He'd been living in England since he could remember. Home was once New York, but his father's work had always taken him around the world. His wife, too. Jud had been something of a surprise; his parents had not scheduled a child into their busy lifestyles, and so as soon as he'd been old enough, he was sent from America to a boarding school in England, and a more settled way of life. Jason, his father, had been schooled in England as a boy and he'd always said it had made a man of him. Besides, it was convenient – with Jud out of the way, his parents could continue their globetrotting.

But some years later, prompted by frequent trips to the UK on business, his father had decided they should spend more time together as a family, just the three of them. 'Time to get to know you again,' he'd once said to Jud. So he'd bought the castle estate in the Chiltern Hills. The plan was to spend school holidays together in England, instead of Jud having to travel back and forth to New York every time term finished. His parents would move to England. Even collect him from school, like the other parents did. It had all seemed so idyllic.

But that was nearly three years ago.

How times change.

And it was hard to separate his feelings for his mother from the nightmare that ensued after she died. Like an open sore, the memory still pained him.

And no one, not even Jud himself, could ever have imagined the cruel circumstances that were to follow her death.

Everything had changed unrecognisably. Jamie Goode was gone – even his name had changed – but slowly, secretly, a new life was emerging for Jud. And as the London skyline gradually hovered into view, he felt a new surge of energy and a sense of freedom.

His father had been right. Things *would* get better, in time.

Soon the black Squirrel HT1 was slowly descending like a demonic dragonfly on to the new heliport at Battersea Park. It had been open for just a few weeks, and the wealthy neighbours in their penthouse flats gazed out of their windows and cursed yet another intrusion into their luxury lives. The great tower blocks of shiny steel and tinted glass rose up either side of the Thames like some futuristic city, the chimneys of the old power station at Battersea the only reminder of a grimier industrial age, when local residents worked hard for their money.

Jud gazed out across the skyline. Where and what would his

next assignment be? His last investigation – a fatal haunting in Shoreditch – had been closed weeks ago, and he knew he'd be due another case soon. Somewhere down there, down among the clockwork commuters, with their everyday deadlines and ordinary lives, something extraordinary was bound to happen again sooner or later. The call would come in from MI5. And when it did, it would be Jud Lester's turn to be dispatched.

His Honda Fireblade waited expectantly for him at the side of the landing pad. He'd had the motorbike from the beginning and it had now become almost a part of him. He knew its potential and was brave enough to reach it. Together they were unstoppable.

The Squirrel landed gently and the blades soon stopped. Jud thanked Gary, his usual pilot and now firm friend, and leapt out on to the rainy ground.

'Good to see you again, sir,' said the man in the hi-vis coat outside. 'Pleasant trip?'

'A blast,' said Jud, sarcastically.

'Your motorcycle is ready and waiting, sir. And here is your helmet. See you next time.'

With a passing nod, Jud threw his rucksack on to his shoulders, squeezed his head into the dark helmet and straddled the bike. Next minute he was gone. Black bike, black leathers, black helmet – he looked like a passing shadow as he wove in and out of the London traffic, bound for the CRYPT. The headquarters of Goode Technology PLC were a fifteen-minute ride away and Professor Bonati didn't like to be kept waiting.

Jud quickly shifted through the gears and opened up the throttle. The Fireblade let rip. He was back in the saddle at last.

CHAPTER 3

MONDAY: 6.02 P.M.

CENTRAL LINE

The jaws began to widen again and the rattling sound started from deep within the ghost's hollow chest.

The second carriage was in darkness. The emergency lighting had failed to come on in here, but the passengers should have been grateful, as the sight now hidden from view was abhorrent.

On hearing the woman's screams, a brave – or stupid – young student stood up to defend her. He grabbed the arm of the spectre, just as the second plague of beetles rose forth. He pulled as hard as he could.

The sharp, bony limb was ripped from the phantom's body with such force, it broke off and plunged straight into the face of the young man. Like a javelin. Right through his mouth. And out the other side.

Suddenly the emergency lights flickered again and the sight was now illuminated like a scene from a horror movie. Onlookers stared, open-mouthed.

Armies of cockroaches hurtled out of the ghost's gaping shoulder socket towards the bloodied student. Like dark globules of blood they poured out. The other end of the arm, its fine bony fingers having pierced right through the man's face, had lodged itself in the headrest behind him, and he dangled limply like a coat on a peg, terror fixed in his eyes. Blood seeped down the detached phantom arm protruding from his mouth. A continuous line of insects frantically marched up it like red ants on a branch. People nearby curled up in their seats, hid their faces and whimpered.

There was nothing anyone could do except hide. And pray.

Hungry for revenge, the ghost threw the woman down on to the floor like a rag doll, and swept towards the dead student. With a sickly wrench, he pulled his lost limb back out of the seat, out of the bloodstained lips of the young man, whose lifeless body slumped over the terrified people at his feet. The spectre reattached his own arm like some child's action figure. A twist, a sickening click, and it was back in place.

He wasn't finished yet.

With a strength that seemed to come from way down inside his skeletal body, he picked up the student by the ankles and dangled him like a pig on a stick. He swung him towards the terrified passengers and croaked:

'Who'll give me a price for this piece of meat?'

Screams were all he heard.

'No?' his voice rasped. 'Oh come on, ladies and gentlemen! What am I bid? It's a fine piece of venison. From his lordship's estate. Shot it meself.'

No one could say anything. Fear choked their throats. The blood-soaked body of the poor man swung up and down the aisle as the ghostly highwayman continued his grisly auction.

'How about you, sir?' he hissed at a man in pinstripes, now pleading for mercy.

'You look like a wealthy gent. What say you? Five guineas? Will you give me five, sir?'

The highwayman was dribbling. A sticky trail of maggots fell from his cracked lips. The plasma that enveloped his frame hung in the air like bloodstained fog.

The man in the suit just stared. And cried like a baby.

'No, sir? Very well then.' With his other hand, the ghost lashed out at the pinstriped man. His bony hand forced its way into his mouth. There was a muffled cry, passengers nearby vomited into laps, and the hand returned out of the mouth seconds later with the man's tongue. Watching his victim's wide eyed attempts to scream a wordless cry, the highwayman began to chomp greedily on the piece of bloodied flesh in his hand.

Food at last.

'Not bad. Bit tough. Needs a good claret to wash it down.' Blackened lips formed a macabre smile across his white face.

Passengers retched again. Vomiting and screaming were the only responses from any of them. Like giant babies in a grubby metal cot.

Then a sudden lurch. A rumble beneath them. Slowly the train began to grind into movement once more. The gruesome butcher roared in anger. Viciously he hurled the body of the student into the corner of the carriage. It struck a row of passengers full on and they crumpled under the dead weight. The cockroaches set to work again: a frantic clicking and cracking. Like a swarm of bees they came to the red nectar that flowed from the student's corpse.

The train began to pick up speed, and soon the comforting lights of the next station swept along the tunnel. As if frightened by the brightness approaching, and with an unearthly scream that chilled the hearts of the survivors, the highwayman turned and made towards a window. He thundered his pistol at the glass and it gave way instantly, lethal fragments descending on to the cowering passengers like deadly confetti.

And then he was gone, returning to the darkness once more. His foul army of feasting insects marched after him.

Amid the wailing and the crying and the shouting came the faint but unmistakable sound of horses' hooves galloping somewhere in the murky depths of the tunnel.

CHAPTER 4

MONDAY: 7.06 P.M.

THE CRYPT

Professor Bonati shot a disapproving glance at Jud over his Armani specs.

'Don't give me that, Jud. You're late. No excuses, please.'

'The chopper was delayed, sir. I couldn't make up the time on the bike.'

'Nonsense. Everyone knows how fast you ride that thing. Suicidal, I'd say.'

Jud gave up. 'I'm sorry, sir. It won't happen again.'

Bonati pushed his chair back and got up from his desk. 'OK. But you know how I feel about lateness!'

He looked irritated as Jud watched him pace up and down. Anger didn't suit him. He was a gentleman. Jud's late mother had always called him a 'silver fox'. Always well groomed, he never lost his composure. If he was fifty, he didn't look it – until moments like now, when the frown at his forehead carved lines into his tanned skin like contours on a map.

He stopped pacing and looked directly at Jud. His steel-blue eyes gazed through silver rims.

'It's about setting a good example to those new recruits in there. Punctuality. It's important, Jud.'

'Yes, sir.'

Bonati looked at him. Jud looked tired. He probably hadn't eaten for hours. Bonati knew all too well that his father rarely bothered with food.

He softened his voice slightly and said, 'So, how was it, J?'

Only two people ever called him J – his father and Bonati. And when they did, he knew they weren't referring to his new name, either. 'J' was a precious link with his past life as Jamie – a past he'd had to try to bury so deep, since leaving prison.

'Home, you mean?' he said.

'Yes. How was it?'

Jud shrugged his shoulders. 'S' all right. Bit strange. We'll get used to it.'

Bonati allowed a gentle smile to show. He regretted shouting at Jud. He could only imagine the atmosphere at home now. Empty. Loveless.

'Any trouble?' he quickly asked.

'What, reporters, you mean?'

Bonati nodded. 'Yes, at the castle.'

'No. Nothing like that. Dad's built a new pad there. Right in the middle of the trees. The Squirrel landed out of sight and I was in.'

Bonati smiled again. 'Good.'

Jud was gazing at his feet, looking pensive now. Sitting still, reflecting like this was never a good idea. There was, after all, so much to reflect on. The last few years had brought him more sadness than most people endured in a lifetime.

Bonati saw the glazed look in Jud's eyes and decided to snap him out of it quickly.

'Still, you're here now, so let's get on with it.' He moved towards the door of his spacious office. 'They're in the briefing room,' he said.

And with that, he swept out of the room and across the shiny tiled floor.

Jud sighed loudly, then sucked up a deep breath, got to his feet and followed the professor out of the room.

Time to start work again.

Jud heard the excited chatter before he'd even entered. Then he saw them. Ten new recruits. 'Zombies', as the experienced agents called them. Once you'd been in the CRYPT a while, and had got enough hauntings under your belt to become a fully fledged investigator – or 'skull', as they were known – teasing the zombies was always a good sport. And here was a new load to pick on, high on the excitement of their first night underground in the vast suite of metal labs that made up the CRYPT.

'Good evening, everyone,' Bonati began. 'Welcome to the Covert Response Youth Paranormal Team. The CRYPT. You've made it, ladies and gentlemen. You've survived the induction course – we've tried to scare you and you've still elected to join us.'

There was a slight ripple of enthusiasm, though everyone tried hard to hide their excitement and relief.

The intensive training that potential recruits had to endure was unlike anything they'd ever encountered. With the entire corporation of Goode Technology PLC at their disposal, Bonati and Jason Goode could design virtual experiences that simulated the most terrifying hauntings. In specially equipped studios, deep underground, the potential zombies were put through all manner of scenarios – in which holographic images appeared without explanation to baffle, shock and even terrify. Under lab conditions, electromagnetic radiation was harnessed, creating magnetic plasma that formed extraordinary images, visible to the naked eye but impossible to explain without the right training.

The question was, could the agents handle it? Were they tough enough? Were they clever enough to work out where and why ghosts like these might appear in real life – and, just as importantly, how to stop them?

Each of the zombies in the room had spent hours poring over

the handbooks and documents that provided their bedtime reading during the induction course. Any one of them could be called upon to explain the existence of ghosts.

According to the CRYPT handbooks, ghosts were physical representations of the disembodied spirits of dead people. Goode and Bonati believed that the disembodied spirits themselves were made of 'dark matter' – that mysterious, invisible and as yet unexplained form that makes up ninety per cent of the universe.

But exactly how spirits took on a *visible* form had confounded scientists and ghost hunters for centuries. Now, though, thanks to the efforts of Giles Bonati and Jason Goode, a concrete theory had emerged.

'You've read the handbooks,' continued Bonati. 'You've learned the theories on which our work is based, I hope.'

The zombies looked nervous. Was he going to ask someone to explain the science? Here, right now?

'And I can assume you understand it. CRYPT agents are recruited for their brains, ladies and gentlemen, as well as their powers of ESP. If you didn't comprehend the science, you wouldn't be here.

'But just in case you need reminding, it begins with atoms.'

Oh no, here we go, thought Jud, leaning casually in the doorway. The professor always began with this kind of speech. He so loved the science, and lecturing like this reminded him of his time on the university circuit. Another captive audience, eager to hear his theories.

'As you all know, each atom contains a nucleus, protons and electrons. Atoms are everywhere. When an atom has more electrons than it should, it gains an electrical charge. An atom with an electrical charge is called an ion. Plasma is a collection of ions that have absorbed so much energy, the electrons within them have separated from their nuclei. It becomes an ionised gas, and as such is one of the most common states of matter in the universe.'

The zombies were nodding dutifully and looking interested.

He continued: 'Neon lights use ionised gas, as do those electrical globes that people love to place their hands on and watch the streams of plasma dance across the sphere. We've all seen them.

'Now, it's already been established that if plasma is of a low enough density, it can pass through walls. And it's called . . . ?'

'Non-collision plasma, sir,' some keen zombie shouted from the back, eager to be the first to answer.

'Yes, indeed. Well, as you know, during our numerous experiments, Jason Goode and I found that the electrical frequency of ionised plasma affected the degree to which it was visible to the human eye. So the greater the electrical charge, the more opaque, or solid, the plasma looked. We found that if we lowered the frequency, the plasma became translucent, or see-through.

'We believe that when spirits enter our world, they harness electromagnetic energy. This explains why there are always higher levels of electromagnetism in the air after a haunting. This energy attracts ionised plasma, like magnets attract iron filings. It's an invisible force, like ordinary magnetism, but it can have a visible effect on particles. It can actually form shapes, as you know. And it can be measured using EMF meters, electrostatic locators and ionisation meters.' The agents' ears pricked up at the mention of the meters. In just a short time they would each be issued with their own equipment - a complete set of field investigation apparatus.

The professor hadn't finished yet. He was proud of the scientific investigations he and his friend had carried out. And this was a rare opportunity to share it all in such detail - with an audience who were willing and able to listen.

'For years people have questioned where this electromagnetic energy comes from. I can tell you that when someone dies, their physical body is buried, and their spirit lives on as dark matter.

But where does the electrical energy our bodies give off disappear to when we die, ladies and gentlemen? You'll know from your school science lessons that energy never dies. So it's not buried with the deceased's body. Instead it remains in the air, moving as an electromagnetic force. And it remains as a residue in the familiar objects and places that once surrounded the deceased person – as electrostatic energy.

'When a disembodied spirit, or dark matter, seeks to return to our physical world, for reasons we'll get to, it draws on the energy it left behind in life. The energy reserves were there all along. They never leave the Earth. They never die.

'Now listen, everyone. This is the most important of all our findings. We found that the electrical charge that a disembodied spirit harnesses can actually *fluctuate*. If the spirit is in a state of rest, the electrical charge is at a lower frequency and so the plasma that surrounds it is invisible – that's why we don't see the ghosts of dead people floating around us everywhere! Hence the phrase "may he rest in peace".

'But ghosts don't always rest in peace, as we know. Some are troubled, angry or even vengeful. And when a disembodied spirit is charged with anger, it can harness even more electrical energy. The plasma that surrounds it becomes more highly charged. And so it becomes more visible.

'And we can see it.'

The professor paused to take a breath and check that his new recruits were still listening. They were, obediently, though no one wished to look too keen. Instead they smiled gently and nodded occasionally to show they were interested. Most were still thinking about the fancy equipment that would soon be theirs.

'Now, incredibly, we found that some ghosts can become as visible and as solid as any living human, by harnessing vast amounts of electrical energy, particularly those who've returned to avenge someone or something – those who seek justice for some wrong committed against them in life, for example. If the electrical energy of the plasma surrounding a disembodied spirit is charged to an extremely high level, then the spirit could even gain the strength of a human, or beyond.'

Some of the zombies were looking daunted now, struck by the sudden realisation that the professor was describing the very real and potentially violent ghosts that they themselves had been recruited to hunt out.

Soon it would be happening for real. No more simulations, just the real thing.

'I hope you're as convinced by our findings as we were,' said the professor. 'Ghosts *can* enter this world, passing through walls in a calmer state, appearing almost translucent at times, but then forming a more solid shape when their spirit is disturbed or angered and the electrical charge is greatly raised, or when they connect with a source of residual energy, like the static electricity in objects around them. You'll have heard the phrase "so scared my hair stood on end"!'

A ripple of nervous laughter broke out.

'If you hear reports that an adult has seen a ghost, then you can bet it'll be because the spirit is volatile – angry in some way, and therefore opaque enough to be seen by anyone. But that's rare. So we need agents like you to sense the presence of ghosts before they become disturbed and ultimately violent. Your ESP is more important than any equipment I can give you.'

Some of the zombies looked proud, others still seemed apprehensive about the responsibility which now fell to them. Few of them truly appreciated the significance of Bonati's research – because, unlike the professor, they hadn't been involved in the endless trials and experiments, the vigils at hauntings, the recordings and measurements. When presented to them in the CRYPT handbooks, the theories seemed so obvious, so simple.

But Jud knew, better than anyone, the magnitude of the breakthrough that Bonati and his father had made. He knew because it affected him more than anyone else. If they could prove scientifically, beyond doubt, that ghosts *could* enter this world and commit violent crimes, then at last there was the possibility, the faint hope, that people would believe he was innocent of his mother's murder, and that his claim that 'the ghosts did it' had been true all along. Jud could clear his own name and live his life as Jamie once again.

But that was still some way off. Though the CRYPT had been proving and solving hauntings for two years now, the sceptics and cynics were still out there. Few people believed the evidence was ever strong enough to stand up in a courtroom.

So the CRYPT kept on investigating and recording and explaining paranormal activity, wherever it occurred, all the time compiling evidence that one day would convince the world they were right.

As Jud leaned casually in the doorway, glancing at the zombies, he thought to himself, *If only they knew the truth . . .*

One day.

Bonati continued, 'You could say – and there are plenty of people who would – that we're an elite group. The country's finest. The experts on whom the entire city above us relies. The superheroes who walk towards the paranormal when all others flee from it.'

Smug grins were now forming on the faces of the zombies in front of him. This was going to be cool.

'But I don't subscribe to that view. And neither should any of you.'

Some faces dropped. Serious expressions returned once again.

'For I know that we are, like our colleagues in MI5, public servants and that is all. Not superheroes; not bounty hunters. Elite maybe, but never indispensable. We are, and will always remain, public servants . . . remember that.

'When crimes happen without any rational, human explanation, then it's down to us to solve them. When violence occurs, when injuries are sustained, without a detectable perpetrator, the CRYPT will be called upon to hunt down the paranormal entity responsible, to understand why it committed its crime in the first place, and to release it from its anger so it may truly rest in peace.

'We have the technology and we have the brains. We know what ghosts are capable of. But it's down to us – to you – to protect the city above us from the power of the paranormal, which floats about us all and, from time to time, reaches out to us in anger and revenge.'

The students listened intently, their gazes transfixed on the professor before them. This was no longer a fantasy. This wasn't some childish dream about becoming a ghost hunter. This wasn't a cartoon. It was *really* happening. They were really here.

The CRYPT only recruited ten agents a year, through discreet liaison with schools and colleges across the country. They scoured the UK for potential agents and they placed subtle advertisements in scientific journals and paranormal magazines too. Recruitment into the training programme was exclusive. To be accepted on to the induction course alone was an achievement – and to have passed it meant something special. But there was little time to feel self-satisfied.

'You'll have read the regulations and the induction handbooks. You'll have signed the contracts and the official secrets declaration. You're ours now, ladies and gentlemen. You belong to us. For the next three years you belong to the CRYPT – and you're going to be living in the shadows, let me tell you.

'Because secrecy is all. It's vital that our work remains under-cover. And there's a very good reason for that. If you've read those handbooks as closely as you should have done, you'll know that one of the most important breakthroughs in paranormal research that we've made – and we've made a few – is that ghosts feed off human fear. The more panic and hysteria at a haunting, the stronger the ghost. We suspect it's due to the energy we radiate when we're frightened.

Your job is to reduce the amount of fear at a haunting. And the only way to do that is to keep a low profile. The fewer people who know about us the better. Discretion, ladies and gentlemen, discretion. Invite your friends along to see you at work and we're all dead.'

Jud was standing behind Bonati, leaning against the doorway. He was gazing at the new recruits in the room. Seven guys, three girls. Ages uncertain, but likely to be sixteen. Zombies usually were. At fourteen, Jud had been younger than anyone when he'd joined two years ago. But then his own entry into the CRYPT had been so very different. So shrouded in secrecy. As it still was.

He studied their faces. They displayed the usual nerves, like freshers on their first day at big school. Except for one of the girls. She was striking – dark-haired, with a pale, unblemished face. There was a composure to her – almost serene. And Jud noticed something oriental about her face. Her sixth sense must have told her someone was looking, as she flashed her dark eyes in Jud's direction. He looked away quickly.

The professor said boldly, 'The CRYPT exists because of the powers of people like you: teenagers with a special gift; that certain something that allows you to sense, to experience, to *connect with* the paranormal. We know the science – we know how spirits can enter this world – but it's you guys who can sense when and where. We don't know why teenagers are more receptive to paranormal activity than others. We don't know why you see more than adults do, though we have our theories. I suspect it's because you have higher energy levels than we do. But you're here precisely because of your gifts. Your talents are valuable to us – and essential to the people in the streets above us, whom we're licensed to protect. But that doesn't mean you can't be replaced. It doesn't mean you're superior.'

Easy, Professor, thought Jud. You've made your point. Message received. No one in the room looked smug now. Faces were deadly serious. *Move on and tell them how good it can be*. How cool it is to ride the Fireblade. How wicked it is to fly in the Squirrel. And then there's the equipment. The gadgets. It's not all bad, sir.

Watching the zombies now, Jud recalled his first evening like this. Bonati had been just the same. Recruit the country's finest. Invite them into the lair – the space-age world of the CRYPT. Then bring them down to earth with a serious lecture about the burden of responsibility they now carried on their shoulders; the need for professionalism and a clear head. The importance of drawing on their powers, controlling them, so they could investigate and ultimately resolve paranormal mysteries before fear and panic spread.

They were investigators, charged with the task of understanding why spirits returned. But they weren't defenceless. Jason Goode had invested hundreds of thousands of pounds in researching 'ghost-busting' equipment of all kinds. His revolutionary electromagnetism neutraliser, or EM neutraliser as it was known, enabled his agents to disperse much of the electromagnetism in a haunted venue. Using the process of inverse interference, the small hand-held device sent negative waves into the atmosphere, combating the positively charged electromagnetism and effectively cutting off the energy source that enabled ghosts to interact with the world.

Vaporising ghosts into thin air took time. Earlier prototypes which Goode and his team had designed had been faster and more powerful, but they'd produced unwanted side effects. They had a habit of scrambling and ultimately destroying any other electrical devices in their range. Not to mention the effect they had on the user. Early experiments had left those in the radius of the machine experiencing blackouts, feeling extreme nausea and tiredness – and suffering from a headache that lasted for a week.

But Goode had not been deterred. Still he invested, and still his technicians developed the machine, until now it was a central piece in every agent's armoury.

The new version, although scaled down and restricted to safer levels, still had the capability to neutralise whole rooms over a period of time, and greatly reduce the amount of paranormal activity within them. But CRYPT agents, especially the newly recruited zombies, harboured a secret wish that one day improved versions of the model would be powerful enough and fast enough to neutralise EM levels instantly, thus serving as the ghost-buster they all dreamed of.

Jud's own EM neutraliser had come in handy on several occasions. Left to work its magic in a room overnight, placed in a specially designed docking station like a phone charger, it had reduced the electromagnetic levels enough to prevent ionised plasma from forming. It was, you could say, the electronic equivalent of an exorcism.

Bonati continued his introductory speech.

'You join an extraordinary group. You're in good company. But the badge you carry, and the oath you swear, will bind you to a set of rules and regulations the likes of which you've never experienced. If you thought school was strict, you've seen nothing yet. We have a code of practice here. A code that . . .'

Bonati stopped. The zombies were distracted. Someone had entered the room, patting Jud on the back surreptitiously and breezing in like he owned the place.

Because he did. Jason Goode, billionaire, IT guru, and the money behind the whole enterprise, now stood before the assembled group.

Bonati quickly stepped back and hid his irritation behind an obedient smile.

'Good evening, Mr Goode.'

He always did this. Always pitched up unannounced. Kept the professor on his toes.

There was a slight intake of breath from the new recruits. Eyebrows were raised. They'd recognised him as soon as he'd appeared at the door. The thin face; the blonde hair, greying at the sides and cropped short to match the grey stubble around his jaw; the dark linen suit; the rebellious T-shirt beneath. And those piercing blue eyes, which now flickered across the room and stared into the faces of each of the teenagers, who gazed back at him in admiration.

'So. You've made it then!' Jason spoke in clipped, rapid bursts, like a machine gun. 'Excited?'

Cheeky smiles broke out again on the young faces, though they glanced back at Bonati and tried hard to maintain their respectful expressions. They'd read so much about these two men. They'd done their homework – read up on their history. How the CRYPT had come into being. How Goode had suffered such tragedy at his castle that night. How his life had been so irreversibly changed by the loss of his wife, and the realisation that his own son had killed her. (They'd no idea that his son was innocent, and now stood just feet away from them.) And how his old friend Bonati had picked him up and driven him on.

But not one of the zombies had expected this man to look, and sound, so *lively*. Almost childlike. His energy filled the room.

'Has he given you the lecture yet? Bored you with the science?' Jason quipped, turning to Bonati and showing him a film-star smile.

The professor shifted uncomfortably and said, 'I was just informing them, Mr Goode, about the nature of their work here and the responsibility they carry. It's important that—'

'Absolutely, Prof! Important stuff.' Jason turned back to glance at the recruits again, and they noticed that his face had changed.

'It's not a game, for sure. But I think you know that, don't you?' Jason's eyes had glazed over. His smile had gradually disappeared. There was even a slight tremor in his voice. 'I know, perhaps more than anyone, how destructive paranormal forces can be.'

The room suddenly fell silent. Jud felt a sickness in his stomach.

Goode was staring over the zombies' heads to the back wall. He sucked his lip and took a sharp intake of breath. 'We can give you all the equipment you need, but it's up to you guys to *understand* them, to connect with them, and, with luck, to send them packing from this world. No one else can do it. It's down to you.'

No one said anything. Bonati looked sympathetic.

Jason shrugged his shoulders and snapped himself out of the chasm that so often engulfed him.

He said more cheerfully, 'And I'm proud of you guys. Proud that you made it. I'm delighted you're here. I'm grateful too. Grateful that you've agreed to join us in the vital work we do.' He was smiling now; brilliant white teeth again. Energy began to radiate from his face once more.

'You're in for a blast, I can tell you. No matter what Bonati here says . . . it'll be cool, I promise you!'

The new recruits grinned and began to relax once again.

Jud smiled. He knew how this speech would be irritating Bonati. He'd known the professor for years. He'd got close to him. He knew there was no question that Bonati shared Goode's passion and determination. They had the same vision. But no one – no one Jud had ever met, or was ever likely to meet – could share the same energy levels as the extraordinary man standing before them. His father. And he knew it made him difficult to get along with at times.

Some said he was a genius. Less charitable voices over the years had called him an obsessive, fast-talking whirlwind of a man, who jumped from one project to the next quicker than a computer, leaving a trail of befuddled acquaintances to scratch their heads and say, 'What just happened?' Jud knew that if his father had been at school now, he'd have been branded ADHD and put on medication to calm him down.

Just like he himself had been.

He'd inherited so many of his father's traits. But standing there, in the room, side by side, no one would ever have known. In the years that had passed since that fateful night in the castle, Jamie Goode had been transformed. His blond hair had been dyed black and left to grow long. And the thick specs that had once framed his blue eyes had been replaced with brown-tinted contact lenses. He was a different person. He was Jud Lester.

'My office is on the top floor,' Jason shouted enthusiastically, waking Jud from his thoughts. 'You're always welcome. It'd be good to see you any time. The view alone is worth the trip up.'

'Any time when you're actually here!' said Bonati, a subtle smile now creeping into his face as he gazed at his impish friend and rolled his eyes.

Jason laughed. 'That's why I've got you, Giles! You keep the cogs whirring. You keep us all going. Damn it, Prof, what would we do without you?' It was Bonati's turn to be patted on the back.

'I've got to run,' Jason said quickly. 'But I just wanted to drop in and say hi. And to tell you how pleased I am to see you here. Genuinely. The job you have is a difficult one. There'll be some very challenging times ahead – but let me tell you, in Professor Giles Bonati, you have the greatest mentor you could ever wish for. I know. So listen to him. Respect him. And do all you can to show him that we've made the right choice in recruiting you.' He moved towards the door. 'See you around.'

As he left, he smiled at Jud.

'Evening, Lester. Going to tell them how it is? Get them motivated!'

Jud nodded obediently. 'I'll do my best, Mr Goode.'

His father winked. And then he was gone.

There was a buzz that remained in the room, a residue of energy, like the ripples in water when a stone is skimmed across it. The zombies were sharing impressions of the man they'd been dying to meet. So that was him. That was the billionaire who'd single-handedly changed the face of global communications technology.

Funny guy.

Bonati called them to order.

'Your gifts are special, as I've said. But they may be fleeting. No one knows how long you'll have them for. No one really knows why such powers of extrasensory perception should be so prevalent in teenagers, and then fade so quickly in adulthood. But it's true, as you know – adolescence is the period of our lives when supernatural forces are at their clearest to us. We see things more sharply, before the tired old cynicism of adulthood shuffles in.

'And if you're lucky, as you guys clearly are, you can be very receptive indeed to the paranormal energies that surround us. You've proved in the entry tests that you've all got it. Now *use* your power. Harness it. Channel your senses. Focus. In the coming weeks and months we'll be helping you to do just that.'

Bonati turned to face Jud. He beckoned him over.

'I've asked Jud Lester to come along and talk to you.'

All eyes switched to Jud. Especially the girls'.

'Jud's been with us for a while, but I'm sure he feels like it was only yesterday when he was sat there like you. I've asked him to come along for a reason. Time and time again, Jud has recorded the highest levels of ESP. He doesn't just see ghosts, he thinks like them. He understands them. He connects with them.

'And he'll inspire you, I'm sure.'

Jud shuffled awkwardly. *OK, Professor, that'll do. Don't big me up too much. I haven't been teased since I left school and I don't need it now.*

'On his entry tests, Jud eclipsed all others in his intake. He's been obsessed with ghosts since he can first remember, haven't you, Jud?'

Jud nodded, with cheeks flushed, and prayed for the ground to swallow him up.

Bonati turned back to face the crowd.

'Sound familiar? Have *you* slept, eaten and breathed ghosts? Have *you* been plagued by sights and shadows that no one else could see? Have *you* heard noises and then found out you've been the only one to hear them?'

Several of the zombies were nodding and smiling in relief.

'Lonely, isn't it? Well that's why you've been recruited. You're not freaks. You're talented. Gifted. And, as I'm sure Jud will tell you, you're no longer on your own.'

With that, the professor turned to Jud and beckoned him to begin.

Red with embarrassment, but determined to deliver the speech he'd rehearsed so many times, Jud stepped up and began.

'Welcome to the CRYPT,' he said. 'Welcome to the world of ghost hunting. If you're feeling nervous, you should be. If you're feeling scared, you should be. I don't know what's round the corner any more than you do. I'm not a fortune teller. But we have to react – and quickly – to the threats that will come at us. No one knows what will come into this world next. But we see things. We feel things – provided we keep our senses sharp enough. We don't know why the spirits call to *us* especially. And we don't know how long we'll have these gifts. But as the professor says, you're not alone any more. You're with people who'll understand you, listen to you, take you seriously. And if you think you're gonna have an adventure like you've never had before . . . you're right.'

CHAPTER 5

MONDAY: 7.42 P.M.

HOLBORN STATION, CENTRAL LINE

'So, let me get this straight,' Detective Chief Inspector Khan said once again. 'You say there was no blast?'

'Yeah.'

'Definitely no explosion?'

'That's right.'

'So how the hell—'

'Look, I've told you!' the woman interrupted. 'We've all told you, but—'

'I know, I know.' The chief inspector was getting exasperated. 'But how the *hell* did the windows blow in? What caused so much damage down there? So much carnage? I need *answers*.'

'I told you, Inspector. It was the—'

'Man in the highwayman's costume with the old-fashioned pistol. I *know*.' Sweat was running down Khan's forehead. None of this made any sense, but panic was already spreading across the city. And he needed real answers. 'This is insane,' he said, half to himself.

The woman continued, 'It wasn't a *man*. It was a . . . a . . .' The word sounded so ridiculous. 'It was a . . . *ghost*.'

DCI Khan clenched his fists tight. This was mad. Insane. He took a sharp intake of breath. His doctor had warned him after his last medical that the ulcer in his stomach couldn't tolerate such stress for much longer. Nor his heart. Too many years with the CID, and especially the last ten at the Met, on homicide and serious crime, were now taking their toll. He fumbled in his coat pocket for his pills and quickly necked a handful.

What the hell was he going to tell his superintendent? Or the world's press? Reporters were beginning to assemble outside, hungry for a headline for tomorrow's front page. Panic was spreading, and fast. He'd got to say something. Silence would only build up people's worst fears.

A bomb?

He *had to* tell them it wasn't a bomb. Anything but that. And yet there was no other reasonable explanation for the horrific scene that had met his eyes when he'd entered the carriage earlier that evening. The sight of the bodies. The gruesome ways in which they'd been dispatched. The jagged glass. The gut-wrenching injuries that had made even the paramedics gag. And those insects. A sea of trampled cockroaches everywhere.

What the hell had gone on in that carriage in the darkness? What foul forces had preyed on those innocent people in that way? And more to the point, *why*?

He clutched his stomach. The ulcer was slowly eating away at him, rotting in a barrel of nervous acid.

Cool it. Deep breaths.

Questions like *Why?* were for the future. Everyone was still trying to work out *what* had happened and *who* was involved. *Whys* were irrelevant right now. Motives were a long way off yet.

Khan glanced in the direction of the escalators, which were still busy with a constant stream of paramedics and fire officers attending the scene underground. The survivors' statements just didn't make sense, at least not to him. In the realms of delusion more like. He'd never heard eyewitness accounts like them. But they *did* match. They all matched. Everyone had said the same thing. And they continued to say the same thing.

He turned back. The woman in front of him looked faint. Her skin was pale, almost a blue-green.

'Please, Inspector, can I go now? It's late. I don't think I can . . .' Her words tailed off as she collapsed into tears again. She started to tremble. The detective chief inspector beckoned to a nearby paramedic, who helped her to her feet and guided her in the direction of the temporary first-aid post now erected in the station lobby.

Khan watched her leave. Her story was just the same as everyone else's, so it must have happened as she said. But here, under the harsh lights of the station, it all seemed like fantasy fiction. Like a dream. A ghost? A highwayman? A duelling pistol?

The world had changed tonight.

New dimensions were appearing. New doors, which should have remained forever locked, were now opening – and something, someone, was coming through into this world.

'This is *fiction*,' he said aloud. *Don't be so bloody stupid. There's always an explanation.*

But the bodies were real. The injuries were real. The grief – so much grief – was real, and would stay with the relatives for ever. Try telling *them* the whole thing had been imagined, he thought to himself.

But the question still remained:

What in God's name was he going to do about it?

The entire Central Line had been closed down and sealed off. Fire officers, bomb disposal experts and a whole myriad of armed police and Special Branch detectives were at work in the tunnels below them, combing the area for clues. The world was waiting to know what had happened. No one had seen anything like it before.

But they would again.

Soon.

CHAPTER 6

MONDAY: 11.06 P.M.

HIGH HOLBORN

Baz and Tariq had been drinking. Two City bankers out on the razz. A few lagers after work, a quick curry, a wine bar, and then that all-important kebab and a stagger down Holborn to Chancery Lane tube station.

Sorted. Good night out.

'Oh, great,' said Tariq, his mouth full of limp lettuce and soapy onions. 'Typical. Bloody typical.' He gazed at the station ahead.

Police tape stretched across the station entrance, and a sign saying 'CENTRAL LINE CLOSED UNTIL FURTHER NOTICE' was taped to the doors. Police officers with Alsatians patrolled the pavement outside. The scent of half-eaten kebab aroused the dogs and sent them straining at the leash.

'What happened, mate?' shouted Baz at one of the policemen.

'Nothing that concerns you, sir. I suggest you go home. You've had too many, by the looks of it.'

'Yeah, that's what I wanna do, isn't it, boss. But I can't, 'coz you've closed the bloody station.' He burped. A foul stench of onions and beer wafted across the pavement. The dogs licked their lips.

'Where's home, then?' another officer said.

'You don't need to know where I live,' said Baz aggressively. 'We've done nothin' wrong. I just wanna get to Liverpool Street.'

'Then can I suggest you take the bus across the road? There'll be another one along shortly.' The officers had seen too many drunks to be bothered by these two jokers.

Baz and Tariq staggered back across the road in the direction they'd just come from. They headed towards the nearest bus stop. Soon a bus arrived and, without even looking at its number or destination, they jumped on it. A brief negotiation with the driver and the two men crawled up the cramped spiral staircase to the top deck. It was empty, so they could sit at the front. They giggled and farted like schoolboys.

As the bus slowly moved away, causing a jolt that pushed the two men back into their seats, Baz noticed something reflected in the front window.

It was the shape of a person. Must be behind us, he thought.

'All right, mate,' he shouted at the reflection. 'How did you get up here? We never saw you come up, mate.'

Tariq turned around and saw the old man. He was coughing. Probably a tramp. Sneaked on with no bus fare. It was hard to see him from the other end of the bus. He'd got some kind of shabby coat on. His face seemed hard to distinguish, almost as though it was fuzzy or out of focus, like a reflection in water. Must be the drink thought Tariq. It was just visible beneath a tattered old hat, which appeared to have three points to it, like a highwayman's would.

'Hey, hey,' Tariq laughed. 'It's bloody Dick Turpin!'

His words caused a reaction from the figure in the corner that neither of the men could possibly have expected. Not in their worst nightmares. It stretched up to its full height and surged towards them. Incredibly, it seemed to be moving *through* the seats, and not around them. It was translucent one minute, like a projected image, then as solid as the men themselves the next. Its wretched face writhed in anger. Tariq's words had stirred something deep within it. Buried deep in the dark recesses between the hollow bones, beneath centuries of injustice and bitterness, a fire of revenge was burning tonight, charged with a renewed strength.

The figure was now emitting an intense glow. Solid flesh was forming. Blood slowly dripped from an open wound that encircled the spectre's neck. The vision that unfolded before the terrified men was truly hideous. Tariq went pale, clutched his stomach and threw up. A putrid cocktail of lager and second-hand kebab meat slopped on to the floor.

Both men, screaming in unison, made for the stairs, jostling and fumbling and staggering in a terrified stupor. They felt the bus suddenly stop.

'Oh God!'

'Come on! Get out, quick!'

But the highwayman had blocked their way.

Slowly his lips parted. His mouth widened. Further and further. A deep, cavernous hole appeared in the centre of his face. Then the rattling sound began, rising from the hollows hidden deep inside his chest.

Baz and Tariq stood frozen like statues. Their dribbling faces were white, like the froth on their beers that night. The rattling sound became deafening, and a wave of insects shot out of the spectre's jaws. Like gunfire they pierced into the bodies of the two men. Screaming, they tried to get rid of them, but it was like trying to stop a waterfall with your bare hands. And still the insects came.

The men fell to the floor, writhing in agony. A blanket of black beetles and sickly yellow maggots covered them and began feasting on their flesh.

The highwayman picked Baz up by the collar with a strength that seemed to be growing by the second. A tidal wave of anger ran through him, bringing an electrical charge that now glowed menacingly.

Deaf to Baz's gargled pleas, the ghost hurled him down the staircase, like a child throws a doll. His head thudded ominously against the metal-tipped stairs as he went down. He landed fatally, his body twisted and contorted at the bottom.

Turning to face a petrified Tariq, still battling against a sea of insects on the floor, the highwayman spoke in a deathly whisper. 'You . . . sir . . .' he croaked. 'What was that you said? How did you address me, sir?'

Tariq's face was slowly disappearing. The flesh was being eaten away by a thousand beetles feasting. Through his muffled screams and retching, the ghost heard him mumble a feeble 'Pl-e-a-se . . . no . . .'

Then the highwayman placed two bony hands around his neck and yanked.

Tariq slumped in a pathetic heap. The flesh continued to be stripped from his body by the frenzied insects. The spectre emitted a chilling laugh, his whole frame now alight with electrically charged plasma. The metal rails on the seats beside him seemed to fizz and glow with an array of tiny sparks.

The red sores around his neck were now even more visible. They glowed red, as though light was leaking out of them, out of the spirit's charged body. Great septic tracks of red flesh that stretched and leaked a glowing pus.

Outside on the street, the driver was now running. And shouting. To anyone. His echoes ricocheted off the dark, empty buildings.

'Help! For God's sake. Somebody! Oh God. Please!'

He'd abandoned the bus as soon as he'd heard the first screams and seen the gruesome figure upstairs reflected in his mirror. Now he glanced back at the vehicle again, abandoned on the pavement. He looked up at the top deck. There, in the window, was a sight that was to haunt his dreams for ever and cause him never to work again.

A hideous figure, an evil spectre around which a demonic reddish glow pulsated and swirled.

There was a burst of sirens in the street.

Something inside the apparition was changing. The glowing began to fade gradually, like dying embers on a fire. The body was weakening, becoming almost translucent. And slowly, incredibly, the figure was sinking downwards – disappearing though the floor of the top deck. The perimeter of its body was merging with the air around it. Its spirit – the dark matter around which the plasma had formed – was departing. Down further through the floor the shape passed, through the chassis of the bus and deeper still through the pavement, on into the sewers below. Among the rats and the worms and the spiders.

Only the sound of the beetles that remained could be heard until the sirens and shouts and cries drowned out the ominous rattling.

Until the next time.

CHAPTER 7

TUESDAY: 8.01 A.M.

THE CRYPT

The retina recognition system was activated. Clearance was given. Jud Lester stepped back from the scanner and waited for the electronic doors to swing open. Seconds later, he was inside Sector 3.

The hi-tech laboratories of the Covert Response Youth Paranormal Team were housed in the third and deepest basement of the building. The first basement, Sector 1, contained the living quarters for the team: lounges with giant flat-screen TVs and black leather sofas everywhere; a silvery steel kitchen with every modern appliance you could imagine (the most popular were always the state-of-the-art coffee machines and juicers); a vast dining room that could seat all the skulls and zombies together, along two vast glass-topped tables running down the centre of the room, fixed to which at regular intervals were black metal rods with stools attached; and then the dormitories – large rooms divided up into pods, or 'iPods' as the skulls called them: small spaces only big enough for a metal bunk, a computer desk and a reclining chair, but packed to the brim with every conceivable form of electronic entertainment. Like a room full of three-dimensional apps. The sleeping spaces were small and purposeful, but they were kitted out like an arcade – like being on a submarine simulation for kids.

Below this floor, Sector 2 housed meeting rooms of varying sizes from small interview booths to the largest conference room, where Jud had welcomed the zombies the night before. When Goode had planned the building with his architects and MI5, an ingenious system of lighting had been installed: between each of the basement floors ran a cavity that stretched the length of the floor and was filled with high-intensity dayglo lighting. The rooms below had a latticework of glass tiles built into the ceiling, allowing the 'sunlight' to flood in. This meant that every room – including the meeting rooms on Sector 2 – offered the agents the illusion of daytime light. Remotely controlled blinds and shades were fitted in each room too, so the fake sun could be blocked out like closing a curtain.

The meeting rooms were furnished in the usual Goode style – minimalist and clean, with a preference for black marble and tinted glass everywhere. Some rooms were large enough for tiered seating in rows, and lecture-style podiums, while others contained more intimate meeting tables and easy chairs arranged in huddles. The most austere rooms in Sector 2 were the interview cells: small spaces with nothing but a table, two chairs and lots of recording equipment. This was where fake hauntings were exposed – the pranksters who thought they could scare the public and fox the agents with their fancy projectors and sound equipment. They'd spend thousands on hi-tech effects, often quite convincing, but under harsh questioning in these police-style cells they always cracked. Their knowledge, or lack of it, would be exposed. CRYPT agents weren't just recruited for their special gifts for sensing the paranormal; if they could sense a real ghost, they could certainly tell when it was phoney, and there wasn't a single piece of sound, lighting or projection equipment they didn't know about. Goode made sure they kept abreast of the latest gadgets.

Below these rooms lay the most secure division of the whole building: Sector 3 – the nerve centre of the CRYPT operation.

Jud walked along the white-tiled, neon-lit corridor, past laboratories and store rooms, towards his own private lab. A second retina recognition scan and he was finally inside.

Several computer screens lined the far wall, and in the centre of the square cell, like a butcher's block, was a clinical white table with a silver laptop on it and two halogen desk lamps. Along the left wall stood a series of lockable cabinets – made of reinforced steel and each fitted with numerous locks. Temperature gauges and dials ran along the top of each cabinet – the 'evidence' cupboards. Filled with all manner of paranormal phenomena, the trophies of ghost hunting: ectoplasm; unidentified limbs and other body parts found at locations and as yet unaccounted for; glass containers housing different forms of ionised plasma; various objects inexplicably charged with record levels of static electricity; and numerous metal trays filled with photographs and video footage of paranormal activity. It was all in there. Enough to frighten even the most sceptical of people, if they ever knew about it. But MI5 made sure they never would.

Like other members of the CRYPT, Jud housed a weird collection of hi-tech gadgets and field equipment in a metal cabinet in the centre of his stark white office: electromagnetic field meters (EMFs), electrostatic locators, ionisation meters, motion detectors, GPS-equipped instruments of scientific testing (or GEISTs), Geiger counters and voice stress analysers. No expense was spared.

And on the bottom shelf, in a specially designed lockable safe, the latest model of the EM neutraliser. The essential tool for every CRYPT agent.

Shaped like a large mobile phone, the black, shiny device was Goode's flagship piece of technology. Every agent had to undergo extensive training on how to operate it, not least because of its destructive powers in the wrong hands, or in the wrong situation.

Jud knew that his father was still, even now, investing yet more funds into the development of new prototypes of the model – newer, more powerful versions that would ultimately eliminate ghosts in one fell swoop, but without the potentially disastrous consequences recorded in earlier trials, not only for all electrical equipment in its vicinity, but for its operator too.

It was a special piece of kit. And there wasn't a day that passed without Jud checking it was still in its place in the cabinet. He'd always been forgetful – usually because he was always in a rush to get somewhere – and so he was paranoid that one day he'd leave it somewhere he shouldn't.

He checked it. There it was.

He sat down at his desk in the centre of his Alladin's cave and fumbled for his remote control inside a drawer. He found it and immediately pressed the switch marked SCREEN. Instantly, the right-hand wall rotated 180 degrees and revealed a giant screen.

He loved that trick. Always made him feel like a Bond villain.

He clicked GPS on his control and a giant globe appeared on the screen. He flipped open the laptop, clicked VOICE COMMAND and said 'Battersea Park Heliport' into the tiny mic. Immediately the view on the giant screen zoomed in closer and closer. The mass of grey and green shapes mingled and distorted until an aerial view of the heliport appeared. Using the control in his hand, Jud zoomed in further still and swung down to reach the horizontal. He gazed across the rainy tarmac.

He keyed in yesterday's date and the time 09:10 hours. Like a DVD on slow rewind, the picture jumped through whole scenes and then settled again. Seconds later the black Squirrel HT1 hovered into view and gently landed. He watched himself disembark and stride out towards his Fireblade.

It was like a music video. All rainy shadows and dark, glossy colours. The black of the helicopter. The black of the Fireblade. The black of his leathers. And the dark mirrored glass of the buildings behind him.

The telephone interrupted his self-indulgent viewing and Jud quickly clicked the conference call button. 'Yes?'

'Yes, *sir*.'

'Sorry. Yes, *sir*.'

Bonati sounded agitated. 'There's a briefing in Lab 6, eight thirty.'

'I'll be there, Professor.'

'Good. Oh, and Jud . . .'

'Yes, sir?'

'Stop admiring yourself, will you. Those screens were not installed so that you could star in your own Bond film. Get a grip, J.'

Lab 6. More field equipment and computers and thirty teenage paranormal investigators all crammed into the room to hear Bonati's briefing. Some of the skulls had been working on various assignments – others, like the keen zombies now seated in the front row – had been undergoing the usual training modules, but all work stopped when Bonati wanted a briefing, and besides, meetings like these provided a rare opportunity for the agents to catch up again. The room was full of chatter.

'Right, morning, everyone,' said Bonati, silencing the crowd as he strolled in. 'And a particular welcome to our new recruits. I hope our skulls have made you all feel welcome?'

They certainly had. After Jud's welcome speech last night, he'd led the zombies into the CRYPT games room – a large space in Sector 1 that resembled an arcade, packed to the rafters with giant TV screens, video games and all manner of home entertainment. Goode had insisted that if his army of teenagers were going to work hard, then they deserved to play hard too.

The skulls had shown the new recruits how to relax, CRYPT style. A sensory overload.

'So then, Professor,' someone called out from the back. 'What's going on with the trains?'

News of an incident on the Central Line had been the talk of breakfast. Theories abounded.

'Yeah,' another skull joined in. 'They said on the news it wasn't a bomb, but the newspapers this mornin' seem to think it was. No one's saying anything officially. What do *you* think, sir?'

'Lord knows,' lied Bonati – he'd already had a call, late last night, but was under strict orders from MI5 to sit on it for a few more hours while they first tried to gather evidence and establish that it wasn't fellow humans who'd committed the atrocities. 'Let's get on, shall we?'

Another investigator shouted out, this time a zombie: 'But some of them are saying it was ghosts, Professor. Some of the witnesses in the papers, I mean. Aren't we gonna do anything?'

Bonati shot him a glance.

'You're new here, so I'll forgive that. But you'll soon realise that we don't take our orders from the tabloids. We don't react until we're told to. The CRYPT answers to a higher authority, and I can assure you, no official orders to act have come through. If they do, you'll be the first to know. Right, let's begin.'

No official orders, thought Jud. He knew what that meant. The professor was in contact with MI5 and Scotland Yard on a daily basis – he must know something. He decided he'd make a point of quizzing him after the meeting.

'I've two matters for you this morning,' continued Bonati. 'In a moment I've some infrared shots of unusual orbs I'd like you to have a look at. They were sent in and corroborated by several eyewitnesses. But first, I have some good news. You'll know the problems we've had with the current batch of EMFs.'

The skulls nodded.

At last! Jud said to himself. His own EMF meter had let him down in both of his last two field investigations and valuable evidence had been lost. Relying on the electrostatic locators was never enough.

'Well, I've asked Dr Vorzek to attend this morning to show us the new batch, which I'm delighted to say has now arrived.'

Kim Vorzek, CRYPT's director of field equipment, was good news. Jud, just like every male skull at the CRYPT, fancied her like crazy. He knew she was in a different league – of course she was; she was probably twice his age, at least – but he could still dream, couldn't he?

The electric door behind Bonati swung across and Dr Vorzek entered, carrying a large metal briefcase.

'Good morning, skulls,' she said, 'and welcome to the new recruits too. Good to see you.'

'Morning, Doctor,' they all chorused. The young men looked like star-struck schoolboys.

Vorzek was wearing her long dark hair tied up, with a few tousled locks hanging down either side of her attractive face, which was adorned with modern designer specs. She wore a pencil-thin skirt with a tight-fitted black top. Her figure was slender, but shapely enough to hold the attention of Jud and his fellow skulls. She had curves in all the right places.

'So you think you know EMFs,' she began cheekily, shaking the boys in the room from their daydreams. 'Well think again. This is the Tri-Axis 333. A new concept in electromagnetics. Watch and learn, ladies and gentlemen.'

A demonstration followed of the instrument's capabilities in monitoring positional changes and detecting energy sources. Paranormal investigations would never be the same again.

'When combined with your locators and ionisation meters, you should have a much more accurate – and reliable – set of readings—'

Vorzek was interrupted by the beeping of Bonati's mobile.

'Yes?' he barked at the voice-activated phone on the desk. Its miniature screen lit up and a face came into view. Jud was unable to make out the person from where he was sitting, but whoever it was, they were important. Bonati leapt up, grabbed the phone and exited the room sharply.

Everyone waited. And the boys tried to ogle Vorzek, subtly.

There was shouting outside from Bonati. Jud couldn't make out much, but he heard him yell, 'Why? Why *now*? Why didn't you say this last night?'

Moments later Bonati returned. He looked anxious. He *never* usually looked stressed, but this time everyone could see beads of sweat on his forehead. There was a mixture of concern and fury written across his face. Jud knew it must have been MI5. An order. A new mission. He knew it. He'd learned to read the signs on the professor's face whenever an official assignment came through.

'Right. This briefing is adjourned, everybody. Something's come up. Something serious. I need to catch a tube to the Central Line. Lester, you're between cases at the moment, aren't you?'

'Yes, sir. I don't currently have—'

'Right. Come on. We need to get to Holborn . . . now!'

CHAPTER 8

TUESDAY: 8.20 A.M.

GREYFRIARS GARDEN, NEWGATE

Jane sipped her mochachino and took another drag from her cigarette.

Ten minutes and she had to be at the office.

This was her regular dose of privacy before the chaos of work began. An oasis of calm. Sitting on the usual bench, in the usual spot beside the rose beds in the quiet of Greyfriars. The great steel buildings of London loomed above the ancient walls that surrounded her. Beyond the trees and the walls, the sound of the rush hour hummed. This was her quiet time, her private moment, before she had to be polite and professional behind a reception desk for the next eight hours.

She took a final drag on her cigarette, threw it on the floor and stamped it out with her stiletto.

Looking up again, she took a sip from the plastic cup. The warm, chocolatey coffee tasted good. She looked across the miniature park at the remains of the wall opposite and let her mind drift. She was thinking about last night's TV, her vacant eyes staring. Gradually she drifted back to reality and focused on the stonework at the other side of the garden. The familiar pattern was clearly etched on her retinas after spending many moments like this, staring ahead and sucking on a cigarette.

She let her eyes follow the pleasing pattern of stones and bricks that made up the great block that faced her. She sipped more of the coffee and began her usual habit of counting the stone rows that sprang up from the ground.

One, two, three . . . nine, ten . . .

Wait a minute.

There was something odd. She couldn't put her finger on it. Was it the stones? Was it the dull grey mortar in between? She wasn't sure, but something definitely seemed different, about five feet up from the ground. She scanned the wall. There were marks - small marks, that looked like stains of some kind. They must have always been there, but she just hadn't noticed. Probably moss, or soot maybe. Or perhaps damp patches. Still, she'd been coming to this bench in this spot for over a year now, and it was odd that she'd never noticed them before.

The really strange thing was, from this distance, if you looked at the marks as a whole, they formed a pattern. It was like someone had drawn a cloudy kind of face and the suggestion of two hands on the brickwork - spread out, like someone held in the stocks.

How weird, she thought.

She got up and walked across the path and over the grass to the wall for a closer look. Perhaps it was graffiti.

As she approached, the pattern remained the same. Clear as anything. Sounded stupid to say it, but it really looked like the top half of a person.

She got up close to the stonework and studied it.

They weren't stains, or moss, or soot. They weren't graffiti.

They were . . . What *were* they? They seemed almost like bumps. Raised parts of the wall. Where each stain had appeared, something was sticking out of the stonework. She looked even closer.

Flesh?

Was this bump sticking out of the wall actually made of *flesh*?

What the hell was she thinking?

She took a few steps back again. Though she knew she was mad for thinking it, something, or someone, seemed to be trapped in the wall. Almost like they'd been cemented in there. But it didn't look solid. Not properly. More like it was a mixture of substances – somewhere between solid matter and gas.

A projection. That was it. Something was being projected on to this wall. She spun around quickly to see what was doing it, and why.

But there was nothing there. Just the usual garden. She glanced up at the high buildings in the distance, looking for a camera or a projector or something – anything to explain what she was seeing. But nothing.

She looked back again at the stones.

And then she screamed.

The strange ripples and bumps set into the wall were beginning to gain a faint reddish glow, with an intensity that grew each second. A shape was moving – towards her.

Someone was coming out of the wall.

There, amid the stones and mortar, a face was appearing from deep within. Like a death mask, the facial features pushed through the bricks, translucent at first – like oil rippling around stones on the road – but becoming more solid with each push through the wall: the nose, the chin, the eyes. Great hollow pools of black, set into a thin, gaunt face.

Jane turned and tried to run, screaming. But it was too late. The body coming through the wall was finding strength. Intensifying. Becoming solid.

And it caught her jacket.

Jane's screams echoed around the park. But there was no one else there. And her screams were drowned out by the traffic that ran between her and the commuters strolling down the other side of the street. They were oblivious.

She was on her own. That's why she came here after all.

But now, on the far side of the park, against the vast stone partition, centuries old, Jane was struggling. And screaming.

A hand was at her hair. It was pulling. Great clumps of her dark brown hair were being ripped out. She was in agony.

The body was almost completely through now, solid and as visible as Jane herself. But stronger – much stronger.

It was a highwayman. But it was different to the spectre that had terrorised Holborn and killed Baz and Tariq on the bus. This figure was smaller. Its face was bearded. Black, needle-like hairs protruded from its bony jaws. Its hair was dark and caked in blood. Somehow it seemed more pitiful, sadder. Grief-stricken.

The black, shadowy pools where the eyes had once been were widening, and glowing. Great mirrored holes in a sickly pale face. As the holes widened further, faces appeared within the sockets. The image of an infant's face in each hole. Sad, withered faces, with cheekbones showing through flesh, and tears of red flowing down them.

Twin children who had loved the spectre in life. Orphaned at the gallows.

The body of their lifeless father now clung tightly to Jane. She was feeling weak. She was losing focus. With her back to the wall, trapped within the ghost's clutches, the park before her was becoming blurred.

As she fought for her last few breaths, she could just make out in the distance two women entering the park. They stopped and began pointing. Their screams penetrated into Jane's ears as she began slipping into unconsciousness.

The hands were around her slender neck. Tightening. Her energy was leaving her. Slipping away.

Her legs fell limp against the spectre's angular limbs.

And then she was no more.

The terrified women in the opposite corner of the park had stooped to steady themselves on the ground. Shock had enveloped them, bringing a dizziness to the head and a weakness to the knees. One had called 999 on her mobile, but was unable to find the words to explain the unimaginable sight before her. She was yelling hysterically into the phone. The other was sitting with her head in her hands and sobbing, peering through the cracks in her fingers at the nightmare that was unfolding.

To their horror, the body of the woman they'd watched die just metres away from them now seemed to fade. As the energy left her bones, her frame was becoming less defined – almost as though she'd become a projection, a holographic image of her former self.

And she was moving. Into the wall. The ghost was taking her. Back through the stones and the spiders and the moss and the dark grey mortar from where he'd come. A new ghost was forged in the crucible of grief and fear and hate. She was in *his* world now. Jane was no more.

Soon the only evidence of her ever being there were an empty coffee cup and a stubbed-out cigarette.

And the ramblings of two terrified witnesses.

CHAPTER 9

TUESDAY: 9.22 A.M.

HOLBORN STATION, CENTRAL LINE

Jud felt something scurry over his right foot. He glanced down and saw a rat quickly disappear into the shadows. He looked up again. The torch strapped to his head shone deep into the tunnel. Slowly he walked on, further into the blackness.

The voice of Bonati faded behind him. He'd remained on the station platform, talking to DCI Khan. Trying to convince him that they knew what they were doing and were acting on orders from an authority far higher than the detective chief inspector.

Khan had been singularly unimpressed when they'd turned up at the station, asking questions, carrying all their fancy equipment and swaggering around as if they were on some film set. This wasn't proper policing as far as he was concerned. But then, as Bonati pointed out, this was no ordinary crime scene.

But Khan knew exactly who they were and why they were here. He'd received the call from his superior just moments before their arrival.

'Khan, MI5 have been in touch. They want to get CRYPT in. It's out of our hands now. They're sending agents round. Be nice.'

Khan knew very well what that meant. Ghost hunters. The policeman in him felt resentful that the case was to be shared with these cowboys. Jumped-up school kids most of them, weren't they? But the off-duty voice inside him, the family man, the ordinary Joe, he felt the fear and dread as much as anyone in the force felt when they heard the word CRYPT. Shrouded in mystery, their agents weren't frightening – they were just kids, after all – but the mention of their name meant that something odd was happening. Something paranormal. Supernatural forces must be at work – it was the only reason CRYPT were there.

And even though Khan would never admit it to anyone, least of all himself, there was a fear rising gradually inside him. A fear of the unknown. A strange, eerie feeling that something was happening, some chain of events had started, and no one really knew how it would end. He felt small – powerless.

And yet just moments ago, he'd watched this plucky kid, this toy ghost hunter, walk voluntarily straight into the same tunnel where the devastation had happened. On into the awaiting darkness, into the unknown; the only person walking towards the danger when everyone else was fleeing from it.

Khan knew Jud was a ghost hunter, a paranormal detective. But he was unaware of his true identity. Jamie Goode remained a safe secret in the heads of just a few agents at MI5, and a handful of reluctant officers at Covert Policing Command, whose job it was to monitor his movements since being released. Few of them believed that Jamie was innocent. Even fewer accepted the idea that teenagers had greater powers of ESP, and that somehow Jason Goode's mysterious agency was going to save the world from ghosts – if there were such things.

But above them in the chain of command, in the secret offices of MI5 and the official rooms of Whitehall, there were people who knew all too well that the possibility of ghosts was more real than some people thought – God knows they'd received enough reports from the public over the years. But they'd managed to keep their investigations secret. They'd never solved them – only hushed them up. An official acceptance that ghosts were everywhere would cause panic. The newspapers would whip up fear and people would be afraid to leave their homes. The economy would be strangled by a nation of cowards.

So when Goode offered to take over this controversial field of investigation, and still keep it underground, MI5 literally jumped at the chance. What was one boy worth in exchange for all the time and money Goode was willing to throw at the problem? Jamie was released. And no one was the wiser.

Of course, the judges in court would always be more difficult to persuade. And in any case, trials were so public these days. How could Jason prove it had been ghosts who'd killed his wife, and not his innocent son, without scaring half the population?

That was the paradox Jason Goode had created for himself, and for Jamie. Prove his innocence and tell the world there really were ghosts at work, and risk panic on the streets; or let them feel safe in the belief that ghosts were fiction and only humans could kill – humans like his own son.

Of course, Jud had worked this out too. Though they never spoke about it, he knew, deep down, that proving his innocence and reclaiming his identity could never be possible – at least not publicly. There was too much at stake. But he lived in hope. Hope that one day, even in secret, a judge would tell him it was OK.

He didn't do it.

Until then he, Jud Lester, like all the other agents at the CRYPT, operated in secret, and took the flak from 'real' investigators like Khan.

'Let them all think we're playing at it,' Bonati had once said to Jud. 'Take the teasing from the coppers on the beat, let them think we're wasting our time. We know better.'

Coppers like Khan.

And yet in the back of Khan's mind – somewhere among the countless faces and files that cluttered his brain from years of criminal investigations – there was a faint feeling that this kid looked familiar. He'd noticed it when he'd first been introduced to him. Then, as he'd watched Jud set off down the tunnel, he'd chewed his lip and gazed down the line with a puzzled expression, wondering where he'd seen him before, or why he felt this way. He thought hard, but nothing came. And then the moment had gone; Bonati was firing questions at him about the witness statements. Khan had turned away, leaving Jud to disappear round the bend of the tunnel and on into the anonymous dark.

And now Jud was alone. Just how he preferred it, though maybe not in such surroundings. If the claustrophobia didn't get you down here in the tomb-like gloom, then your imagination would. The voices of his companions had stopped echoing down the tunnel.

Silence.

But Jud kept walking, further, deeper, lower. This was what he loved. No courage – no glory; that was his motto. No challenge – no thrill.

Another few steps and he was there, right where it happened. The shards of glass beneath his feet, the gruesome, metallic smell of spilled blood – he knew this had to be the place. He could sense it.

He took off his backpack and set it on the dark, grimy floor. Something scurried away quickly. He opened the bag and took out several instruments. His flashlight moved momentarily across each one. He switched on the new EMF meter – surely with so much paranormal activity down here, the electromagnetic levels would be off the scale. His electrostatic locator would prove invaluable too. Next he unpacked the motion detector, and his hygrometer for testing humidity. Finally he took out the Geiger counter, for radiation readings. He was leaving no stone unturned. He wanted to go back to Bonati with a set of readings the like of which he'd never seen. His extrasensory perception, what he felt – though it often directed him to haunted locations with the accuracy of a guided missile – he knew it wouldn't be enough. He needed actual evidence, numbers and readings on meters. Show the zombies at the CRYPT how it's done.

He took off his headlamp and replaced it with the infrared sights he'd brought. He switched on the miniature video camera strapped to the side of the goggles above his left temple and began to explore the section of tunnel in detail, treading back and forth, across the rails to each wall, up and down. He watched the needles on the meters carefully for any readings that might indicate some kind of anomaly.

Nothing.

Typical. Bloody machines. He could sense a presence. It was always so difficult trying to explain to others, especially adults, just what he felt at times like these. But he could definitely feel something, an almost tangible vibe, like the atmosphere in a room after a fight.

He held the electrostatic locator to the wall and moved steadily up and down a few steps. The needle began to rise. There was definitely a residue of static electricity within the brickwork. Unsurprising, given the currents down here and the frequency of the trains passing, but still unusually high.

He studied the blackened walls of the tunnel closely. Felt the fluctuating temperature of the stones. Sucked in the atmosphere.

And then he saw the stains.

The infrared sights had illuminated the blackened walls. Dark reddy-brown splatters. The blood of passengers. A rank smell in the air. The foul aroma of old blood. His feet crunched over more broken glass. Though his equipment continued to show no evidence of the paranormal, the natural sensors in his body were ablaze with activity, sending an icy prickle down his spine.

The EMF at his side registered normal. He'd been to some hauntings when the electromagnetic readings had gone off the scale. Needles had gone haywire, or digital numbers had scrambled and settled on mG levels over a hundred. Ghosts gave out electromagnetic energy. Yet there were no traces here. He *had* to go back with something more than feelings. *Anything.* Radiation levels? Sudden drops in temperature?

Nothing.

He placed his instruments into his bag and went further into the tunnel. Deeper. Solitude was creeping up on him. It wasn't fear exactly, but remoteness – a growing feeling of abandonment. Like he was the only human left in some strange, post-apocalyptic world, deep underground. His mind began to race, as it always did. He didn't mind being alone – God knows he'd been on enough vigils to feel at ease by himself in dark surroundings – but somehow this was different. He knew he wasn't in a house or a church now. He wasn't in some remote bedchamber in a stately home. He was several meters underground in a black, rat-infested gloom, with nothing to report back to Bonati.

Nothing.

There was a rumble in the distance. A train in a neighbouring tunnel, he thought. He carried on searching.

The sound grew steadily to a thunderous roar that echoed around Jud's ears and sent shockwaves through the metal rails at his feet.

They'd closed this stretch of tube line.

Hadn't they?

Oh God.

Hadn't they?

The noise took on a metallic ring. Metal rims sliding along rails. Getting closer.

Up ahead, at first very faint, but unmistakable, a light was creeping around the bend in the distance.

It could only be a train. But in *this* tunnel?

Jud froze. For the first time in his life, he actually froze.

Running was pointless. He knew that. He could never outrun a train, even if it was braking. It took yards to bring a train to a halt, and he didn't have yards to spare.

But he ran all the same. Grabbing his bag of instruments, Jud began the run of his life. The run *for* his life.

A deafening sound of squealing brakes rose behind him, ever nearer.

Run.

There, ahead, growing brighter with every step, were the lights of Holborn station. There, several metres away, was sanctuary. Safety.

Behind him lay death.

And still the train moved. The great battle between speed and brakes, momentum and inertia, raged on. Getting closer.

And then he fell.

His right shoe had become caught between one of the bars that ran across the rail fixings. It yanked him back. He was in agony. The rucksack on his back lurched sideways and something slipped out on to the ground with a quiet thud that evaded his hearing.

It was his EM neutraliser. He hadn't noticed.

The force of the rest of his body moving on while his foot had remained lodged brought a searing pain to his whole frame. Frantically he tried to free his foot. His leather boots were thick and heavy. He winced in pain but kept wriggling. It wouldn't budge. The aching grew, but this was nothing, he thought, when compared to what was about to happen to him.

Any second now.

Anger grew inside him. This was not how he was meant to go. Not now, not here – not like this. He fought away tears. Courage had never left him before, but a feeling of panic now set in. The train was closing in on him.

This was it. His time. Tears crept slowly down his darkened cheeks as he still wriggled and wrenched frantically, trying to release his foot. It was agony. He pulled and yanked, pain soaring up his leg from the inflamed ankle, locked tight beneath the rails.

It still wasn't budging.

He stared into the tunnel ahead and tried hard to imagine his spirit released from the material body in which it was forged – a body destined to be so horrifically crushed, any second. He closed his eyes and waited for death to come.

An image of his mother slowly drifted into his mind. Her tender face. Forgiving. Understanding. A gentle hand on his shoulder.

Then darkness.

Bonati stood frozen, staring into the tunnel. What would he tell Jason?

How could he tell a man who'd already lost his wife that his son was killed too?

His mind was made up. Without a warning to anyone, he leapt off the platform edge, down on to the tracks. Like a man possessed he ran towards the slumped figure in the distance, ignoring the bright headlights beyond. The boy in the tunnel was like a nephew to him. He wasn't going to let him slip away without a fight.

'NO!' yelled Khan. 'Come back, man! What're you doin'?'

Standing on the platform seconds earlier, they'd heard the sound of the train, just moments after Jud had heard it himself. There had been yelling, arguing and frantic shouting to station staff. Angry questions as to why the tunnel had not been closed down properly had echoed around the platform. A shocked station official, sweat dripping from his face, had grabbed a walkie-talkie and ranted into it. Muffled voices full of panic were all that Bonati heard.

The tunnel had been closed. Officially. All drivers knew it was off limits. Trains had been cancelled, or diverted from the previous stop. This *could not* have happened.

But it *was* happening.

Before their eyes, the CRYPT's brightest star and, though no one knew it, heir to the entire empire above it, was going to lose his life tragically, gruesomely. Prematurely.

Bonati ran. He ran for Jason. He pictured his friend's face, greeting the news of a second tragedy. He *had* to save the boy.

Khan jumped after him, his weak heart pounding inside his chest.

'Get help!' he shouted over his shoulder at one of the station staff. 'NOW!'

He landed awkwardly on the rails and a sharp pain soared up his leg as he ran. He roared in anger, but still he limped on after the professor, who by now was yelling at the top of his voice:

'Jud! JUD! Get up! Come on!'

Up ahead, Jud lay motionless. Consciousness had left him.

Behind him the train squealed.

Bonati stopped and fell to his knees.

Khan turned and limped frantically back towards an alcove set into the tunnel, which he'd passed seconds earlier. But there wasn't time. He'd never reach it.

They braced themselves.

Shut their eyes.

Held their breath.

And then, with a grinding judder, the train stopped.

The space between metal and flesh measured no more than twelve feet in the end. Twelve feet – the difference between life and death.

But it was enough. They were unscathed.

Desperate to regain their breath, the men drank in large gulps of sooty air and steadied their nerves. Khan waited for his heart to surrender; but it didn't. He and Bonati grabbed Jud, his rucksack still on his back, released his foot from the trapped shoe, and lifted him in the direction of the platform, panting and heaving.

They sat him down against the wall, and as the blood rushed to his head, he slowly came to. Wearily he looked around.

He'd made it.

He rubbed his forehead and whispered, 'Thank you, Mom.'

Khan's mobile phone beeped – the signal had started to return now they were out of the tunnel – just two bars, but it was enough. Voicemail.

He listened. His face fell.

'What?' said Jud wearily. 'What's happened?'

Khan put the phone slowly into his pocket, and stared into the darkness of the tunnel ahead.

'Well?' said Bonati. 'Tell us!'

Khan wasn't sure how to convert the short message he'd heard into words that sounded reasonable. It was so inexplicable.

'An incident's happened. Over at Greyfriars.'

'What?' said Jud.

'In the garden. A girl's . . . er . . . gone missing.' Khan was shaking his head.

And thinking about the consequences of what was happening around him.

The consequences for him.

'Come on, Khan, quickly!' Bonati said impatiently. The train was pulling slowly into the station behind them. They had to deal with this crisis before another one engulfed them. 'Quickly. What's happened? Is it like the others? Is there an explanation? Tell us, man.'

Khan glanced quickly about him: station officials and police officers all around. Crowds were coming to see what all the fuss was about – which crazy guy had jumped in front of a train this time? With so many people near, he couldn't convey the details of the voicemail – and risk spreading yet more panic.

He chose to keep quiet.

'It's nothing. Unconnected. Don't worry about it.'

But Jud could see it in his eyes – fear. He recognised the signs.

Bonati thought for a moment. There was no point in grilling

Khan now to get more information. He knew that if this incident in Greyfriars had paranormal elements, he'd get his call from MI5 anyway. He didn't need this copper to tell him.

'Come on,' he said. 'Let's deal with one crisis at a time, shall we?' And he felt his own phone vibrate in his pocket as a single piano chord struck to indicate a text message. He knew who that would be from.

One thing at a time.

'So, tell us what you found in the tunnel, Jud,' he said, ushering them both to a quieter corner of the platform.

'There was nothing. I mean, I felt so much – felt a presence, you know, a real atmosphere down there . . .'

Khan allowed his eyes to roll momentarily towards the ceiling in mockery. All this 'feeling' stuff. He'd heard these wannabe investigators were obsessed with their senses. How they felt. What they saw in their mind's eye. Imagination, that's all it was. Strong hard facts were what was needed. And did this kid have any?

'Come on!' he said. 'Facts, boy. Facts!'

'OK, OK,' said Bonati, sensing trouble was brewing. 'Just let him speak.'

Jud continued, 'But the readings showed nothing strange, sir. Nothing at all. No signs.' He looked at the floor, defeated. 'I'm sorry.'

Bonati patted his shoulder.

'It's all right. God knows you tried.'

Jud looked up at him, 'But there's something down here, Professor. Something very bad. I can *sense* it.'

Suddenly there was a cry from the train, which had now inched its way slowly into the station.

Officials had raced into the driver's cabin when it had stopped, to find out why the train was on the line when it shouldn't have been. But one of them had leapt straight out again and shouted, 'My God!'

Bonati went straight over with Khan, who was still limping. His ankle had swollen up inside his dirty boot. He grabbed the door frame and followed Bonati up into the cabin. Jud followed, approaching the train that had so nearly killed him.

The sight inside the cabin was gruesome.

The driver lay slumped in a corner. Rivers of blood poured from a gaping wound in his chest. His eyes were open but life-less. His rigid face was contorted with fear. Fixed like some gruesome waxwork. Three passengers from the carriage behind had forced their way into the cabin earlier and attempted to drive the train themselves. Now they simply stood over the body and stared at the people entering, bewildered. The crowd inside the cabin just gazed at the pitiful body of the driver. No one said anything at first.

Police officers entered. Khan motioned to them to escort the passengers out of the cabin and on to the brightly lit platform.

The three dazed men stood by the train, handcuffed and in shock. They shook their heads.

'It wasn't us!' one of them shouted. 'We tried to save the guy!'

'We've done nothin'!' another cried, his body trembling.

The situation was enveloping them like some gruesome nightmare.

Khan began, 'No one's accused you of anything . . . yet. But I hope you can shed some light on what went on in that cabin. Someone start talking!'

They looked at each other.

One man said tentatively, his body shaking with shock, 'There was this . . . thing. Oh God. It was . . . I dunno. Something entered the train.'

'What're you talking about?' said Khan, a wave of nerves rising up his body like acid from his rotting stomach. This was beginning to sound horribly familiar.

'Where?' he continued impatiently. 'How could something

have entered the train? You were in a tunnel, for God's sake!'

The men said nothing. Their faces had paled. One of them slumped to the floor.

'Come on!' shouted Khan, sensing he was close to a confession. 'I want answers. Who did it? Who did this? It must've been you!'

'That's enough!' commanded Jud.

Khan swung round and glared at him. 'I *beg* your pardon?' he said coolly.

'Don't be stupid!' Jud was shouting now. 'Can't you see? Hear them out. Don't just assume they've done it. What's the matter with you people?'

Bonati grabbed Jud. He knew what was happening. He could sense Jud's temper boiling over, like a crucible of molten steel.

'I think you've said enough, J,' the professor said calmly.

But Jud was having none of it. He knew – better than anyone else – what it meant to be accused of something you hadn't done. To be ignored. To have your defence dismissed in this way.

'Listen!' he yelled again at Khan, 'Listen! Let them speak! Let them tell you what happened. You don't know, any more than I do, what went on! You can't just assume—'

'Right, that's it, Jud,' Bonati said. 'Come with me. You need to calm down.' He pushed him away from the scene, in the direction of the exit.

Khan showed no emotion. Abuse like this was nothing, almost comical from this hot-tempered kid. He turned back to the three men, now sat on the ground, looking dizzy and disorientated. If the nightmare they'd just witnessed hadn't shocked them senseless, then the prospect of being charged with murder would.

'Talk to me. Now!' said Khan, angrily. 'If it wasn't you, then who was it?'

A few feet away, Jud wrestled to free his arm from Bonati and stood listening intently.

One of the men on the ground arched his neck upwards to face Khan. His eyes were red and swollen. He was shivering. His cheeks were splattered with the driver's blood.

He said, 'It was a figure. I dunno, I mean it was all so weird. It was like almost glowing. It wasn't really there at first. Like a projection or somefin'. It came right through the window. I mean through the carriage somehow. It was after the driver. It must've been. We saw it head straight for him. But it kinda grew, became solid, like. I dunno, it was like we were watching a game or something, like on a computer. First it was like a picture, then it was sort of a *real* person.

'Threw the poor guy to the floor it did. Like a doll. It was so strong. The driver, like, kept shoutin' about the tracks, but . . . like . . . then I saw . . .'

The man stopped. He was shaking his head pitifully. Another of the passengers now started shouting.

'Weird thing. I ain't seen anything like it. It was just so . . . horrid. All skin and bone . . . like, I dunno . . . evil or somethin'.'

Jud closed his eyes. He knew it. He could sense it in the tunnel. An evil presence of some kind had been here. And left a trace of something horrific, like a foul stain in the air.

'Yeah.' The third passenger joined in. 'I tell ya, it was gross. Like a horror film. D'ya know what he did? I can't get it outta my head . . .' He began whimpering. Like a kid, plagued by the gruesome images of a nightmare from which he'd just woken.

'Shoved his hand . . . all bony like . . . straight into this bloke's chest. The driver just screamed. And screamed. He'd got no chance. And then the ghost thing ripped something outta him. I mean actually out've 'is body . . .'

'An' I tell you . . . I mean, I swear it was 'is heart.'

CHAPTER 10

TUESDAY: 10.47 A.M.

THE CRYPT

'Let's go through everything again. We've got to keep rational.' Bonati tried to calm the voices in the room. Everyone was shouting. Tempers were running high.

Deep underground, below Goode Technology Plc, members of the CRYPT had gathered in Bonati's office. He ran through the situation again. While they'd been waiting for Jud in the tunnel that morning, DCI Khan had briefed Bonati about the incident on the bus on High Holborn. The bus driver's hysterical ramblings sounded like they belonged in a horror movie. A glowing figure inside the bus. The screams of the two men. But there were so many coincidences when his account was compared with the eyewitness statements taken from the passengers on the tube. The face. The cockroaches. Was it the same man? The same 'ghost'?

'The public aren't going to accept what they're being told for much longer,' said Jud. 'There's too much panic around. Too much horror. The police said they were looking for a gang of masked men. What's that all about, sir?'

'Well it's better than saying it was a bomb, Lester,' said Nik Jones, another member of the CRYPT, and someone with whom

Jud had never seen eye to eye. His arrogance irritated Jud. And it was Nik who usually led the charge to wind him up – see if they could get him to blow in the usual way. Watch his eyes go. See the muscles clenching in his jaw. Then sit back and watch the fists fly. Jud's outbursts were well known at the CRYPT. Jud-baiting had become a sport, thanks to Nik.

'But it wasn't a bomb, was it,' interrupted Dr Vorzek, sensing a squabble brewing. 'We all know that.'

Bonati looked pensive. He knew more. The text message at the station had been from MI5, as he'd expected. The call he'd made as soon as he'd returned to the CRYPT had proved his worst fears. Khan had been cagey; he hadn't told them everything. Not by half.

The incident at Greyfriars had been appalling. The accounts from the two women who'd seen it happen seemed too strange to believe – at least for ordinary policemen like Khan. But MI5 and the agents at the CRYPT knew all too well what powers the supernatural world could unleash. Anything was possible. Even people disappearing into walls.

It was time to brief the agents in the room. But Bonati knew it wasn't going to bring calm to an already anxious crowd.

'Right, everyone listen. Keep a cool head. Think about what I'm saying and let's find some answers. It's not just trains and buses now. It's happened again. Earlier this morning.'

They shot looks at each other across the room. The situation was slipping out of control. And they all knew it.

'Greyfriars?' said Jud.

Bonati nodded. 'It was a girl. Witnesses said they saw her disappear.'

'What do you mean, *disappear?*' said Nik.

Bonati stood up. 'Just what I said,' he sighed, exasperation escaping from his voice. 'She *disappeared*. Into a wall, apparently. Something pulled her into it and she was gone.'

Silence descended. Agents looked at one another. This wasn't a game. It wasn't some simulation cunningly devised by Goode and the professor. This was really happening. The fatalities were real. Several lives and much carnage. Panic was seeping into the city. Into people's lives. Commuters were scared to use the tubes. Questions were being asked on news programmes. Newspaper headlines were setting people's minds racing.

And though the majority of the public in the city streets above them were ignorant of the CRYPT's very existence, the agents inside knew it was up to them to find answers. To solve this case before even more people fell victim to the powers that were plaguing the city.

Whatever they were.

Every channel the night before had been crammed with reports about the 'London raids', as they were now being called. DCI Khan had submitted the briefest of press releases as soon as he'd returned to Scotland Yard from the tube station that morning. Few details were given, but enough to make the public worry.

'DCI Khan, chief investigating officer, says the case is moving forward very quickly. Fresh evidence is coming in by the hour. Those responsible for the recent atrocities will be caught and justice will be served. In the meantime, the public should exercise vigilance and report anything suspicious to the police authorities immediately.'

After submitting the press release, Khan had called Bonati and said, 'Get this sorted, or God help us all.'

Khan knew, as did everyone at the CRYPT, that the supernatural still held a real fear in people's minds – a fear of the unknown – and if ghosts really were crossing into this world to cause carnage, then where would it end? He needed an explanation.

And soon.

Now here they were, the greatest researchers into paranormal activity, all crammed into the professor's office, and not one of them had an answer. Because not one of them had any evidence. Nothing. But news of Jud's narrow escape from death in the tunnel had spread right around the agency and had made everyone hungry for action. Even revenge.

Bonati continued, 'We need to get a grip on this. We have the expertise and the technology to solve it, and fast. But we must keep a cool head. What we need is *evidence*. Both sensory *and* scientific. We need to be on the ground, out amongst the people, collecting accounts and taking readings.' He stood up. 'I'm not going to let some second-rate newsreader tell me what's going on. I want to know first.

'Now, I know we've got other cases ongoing – and it's right that they continue. There's the case at Goldsmith's College, which I know some of you are still on, and the work up at Highgate Cemetery, which never seems to end. Is the investigation at Morden complete?'

A few agents shook their heads and looked embarrassed.

'This has gone on too long. Get it resolved soon! Parishioners are too scared to enter the church now. I've had the dean on. Find out what's going on. There's always a reason. You know that.

'At the moment – and the situation might change – we don't need every agent on this one anyway. I suggest those who are involved in other investigations continue their work. Besides, we don't know if they're connected to this case. And we can't take chances. Dr Vorzek, do we have enough equipment to supply everyone for field investigation work? The second batch of neutralisers has arrived, yes?'

'It has, yes. We're fully functional.'

'OK, let's do this.'

The agents still involved in cases left the room. Nine remained. Bonati dispatched them in the direction of the various locations across town. New equipment, new resources, the latest technology; he knew Jason Goode would throw everything he had at this one. The latest batch of EM neutralisers and the new delivery of Tri-Axis 333s had all come at the right time. The revolutionary EMF meters would deliver what Bonati wanted – some kind of tangible trail they could monitor and track.

'And remember, everyone,' he added as the agents got up to leave. 'You can have all the equipment in the world, but it's no good if you're not awake and your senses aren't ready to receive. So stay alert! And for God's sake, take your neutralisers with you. They may not zap the ghosts into oblivion, but they'll slow them up, that's for sure.'

They could take no chances. There was no room for mess-ups. The world was watching.

Jud was dispatched to Greyfriars Garden, Newgate. Much to his frustration, he wasn't going alone. He liked to be a free spirit when conducting paranormal research – his own boss, able to research where and when he liked – but Bonati had asked him to take Bex De Verre with him.

Bex was a brand-new recruit to the CRYPT. Attractive, sassy and young. Her mother's Chinese ancestry gave her an exotic look that most girls her age would die for. She'd grown used to their jealousy, and the constant attention from the boys – just like Jud who'd clocked her on the first day.

And she was clever, too. Perhaps the only one in the new intake to attain anything close to the grades Jud had achieved on his own entry tests. (He'd said at the time it was ridiculous him having to sit any tests at all, given the circumstances of his entry into the CRYPT, but his father and Bonati had insisted that he be treated like everyone else. It was essential for his cover.) If anyone could match Jud for quick thinking and intelligent conversation, Bex could. Bonati thought they'd make a good team.

Jud opened up the throttle and stepped through the gears. His ankle was still raw from his fall in the tunnel, but he wasn't going to let Bonati tell him he couldn't ride. Not now. He let the

Fireblade rip through the traffic. His dark brown eyes stared through the visor with steely determination. If he was stuck with this girl, she was going to have to understand how he worked – and how he travelled. He wasn't about to slow down for her, or for anyone. The Honda accelerated up Kingsway.

'Not bad,' came a voice from the headset in his helmet. 'I reckon the Suzuki GSX has got more throttle than the Fireblade.'

Jud felt a mixture of anger and admiration. Here was a girl, seated behind him, clinging to his chest, who was challenging his Fireblade. And she knew about GSXs – the best bikes to challenge his Honda. Was she cool, or was she going to be trouble?

Jud thought he'd find out. Ignoring her comment, he pulled up to the next set of lights. He waited for the red to change to amber and green, then, kicking through the gears again, his ankle throbbing inside his leather boot, he opened up the bike for the fastest fifty yards he could manage.

That'll scare her into submission, he thought.

'Like I say,' she said, unfazed, 'not bad. I still think the Suzuki is better, though. Just wish they did it in pink.'

Jud smiled. She'd got a sense of humour too. Could be fun.

CHAPTER 11

TUESDAY: 11.02 A.M.

MARBLE ARCH

John Silverman, MP, walked up the steps at Marble Arch tube and on to the rain-soaked pavement. Ahead of him, the plastic sheeting that surrounded the vast construction site flapped in the wind. The great oaks in Hyde Park beyond swayed and rattled.

It didn't look much. Just mounds of extracted earth, scaffolding poles and diggers everywhere, but Silverman could see past all that. Trees were being felled, pavements diverted, and the closely cropped turf that lined this end of Oxford Street was being ripped up and replaced with cement foundations. The large pond and fountains that had once provided an oasis for commuters and pigeons on the corner of Edgware Road was now just a muddy hole in the ground.

Silverman felt a surge of excitement and adrenalin run through his body. This was his moment. At last he had the chance to do something big. To make some serious money.

Lucien Zakis was waiting for him beneath Marble Arch, as arranged. He was flanked by two well-built men wearing sunglasses – pointlessly, considering the English weather. Though it was only September, the rain felt almost wintry. Zakis wore a cashmere overcoat, peppered with damp dots from the rain. He was in his early forties, but his black, greased-back hair, and his dark Mediterranean skin, carefully studded with designer stubble, made him look younger. There was something about him that exuded money and power.

He was a third-generation Zakis. His grandfather's company, Zakis Hotels, had grown to become one of the biggest chains in the world. There wasn't a single major city in Europe that didn't boast a Zakis hotel. And they were always in prime locations – the Zakis family had enough money to buy land wherever and whenever they chose. Everyone had a price. They always did. Whether it was another business, a city park, even a government building, the Zakis company would relocate it and seize the land as their own. The money that changed hands in planning offices, parliamentary rooms and fancy restaurants amounted to millions each year. Anyone could be bought.

John Silverman was the latest pawn in the game. He worked for the Ministry of Transport. A big fat share in the new hotel suited him nicely, and in return he was able to pull strings and rubber-stamp the plan to restructure the whole roundabout and traffic system at Marble Arch. The intersection between Oxford Street, Park Lane, Bayswater and Edgware was one of the busiest junctions in the whole of London. That was where Lucien had decided to build his hotel. Right in the centre.

So that was where it was being built.

Silverman walked across to the main arch beneath the monument and shook hands with Zakis. His dark hazel eyes penetrated into Silverman and he smiled.

'Pretty good, uh? A quick start, yeah?'

'You certainly don't hang about, Mr Zakis. Permission was only granted last week.'

'An act of kindness for which you'll be rewarded, John. I'll see to that personally.'

It was really happening for Silverman. Years of applying for senior posts at Westminster, years of rejection, no promotions and then eventually a junior post at Transport was all he had to show for twenty-three years as an MP. But he had friends. And in high places too. And some of them could be bought, just as easily as he could. He'd become the crucial link in the chain. The route through which Zakis could do his deals and still remain at a safe distance.

And now, finally, he'd got his break. He turned back towards the site and imagined the plaza and fountains, the marble floor, the lions' heads, and the great glass tower soaring skywards. He pictured himself in the casino, in the private members' club.

Silverman was to be part owner. Secretly, yes, but the money would soon be rolling into his offshore account in Switzerland. An account personally set up by Lucien. At the Zakis bank in Zurich. Of course.

'And the application for the car park in Green Street, John? Granted, yes?' Zakis was holding Silverman's arm, and smiling at him.

'Well, as you know, there were many objections, but I'm dealing with them. We will get it. There's so much red tape, you know.' Silverman laughed nervously. Zakis gripped his arm even tighter. He pressed his fingers right into the sinews. The pain was registering now. Loud and clear. But Zakis kept smiling.

'Of course you'll get it. You can do anything, John. I know that. And I'm grateful to you. The Zakis family are grateful people. We treat our friends well.' He started to laugh. 'Not so much our enemies though, uh?' He turned to look at the men either side of him, who stared at Silverman, smirking. One final squeeze of his arm, which sent a nervous tingling sensation right down to his left hand, and then Zakis released him.

'OK,' he said, with a sinister smile. 'Let's have that lunch I promised you.'

CHAPTER 12

TUESDAY: 12.18 P.M.

GREYFRIARS GARDEN, NEWGATE STREET

The quiet solitude of Greyfriars Garden was shattered.

The paths that ran through the rose beds were crammed with people: police investigators, liaison officers, medics, park attendants, council officials, building surveyors and structural engineers – all seeking answers to the bizarre story that was unfolding. Eyewitnesses were being interviewed and then reinterviewed inside a neighbouring building. Beyond the walls of the garden reporters and photographers wrestled for the best vantage point, the best image and any exclusive comment they could get from anyone in the know. The pavement along Newgate Street was lined with television vans. Giant satellite dishes pointed skywards, transmitting fear across the globe. Coffee-fuelled presenters talked expressively into cameras, recounting the strange and gruesome facts they'd gleaned from shocked bystanders. Stories were being embellished. Drama was being created. Fear and panic were freely handed out to anyone who'd listen. And they *were* listening. Across the country people watched the live images. A news special on BBC1 had split the screen into four sections, one showing an excited newsreader in the studio, and the others the three different locations where the incidents had taken place: Holborn tube, High Holborn and Greyfriars Garden. In every place the image was the same – a mass of people, cameras and microphones, yellow tape emblazoned with POLICE INCIDENT and metal barricades keeping the public out.

The text that ran along the bottom of the screen said the same thing on most of the news channels: LONDON RAIDS – BREAKING NEWS – INCIDENT AT GREYFRIARS GARDEN . . .

'Experts' were drafted into newsrooms to dream up their own answers to the pressing questions on everyone's lips – why, how and who? No one was talking about a bomb. The police had been clear about that. But no real explanation had been forthcoming from Scotland Yard – not yet, at least. Another press conference was scheduled for 3 p.m. Until then, official sources only talked of 'raids' – possibly the work of a radical group of protesters or religious fanatics. No group had yet admitted to the crimes. But news commentators and their invited guests all agreed that whoever was responsible for these atrocities must have had access to unlimited funds. The kind of technology needed to create the special effects described by eyewitnesses at the scene would have cost millions and may have taken years to develop, according to experts interviewed. The holographic images outside the train. The 'masks'. The projections on to the wall that the witnesses had seen at Greyfriars. Theories abounded. Excitement was mixed with fear. Across the globe, viewers would be watching the three o'clock press conference and expecting real answers this time.

At Greyfriars, the public were fenced back across the other side of Newgate Street. Lining the dark, sooty walls of what was once Newgate Prison, they stared at the mass of activity opposite and swapped theories about what was going on. The road had been sealed off to public traffic. Only vehicles with official authorisation were admitted through.

The sound of a motorbike approaching from Holborn Viaduct came into earshot. The throaty rasp of the exhaust echoed around the high-rise buildings, creating a monstrous growl. The crowds turned to see Jud Lester and Bex De Verre arrive on the Fireblade.

Jud panicked as soon as he saw the TV cameras and the mob of reporters and presenters. The world's eyes were focused on Greyfriars, and he was about to enter its gaze. He didn't need this.

They parked the bike and dismounted.

'Come on,' said Bex, seeing Jud standing there, still wearing his helmet and staring at the crowds. 'Let's go.'

Nervously he removed his helmet, and they locked them both in the giant panniers that flanked the bike.

Trust the new look, a voice said inside his head. *No one will recognise you here.*

He ran his fingers through his black, shiny hair. His stubble was visible now – he hadn't shaved for two days. His eyes, now tinted brown with the false lenses, looked tired. Shadows lay beneath them. The stress was beginning to show. Beside him, Bex flicked her long dark hair and adjusted her leather jacket. They could've been a celebrity couple. Two trendy presenters, here to catch the gossip and entertain the folks at home with their sharp reporting from 'live at the scene'.

But they weren't celebrities. The crowds opposite, and the viewers back home, would never have believed what they actually were – and Jud liked it that way. It was how he always worked. It was vital that the work of the CRYPT remained confidential. Bonati saw to that. If word got out that paranormal investigators were at the scene, panic would be heightened. Jud knew just what that would mean. Memories of his father's efforts to create the PIT with Bonati were a constant reminder of how fear could spread. That was why they were shut down the first time. There was no way they or MI5, would allow the same mistakes to be made again.

Secrecy was everything.

Especially for Jud.

They left the bike and moved towards the mass of vans and reporters. Jud looked at the floor, allowing his hair to flick over his forehead and cover his face. Detective Chief Inspector Khan appeared behind one of the lorries. He looked mad.

'Where the hell've you been? Look, Lester, I know you've had a bad morning, but this isn't a stroll in the park for me either. I want answers. I don't care what you do, where you go, or what you need. You can have any resources you want.'

He walked right up to Jud and gazed into his eyes. His expression had changed.

Jud held his breath.

DCI Khan whispered, 'But if I don't get answers from you soon, I'll close you down. You think you're working for MI5. You think ordinary coppers like me don't matter, uh? Well you're not the only one with friends, you hear. Scotland Yard won't be made to look like fools. You can play your little spy games, sure. You can dash about on your shiny motorbike. But meanwhile I'm the one who's gotta face the cameras and have some answers.

'And believe me, I need something to say. *Anything*. You better give me something soon. And I don't want no airy-fairy feelings stuff. I don't care if you felt hot or cold, or what you think you heard. Understand? I want *facts*. Evidence. Or we'll see who's working for who.'

'For *whom*,' said Jud.

'What?' said Khan angrily. 'Oh shut up.'

Jud smiled as he watched him storm off. Stupid copper. Didn't he realise how pointless his threats were?

The boys from Scotland Yard had always resented the agency. Few of them had ever taken them seriously. Jud might take his orders from Bonati, who answered directly to MI5, but on the ground – day to day – it was coppers like DCI Khan he had to work alongside. That was the deal. MI5 would control from a distance and deploy CRYPT agents when necessary. Covert Policing Command would monitor Jud's movements from the shadows, but as far as the public were concerned, Scotland Yard were in charge of every investigation. And making them understand the realities of the paranormal was always hard. They'd no imagination.

But how dare this copper vent his anger on him! It wasn't the CRYPT who'd done this. Like every policeman, DCI Khan felt the usual desperation when a case was slipping further and further out of his clutches. Every phone call from MI5 was an interference as far as he was concerned. A nuisance. 'Proper policing' was what he always said worked. Not cowboys on motorbikes.

But how else could Khan investigate here? Just like at the tube station, this was no ordinary crime scene. There was no suspect. No motive. No evidence, other than the gruesome accounts of the people in the park. And this time there was not even a body to inspect – just frantic talk of a woman who was 'here one minute and gone the next'. Vanished into a wall – apparently.

This was madness. Khan knew that as the chief investigating officer, the three o'clock press conference was *his* problem. A conference in front of the world's media. And he had nothing to tell them. *Nothing*. Everyone would be watching. He'd less than five hours to come up with something.

Jud saw him grab his stomach as he walked off, and reach for a bottle of pills in his coat pocket. He was mumbling something about babies in a crib. Jud knew exactly what that meant. The few officers at Scotland Yard who were actually aware of the agency's existence often referred to Bonati's team as the 'crib' instead of the CRYPT – obviously a dig at their young ages. Jud had grown used to it by now, but this Khan guy really got under his skin.

He turned to Bex and together they fought their way through

the scrum of reporters and cameramen, in the direction of the garden. The brief from Bonati was clear: get to the garden, inspect the wall, then get into the building where the witnesses are and don't leave them until you've compiled a full picture of the scene. Then, later, when the crowds have moved on, take readings for the entire garden. Be discreet. It was the usual cover story: they were accident reporters, working freelance for the police. Under MI5's orders, Khan had reluctantly given them access to all areas.

Jud and Bex moved towards the wall. The backdrop of ancient stones looked strange, flanked by the modern office blocks. The moss-covered bricks and darkened mortar were a reminder of an older, grittier London. A city of soldiers and smugglers, thieves and pickpockets. And ghosts. The tube station had seemed such an unlikely place for a haunting, but here in the garden, with the small stretch of Roman wall towering over them, shadows of the past seemed at home. Anything was possible.

But the story Bonati had relayed to them before they'd been dispatched, seemed unimaginable – even to Jud and Bex. A woman disappearing into a wall?

No wonder there was such an atmosphere in the garden. They'd noticed it as soon as they'd cleared the frenzy of reporters on the street and entered the precincts of Greyfriars. There was a residue. A cold, macabre mood. They could feel it. They were sensitive to it – more than anyone at the scene. That was why they were in the CRYPT. Bonati had often said: it doesn't matter how much equipment you've got with you, always begin with your senses. Listen. Look. And *feel*.

Footprints are always left behind. Not visible markings on the ground, but traces of energy; a drop in temperature; an electro-magnetism in the air, or a feeling of a presence. Bex shivered slightly as they walked even closer to the wall. The temperature had definitely dropped.

Jud placed his hands over the stones. Moving from left to

right, he stroked the bricks with his fingertips. Nothing; just ordinary warmth – like all buildings and structures in London, the wall was a radiator for heat. But then the stones dropped in temperature. He could feel them getting colder. They were icy in places. He beckoned to Bex and she moved across to where he was, placing her hands over the same spot.

'It's freezing,' she whispered.

'Exactly. Something's been here,' said Jud. 'Something's happened here. You can feel it. Sense it.'

'There's a fear in this garden,' said Bex. 'I noticed it as soon as we came in. An emptiness. Like a hole – in the air.'

'Often happens like that,' said Jud, still tracing his hands over the patch of wall, trying to identify where the temperature rose and fell. 'There's often a hollowness, like a vacuum almost. A shift in the elements. Like something's missing.

'Come on. Let's get the equipment.'

Bex said, 'What about the witnesses? Don't you want to speak to them first?'

Jud looked unimpressed. 'You're new at this. You've got a lot to learn. We don't do it like that. We don't let ourselves be persuaded or influenced by what other people have seen. Not yet, at least. We *will* listen and take all the statements we need, eventually. But not yet. We keep our minds clear. And open. We just look, listen and feel. Soak it up. Trust your emotions . . . then we take readings. And *then* we interview.'

Jud headed back towards the mob of reporters and the motorbike parked beyond them on the street. Bex followed.

As he pushed his way back through the crowd, there was a shout from somewhere.

'Hey, wait a minute. I know you, mate!'

Jud quickly turned.

One of the reporters was looking straight at him.

'You!' he said. 'It's you. I've seen you before, mate.'

Jud froze.

His heart was speeding up. Hands getting clammy.

Did this guy know something? Jud had always known that one day his real identity would be revealed, but not here, not now – in front of the world's cameras.

He quickly turned his face away.

The reporter followed him.

'I know what *you* are.' The man grinned at him, a sneaky grin, as if he knew a secret and he was just about to tell the world.

Is this it? thought Jud. He waited for his real name to be said . . . If it came, he knew he'd have to deny it. Try to talk the man down. Convince him he was mistaken. He spun round and tried to keep calm.

'Sorry, you talking to me, mate?'

'Yeah, sure I'm talkin' to you. I saw you at that place last year – you know, what was it called?'

Jud held his breath.

'All Saints?' the reporter shouted. 'Was that it? Yeah, it was! You know, where that ghost was. Hell of a story at the time.'

Jud felt the sinews in his arms relax. He unclenched his fists – though he'd not even noticed they'd tightened to show white knuckles.

It was going to be OK. This joker might have recognised him from an earlier haunting; he might even know all about the CRYPT, but he'd no idea who Jud really was. Jamie Goode was to remain safe inside – at least for another day.

But people were starting to listen now. They'd gathered around them, curious as to what all the fuss was about. Bex had tried valiantly to push them away, but there were just too many.

Though Jud felt relieved that the man had only recognised him as a ghost hunter, and not for who he really was, this was still dangerous for the CRYPT. Bonati and his father had told him so many times about what had happened before. How their PIT operation had gone wrong because too many people had panicked. How the mere mention of ghost hunters had sent fear through the streets. He *had* to keep this under wraps. He had to silence the man.

Jud's temper was building, like it always did, but after the morning he'd had down in the tube station, he was feeling especially uptight. His nerves had been shot down in that tunnel. And now the shock of thinking someone knew his real identity was tipping him over.

He clenched his fists again. This time deliberately. He had to silence this fool.

Bex grabbed his arm from behind. She sensed he was getting wound up. She'd already heard about Jud's angry outbursts back at the agency. His temper was well known. 'Come on,' she said. 'Leave it. Like, just play it down. Let's go.'

Jud breathed deeply, turned to face the man and said, 'What're you talking about? Sorry, I don't know what you mean, mate. You're thinking of someone else.' He began to walk away with Bex.

But the reporter wouldn't let it drop.

'I'm not thinking of anyone else, mate. It's you, isn't it? I know exactly who you are and what you do. I was at the church. I saw what you did. All them machines, like. Those readings. All that science stuff.'

'Yeah. I'm an accident reporter, aren't I? I take that stuff to accidents and crime scenes. Big deal.'

'No you're not. You're a GHOST HUNTER! That's what *you* are! You're looking for ghosts, aren't you! This woman disappearing. This mad story. You actually believe it all, don't you. It's ghosts, isn't it, mate? That's why you're here.'

Chaos broke out. Other reporters surrounded Jud as he tried to walk away. Microphones were thrust into his face. The loud-mouthed reporter who'd started the outburst was still following Jud like a bad smell. Shouting after him and hounding him for a comment. Bex tried to intervene and get amongst them, but it was no use.

Jud stopped. He'd heard enough. The man needed silencing.

One strike was all it took. He smashed his fist into the man's face and he dropped like a stone, clutching his bloodied nose. Red trickles oozed through his fingers and dripped on to the pavement. His face was a mush. He shrieked in pain. The clicking of cameras intensified, like a plague of locusts. Lenses flashed in Jud's face, blinding his eyes with blue dots.

It couldn't have been worse. It just couldn't, and Jud knew it. The truth about the paranormal investigation was out. Those rumours of someone disappearing, they were true. Now the scaremongering stories of supernatural body-snatchers would spread like wildfire across the media – they'd lap it up – and each investigation scene would be crowded with people, half terrified, half intrigued, all anxious to know more. The police would never be able to keep them back.

And as everyone at the CRYPT knew, that meant disaster for their field work. Taking readings in locations where hauntings were reported was difficult enough, but with hordes of inquisitive onlookers, it was almost impossible to get any sort of reading that was reliable. The air conditions, the temperature, the electro-magnetic energy, the static electricity levels – everything changed when there were people around, especially when they were pumped up and emotional. The readings would be meaningless.

Not to mention the agents' ESP powers. Detecting traces in the air of paranormal activity – a sound, a shape, a drop in temperature, a mood shift, a chill in the atmosphere – all these things were masked when too many humans were present. They had to work alone. They had to work undercover. That was why Bonati had already insisted that the garden should be empty when Jud and Bex arrived.

And then there was the matter of Jud's violent outburst. It had been caught on camera. A lot of cameras, all piping images back to excited newsreaders and expert pundits in studios.

Jud's photo would appear in every newspaper. Someone would recognise him – see who Jud Lester *really* was.

He was finished. Game over.

CHAPTER 13

TUESDAY: 2.38 P.M.

THE CRYPT

'Don't give me that! Don't start your usual excuses, J.'

Bonati was pacing his office. Jud stood firmly in the centre of the room, eyes fixed on the wall ahead. He'd already tried to explain how he'd been provoked. How the reporter had wound him up. How he thought his cover was about to be blown.

But he shouldn't have let himself be provoked, Bonati had said. That was just the point. He was too easily wound up.

'I suppose you took no readings at all, before you started your fight?'

Jud shook his head.

The professor rarely lost his composure; he was always calm and steely, even when the pressures of the CRYPT were mounting. But this time he couldn't hide his concern. Things were slipping out of control. It was essential that his agents were self-disciplined and methodical. And now this.

'You *knew* you had to control that temper of yours – you knew right from the start that your place here was conditional upon you managing your anger. That's why we sent you on *courses* for it. What a waste of money! Did you no good at all.'

'But sir . . .'

'No. I think that's enough. We've invested in you. Because we knew, more than anyone here, how much you've been through – and what it did to your temper, Jamie.'

Bonati had not used his real name for a long time. Jud felt a sickness in his stomach. Somehow hearing that word brought a new reality to the situation. It made it seem even worse.

This was serious now.

His head began to throb. His ankle too. Any more pushing from Bonati and he was liable to go again. This time the professor would get it.

But Bonati continued: 'Look, you've got to meet us halfway. Why can't you understand that? You've got to keep your end of the bargain. Keep your head down and stay out of trouble – wasn't that what we said? What *you* said!'

Then his voice lowered. He spoke in an angry whisper.

'All I can say is, it's a good job your father's not here right now. You know what this means to him, Jamie. You know how every day he worries that someone's going to see you. Identify you.

'And now you're going to be plastered across every newspaper in the land.'

Jud stared at the floor. There was nothing left to say. Like Bonati said, his father would've bawled him out, no question – out of worry more than anything. There was no way Jason Goode could contemplate losing his son again. Especially as he believed, just like Bonati did, that Jamie hadn't committed the crime he'd been charged with. He was innocent. Always had been. And to lose him now . . .

'Then there's the CRYPT,' Bonati carried on. 'You may have blown your cover. Maybe blown it for all of us. You know that, don't you, Jud? How can we work undercover now?

'Look, I've told you – and no doubt your father has too – about how important it is to keep the agency under wraps. The

CRYPT *has* to be discreet. We've been through this so many times before . . .'

'I know, sir.'

'The CRYPT was given its licence from MI5 on the strict condition that it remained a *secret* organisation. You know the trouble your father and I had when we first set up the PIT. The paranormal still holds a real fear in the public's mind. As soon as they know there's an actual organisation devoted to investigating paranormal activity, we'll be inundated with everything from hoax calls from crackpots wanting to see what we do, to panic-stricken demands for us to investigate every squeak in the attic or door slamming in the wind. It'll be chaos, J.'

Jud fell silent. He braced himself. He knew this might be one outburst too many. His record for controlling his temper at the institution was not a good one. But then that wasn't new.

Losing his temper was something he had always struggled with. Ever since his parents had packed him off to boarding school – that's when the trouble started. Resentful and feeling like he was unwanted, Jamie had found those first few months at school horrendous. But unlike some of his classmates, who cried like babies with homesickness, Jamie just felt angry for being abandoned in this way. And his anger often led to arguments and even fights. His school reports had been peppered with comments about his temper.

And it was those same reports that had been dragged up in court. The prosecution had made such a big deal about his temper. It had been a recurring theme throughout his trial. It was suggested that it was in one of these violent moods that Jamie had lost control and fought with his mother, pushing her over the battlements and causing her death.

All untrue. All lies. But so difficult to prove otherwise. His school record didn't exactly paint a picture of a passive, easy-going boy who loved his parents. And the accounts of his teachers and friends didn't help either.

And now here he was, in trouble for losing it again. But as Bonati knew better than anyone, here was a boy who had more reasons than most to be angry.

If he could have started again - wound the clock back for Jamie, begged Jason not to send his son away to boarding school in England, he would have done so. Things might have been so different.

Since arriving in the CRYPT, Jud had endured hours of counselling - it had been a stipulation of the order, part of the deal to allow him out. All those crappy sessions with the therapist, learning how to manage his anger. Let it go. Release the tension. Count. Breathe. Do anything, just don't get mad.

But there was so much to be mad about. The therapist, just like all those before her, could go home to her normal house, with her normal family, and her normal life. Jud, Jamie, J - whatever the hell his name was these days - had to remain underground in the CRYPT with a father he called sir and a family of strangers. Just like in the institution.

Back there, whenever he'd tried to protest to fellow inmates and staff that his mother had actually been thrown off the battlements by a ghost, that he'd seen it all happen and had suffered nightmares ever since, he was always subjected to the usual teasing, beating and locking up, in that order. And it was in the solitary confinement that followed when the nightmares took hold and often stretched into daydreams. Gruesome faces, black shadowy wretches scampering up the tower, dragging his mother behind them like a rag doll. Their hideous screeching that rattled around the stone turret. And then the chilling scream of his mother as she fell from the top.

But the teasing continued.

'That Jamie Goode, he's off his rocker, man. I mean, 'e's mad. Totally.'

No one - no one except his father and Bonati - ever believed that he was innocent of the worst crime there is. The thought that it was ghosts who'd killed his mother seemed ridiculous to everyone else.

And the result: he developed a tough skin like a suit of armour most of the time; self-preservation kicked in and he became a survivor. But there were still times – even now, in the CRYPT, where he was semi-free – when the blood rose up in his veins, his heart thumped like a machine gun, and the anger-fuelled adrenalin let rip.

And now it had happened at Greyfriars. The horrifying thought that the truth was going to come out of that rat-faced reporter. His stupid, sneaky face. His 'I know something you don't know' kind of grin. He'd needed silencing. Jud had known that. So he'd let rip.

And now he found himself in trouble again. Only this time it was different. It wasn't some brawl with another offender, or a row with a guard, which twenty-four hours in solitary would fix. It was his liberty that was at stake. Locked up in the institution, they couldn't threaten to remove his freedom. He was already banged up. But now that he was out – albeit under close surveillance – everything mattered more. Being in trouble mattered. He was beginning to care again.

Bonati was still pacing.

'And of course Covert Policing Command have been on. You didn't think the CPC would ignore what's happened, did you? Or MI5 for that matter. Huh? Are you listening?'

Jud nodded, but continued staring at the wall. He was remembering the ugly mesh fences that had surrounded the compound outside his room at the institution. How he'd imagined scaling them one day, and running. Would he be staring for hours at the same view every day once again? Was he going back?

The professor continued. 'As you well know, your release from prison was absolutely conditional on you following the bail conditions – which meant abiding by the curfew, reporting in to the CPC, and – above all – keeping a bloody low profile.'

'Yes, sir.'

'So what d'you do? You get into a fight in front of the paparazzi and get yourself plastered all over the newspapers like some bloody celebrity. *Very* low profile. Well done.'

Jud was gazing into nothing. Thinking thoughts but knowing better than to voice them now. Bonati was in no mood to listen to some sob story about how no one understood him, or appreciated what he'd been through, or truly knew what he'd seen that night at the castle.

The professor sensed that Jud was drifting into his own world again. 'Jamie!' he shouted. 'Listen to me!'

There was a knock on the door.

Bonati shut up suddenly. He looked embarrassed. He shouldn't have been so careless with Jud's real name. If keeping a low profile was so important, then why was he yelling it across the room for the whole world to hear? He was a hypocrite, and he knew it.

'Yes?' he snapped angrily, in the direction of the door.

Dr Vorzek entered.

Jud and Bonati exchanged furtive glances. Had she heard? How much?

Silently they agreed to say nothing further and waited for her to speak.

'Sorry to intrude, Professor, but I wanted to remind you about the news conference.'

'Oh yes,' said Bonati. 'Time?'

'Three o'clock. We've got ten minutes.'

'Thanks, Kim. I was just telling Lester here how his little outburst this morning might have cost us the whole operation.'

'Ah.' Vorzek tried to look sympathetic. She knew, like everyone did, how Jud struggled at times. Of course, she didn't know why. She thought he'd just always been a hot-tempered kind of kid. Typical teenage boy. But she'd offered him more sympathy than most of the adults in his life had ever done. She was good news. And he was certainly glad she'd just walked in.

Bonati began again, this time in a softer voice. And this time making sure to keep much of their previous conversation under wraps.

'Jud. I'll cut to the chase.'

Here we go, thought Jud. Time to leave.

'I've thought about it. And I've chatted to Mr Goode, too.'

'What? You have?' said Jud quickly. That was a surprise. Why hadn't Bonati said so at the beginning? 'And what did Mr Goode say?'

Bonati shook his head slowly and shrugged his shoulders. 'I think you probably know what he said, Lester . . . but there is a lady present, so I'm afraid I can't repeat most of it.'

Vorzek didn't appreciate this sudden sensitivity. Bonati may have intended to sound polite and chivalrous, but patronising and bloody stupid were the words that came to her mind. Still, she kept silent.

'Oh,' said Jud.

'I told him about what happened at the tube station, Jud. How we nearly lost you under that train. He was more concerned about that.'

'Oh.' In the frenzy of Greyfriars, Jud hadn't been thinking of the experiences at Holborn tube, though his painful ankle served as a regular reminder. The nurse at the CRYPT had given him a once-over as soon as they'd returned from the tube station and given him the all-clear – just a sprained ankle. She'd said he had been lucky, though that was the last word he would have used to describe his day now.

Bonati continued, 'Mr Goode said – and if I'm truthful, I think he has a point, Jud – that you can't be blamed for losing your cool if moments earlier you'd faced a train head on and nearly died.'

Jud shrugged. Vorzek tried to smile at him but he didn't look up.

'So, given all you've been through,' Bonati said, glaring sympathetically at Jud across the room, 'Mr Goode has advised me to allow you to continue at the CRYPT and we'll take our chances with what happens next. See what the papers do with it. If you've blown our cover, then it won't be just you who's out of a job. It'll be all of us. There'll be no point in continuing. Either we'll scare the city to death and be shut down, or the sudden interest in what we do will mean every investigation scene ends up looking like Wembley stadium and we'll never get a single reading that counts.'

The professor walked closer to Jud.

'So, one more little indiscretion, one more outburst, and we'll send you back to where you came from. *Straight* back. Understand?'

Bonati stared knowingly into Jud's eyes. Message received. He understood. The metal fences, the solitary confinement. His freedom was fragile, like a bubble.

'Giles?' It was Vorzek's turn to speak. 'Will the reporter be pressing charges? Is there a case? What did Khan say?'

'I was coming to that. Khan's told me he won't allow an assault charge against you; he'll say you were provoked and pushed. He'll charge the reporter with causing an affray, if – and bear in mind you have no choice about this Jud, so don't react in your usual way – *if* you manage to come up with proper evidence and an explanation for the atrocities around us. You've gotta find some answers, and quick. But if you screw up, he'll have you in court quicker than you can say "boo", and you don't want an assault charge against your name, do you?'

Jud shook his head solemnly. He knew what that would lead to.

'I've had to send other agents to Greyfriars now – to continue the tests and talk to the people, like *you* should have done. Just hope they come up with some real evidence for you. One thing's for sure, Jud, I bet *they* won't lose their cool.'

'They won't,' said Jud. *Because they don't have as much to lose as I do,* he thought. The prospect of being identified as Jamie Goode had rattled him. He'd never come that close before and hadn't realised how much he appreciated his freedom – albeit a limited freedom – until it had been threatened again.

Jud's thoughts were interrupted by the ringing of Bonati's phone.

'Yes? The press conference, I know. Kim's told me. We're on it.' Bonati replaced the receiver, then pressed the intercom button and sent a message around the CRYPT's labyrinth of speaker systems.

'Will all available agents report to Level 3, Office 1 immediately, please.'

Jud was happy they'd been interrupted. A huge sense of relief was beginning to grow inside him, cooling the anger and frustration like water on a fire.

A few minutes later Bonati, Vorzek and Jud were joined by an army of CRYPT agents. The giant screen had been lowered against the left wall and Bonati was fiddling with the remote to find the correct channel.

Questions were buzzing. What was Khan going to say? Would the agency's cover be blown for ever? Radio and television news channels had picked up on the story within minutes of Jud's fight in the garden. The bloodied face of the reporter had been plastered across the lunchtime news. And so had Jud Lester's.

The front page of the *Evening Standard* would be running with: NOW THEY'RE LOOKING FOR GHOSTS.

The screen showed the tail end of a dull programme about decorating. As the credits rolled, more zombies and skulls entered the room, arguing about what the hell the police would say now that the world knew ghost hunters had been called in. David Blackwell, a second-year skull who'd never liked Jud, called across the room, 'You should've kept your temper, Lester. You should've walked away.'

'Tryin' to impress the girl, were you?' shouted Nik. He'd seen Bex De Verre and felt aggrieved that Jud should be paired up with her.

This was too much. Less than seven hours ago, Jud had been trapped in a tube tunnel, seconds away from death. Though the threats from Khan to charge him with assault and the following lecture from Bonati had quietened him, to face anger and ridicule from these guys now was just too much. He leapt from his seat in the corner and flew at Nik.

'That's enough!' Bonati moved swiftly to intercept Jud. 'What did I say? What have we just been talking about? Eh? We've seen enough violence today, Lester.' Then he turned to the students who'd been goading him.

'And *you* need to grow up. We're a team. I appointed Jud to this assignment and I don't blame him for the way things have turned out. Anyone who does should see me after this meeting, so I can put them straight.'

He moved back to his desk.

'Now shut up and listen – Khan's on.'

They turned to face the screen.

'And now we go live to Scotland Yard, where I'm told the chief investigating officer will make his statement.' The picture behind the newsreader increased to full screen and viewers saw a conference room crammed full of reporters. DCI Khan was seated at the front, surrounded by microphones and flanked by an army of police officers and officials.

There was shouting in the press room. Tempers were running high. Reporters wanted answers.

Khan tried to settle them down. 'Good afternoon, everyone. And thank you for coming. As you know, there was a further episode today in the ongoing investigation relating to the London raids. The incident took place at Greyfriars Garden, Newgate Street, this morning. It is believed that between approximately 8.15 and 8.30 a.m., a woman was abducted from this location.

Eyewitness accounts are mixed as to the circumstances in which she disappeared. We're still gathering evidence. More details will be made available in due course.

'At this moment in time we cannot say for certain that there is any link at all between this incident and the atrocities seen yesterday at other locations in central London. We have no conclusive evidence to link these crimes. Yet. But we *will* find answers.'

The shouting began again. This wasn't enough. It was a joke. The world was expecting more. Reporters shouted at Khan.

'You'll have to do better than that!'

'This is nothin'!'

'Have you got no leads, no theories?'

The detective chief inspector stood up and tried to raise his voice over the din.

'That is all I can say at this moment.'

The crowd shouted even louder. No one was satisfied.

Khan tried again. 'In the meantime . . . I said in the meantime, may I urge the public not to panic. We're doing everything in our power to catch the perpetrators of these crimes. And we're deploying all our resources to make London as safe as possible—'

'But you're failing!' someone interrupted him from the back.

Khan ignored this and carried on. 'People should go about their daily business as responsibly as they can. And report anything suspicious to the authorities.'

He looked down at his notes. He was sweating. He took a glug of water from a glass beside him. The ulcer in his stomach tugged and heaved.

He continued again. 'Now, I am aware that after the abduction took place, a minor altercation occurred in Greyfriars, in which a member of the press was assaulted by another man. You'll have heard that the assailant has been described as an "investigator".

'He does not work for the Metropolitan Police, but he *was*

there in an official capacity. It's true that he is what is known as a psychic investigator.'

Vorzek shouted at the screen: 'What? Why did he say that?'

Bonati looked resolute. He'd already had a conversation with Khan and knew precisely what he was going to say.

'There's nothing else he could do, Kim. It's already out there. People know. Some of them saw what happened, for God's sake. But we don't have to say where Jud and Bex are from, or who they actually work for. You know the procedure. We've done it before.'

Vorzek nodded and they watched the screen.

The shouting rose again in the press room. Reporters and photographers all had their own views on what that meant.

'You looking for ghosts now?'

'Is it true what they're saying?'

'What the hell's going on, Detective Chief Inspector? Do you believe in witches now?'

Khan looked awkward. He was blinking. He shuffled his papers unnecessarily. Bonati was watching anxiously. *Remember the script, Khan. Don't get sidetracked.*

Khan continued. 'I've commissioned a team of experts, which includes psychics, to look at the crime scenes for us. It's not unheard of – we've done it before. We work with anyone who will help us to understand the circumstances that lead to crimes, the way people think and what motivates them: psychic mediums, psychological profilers, anyone. We wanna get to the truth.'

The buzz in the conference room rose again. Someone shouted the word 'ghosts' and another yelled out 'hauntings'. The public, in their living rooms, offices and shops, would be watching and listening to this.

Bonati and Khan had rehearsed the speech – tried to keep it low-key and calm. No mention of ghosts or hauntings. Just ordinary policing and investigation work. But they couldn't prevent the reporters from stirring it up. The hacks wanted their front-page stories. Something sensational. It didn't matter what Khan said. They'd already written their headlines.

'Cut the transmission!' Bonati shouted at the screen. 'Come on, Khan! End of conference. Back to the studio!' He knew that if the cameras stayed live for much longer, the viewing public would hear even more references to ghosts from the scare-mongering journalists, and then the fear would spread. Just like it had before. Just like with the PIT.

Yet more uninvited questions came from reporters.

'Are you *actually* saying a ghost did this?'

'Are we being attacked by spirits?'

'Do you believe in the devil, Inspector?'

'Is evil at work here?'

Khan asked for silence. Bonati could see that he looked angry.

'Ladies and gentlemen, I do not believe that these crimes were committed by anyone or *anything* other than cruel, callous humans. I believe Man is capable of evil, without the need for anything supernatural. But it's essential that I conduct an investigation that is thorough and leaves no stone unturned. And if psychics can help provide answers, then so be it.'

He looked over the heads of the frenzied reporters at the cameras at the back of the room – and straight into the faces of the viewers.

'There really is no need for alarm. Let the newspapers say what they wish – ghostly hauntings make for a good story, I've no doubt – but thirty years at the Met have shown me that humans can be ingenious, resourceful and determined in their desire to cause harm and spread mass fear. Whichever person or persons are responsible for this – and rest assured we shall find and punish them – they will be intent on spreading panic across our city, and the suggestion of ghosts will only help them to achieve this goal. Let's remain calm and rational. Let's not allow our imaginations to get the better of us. We must deal in facts only.'

Khan stood up. 'That's it. That's all I have for the moment. I'll keep you informed of developments as they occur. Thank you, ladies and gentlemen. Thank you . . . thank you. Nothing further.'

He made for the door, ignoring the shouts and cries for more information. The room descended into chaos.

'Come on!' yelled one of the skulls in Bonati's office. 'Cut! Back to the studio!'

Eventually the screen returned to a dazed-looking newsreader, who tried to carry on with the rest of the day's news.

Bonati pressed his remote and the giant screen went black. The room was silent. Everyone looked at each other. No one really knew where this was leading, but they all knew it was heading somewhere.

Vorzek sensed the tension. 'Khan did all right, I thought.'

'Not bad,' said a skull. 'Could've been better, but could've been so much worse, sir.'

Bonati just stared at the blank screen. 'Yes,' he said. 'But the question still remains, ladies and gentlemen: what the hell is plaguing this city?'

CHAPTER 14

TUESDAY: 6.07 P.M.

ST SEPULCHRE'S CHURCH, HOLBORN

The Reverend Mark Painter, curate of St Sepulchre's Church.

It sounded good.

Mark said it again to himself. *Curate of St Sepulchre's.* Two months into the job and the title still sounded impressive. He'd been appointed to St Sepulchre's, straight from theological college for his four years of curacy before becoming ordained as a vicar.

And now here he was, robed up and ready for his first evensong. He was in the driving seat. Tonight would be his first chance to lead a service, and not just help the vicar, Nigel Stanton. As friendly as his mentor was, Mark wanted more than anything to lead a service himself – it was why he went to college.

And here was his chance. At last.

He turned to face the altar and prepared his notes once again. Fourth time of checking. He glanced at his watch: 6.07 p.m. The congregation would begin arriving soon for the seven o'clock service.

There was an air of anticipation about the place tonight. The flowers he'd ordered had arrived and looked magnificent at the entrance and up on the altar. The brass rails leading to the pulpit were polished so you could see your face in them. The newly restored flagstones were free of blemishes, save for the red and blue swirls cast down from the stained-glass windows as the evening sun poured through them. And the uniform rows of polished oak pews gleamed beneath the chandeliers above. Their symmetry pleased the obsessive young curate.

He decided he had time to run through his address just once more, this time from the pulpit.

He climbed the stairs and laid his notes out across the lectern at the top, smoothing his hands gently over the pages and straightening their corners. He looked up. The church always seemed more daunting from this viewpoint, but he'd practised so many times and didn't feel fazed by the great space around him. Tonight this was *his* theatre. *His* audience. And the address he'd planned was going to be the best of his career so far. The funniest, the cleverest and the most sincere.

'My good friends, I'm going to begin tonight by asking you a question. When was the last time you—'

He stopped.

What was that?

A noise. Hard to make out exactly. It was so faint.

A bell?

A siren?

St Sepulchre's was right in the heart of London. Mark knew it could've been any number of different elements that made up the usual hum of city life. He carried on.

'I want to begin by posing a question. When was the last time you said to yourself "I wish I'd done that"? A time when you said—'

There it was again. What *was* that noise?

He glanced down at the pews and the pillars. He was sure the sound wasn't coming from outside. It was *inside* the church. Was it Duncan, the verger, coming in to help him set up? He was due any minute.

But it was a bell. Definitely a bell.

Mark descended from the pulpit and slowly walked down the central aisle. The noise had come from his left – and not far away.

'Hello?' he said. 'Anyone there? Duncan? Is that you?'

Silence.

'Is there someone there?'

Nothing.

Mark had worked in and around churches all his life. He'd been a choirboy and an altar server, a sidesman and even an organist on occasion. He was no stranger to working in the quiet solitude of empty churches, and such places had never unsettled him. But now he felt alone. Acutely alone.

He walked back towards the altar.

The bell sounded again. He spun around.

It couldn't be. Surely.

The sound was coming from the same place each time. The same spot, not far from where Mark was now standing. He suddenly felt a chill inside.

It couldn't be. Not there.

He went to look. There was an ancient handbell kept inside a glass cabinet on a pillar near the front pews on the left.

Don't be stupid. How can it ring itself? This is madness, he thought. *Get a grip.*

The bell hadn't moved. Of course it hadn't! It was still in its sealed cabinet. But there'd definitely been the sound of ringing. He'd *heard* it. And it seemed to have come from this direction.

He looked into the cabinet.

Nothing. No movement, no sound.

He walked around the pillar, shuffling past the pews that butted up to it.

Still nothing.

Suddenly he felt cold. Had the heating gone off? A new system had only just been installed. Surely it hadn't packed up already.

104

He walked over to a radiator. Hot.

He returned to the bell and felt distinctly cold again. Almost like he was walking through the chilled section in a supermarket.

He stared at the cabinet. He saw his reflection in the glass and the altar behind him. He looked tired. There were dark circles beneath his eyes.

He looked deep into his own reflection. He saw his eyes widen.

Trick of the glass.

But they were still widening. Large ebony spheres in his face, which caught the light. They seemed huge.

Still a trick of the glass.

Quickly he looked away and felt round his eyes. Normal. *Just a reflection, you fool.*

The solitude of the church and the growing darkness outside were playing tricks on his imagination. Maybe his nerves were finally getting to him.

Then the bell sounded for a third time.

A faint but unmistakable ring, from deep within the case. He glanced into it again. The bell appeared to have gained a reddish glow.

It couldn't have. Trick of the light.

His eyes refocused and he saw his own face again, mirrored in the glass.

He saw the great dark pools where his eyes should be, only this time they didn't shine. They were empty sockets. And they were growing. He saw his cheekbones shrivel. He grabbed his face. It still felt normal. But the hand he'd used to touch his skin looked hideous in the glass. Gnarled and shrivelled. Flesh was peeling from his knuckles. He glanced quickly down at his hand – it looked normal.

And then it happened.

With a sudden crash the glowing bell rose up from its position and began rocking frantically to and fro. The noise was deafening. Tiny electrical sparks seemed to dance across the metal surface. Within a split second the glass case exploded into a thousand fragments and the bell struck the curate full in the face. His nose exploded. Blood splattered across the remains of the cabinet, and all the way down the pillar as he fell.

He struck his head on the stone floor and passed out.

The bell landed with a booming crash on the floor beside him. The metallic ringing continued as the curved brass rolled back and forth over the hard stone, the glowing sparks fading gradually. Soon it fell still. And silent. The curate's blood slowly seeped across the stone and framed the outline of the bell.

There was a sound. At the rear of the church. An iron door handle rattled.

It was the verger. Duncan Greenford entered.

'Hello? Mark? I'm here,' he shouted politely from the back.

The curate was probably up at the altar, preparing his speech, Duncan thought. He walked tentatively down the central aisle, wincing at times. His hips had been slowing down of late – he'd refused to let on to anyone that the job was getting to be too much for him, now that the arthritis had set in.

'Sorry I'm late, Reverend, you'll never guess who I bumped–'

He stopped. He pulled a handkerchief from his pocket and retched into it. He closed his eyes, then reopened them.

The sight was horrid.

The young man's face was covered in blood. There was little left of his nose. Just a pulpy mass of red flesh, which continued to leak on to the flagstones beneath him.

'Mark. Oh Lord! Mark, can you hear me?'

He knelt down slowly, bent over the curate and listened for a breath.

He *was* breathing. Duncan felt for a pulse. Faint, almost imperceptible, but it was there. Slow and steady.

Whatever had just happened, whoever had done this, the police would find out. But right now, Duncan just wanted to wake him up.

'Mark! Can you hear me, Mark?'

Nothing.

'Duncan?' His wife entered the church. 'Duncan, what's happened?' She was moving down the aisle.

'No! Mary! Wait—' But it was too late. She'd seen everything.

She screamed and began to shake uncontrollably.

'Oh God. No! Duncan, do something!' she sobbed, loud sobs that echoed around the empty church.

The sound of his wife's crying shook Duncan into action. He reached for his mobile phone and, with trembling fingers, dialled three nines.

CHAPTER 15

TUESDAY: 7.31 P.M.

HIGH HOLBORN

'I'm already on my way, sir.'

'Good. That's fast, Jud. Now, I want results this time. I told Detective Chief Inspector Khan you wouldn't leave the church until you'd got something. And I don't care how long it takes.' Bonati's voice rattled around Jud's bike helmet.

When the orders had come in, Jud had grabbed his bag of equipment, still packed from his visit to the tube station, and sped out of the CRYPT as quickly as he could, denying Bonati time to send Bex with him again. It was too late; he'd already gone.

Bex wasn't bad, as zombies went, and a female one at that. She was all right, he had to admit – her great looks had certainly been a welcome addition to the CRYPT. The other skulls had all been talking about her. But when it came to work, Jud preferred it alone; it gave him more freedom.

If he'd thought about it, Jud would have realised that he'd become obsessed with freedom. But not just freedom to live – freedom from relationships of any kind. After everything that had happened in his life, he found it hard to make any kind of friendship – working or personal. Having to make small talk, thinking of polite things to say, sharing his thoughts with someone else – it just confined him, caged him in. And there would always be so much he couldn't tell a friend anyway. Not making friends meant not having to lie so much, about who he was, and what he'd been through. Jud was his own boss and he preferred it that way.

He opened up the throttle and sped along Fleet Street. The rasp of the exhaust spat into the evening air. At Ludgate Hill he turned up Old Bailey and reached the junction at the end in just a few short seconds. The great edifice of the old court towered over him. As he approached the church on the other side of Holborn, he saw the flashing lights of the ambulance and police cars, bouncing off the steeple and flashing past the gravestones. Suddenly the images of that fateful night at the castle flooded his tired mind, as they so often did whenever he saw blue flashing lights and ambulances.

The way the castle had been floodlit, the blue lights leaping from the police cars on to the old stone walls and flickering past the cold body of his mother, slumped on the hard ground beneath the tower; the noise of the sirens; the shouts from the paramedics; and then the blinding lights of his father's Maserati as it swung through the arches and swept into the quadrangle.

Jud shook away these macabre thoughts before they took hold. He'd been revisiting the past too many times of late. Maybe it was the new intake of first-years. He'd been thinking about his own entry into the CRYPT. And now, one year on, though he was a well-respected agent, and the one every zombie aspired to be like, inside he was no stronger than before. The memories of what had happened to him still ran deep. Only Bonati and his father understood, and the opportunities to talk to them were few – especially now the new intake of agents was here, all needing attention.

As he waited for the traffic to clear so he could cross Holborn, he breathed in deeply and told himself to get a grip. The day's events were bound to have affected him. But he had a job to do. A reputation to live up to, and Bonati was counting on him. *Get a grip.*

A small crowd of people stood outside St Sepulchre's – the modest congregation who'd turned up for the service only to be refused entry by a confused and anxious verger. No details had been offered.

Parking the bike quickly on the road beside the railings, Jud removed his helmet and ran through the gates into the church. Luckily there were no reporters there. Yet.

The paramedics were just lifting Mark Painter on to a stretcher. They'd managed to rouse him, but he was clearly delirious – shouting something about a bell; saying it had struck him in the face.

As Jud approached, the paramedics pushed him away, saying it was vital they got the patient into the ambulance to run tests as soon as possible. The injury sustained to his head had caused some delirium, judging by his strange ramblings about a bell coming to life. They wanted him in hospital *now*. The questioning would have to wait.

The curate was shouting all the way down the aisle towards the door.

'The bell! The bell! It's ALIVE!'

Jud walked towards the huddle of policemen at the front of the church. They crowded around something on the floor. It was clearly a large brass bell, bloodstained and dented.

'Jud Lester, I suppose? The detective chief inspector said you were coming,' an officer said.

'I want no trouble from you,' said another, with a smirk across his face.

Jud's reputation had preceded him, thanks to the earlier incident at Greyfriars. Now the world was full of jokers.

'I take it this was the instrument that injured him?' asked Jud, pointing towards the bell on the floor.

'Well, it looks like a bell to me. What d'ya think, Gary?'

'Yep. I think it's a bell,' nodded the other officer, and they tried to show the most sarcastic faces they could. Who was this kid in his black leathers, anyway?

Jud wasn't going to be riled again. He sniffed out a chuckle and smiled.

'But the assailant's long gone,' said the first officer.

Jud turned to Duncan Greenford, who was comforting his wife in a nearby pew.

'Were you the person who reported the incident? You found him, yeah?'

'That's right.'

'And there was no sign of anyone else here? You saw no one?'

'I saw no one. I've already told the officers this. I saw no one, I heard no one. I came to help Mark get ready for the service. The vicar's visiting relatives in Birmingham this week, so Father Mark is in charge . . . *was* in charge . . . I found him out cold on the floor over there.' The verger looked shaken. In his seventies, his face was lined and worn at the best of times, but he now looked pale and his fingers were still trembling slightly. Beside him his wife dabbed at her red eyes with a wrinkled tissue she'd retrieved from up her sleeve. Clearly they needed to go home, but would this man be up for questions later? Unlikely, by the looks of him, thought Jud.

Though he rarely liked to interview witnesses before he'd had a chance to scour the scene for himself and allow his senses to work freely, Jud knew he should ask a few questions of Greenford now, and then let him go home and try to recover from what he'd seen.

'OK,' he said, glancing back towards the place where the bell still sat on the floor. 'So tell me about this bell, Mr . . . ?'

'Greenford. Duncan Greenford. I'm the verger here.'

'I see. It's obviously an antique. I take it it belongs in this cabinet up here, yes?'

'That's correct. It's the Execution Bell.'

Jud stopped. He turned round to face Greenford.

'What did you say?'

'I said it's the Execution Bell. Read the sign. It'll tell you everything.'

Jud looked at the broken cabinet still fixed to the stone pillar and read the great marble plaque next to it.

THE EXECUTION BELL

This bell was rung outside the condemned cell at Newgate by the bellman of St Sepulchre's at midnight on the eve of an execution, when he recited the following lines:

> *All you that in the condemned hole do lie,*
> *Prepare you, for tomorrow you shall die.*
> *Watch all, and pray; the hour is drawing near*
> *That you before the Almighty must appear.*
> *Examine well yourselves, in time repent,*
> *That you may not to eternal flames be sent,*
> *And when St Sepulchre's bell in the morning tolls,*
> *The Lord above have mercy on your souls.*

He looked down at the bloodied bell lying on the stone floor. What story was it trying to tell him? Who, or what, was trying to communicate? And why now? If the curate's ramblings were to be believed and the bell had sprung to life and launched itself at him – and certainly the verger had said he saw no one else in here who could've done it – then there was paranormal activity at work for sure.

Jud decided he wasn't going to budge from this place until something else happened. He wouldn't miss it, not this time. He looked at his watch. Two minutes to eight. Four hours and it would be midnight. The sign said the bell was rung at midnight on the eve of executions. If anything was going to happen tonight, it made sense to Jud that it would be then.

But why had the bell rung earlier, as the curate said?

Was it summoning someone?

It was going to be a long wait, but he was determined to catch something. Some movement, some temperature change, some sound, even a sighting maybe. This bell was significant. Something was stirring. And he would record it.

'Has this ever happened before?' he asked Greenford.

'Of course it hasn't! What kind of a question is that? And who are you anyway? You don't look much like a police officer to me.'

'I'm not,' said Jud. 'But I can let you go now. I think we've got everything. Please, take your wife home and have a stiff drink.'

Greenford got up and moved past him.

'I don't drink,' he said sternly. Then he left the building, holding his wife's arm, and looking back over his shoulder as he went.

Jud told the police officers that they too could leave the building. This investigation might take all night, he said.

They replied that they needed the bell to be bagged up and taken with them to the station. It was, after all, an offensive weapon now.

'Sorry, guys. Not possible, I'm afraid.'

'You what?'

'I said not possible. This bell is significant. And I get the feeling it's not finished for tonight. I need to watch it.'

'You need to watch it?' one of the officers said, smirking. 'Don't tell me, it's going to leap up and dance a jig, is it?'

The two policemen laughed as they left, shaking their heads.

'You better keep your fingerprints off it, though,' shouted one of them over his shoulder. 'Or you'll be facing a charge of vicar-bashing.'

Jud watched them shuffle out of the door at the back. He heard the great metal latch close with a clunk.

He was alone.

He went back and examined the handbell closely. There were bloodstains on the edge where presumably it had struck the curate across the face. But how had it moved? What had moved it? He picked it up, grasping it with the end of his sleeve so as not to disturb fingerprints, or leave his own. It was heavy. A solid brass bell with a wooden handle – these things didn't move by themselves. Something had moved it. Some force. Some energy.

He decided to return to the bike to fetch the rest of his equipment. He left the church and came back a few minutes later carrying the two large metal panniers, which detached from the bike and served as briefcases. Entering the church for the second time, he was suddenly aware of the silence. The traffic outside was dissipating, but there'd still been noise out there. In here there was nothing. But it couldn't be described as peaceful. There was no feeling of calm, or serenity, like you'd expect in a church. Not tonight. Somehow the atmosphere was restless, awkward, unsettling. Jud wondered if it was always like this here. It wasn't anything he could see especially. Apart from the broken case on the pillar, everything looked in order. But there was something almost tangibly sad about the place tonight. Angry even. His ESP was running into overdrive. Emotions, moods and shifts in the atmosphere were coming to him. Through him.

He sat on a pew and breathed deeply, allowing the residues of whatever had been in there to soak into him. Whenever paranormal activity occurred it always left a residue. Not just the electrical energy left floating in the ether, but a feeling, a trace of something left behind. A mood. If you sat still and opened your senses to possibilities, you could usually detect it. Jud often described it as being like an odour that lingered. But one that you felt, rather than smelled.

Here, in the solitude of St Sepulchre's, Jud felt discontented. Not frightened, but sad.

There was a feeling that it was too late. Something was too

late. He sensed that something was unstoppable now. Like being on death row. Being sentenced to death.

That was it.

Whether it was the sign on the wall he'd just read, or something else, he wasn't sure, but there was an overwhelming feeling of impending doom. The eve of the execution. The last night for the condemned.

There was a sadness. You could feel it. Almost touch it. There was real paranormal residue left in the church. Jud was certain.

Quickly he got up, unpacked the cases he'd come in with, and laid the equipment out on a pew. The Tri-Axis EMF meter was connected wirelessly to his laptop, which he set up alongside it. He wanted to record everything so he could consider the data back at the lab. Within a few moments the meter was registering a normal EMF reading of 5mG. Pocketing the EMF and his electrostatic locator, he moved around the church. Same sorts of numbers: 7mG, 3mG. As he approached wiring in the walls, microphones or amplifiers the meter showed slightly higher readings of 14mG and 21mG. This was normal. The presence of electrical appliances meant greater electromagnetic radiation. He walked on. The meter returned to lower numbers again: 7, 5, 2. And then - 96mG.

He was near the pillar. Near the cabinet that had housed the Execution Bell.

He stood over the bell itself.

The digital numbers scrambled on the meter's screen, then settled.

147mG.

He took out his electrostatic locator and held it near the cabinet. The needle went crazy.

There was real energy here. A radiation. Far beyond the levels for normal environments, even churches, which often recorded higher levels, given the spiritual activity they housed. But this was different. It seemed so physical. There were no discernible appliances nearby that might give off anywhere near that kind of radiation.

It *had* to be something else. Something paranormal. And the bell was at the root of it. Something or someone had heard its call.

And they were coming for it.

CHAPTER 16

TUESDAY: 8.37 P.M.

THE DORCHESTER HOTEL, PARK LANE

'Another Moët and Chandon. And see that it's colder than the last one.' The waiter returned to the bar and Lucien Zakis crammed a fistful of olives into his mouth.

'Order anything you like. I'm feeling generous.' He grinned an ugly grin at his guests around the table. 'Tonight we celebrate The Tyburn – London's finest hotel. We'll show this country how to do it.' The Dorchester staff smiled discreetly and hid their disgust.

Seated around the large circular table in the private suite were architects, surveyors, interior designers and construction managers. All on the Zakis payroll – Lucien's army of yes-men. Together they would build the greatest hotel ever seen. And it would be right here, in the heart of the greatest city in the world.

Zakis continued his premature victory speech, ignoring the fact that the building was months away from completion.

'The Tyburn will symbolise all that is best in hotel accommodation and luxury living. Fine dining, first-class health spas and treatment centres, fast and efficient service and, of course, the glamour and glitz that go with Zakis Hotels. No one does it like Zakis, huh?'

The assembled group nodded and laughed obediently, then curled their lips and disguised their own thoughts inside their champagne glasses. Lucien was a bully, a crass and thuggish dictator, but he and the Zakis dynasty paid their wages – and handsomely. As Lucien's own team of consultants, they were all on six-figure salaries. They travelled everywhere with him, built every hotel with him, wined and dined with him. And now the cavalcade had rolled into London for the next project.

'As we speak,' continued Zakis, 'as we sit here sipping champagne, my boys are down there working round the clock. We *will* be ready. You should see the floodlights.' He grinned. 'Like Wembley Stadium down there. I tell you, guys, Zakis builders don't sleep.'

They laughed with him as he raised his glass for a toast to the construction team.

'To my night owls. May they never stop until we're done.'

After they'd drunk the toast, Julia Dubois, Lucien's new interior designer, spoke up.

'Mr Zakis, did you receive the mock-ups for the presidential suite?'

'I certainly did, my darling.' He grinned at her. 'But I want black marble rather than grey for the bathrooms.'

'I think we looked at black and decided that it was too—'

'I'm sorry, you didn't hear me right.' His faced had changed. 'I *want* black.' He turned to the waiter, who'd arrived with the Moët. 'Yeah, that feels colder.'

Miss Dubois looked down at the menu. Her cheeks flushed. Conversation over. She wouldn't try that again.

'Did you get the parking application you wanted, Mr Zakis?' said Brian Jackson, chief architect. 'Spoken to Silverman yet?'

Zakis downed his champagne and nodded. 'He's a puppy. Don't worry about Silver. He'll do what we want. Puppy wants his bone. You'll see. A three-storey car park with full valeting service and chauffeurs will rise from the ground in Green Street.

And puppy will get his treats in return. I don't care what's there now. I want it to happen. And it *will*.' He glugged his drink and said, 'Right, you guys, let's order.'

Suddenly his phone rang.

He quickly picked it up. 'Zakis here.'

The voice at the end of the phone seemed shaky.

'Mr Zakis, sir. It's Miles Harrison. There's been . . . er . . . an accident.'

'What?'

'There's been an *accident*, sir.'

'I heard you! What kind of accident? What do you mean, Harrison?'

'Here at the site. One of the labourers, sir.'

'Spit it out, man!' Zakis slammed his fist on the table. 'Speak, you dumb bastard!' Glasses bounced and cutlery clinked against china. His guests shot anxious looks at one another.

'Tell me NOW!' he said.

'I don't know what to say.'

'Then I suggest you think of something quickly or you're fired. Speak!'

'Well, it's Yuri. He's one of the construction workers we've just hired. You know, the new lot that came over from—'

'Yes! Get on with it.'

'Well, he's . . . er . . . he's . . . dead, sir.'

Without showing emotion, Zakis stood up quietly and left the table. His guests said nothing. He walked discreetly out of the restaurant and into the foyer. Finding a quiet corner, he sat down and said, 'Talk to me.'

'I just can't explain it, sir,' said Harrison, with a tremble in his voice.

'What're you talkin' about? Spit it out Now!'

'OK, OK. He's . . . he's been . . . well . . . *hanged*, Mr Zakis.'

CHAPTER 17

TUESDAY: 9.01 P.M.

MARBLE ARCH

The black Mercedes sped through the London traffic.

Zakis stared out of the rear window, his mobile phone pressed into his cheek. The orange glow from the streetlamps flickered across his face, alternating with the shadows. His eyes were determined and his cheeks shone with perspiration.

'Like I said. You talk to no one. You ring no one. You wait till I get there.'

Harrison was still panicking. 'But the police, sir. Shouldn't I call—'

'I've told you! You do nothing till I'm there. No one leaves the site. And no one enters. Got it? You get the gates ready. I'm coming.' Zakis ended the call and hurled the phone into the footwell of the car. 'Damn!' he shouted.

The bodyguard next to him said nothing. The driver glanced at Zakis in his rear-view mirror but kept silent too.

Minutes later the limousine swept around the traffic system and disappeared through the gates in the high wooden boarding that encircled the construction site. A security guard hurriedly shut the gates again and ran back into his Portakabin.

Zakis got out of the car. Miles Harrison, his duty manager on site, ran to the car.

'I'm sorry, sir. I'm sorry to have to disturb—'

'Shudup! Take me to the place.'

Harrison led Zakis and his men around past the cabins and site offices to the vast crater in the ground that was the foundations of the hotel. Giant steel struts, many metres high, rose up like colossal metal totem poles: a temple to greed.

'There!' shouted Harrison, fear in his voice. He was pointing to a distant strut in the far corner of the plan.

'What're ya talkin' about? Where?' demanded Zakis.

Harrison led him closer.

And then Zakis saw it.

A body. Swinging.

Halfway up the massive steel girder, metal branches stuck out horizontally in several directions – the mid-section of the building's frame. Swinging from one of these was the body of Yuri Kozlosky.

The scene resembled some futuristic gallows – all steel girders where they would have been wood.

But the body was real, and it swung in the breeze as the great tarpaulins rattled behind it. An expression of terror was etched indelibly on Yuri's face. His skin was greying, drained of blood. And his limbs were lifeless, dangling like a rag doll's.

Zakis went silent for a moment. No one said anything. His henchmen either side of him shuffled uncomfortably and sucked on their cigarettes.

After a few long seconds, Zakis turned to face Harrison and said slowly, 'I'm going to ask you one question. And your future depends on it. You tell me the truth – you live. You tell me lies – you join him up there. Now . . . who did this?'

Miles Harrison was twitching. His eyes were blinking quickly and the shirt around his thick neck felt like it was tightening. He glanced quickly at Zakis's bodyguards, as each one finished his cigarette and flicked the stub at his feet. Tobacco smoke rose up into his nostrils. He opened his mouth and stuttered:

'I . . . I . . . er . . . I mean, er . . . well, put it this way, sir . . . they weren't *human*.'

'What?' Zakis had gone pale.

'I mean, er . . . well, all the men who saw them said the same thing.'

'Which was?'

'*Ghosts*.'

Zakis walked right up to him. He was so close, Harrison could smell his breath: champagne and salty olives. The site manager glanced at Zakis's men, who had followed him and stood either side of him. He knew this was it. Whether his boss thought he was joking, drunk or stoned, or so scared he'd lost his mind, he couldn't tell; but either way he was finished.

In a slow, deliberate tone, Zakis said, 'If that's a lie, Harrison, then God help you. But if it's the truth . . . then God help us all.'

CHAPTER 18

TUESDAY: 11.51 P.M.

ST SEPULCHRE'S CHURCH, HOLBORN

Jud sat and waited. His eyes were tired. His head felt like it was filled with thick soup, heavy and dizzy.

The EMF meter had fluctuated over the last few hours but had still remained well beyond the usual levels for a church, particularly out of hours when there were no speakers or microphones in use and the heating and lighting were at a minimum. The readings shouldn't have been this high. But when Jud approached the pillar and the bell – which he'd now replaced back inside the open cabinet – the electrostatic locator went crazy.

The bell showed extreme levels of electrostatic energy.

He'd also taken temperature readings. The LCD display on his thermocouple thermometer had shown that the temperature dropped dramatically in the vicinity of the bell, confirming his worst suspicions that the curate's ramblings were accurate and the bell really had moved by itself.

Suddenly the meter registered movement. The energy source, which had remained in the same area constantly, was shifting. Though the levels near the bell still remained high, the readings had dropped from the mid hundreds to 86mG. At the same time, Jud noticed as he patrolled the central aisle, there were now higher readings towards the rear of the church, near the main doors – where the levels had previously been at their lowest: 43mG . . . 68mG . . . 101mG. Something was moving.

Or *approaching*.

Jud felt a sudden drop in temperature where he was standing – he didn't need his thermometer to register it. He glanced across at the Geiger counter too. Radiation levels were changing.

He was facing the door of the church. Was someone, or something, coming in?

Hurriedly he double-checked to see if his motion detector was still on. He grabbed his thermal imager, pointed it in the direction of the door and switched that on too. He moved to the light switches and dimmed them all. Moonlight gradually seeped in from the heavy stained-glass windows above him. It gave the church a mystical, ghostly feel, but there was enough light to see by.

The video camera was in position. He was primed and ready.

Come on. Do your worst.

He checked his bag for his EM neutraliser, just in case. You never know.

It was gone.

He emptied the entire rucksack on to the floor of the church. Gone.

He glanced at his watch. A few more seconds and it would be midnight. There was no point in leaving, just because he'd left it behind. He might not even need it.

But he was sure he'd packed it that morning. He remembered opening the safe, taking it out and placing it in the bag.

So where was it?

A large clock, up near the choir stalls, suddenly began to chime.

Midnight.

He turned towards the door and held his breath.

Nothing.

Then, gradually, something appeared.

Something – or someone – was coming *through* the great oak door, and yet it had remained bolted shut.

At first it was a strange grey mist. Cloudy and unclear.

And then he realised.

He was looking at what seemed like a projected image of a shoe, a black buckled shoe, followed by a white stocking and black breeches. The limbs were visible, yet lucent. A transparent body passing through the door right into the church.

It was the spectral body of the bellman.

It wore a dirty white shirt with an old leather tunic of some kind – like a long waistcoat. Its black brimmed hat shadowed its face at first. But then it lifted an old lantern it was carrying, up towards its head.

For the first time since joining the CRYPT, Jud felt scared. It was unlike any face he'd seen. So gaunt; so withered. Prominent cheekbones pushed through grey, mottled flesh, and between them lay – nothing. No nose. Like the gaping hole you saw in the centre of a human skull. A skeletal, bony outline of where the nose once was.

And the figure was slowly becoming more solid. The translucent effect that had first made it seem like a projection, or a holographic image, was now gradually changing, becoming opaque.

Jud knew, from past hauntings, what was happening. The electrical charge of the ionised plasma that formed the shape was increasing. Deep within the microscopic atoms, particles were gaining strength – whole molecules were becoming solid. The bellman's disembodied spirit – the strange, elusive dark matter that Bonati had written so much about – was right here, in the church. And it was drawing energy from somewhere. Forming a shape.

It was the eyes that struck Jud the most, and brought a sickness to his stomach – horrific balls of crimson, sunken deep into bony sockets. Blood red, with an electrical glow. Like open wounds: swollen, inflamed; and in their epicentre, large black pupils that darted across the church, searching for the bell.

His bell.

The bellman moved mindlessly. Unquestioning. Unthinking. He was obedient to some invisible force. The spirits had summoned him and he'd answered their call. Jud slunk into the floor space between the pews and peered over the edge.

The ghost's walk may have seemed mindless, but it had direction and purpose. He knew where he was going. It was habitual. The route he'd taken so often in life. Now, encased in plasma, his spirit could re-enact it all.

But why? And why now?

His eyes darted in Jud's direction.

A shaft of yellow light suddenly pushed through the windows and swept across the church, startling the ghost. A passing car outside. The ghost paused. The light ran through him, his body not yet fully solid. He stared upwards, and made a sound. Impossible to make it out. A raspy kind of clicking. Almost insect-like.

He checked his lantern, lifted it before him and walked further into the church. Further towards Jud.

The cold of the hard stone floor penetrated into Jud's legs as he knelt down between the pews. He was pointing the thermal imager at the apparition. The body was framed in blue as it shifted. A cold temperature surrounded it. But the energy readings on the EMF meter were higher than ever. The ghost was sourcing energy from somewhere. Perhaps the lantern. Jud studied it closely. The candle inside the black metal frame flickered with an intensity unlike any other he'd seen. The flame burned red, the colour of the ghost's eyes. And it was getting brighter. The electrostatic locator was now giving readings higher than Jud had ever seen before.

On the bellman moved, deeper into the church, further down the central aisle. It was now just a few feet behind Jud's pew. And getting closer. Jud remained still; statue-like. But he had to follow the ghost's movements. He had to keep facing it, otherwise the miniature video camera, strapped to his temple, would miss it. But cramp was setting into his knees. He was twisting awkwardly to keep the ghost in view. He shifted to release the pressure on his kneecaps and caught the pew behind him. There was a clonk of heel against wood.

The bellman stopped.

He faced Jud. He was staring just above his head.

Jud slunk even lower between the pews, almost out of sight. The red eyes of the bellman darted left and right, up and . . .

He didn't look down.

Jud's heart was thundering inside his chest.

If only he hadn't lost his neutraliser.

The ghost kept the lantern still raised to shoulder height and moved slowly on. Past Jud's pew. On towards the bell, which sat expectantly for him in the broken cabinet. Jud noticed it was now gaining a reddish tinge. A culmination of millions of tiny electrical sparks fizzing across the surface of the metal.

Setting his lantern down beside the cabinet, the ghost lifted the bell with both hands. Jud could see that his fingers were smoky white. Pure bone; no flesh.

His eyes swelled up even larger and the black pupils danced about. His mouth parted and the scratchy clicking noises returned. They weren't words. At least not to Jud. But there was a pattern to the sounds. It was almost like the bellman was reciting something in a language unknown. A language of whispers and ticks; of clicking and retching.

Jud listened closely, desperately extending his invisible antennae, using his ESP to reach out to the ghost's message.

Come on. Concentrate. You can hear it.

The sound, indistinguishable at first, began to fold into something coherent. Jud strained to listen in, his whole being fixed on the strange clicks that flowed like waves from the spirit world into his ears.

And then he heard it. In life the bellman had recited the lines so many times that now, in death, his spirit could repeat them still. In its own way. The clicking sounds rang around the hollow cavities of the ghost's head and awoke memories within it. Jud finally heard his cry, and it chilled him to the bone.

> *All you that in the condemned hole do lie,*
> *Prepare you, for tomorrow you shall die . . .*

The bellman lifted up the great brass bell. His withered arms found strength. His body was becoming fully opaque now – as solid as Jud's. But stronger, so much stronger. The plasma was transforming into solid matter.

Electrostatic energy, left as a residue on the bell after years of handling by its owner, was now feeding him. It was *his* bell, and it was repaying him.

Jud quickly looked at the EMF meter and the electrostatic locator. The levels were still rising. The thermal imager showed that heat was shifting – channelling from the bell into the cold, empty shell of its master.

His prize claimed, the bellman backed away from the cabinet. He held the bell in one hand and picked up the lantern in the other. Instantly the flame within it rose to an even brighter red. It blinded Jud. He shifted backwards and placed a hand before his eyes. His foot caught a leather prayer cushion, which was hooked on to the pew behind him. It fell to the floor. There was a soft thud. But it was enough.

The bellman had heard it.

With the lantern still dazzling, the ghost shuffled towards the sound. He lowered the lantern. He peered over it. His eyes grew wider and burned red.

He hadn't just found the bell tonight.

He'd found a new source of energy too.

Jud.

CHAPTER 19

WEDNESDAY: 12.07 A.M.

ST SEPULCHRE'S CHURCH, HOLBORN

The light from the bellman's lantern was too bright. Jud was helpless. Blinded by the intense flame, he could see just black silhouettes in front of him. He pulled his hands away from his eyes – which he then closed tightly to protect them – and launched his fists in the direction of the ghost. Pummelling into space. Jabbing. Punching.

He wasn't going to go down easily. Though he was scared, his temper alone would see him through. He was known for being tough in a fight, and this was no exception. Man or ghost. Flesh or spirit. Jud would have them.

But he just couldn't see – anything. Like when you come into a dark room from the bright sunlight, he only saw shadows. He stood up and launched himself blindly again at what he thought was the ghost.

The clicking noise from the bellman's mouth rose to a poisonous clatter, like a rattlesnake aroused.

Jud stooped and fell into the pew in front of him. He landed on the stone floor, hitting his head. A throbbing pain came to his skull but he was still conscious.

And then something pulled his leg sharply.

It was the ghost. Finding the bell at last had given him extraordinary strength. He was screeching and scratching. Animal-like sounds emitted from the gaping hole in his face. Savagely he grabbed Jud's feet and dragged him out of the pew into the space of the central aisle – like a child flings a rag doll around. Jud weighed nothing. He meant nothing. Just food.

Jud's head felt like it was in a vice. His eyes throbbed behind the thin skin of their lids. His body felt frozen from the cold of the stone floor. For the first time in his life, he was at the mercy of someone else. No control. No power.

But anger was overcoming fear within him, forcing his body into frenzied action. He lashed out and kicked.

The bellman's grip was too tight. Hunger was fixed in his red eyes. Mucus dribbled over his cracked lips. Determined cries rang around his empty head . . .

Batter him with the bell. Drive the hard brass into his skull. Pound his flesh. Make the meat soft and bloodied. Silence the wretch.

And then devour him.

He brought the bell down and caught Jud on the shoulder. The pain was searing. Agonising.

The ghost raised the bell once more. This time he would go for the skull and turn this wriggling prey into a still corpse. Then, while the flesh was still warm, he would have his meal.

His eyes slowly recovering, Jud could make out the yellowy shine of the brass bell climbing higher towards the dark roof above him. Like a guillotine rising before its fatal descent. He wriggled and squirmed. The pressure on his legs felt like a dead weight crushing him into paralysis. The ghost's power was immense. The pain from his shoulder rose.

The bell began to lower . . .

Jud tensed every muscle in his body as he waited for the end to come.

There was a deafening crash.

Behind them.

The sound of heavy wood striking stone; and the sound of an engine. The bell fell from the hand of the startled bellman. It landed on the lantern, smashing it into pieces and extinguishing its deadly flame. The bellman let out a cry of anguish that echoed up to the rafters above them. Jud covered his ears from the deafening howl.

Bright lights swept across the church as the engine still roared.

It was Bex.

She'd forced the great door open by using her own bike as a battering ram. Leaning back in the saddle, and revving the engine to its full extent, she'd forced the door off its hinges as the great front tyre bulldozed into it. She was inside.

She turned off the engine and allowed the bike's headlamps to search the church. She saw the apparition. He was moving across the pews, through them, emitting a strange, frantic clicking noise.

Quickly she grabbed her neutraliser from her bag and switched it on.

The sound of the door crashing and the strange roar of the bike had truly shocked the bellman. The breaking of the lantern had clearly weakened him too. Now the neutraliser was working its magic and dispersing the EM levels within the church. The energy source was reducing. The ghost was weakening gradually. Becoming translucent again.

But it had taken the bell.

Jud watched it slink off in the direction of the choir stalls, now just a cloudy image. The bell had changed too. Deep inside its structure, molecules were altering. The spaces between them were growing. Solid particles were weakening, becoming plasma. Then further still, transparent.

The ghost and his treasured prize passed right through the walls of the church, and out into the dark night, where they melded with the air and diffused into dark matter.

Until next time.

Jud struggled to sit up. Dazed, confused and in pain, he looked up and saw the approaching figure of Bex.

'I know you like working alone,' she said, 'but I was bored.'

CHAPTER 20

WEDNESDAY: 12.14 A.M.

NEWGATE STREET

The ghost had answered the spirits' call. Now he had a job to do. A job he'd known so well in life. Ring the bell and summon the spirits. Call all the condemned men who'd once made that one-way journey from Newgate prison to the gallows at Tyburn.

The spirits had urged him this far. He'd been called. It was his time. Just like in life. Midnight was his time. And it was late. Feasting would have to wait.

Fleeing St Sepulchre's, he swept around the side of the church and entered Snow Hill, retreading the familiar steps down towards Newgate Street. Steps he'd taken so many times before. The beloved bell was clasped in his skeletal hand.

And it was feeding him with energy once more. Though he'd lost his lantern, there was enough life in the bell to give his spirit form. The plasma now darkening once again from a cloud to a solid figure, the bellman slowly moved on in the direction of Newgate.

The streets were deserted. Not even a black cab or a riotous group of drinkers walking homeward from a club. No one. Nothing. Solitary rays of moonlight struck iron railings and signs, giving them a silvery sheen along the bellman's path.

In the distance, the great dark edifice of the Old Bailey stared down at him. Reaching Newgate Street, he looked across at the buildings opposite. His eyes didn't see the courtrooms and offices; the office blinds at the windows; the signs over the doors. He saw only the prison fixed in his memory. Newgate Gaol, as it once was. The place of torture. The home of pain and misery, anguish and fear – the cells in which the sentenced men lay hungry, desperate, afraid.

In the empty spaces of the ghost's hollow skull, indelible memories lingered on, and projected the old image of the gaol. It was so real.

And it was his time to remind the condemned of what would befall them in the morning. The gallows awaited them.

Time to do his duty.

The bellman crossed the street towards the prison, more hovering than walking.

Nearing the walls of what was once the prison, he swung his skeletal arm skywards and rang the bell. The clicking sound emitted from his mouth again. A deathly version of the old rhyme that once wove its way through the bars and into the dirty cells of the men who would hang in the morning.

Up Newgate Street two students were singing. Arm in arm. Laughing and joking. Swapping jokes and giggling drunkenly.

They'd had a great night.

But it was a night that was about to change.

CHAPTER 21

WEDNESDAY: 12.29 A.M.

MEDICAL ROOM, THE CRYPT

Jud sat on the edge of the bed. The nurse was assessing the damage to his shoulder. Purple bruises had already appeared right across the joint. It was swollen and puffy, but he was still able to raise his arm, despite the pain. No lasting damage. Just heavy bruising and some serious soreness for a few days. It could've been worse. Much worse, but Bex's sudden arrival in the church, crashing through the door on the bike and using her neutraliser, had meant that Jud had escaped death for the second time in twenty-four hours. Must be a record, he thought.

'Do you believe the curate, then?' said Bex. She was sat on a chair across the room, her feet propped up on a nearby bed. Her eyes looked tired – the piercing pupils had lost their shine, and there were dark shadows beneath. 'Do you think the bell really came to life?'

'Don't you? I mean, it's about as believable as a ghostly bellman coming through the door and beating me up.'

'Yeah, I suppose. But why the bell? I mean, why now?'

'It was an execution bell, like I said. It was used by the bellman on the eve of an execution. That's what it said on the plaque. He'd ring it across the road, outside Newgate prison.'

'To tell the prisoners to start praying.'

'Exactly,' said Jud. 'To tell them they were going to be hanged in the morning, and that now would be a good time to start repenting.'

'Wouldn't do any good, though, would it?' said Bex. 'I mean, they were still going to be hanged whether they prayed or not.'

'Yeah. But it might've made the difference between going to heaven or hell when they finally faced the drop.'

Bex watched Jud as he spoke. Though he was exhausted and filthy and injured, he still had the same appeal she'd noticed when he'd entered the meeting room on the first night: his dark eyes; his black, shiny locks that touched his forehead; the defined line of his jaw. He had the face of a model, though she would certainly never tell him that. He was arrogant enough. He was hot-tempered. He was rude. But beneath all that, Bex could see he was just as insecure as anyone else at the CRYPT. Probably more. She didn't know what it was, but there was something vulnerable about him. Like a small boy struggling to know who he was, or what he was supposed to do. He was, after all, still only a teenager, like they all were. But Bex looked older, like most girls did.

Jud was different. Though his brain may have been advanced, and he had the courage of a battle-scarred soldier twice his age, he was still a boy. And at times, his face showed it.

'Right, Jud, the ice pack should reduce some of the swelling and bring the bruises out,' the nurse said, rousing Bex from her thoughts and making her feel suddenly embarrassed to be staring at him.

'Thanks,' said Jud. Then he turned to Bex. 'Have I said thanks to you yet?'

'What?'

'I mean, you know, have I thanked you for coming to the church? At the right time like that.'

'Yeah, of course,' she lied. 'So, this bellman. Do you think he'll come back?'

'Dunno. He dropped the lantern – which seemed to be a source of energy for him. And the neutraliser would have helped. But I think the bell would have given him some strength. No idea where he went, but I just don't think he'll come back tonight. He was weakened. And it's after midnight now anyway, so it's too late.'

'Too late for what?' asked Bex.

'To ring the bell. It said in the church, don't you remember? I showed you the plaque on the wall before we left.'

'Yeah, I remember. I know. He rang it outside the prison. But why tonight? Why now? There haven't been hangings in this country for decades. We don't need a bellman any more. There's no condemned men left.'

'I know.'

'But there's gotta be a connection to the others, Jud.'

'Of course there has,' said Jud quickly. Tiredness and impatience were creeping up on him. It had been quite a day. 'But what is it? Why the *Execution* Bell, Bex? It's worrying me.'

She helped him get his shirt back over his bandaged shoulder. His skin felt soft, but the muscles in his arm were tight and sinewy.

'Ow!' he shouted as she caught the bandaged area.

'Sorry.'

He brushed her aside. 'I can do it!'

She returned to her chair. A few embarrassing seconds passed between them and then she said, 'Well at least we're safe now. And you've got all that data for Bonati. Surely he'll be happy with that.'

Jud shrugged his good shoulder. 'Dunno what the cameras and meters have recorded yet.'

'I'm sure they're full of evidence,' she said, consoling him. 'You did what he told you to, Jud. You stayed until the ghost was gone. You did it. You'll be back in Bonati's good books tomorrow.'

'Yeah,' said Jud. 'We'll see.'

CHAPTER 22

WEDNESDAY: 12.33 A.M.

NEWGATE STREET

It was late. Half an hour past midnight. But the ghost kept ringing the bell. His arm lifted and swung up and down without thought or control. Like a pendulum. The harbinger of death. The signal that said *death is coming in the morning*. Deep inside the cells of Newgate Gaol, the ghosts of prisoners long gone heard the bellman's call. Loud and clear.

The two students down the street, Saskia and her boyfriend Paul, stopped momentarily. The sound of the bell had penetrated through their drunken singing. It made no sense to them. What was that noise?

'Time at the bar, ladies and gentlemen, please, I thank you!' shouted Paul. Saskia laughed and held his arm snugly. They ignored the sound and carried on walking down Newgate Street.

The bellman was now standing outside the Old Bailey – the central criminal court built on the site of the old prison. The great dark stone walls, the pillars, the cellar windows – it was all as forbidding as the old gaol had been.

The spectre rang the bell again. The metallic sound seeped in through the cracks in window frames and blew through empty corridors inside.

Something stirred.

Something deep within the bowels of the building, deep below ground. Within the cells that stretched up to the pavement for light, the ghosts of condemned prisoners were awakening.

And this time they would not sit and listen to the bell that heralded their doom. There would be no praying. Not this time. They were free. They were dead already. And in death they could float through walls, move through bars and out into the chill of the night.

To strike terror.

The ghost kept ringing his bell. The spirits were summoned.

Drunk and oblivious, Saskia and Paul approached. They could see a tramp up ahead. A sadly dressed figure, shuffling around. Loitering, with nowhere to sleep.

But why was he carrying a bell? Was this what they'd heard? Where had he got it from?

The old tramp had his back to them as they came nearer. He was wearing strange clothes. Was this some kind of fancy dress?

'Been to a party, mate?' Paul said, from a few feet away.

The bellman turned around.

They saw his face.

'What the hell . . .'

They froze. That skeletal jaw. The blood-red eyes, distended and pulpy. And glowing like lights, flickering with an electrical kind of intensity.

Saskia screamed.

'It's him! Like on the train. Like they said in the papers. Oh God!'

She hid herself in Paul's arms as they turned quickly to run back up the road. There was a smash. Like breaking glass.

'Come on!' Paul cried.

The ghost was approaching.

'Move!'

Paul tugged Saskia back towards the way they'd come. But she wouldn't budge. She kept screaming: 'Get it off me! Paul! Get it off!'

He looked down. His heart sank.

Something was holding on to her right leg. She was crying and screaming, her face buried in his chest.

There was something preventing her from moving.

It couldn't be.

It *was*. A hand. A mottled grey skeletal hand. And an arm. Bloodied and stripped of flesh. There was broken glass around it. Paul saw the smashed cellar window through which the arm had thrust itself.

It was the ghost of a condemned man, rising from the depths of the prison cell below ground.

Saskia's perfume had drifted through the cracks in the cellar window. As the bell sounded, he'd smelt flesh. He would have it.

Paul tried frantically to pull Saskia towards him. She was still screaming – deafening cries that echoed around the deserted street and bounced off the cold, empty office blocks. Up Snow Hill across the street, lights were coming on in flats.

'Oh God. Help me! Help me, please . . .'

Paul was crying. And shouting. He was losing his grip. Saskia was slipping away from him, being pulled inside. Now she was on the floor. Her legs were being dragged inside the cell. The emaciated limbs of the prisoner had found a colossal strength.

The bellman was upon Paul. He brought the bell down. A heavy blow that struck the student on the back of the head. He fell like a stone. Out cold over the disappearing body of his girlfriend, who kicked and screamed and bawled.

Then she was gone – dragged through the jagged edges of the broken window, her skin ripping like paper blotched with crimson ink. Deep into the cells of the old gaol. Paul was deaf to her screams. Blood-curdling, pitiful cries of terror.

The prisoner was consuming her.

The bellman grabbed the body of her boyfriend, who lay still, blood seeping from his head on to the grey pavement, next to Saskia's abandoned handbag. He began to drag him across the ground, in the direction of St Sepulchre's. A reddy-brown trail stained the paving stones in his wake. The red eyes of the bellman intensified once again. Now he would have his meal.

But the ghost's bell-ringing had roused other spirits in the bowels of the Old Bailey. And in the rooms that were once cells, they were returning. Apparitions were becoming visible. Mist was swirling in the old rooms that lined the street. Bones were appearing. Limbs. Faces. Coming through walls, rising from the ground. Condemned, hungry souls.

One by one, cellar windows cracked. Shards of glass fell on to the pavement. The old bars of the gaol had long gone and the thin sheets of glass were collapsing. Fists were appearing. And arms. The prisoners were escaping.

Dozens of lifeless captives streamed out on to the road. Hideous spectres. Thin, wasted bodies still in shackles. Out they poured. They were clicking in the same way the bellman had done. Foul, insect-like noises that whispered down the empty street. Like locusts they came.

They were making for St Sepulchre's. Their prize, the body of Paul, still being dragged behind the bellman as his skeletal frame shuffled across the street.

There was an angry scrum of souls as they caught up with the bellman in the churchyard of St Sepulchre's, amidst the gravestones. Like lions skirmishing over a wildebeest, they fought each other, battling to get to the flesh of Paul's body.

Up ahead there were flashing blue lights. The residents of Snow Hill had heard Saskia's screams. They'd peered through their curtains. And wished they hadn't. The sights that had met their eyes were horrific. Like staring at a horror movie on a panoramic TV screen. That poor girl. Seeing her being dragged through the broken window into the dark cells beyond. Her body ripped and torn. Those screams. And the boyfriend who'd been with her. His desperate attempts to hold on to his girl. Then being silenced by the deathly blow of the man with the bell.

And the army of ghosts that had rallied out of the cellars.

The police telephone operative had received the same panic-stricken message from several trembling voices. Ghosts. Carnage. Terror. The words had been the same. The accounts hadn't differed.

This was happening for real. Newgate was under siege tonight.

The growing sound of sirens and the emerging blue flashing lights unsettled the weakened spirits of the prisoners. They dispersed down into the grassy graves in the churchyard.

But they would be back.

By the time the police cars had screeched to a halt and the officers had raced into the churchyard, all that was left was the half-eaten corpse of a man.

CHAPTER 23

WEDNESDAY: 7.33 A.M.

THE CRYPT

'I bombed, sir. Failed! I've had it. I can't do this any more.'
Jud rubbed his sleepy eyes. The nurse had sent him straight to
bed after tending his wounds in the medical room. He'd slept
like a baby.

Until the news had come. Bonati had called to inform him of
the fatal attacks at Newgate, just moments after he and Bex had
left the scene.

There was an exasperated sigh at the other end of the phone.
'Jud, will you please calm down and just listen for a second?
You're the best investigator I've got, but by God you're impossible
sometimes! I know you feel bad about the couple who died. We
all do. It was *appalling* what happened. Dreadful. But you couldn't
possibly have known that was going to happen. And let's face it,
you needed to get back here to sleep, like you said. Doctor's
orders. It'd been a marathon day, Jud . . . What I'm saying is stop
blaming yourself.'

That was a phrase the professor had used on more than one
occasion. Jud suffered from bouts of guilt like this regularly. But
the cause was usually very different – it was his mother's death.

He hadn't done it. But he hadn't been able to stop it either. And now he had to live with the guilt.

The emotion was a familiar one to Jud. He was well versed in self-loathing. He made it an art form.

Jud said, 'Let someone else do this. They can have it. I don't need this any more.'

Guilt burned into him like a branding iron, as he tried to imagine the horror the two students must have faced moments before their brutal deaths.

After he'd gone.

Should've stayed. Should've followed the bellman. Should've seen where he'd gone to. Seen if he really had disappeared from the scene.

He sounded resigned. He was resentful of the pressure on him – pressure to succeed, pressure to solve the mystery of the London raids, pressure to prove himself time and time again. Pressure to keep his identity secret.

'I give up.'

'You're not responsible!' Bonati said sensing his despair. 'You said you'd stay in the church until you'd got something for us, and you did just that. I've thought about this. I've had plenty of time to think about it since Khan rang me in the middle of the night. You did everything you were asked to do, and more. The killings outside were out of your control. You had no idea this bellman figure would return. You can't blame yourself any more. It's time to toughen up. There's a case unfolding the like of which we've never seen before. There are forces at work in the city bigger than anything we've encountered in the past. And we need everyone to stay focused. Including *you*.'

'But—'

'No!' Bonati was getting impatient now. He understood the complex feelings inside Jud's head – God knows he'd been through so much – but there wasn't time for this self-indulgent wallowing. They had to get on and find out what was happening.

And quickly. 'As a member of the CRYPT, you did all that was asked of you at the time. Your mission was to get there, set up the instruments and wait for evidence. You got it. And you left with a nasty injury.'

'Yeah, but the attacks outside? I mean, what happened afterwards. I should've been there. It's my fault!'

'OK,' snapped Bonati. 'If you want to insist on this blaming game, then blame yourself for forgetting your instrument. That's the only thing I feel angry about. Your neutraliser. You didn't check you had it with you. You should've done.'

Jud suddenly remembered the panic that had filled his mind as he'd frantically tried to find the instrument in his bag.

'I . . . I mean . . . I don't know what happened to it. I swear I checked it before we went to the station yesterday morning. It was—'

'I know. You had it in the tube, and that's where you left it.'

'What?'

'One of the station officials found it a couple of hours later. He contacted the police. He thought it was a bomb or something. Luckily Khan attended the scene, right after he sorted out your brawl at Greyfriars. He guessed it must have been something to do with us, and arranged for it to be couriered over here. But by the time it arrived you'd already left for the church.'

'I'm sorry, sir,' Jud said quietly. 'Have you got it?'

'Yes. You can collect it later. You won't need it today anyway.'

'What?'

'You're still on the case, Jud, but I'm not sending you to the scene of the crime yet. It's plagued with TV vans and reporters. It's chaos out there. I can't let you near St Sepulchre's. I don't want a repeat of yesterday at Greyfriars.'

'But—'

Bonati ignored the interruption at the other end of the line. 'What I want instead is for you to get into the labs now and start analysing the evidence you've picked up. Not just the readings, but what you saw with your own eyes. What you felt. The circumstances. The history. If, as you said, it really was a bellman, coming to ring his execution bell, I want to know why he's chosen to do it now. I want to know what was on that plaque you mentioned. I want to know everything there is to know about Newgate prison and about the wretched souls who were in there. I want a bloody history lesson, Jud. You've got to solve this. I'm relying on you.'

'OK, sir.'

'Because they're out!'

'Yeah, I know, sir.'

'And the only way we can send them back is by understanding why they came here in the first place. Why they're attacking us. You know the score, Jud. Ghosts never come back to this world without a reason.'

'I know, sir.'

'So find it!' replied Bonati briskly. 'It's down to you to sort this. Now get up and get a grip, J. I want you to find out more about the executions. Where they happened. I want a complete history lecture. And I want it by lunchtime.' He paused. 'Leave the world's media to me. The country's gone mad – just switch on your TV and you'll see that.'

Bonati rang off.

Jud placed the phone on his bedside cabinet and sat for a moment staring at the opposite wall of his room. It could've been so different. He was going to wake up and have breakfast in the college with Bex. Then they were going to head straight to Bonati and impress him with all the evidence they'd collected in the church.

What a difference a night makes, he thought.

A night of carnage.

But he was still the lead investigator on the case. Sidelined into a research job indoors maybe, away from the prying eyes of the media, but not off the case. And there was so much researching to do.

He switched on the TV.

The news reporter was standing outside St Sepulchre's. Jud recognised it instantly: the black railings that encircled it; the lichen-encrusted gravestones that rose up from the grass. But this time there was a large white tent erected at the rear of the churchyard, near the church door. The kind seen at crime scenes when there's a body – or the remains of a body – still being investigated. Jud could see armies of other reporters either side of the man who was talking. Each of them was shouting into their own camera, sending back panic-stricken stories to their own loyal viewers at home. Wherever they were. The noise was so loud, you could hardly hear anyone.

'Back to you in the studio!' shouted the reporter over the din, and the picture switched to the newsreader. A large screen behind her read: THE LONDON HAUNTINGS.

So it's official, Jud thought. No more raids. They're calling them hauntings now. Ghosts were on the agenda. And Jud knew better than anyone what effect that word had on the general public. He'd heard his father and the professor talk of the PIT in the early days, and the mixture of fear and intrigue that surrounded it. The panic that often swept through the villages and towns where hauntings were recorded. And the crowds of anxious locals who came and watched the agents at work, rendering their meter readings and recordings close to useless.

The CRYPT *had* to be more secretive than that. It was essential they could go in and out of hauntings unrecognised.

Bonati had always said that detecting ghosts, investigating paranormal activity, was hard enough without the crowds – and it was almost impossible when they were there.

What would happen now, with the press whipping up the story, and spreading fear across the city?

What was it about ghosts that captured - and terrified - people's imaginations? Jud asked himself. He'd been at the CRYPT for over a year now. He'd seen so many different apparitions. Heard different noises. Smelled odd smells. But these things had only raised his curiosity. None of them had *scared* him. The gardener in the grounds of the old mansion in north London - his thin face, and the wound in his neck where the axe had fallen. Or that grey lady who'd scared the family so badly over in Kensington. Her wispy frame had haunted the corridors of that home, and terrified the kids. And then that old man who'd flatly refused to leave his house in Putney, despite dying there three years earlier.

The people involved each time had been so frightened by their experience - *real* fear. Fear of the unknown; fear of death itself. There was something about these apparitions that often reminded people of their own mortality, Jud thought. They'd come from the land of death, back to our world. Messengers from another place - a place we were all destined for.

Jud had seen it so many times, but hadn't felt the taste of fear himself since he'd joined the CRYPT.

Until last night.

The hideous face of the bellman drifted into his mind again. Those red eyes. The pallid skin, and those gaunt cheekbones.

But why? Why now?

Jud knew that every haunting he'd ever visited had been caused by something. Ghosts always came back for a reason - an injustice of some kind that prevented the spirits from resting in peace. You just had to find the trigger. And Jud and his team had usually been able to do just that - and release the spirits from their sentences, so they could rest in peace again. Wrongs had been righted. Accused spirits had been forgiven. And they'd always dispersed back into the air after that - as translucent plasma, and then joining the invisible dark matter that surrounded us.

It was rare to have to use the EM neutralisers at all. The CRYPT handbooks made it clear that neutralising the electro-magnetic energy at a haunting was always the last resort. It was better to try to empathise with ghosts, find out why they were here, right the wrongs that had plagued them, and help them to disperse naturally into the air. Cutting off their energy source was an aggressive tactic, and one that should only be used in cases of extreme danger.

It was better to try to understand them. Listen and feel. Allow your extrasensory perception to soak up the mood of a place and uncover the secrets that often lay within.

But the hauntings Jud had investigated up to now had been adventures. Thrilling. Exciting. He remembered them all, but there were some that touched him more than others. The poltergeist in the pub cellar who'd thrown the bar stools around every night. He'd used his neutraliser then, but it had taken days to reduce the high levels of energy that lingered in that cellar. The whole room was alive.

And the screams that still echoed in that hotel room in Bayswater, on the anniversary of the death of the young mother there four years previously. Her howls had filled the hotel – and emptied it of guests the next day.

And the sad little boy who'd sit on the steps of that terraced house in Camden – the house that was his home in 1870. He often returned looking for his mother.

It was all awesome. And Jud had been right in the thick of it. His special gift for sensing supernatural presences had never scared him. But last night was different. So different. There had been an intensity to the bellman's whole presence that he'd not seen before. An anger. A fury that seemed to drive the levels of energy up to unimaginable degrees. And the ways in which innocent people were now being so brutally dispatched. Fear was eating into people's minds. That was obvious just from the terrified faces of the onlookers who'd lined the streets behind St

Sepulchre's when he'd watched the TV report. They'd looked bewildered. Like rabbits in the headlights.

Jud shivered. This wasn't a fantasy. Or an adventure like the others. There was real danger this time. The spirits that were haunting London had broken into this world and were making physical contact. These weren't apparitions, or hallucinations. They weren't visions that gently drifted in and out. They'd had physical form. When Jud had fought with the bellman, his hands and feet had touched, kicked and punched him.

He'd been real.

This was *all* real.

His thoughts drifted back into the room. The newsreader was still going on. 'We'll bring you the latest on the London hauntings as we receive it throughout this programme, but now,' she said patronisingly, 'the rest of today's news . . .

'It will be the greatest hotel ever seen. A jewel in the crown. A haven in the heart of the metropolis. Such are the claims of Lucien Zakis, world-renowned hotelier. Plans for his new luxury hotel at Marble Arch are now well under way. Our reporter Giles Olson is at the site of the new Tyburn Hotel.'

Jud switched it off. Some fat cat getting rich again. He'd never stayed in a Zakis hotel, but he could guess what they were like. The same as every luxury hotel: a temple to money and greed. Did London really need another one?

He got out of bed and dressed carefully, wincing in pain as he tried to pull a shirt over his bandaged shoulder. He deserved it. A painful reminder of how he'd goofed last night.

His mobile rang again.

'Jud? Are you up?'

'Yeah.'

'How's your shoulder?'

'How d'you think it is, Bex?'

'Have you seen the news?'

'Yeah, I have. You don't need to tell me—'

'I wasn't going to. I've spoken to Bonati. He just rang. Said he'd already spoken to you.'

'Yep. So are you going to St Sepulchre's then?' asked Jud.

'No,' said Bex. 'I've been told I've gotta stay here and help you research.'

Jud was irritated. He hated working with others, especially in his own lab. But if he had to be landed with anyone, it might as well be Bex.

'Oh, great,' he said sarcastically. 'So I'm stuck with you again, am I?'

Bex laughed.

'By the way, I s'pose I should thank you again,' he said. 'I'm glad you turned up last night. It could've been worse.'

'Just be thankful I brought the neutraliser. Can't believe you forgot yours.'

'I didn't forget it! I just didn't know it wasn't in the bag,' protested Jud. 'Didn't know it had fallen out, did I!'

'Yeah, well, I suggest it'll be the first thing you check for next time you go out.'

'OK, OK. You're beginning to sound like Bonati!'

Bex laughed. After seeing Jud in such danger the night before, she was happy to be enjoying a laugh with him now. He rarely sounded so relaxed. Perhaps it was the tiredness kicking in.

'Listen,' said Jud, sounding more serious now, 'if we don't find what's causing these ghosts to attack, then I'm off the case for good. I won't get any more chances from Bonati. That's why I'm still on it. He wants me to solve it.'

'You will,' Bex said reassuringly.

'So, you comin' to the lab today?'

'Yeah,' said Bex. 'But I'm going for a run first. Said I'd meet someone. I'll see you later.'

'Who?'

'Why do you need to know?' said Bex, playfully.

'I don't,' snapped Jud.

'It's just Grace. You know, one of the others I started with this year.'

Jud knew exactly who she meant. He'd seen her in the briefing room on day one, chatting to Bex. Like all the other boys, he'd noticed her long blonde hair first.

'Where are you going?' he asked nonchalantly.

'Ooh, another question,' she said. 'Just for a run, Jud. We're trying to keep fit. Thought we'd go round Hyde Park.'

'I don't know how you've got the energy for a run after yesterday,' he said.

'Well, I'm not a boy, am I? Girls are built differently.'

'Yes, I'd noticed that,' Jud said cheekily. 'Breakfast at nine thirty, then?'

'Yeah, OK.'

'Then we've gotta get into the lab. We have to solve this, Bex. I just hope we can.'

'We will,' she said soothingly. 'I've got a good feeling about today.'

CHAPTER 24

WEDNESDAY: 8.40 A.M.

HYDE PARK

'You're so lucky!' said Grace.

'Why? What are you talking about?'

'I mean to be paired up with Jud. On the case. How did you manage that one?'

'Well, he's all right, I suppose,' said Bex. She quickened her pace and ran on ahead, flushing slightly.

'Hey,' shouted Grace. 'I thought you said you hadn't slept well. I thought you were tired!'

They ran on.

Jogging in Hyde Park – it was what Bex had dreamed of doing when she first heard that her application had been successful and she'd be moving to London. Back home in Oxford she'd often jogged in the mornings. But to jog in Hyde Park, it's what everyone did. And now she'd found her new friend Grace, another zombie at the CRYPT, she could come running here every morning.

'So, come on,' said Grace, puffing slightly to keep up. 'What's he like? We're all dying to know.'

'What do you mean?' asked Bex innocently.

'You know. His temper an' all that. It's well known. Bit of a head case is Jud. So they say.'

Bex said quickly, 'He's not mad. He's just passionate about what he does. He's bright though. *Very* bright . . . but he's lonely, I reckon.'

'That's it,' Grace said. 'Definite. You fancy him. No question,' and she giggled.

They stopped at a bench to catch their breath.

'Did you hear about last night, then?' asked Grace. 'I mean I couldn't believe the news. Did you see it? It was like chaos, you know. At that church. It was mad. What did they call it? St Stephen's or something?'

'St Sepulchre's.'

'Yeah. That's it. It was horrid what they did.'

Bex looked at the ground. 'I know,' she said. Grace had no idea that she had been there too. At the church. She'd no idea that it had been Bex who'd crashed in and saved Jud from death.

'I heard he was there last night. Is that true?'

'Who?'

'Jud, stupid!'

'Dunno.'

'I heard he was there and ran away. Got scared or something,' Grace whispered.

'He didn't!' snapped Bex. 'I don't believe he was scared.'

Grace smiled. 'You've got it bad, girl.'

They giggled and started running again. Passing other joggers, and dog walkers, all grabbing a moment's calm in the awaking metropolis. The steady hum of commuter traffic penetrated the oasis of trees that surrounded them. London had risen for work again. But the city was scared. There was a tension in the air. Even here in the park. Fewer joggers today. The faces of those who did brave it out seemed preoccupied. Some were stopping to talk anxiously to each other, mirroring Grace's horror and disbelief about the previous evening's events.

'So where's it going to end?' said Grace. She was lagging behind again.

Bex shook her head. 'Come on, slowcoach! Keep up!' she shouted over her shoulder.

Grace turned on the pace and sped past her friend, laughing. 'Who's the slowcoach? Race you to that pavilion up there.'

Bex followed on. 'I don't know what's going to happen, Grace,' she shouted after her. 'But I do know that Jud and I are gonna solve it. We'll crack it today. We're gonna find out what's causing all this.'

'You're so lucky,' said Grace up ahead. 'I wish I was on your case. It's a big one.'

'It's certainly turning out to be. You're up at Goldsmith's, aren't you?'

'Yeah. There's some weird things happening there. But it's not connected to what you're doing.'

'You *think*,' said Bex. 'None of us really know what's going on.'

'S'pose so. Are you going to the church today? To, what was it . . . St Sepulchre's?'

'No, we've got to stay in and research. Collect the evidence and go through it. Find a connection – you know the routine.'

'Stuck in a room researching with Jud Lester all day. You poor thing,' Grace said enviously. 'I'll swap if you like!'

Silence.

'Bex? I said I'll swap with you.'

Nothing.

Grace stopped. She looked behind her.

'Bex?'

Where was she?

Grace spun right around, looking across the park. Right – left. People going past. Traffic noises in the distance. Trees. Bushes. The pavilion.

Where was she?

'Bex! Stop foolin' around, will you! Ha ha! Now come out!'

157

Grace was stood in the middle of the path. 'BEX!' she shouted again.

A woman came around the bend, past the old pavilion where Grace now stood. 'All right, luv? Lost somebody?'

Grace was going pale. 'This is gonna sound *really* weird,' she said, 'but I was with my friend just now and she's . . . well, she's, like, gone.'

'What do you mean, *gone?*' said the woman. 'Was she with you just now?'

'Yes! I mean literally a second ago. We were talking. She was racing me.'

She knew it didn't make sense. The woman looked puzzled.

It seemed like time had stopped. Grace's stomach lurched and her heart was beating so fast it felt like it was overtaking time. Everything else was in slow motion.

Strangers looking at her. More and more people coming over. Faces looking sympathetic. Questions asked.

'Bex!' she yelled. Others joined in.

'Bex!'

'Bex! Hello? Are you there, love?'

They started searching. Joggers in separate little worlds, cut off by iPods and radios, but now united in a search, that was getting frightening.

And then they heard it.

A girl's scream.

From the bushes. Behind the old pavilion.

The sound froze them all. They stopped. Someone started crying. Grace yelled a desperate cry: 'Bex!'

A tall, thickset man in his twenties joined them. He'd heard the scream and had sprinted over. 'I'm a police officer,' he panted. 'You stay here. I'll go in. Wait there.'

Grace moved to go with him.

'Wait there!' he shouted. 'Nobody this side of the pavilion. Move back!' He disappeared into the bushes.

Grace was being comforted by other people in the park – the crowd was now swelling. But she pushed her way through them.

'Hey, luv. Come 'ere.'

'You heard him. Stay back!'

She ignored their shouts and ran in after the police officer. If her friend was in there, she wasn't going to wait around. She disappeared into the shadows behind the hut.

It was a large rhododendron bush. A mass of tangled green, with a huge oak behind it. Its canopy smothered the ground in shade. A dark corner of the park.

Then they saw her.

It was pitiful. Bex was slumped over the gnarled trunk, her face buried in the soil.

She wasn't moving. The police officer quickly rolled her body over. Her face was pale beneath the muddy stains. There was a reddish bruise across her temple. She'd hit something. Or something – someone – had hit her.

Grace fell to her knees and began sobbing – great bursts that welled up inside her and choked her throat.

The officer was checking Bex's wrist for a pulse.

Nothing.

He opened her eyelids.

No reaction.

He knelt down and listened carefully for a breath.

There was something. He was sure.

He felt around on her neck for a pulse again.

Nothing. Then . . . a faint tap against his fingertips. An almost imperceptible thud from deep within Bex's veins. And another. And another.

She was alive.

'Quick!' he shouted to Grace. 'She's still with us. Ring for an ambulance.'

Grace raised her head, which had slumped on to her bent knees. There was hope.

159

'Now!' the policeman yelled at her.

Startled, she scrambled to her feet and rummaged in her tracksuit pockets. No phone. It must have fallen out. 'It's gone,' she cried.

'I haven't got mine either,' said the officer. 'Go and tell someone, for God's sake. Quick!'

She ran out of the bushes, past the pavilion and on to the path.

'Well?' people shouted. By now there was a large crowd gathered on the path.

'She's alive. Just about. Call 999, someone, please!'

'Already done that,' a woman cried out. 'They're on their way.'

Relieved, Grace ran back into the bushes, where the officer held Bex.

The sight of her friend, still lying unconscious, brought a stabbing surge to her stomach. She began shaking. Great uncontrollable rattles that began inside her chest and sent her limbs shuddering. The policeman moved to her and hugged her until her vibrating body calmed.

'But . . . but . . .' Grace sobbed, 'How? Who did this?'

'Dunno,' said the officer. 'But she must've put up a good fight. Look at the floor.'

Grace glanced down. Her tears formed bubbles around her eyes, which made the ground seem blurred. She brushed them away.

There were marks in the soil. There'd been a fight. Leaves and stones were disturbed. But the footprints in the ground seemed strange. Like they were in a pattern. A circle.

'Oh, Bex,' she cried. The officer grabbed her again before she fell.

Then Grace heard it.

At first it was just a whisper. A faint whisper that rattled through the leaves of the great oak above them.

It sounded like *Doo . . . v-a-l.*

She spun around.

D-o-o-v-a-l. Dance with Dooval.

She looked around again. Saw nothing.

Dooval . . . D-o-o-v-a-l. Will you dance with Dooval.

Grace screamed. 'What was *that*?'

'What?' said the officer. 'I heard nothing.'

'There was a voice. A whisper. I tell you, I heard somebody whisper. I'm sure I heard someone.'

'Just your imagination,' said the policeman. 'Now come here and sit with your friend.'

'But . . . but I swear I—'

'Come on,' said the man. 'You're in shock. That's all. The mind plays tricks sometimes. There's no one else here now.'

The whisper had seemed so real. Though the words made no sense to Grace, the voice was so chilling. So callous. And it came from nowhere. Like it floated in the air. She'd heard it. She knew very well her mind wasn't playing tricks. It was precisely because she could hear such things that she'd been recruited into the CRYPT. It wasn't her imagination. It was her ESP. But with her friend lying cold on the ground, right here, right now, it all seemed different. Scarier.

A foul smell was lingering too. Like rotten meat.

People were now pouring into the clearing in the bushes and the police officer tried to keep them back.

'What's happened?' someone shouted. 'What's . . . oh my God. No! Oh God.'

There was screaming. People ran out of the bushes back on to the path, crying. The officer went out to calm everyone's fears.

At the other side of the pavilion, the crowd of curious onlookers was swelling.

There were more shouts.

'What's happened?'

'Is somebody in there?'

'Has something happened?'

'Did anyone see someone running from the bushes?' the officer said, trying to stay calm, ignoring their questions.

No one had.

'Anyone? Something, *surely?*'

Nothing.

He continued, desperately, 'What just happened in there cannot have happened by magic. Someone *must* have seen something. There was a fight. There were other footprints. I saw them.'

No one offered any explanation. They just looked confused and bewildered and scared. *Really* scared. They huddled together round the bench, their eyes darting towards the pavilion and the dark bushes beyond it. There was a chill in the air. The clouds had drawn in, painting a grey sky overhead, and the treetops swayed. The comforting sound of commuter traffic in the distance was being drowned out by the gusty breeze as it rattled the leaves.

'It's them ghosts!' someone shouted out. 'Them bloody ghosts! None of us are safe now!'

'Don't say that! Please don't say that.' A young woman shouted.

'You're right. It's them evil spirits. I said it would happen again.'

'Calm down! Look, I'm a policeman and I can assure you it's got nothing to do with ghosts at all. Nothing, d'you hear?'

Someone shouted at him, 'Do somethin'.' Others joined in, venting their panic at the man who should've had the answers.

'Yeah. What the hell are you guys playin' at?'

'Is it safe here or not?'

'You guys said you'd sort it out. Protect us. Rubbish! You've no idea what's happening.'

More frantic shouts from worried people. Arguments broke out as panic spread and rational thoughts were chased away. Anger was rising in the park. The crowd was still growing.

The policeman tried desperately to calm everyone down, but he was being pushed now. People were losing control. They had to blame something, somebody.

The officer tried to shout over the cries: 'It's not ghosts. I tell you, there's *no such thing*. Listen to me!'

The crowd was gradually calming, though some people were still shouting and pushing and swearing.

'Listen to me! The injuries in there *cannot* have happened by themselves. No ghost could've done that. You've got to stay calm. People get attacked sometimes. It's wrong and it's tragic and we'll find who did it, I promise you, but it's *not ghosts*. Now move on, *please*.'

There was a siren in the distance. A car was racing into the park.

Grace stared at Bex and stroked her cheek. 'Don't worry,' she whispered. 'We'll get you sorted. Stay with me. Stay, Bex.' Her tears fell on to Bex's mud-stained face. The bruise on her temple looked swollen and sore.

The car drew up and a familiar figure stepped out on to the dusty path.

'Right,' he said to the officer. 'What's going on?'

'In there. It's a girl. She's alive. Just.'

They entered the clearing.

'I don't believe it,' said Detective Chief Inspector Khan. 'It's her.'

CHAPTER 25

WEDNESDAY: 9.51 A.M.

THE CRYPT

Jud found a table in the corner of the dining room and set his tray down. He couldn't remember the last time he'd eaten. He began tucking into his hot breakfast. Bacon, eggs, beans, fried bread. The works.

But where was Bex?

She was supposed to meet him for breakfast at 9.30. Probably binned the idea of the run and gone back to sleep, he thought.

Nik Jones walked past his table followed by two loyal buddies. They stared at Jud.

'Good fight, Lester. Like I said, trying to impress the girl were we?'

'Yeah, nice one,' added his buddy. 'Didn't know Bonati recruited street fighters.'

Jud ignored them and looked down at his food.

'Don't understand it, though,' said Nik to his mates. 'If I'd been caught fighting like that, I'd have been kicked out.'

'Yeah, I know. Somebody thinks he's special.'

'S'pose so,' smiled Nik.

Anger was rising inside Jud. Just what Nik wanted. The bacon was struggling to go down. He chewed through clenched jaws, but he wasn't going to take the bait. He'd ignore it this time. He knew he'd get it in the neck from the jealous ones. He always had done.

More agents came across once they'd seen what was happening, skulls and zombies.

'Hey, look here. It's the golden boy. Bonati's buddy!'

'Well, well. The one and only.'

Jud looked up. 'All right, guys,' he said as politely as he could manage. 'Nice one. Now can I just eat?'

They weren't content with that. They wanted to see more. They wanted to goad him. See if they could light his fuse. See if the rumours about his temper were really true.

'Tell me, Lester,' someone said, 'did you sleep well?'

'What?' said Jud.

'Did you sleep all right, after last night, I mean. You know, after you ran away . . .'

Jud slammed his cutlery on the table. He stood up. He was about to silence this idiot. Then he saw someone over his shoulder. Coming through the door. It was Bonati. He was heading straight for Jud. He looked pale. Haggard.

Jud sat down quickly. The crowd around him saw the professor coming and dispersed.

Bonati looked pensive. Something was wrong.

Jud stood up as Bonati approached his table.

'Something's happened, Jud,' the professor said sombrely. 'It's Bex.'

A sinking feeling struck Jud's stomach. 'Sir?' he muttered.

Bonati sat down. Jud pushed his discarded breakfast to one side; he'd lost his appetite.

'She's OK, Jud, but she's been involved in a . . . serious accident.' He was glancing around the cafeteria and speaking in hushed tones.

'Accident? Where? How?' The concern in Jud's voice surprised them both. Bex had been thrust upon him by the professor, and he'd resisted having to take her to Greyfriars the day before. But the news still shook him.

'Hyde Park. She was out running with a friend.'

'Grace. Yeah, she told me. Is she OK? Is she in her room?'

'She's been taken to St Thomas's.'

'To hospital?' said Jud, standing up. 'What the hell happened? Did she fall? Is it bad?'

A few other agents heard him and turned to look in his direction.

'Keep your voice down,' whispered Bonati. 'It's bad enough. But she's OK. She's had a CT scan. They think there's no permanent damage.'

'A *head scan*? What happened?' asked Jud, sitting down again, glancing over at the others.

'I don't know much yet. Details are patchy. But she was struck on the head, apparently. Attacked. The blow knocked her unconscious.'

'*Unconscious*?' said Jud. 'She's awake now, though, yeah?'

Bonati shook his head. 'I don't know, J.'

CHAPTER 26

WEDNESDAY: 10.08 A.M.

MARBLE ARCH

The cold grey corpse of Yuri Kozlosky lay prostrate on a metal shelf deep inside the site storage container.

His eyes were closed. His pallid face bore no expression. His lips were pursed and dark red. At twenty-one his skin was blemish free – no wrinkles. There was a trace of dark stubble across his chin.

It had ceased growing.

The only traces of the nightmare that had brought him to this cold, austere room were the rings around his neck. Deep scarlet tracks cut into his flesh. Congealed blood had dribbled from the wounds and set hard on the metal shelf.

Half-empty bags of fixings and boxes of used tools surrounded him. Lifeless and abandoned. Like him: materials of the building trade, now surplus to requirements. Tools he'd have treasured in Ukraine. Now he lay among them. Spent. Discarded.

Outside, the door had been firmly locked. No one had been given access. No one except Zakis and Harrison.

Zakis had ordered the body to be taken down immediately and kept in the storage container until he'd had time to think. Harrison's protests about leaving Yuri in position so the police could investigate had been quickly silenced by his employer's cold-blooded threats. 'You stay quiet – you stay alive.'

Though it had happened during the night shift, there were still over twenty staff on site. And they'd all seen it.

They'd never forget it.

Everyone knew how it had happened; everyone except Lucien Zakis.

Zakis paced up and down the site office. Harrison sat in a corner staring out of the dusty window at the great metal spires that rose up from the ground, and the dark grey skies beyond them. The strut from which Yuri had been hanged stood proud, flanked by the others: an ominous reminder of the night's gruesome events.

Zakis said, 'Are the men all still here? No one's left?'

'That's right, sir. No one's been allowed to leave. When the shift finished at eight, I told the men to wait in the cabins for further instructions. They're still in there.'

'Good.'

'But they're angry, Mr Zakis. Angry and frightened. They wanna know why. Why him? Why here?' Harrison's voice was still trembling from the shock of the gruesome events the night before, and the need to break the news to Zakis. It was early, but he needed a drink. The half-full bottle of whisky was calling from the filing cabinet behind his desk. If he didn't have a swig soon, surely his nerves would fail him.

Zakis ignored Harrison's panicky questions. He was still thinking. 'And the new shift? They've been turned away, yeah?'

Harrison nodded obediently, fidgeting. 'I still think we should contact the police, sir. The men and I feel we should—'

Zakis made a move for him. 'The men and I feel . . .' he mocked. He picked Harrison up by the collar and rammed him against the wall. A pathetic sigh escaped from Harrison's lips as the thin metal frame of the cabin reverberated around them.

'You listen to me, you little worm!' yelled Zakis. 'I don't care!

D'ya understand? I don't care how they *feel*. I don't care what they think. I don't care what they saw. I only care about what they *say*. They're my men, d'ya hear? Mine. *You're* mine. You signed your life over to me when you joined the firm. Understand? And now it's time to be good boys and keep loyal to Daddy, uh?'

His finger jabbed into Harrison's chest. The site manager was twitching and blinking. His eyes looked shattered and his face worn. Just a quick swig. A stiff gulp of the amber liquid would coat his throat and stiffen his resolve for the day. But Zakis wasn't budging.

'Now, I'm going to ask you one more time. And I want you to start from the beginning. Don't leave anything out. I wanna know how the hell this punk got up there in the first place.'

He released his grip on Harrison, lit another cigarette and returned to the desk.

Harrison sank down on to the plastic chair and stared at the floor. He was shattered – mentally, physically, emotionally. It had been the worst of nightmares. A night from hell. And now Zakis was demanding he go though it all again – for the third time. He closed his eyes; they stung with fatigue. He thought of home. His wife. The kids would be at school now. He'd called Julie last night, moments after calling Zakis. He'd tried to sound rational and calm – said he'd have to work right through the night to meet a deadline for a delivery today – but she'd sensed fear in his voice. He'd told her everything was fine – that they were just behind schedule – and that he'd call her again in the morning.

But he still hadn't.

'OK,' he said, sighing. 'OK, sir. I'll go through it again. It was just before eight p.m. The new shift was turning up. I was checkin' them in, and setting up the jobs. I came back in here to collect my workbook. There was a shout. Then someone ran to the cabin and banged on the window behind where you're sitting. It was one of the workers. One of the new lot. He was terrified. Eyes wide and all pale, like. He was yellin' at me to come outside.

'I ran out. He was screaming. I couldn't understand him. Polish? Ukrainian? I dunno. Anyway, I couldn't work out what he was sayin', but he was certainly screamin'. An' pointin' – over to where it'd happened. There was a crowd of men gathered. I didn't know what they were lookin' at, at first. I dunno, I thought it was maybe a sort of protest or somethin'.

'But when I got closer, I could hear some of them cryin'. Like babies, you know. I've never heard anythin' like it.' Harrison was gazing out of the window again, eyes glazed over. His lip was quivering.

'*Come on!*' said Zakis. 'Get on with it, man!'

Harrison continued. 'Luckily one of the men could translate. I think it was Kravec. He came up to me and started shouting and pointing. He was swearing and screamin' like. "There! Up there! It's Yuri!" he kept sayin'.

'An' that's when I looked up, see . . . I mean that's when I saw 'im. All the guys were talkin' in whatever language it was. But Kravec, he kept sayin' the same thing. "Ghosts! We see ghosts, boss. They come! They take Yuri!"'

'How, for God's sake?' interrupted Zakis. This sounded ridiculous. Like some kid's crappy sci-fi cartoon. It didn't add up. 'How did they take him?'

'I told you, I didn't see it meself, Mr Zakis. But they all said the same thing. The ghosts come up outta the ground. Men. Dozens of 'em. In dark coats, like. They took Yuri. They climbed the scaffold with 'im. They strung 'im up.'

'And no one *did* anything? They all just stood there and watched it happen?' shouted Zakis.

'Well, they said it all happened so quickly. One minute Yuri was there, chattin' an' stuff. And the next minute, these ghosts just appeared. Kravec said the soil started to break up around 'im. On the ground, by Yuri's feet. The stones were shifting. There were cracks an' stuff. Some of the men said they thought it was an earthquake. And then these weird things rose up. I dunno, Kravec said they were sort of, well, cloudy. Like not really there? At first. Then he said they seemed to grow stronger. He said they all heard these clicking noises or somethin'. Some weird sounds. The men ran as soon as they saw them comin' up outta the ground. But poor Yuri. They grabbed 'im before he could get away, see. He had no chance.'

'So the men ran?' Zakis was now staring out of the window at the site, which looked quiet and abandoned. It all seemed so unlikely. Almost like the men had all been smoking something strange, or were so drunk they were seeing things. But Harrison wasn't a liar. A bit lazy, and Zakis knew he liked a drink, but he wasn't a liar.

'Yeah. They ran into the cabins, sir. They've all read the newspapers, Mr Zakis. They know what's goin' on. They'd been chattin' about ghosts an' stuff all day, before it even happened. It's on everybody's minds, sir.'

Zakis stood up. 'And that's exactly why we've gotta keep a lid on this! You imagine! Even you, Harrison, surely you can picture it? Ghosts rising from the ground at Marble Arch! We'd be finished, uh? The site'd be closed. Police, firemen, health and safety – and then there's the press. We'd be closed down. The site would be condemned. Plans for The Tyburn would be dead. We'd never get it off the ground. Not for months, anyway.' He slammed his fist on the cheap desk. He was mad. He lit another cigarette and gulped the smoke down. It resurfaced through his nostrils like a dragon.

'But–' Harrison tried to interrupt.

'No! You've said your piece! You've done your job. Now listen to me. This is how it's gonna be.'

Harrison fell silent.

'Where's this punk from?'

'Who? Yuri?'

'Yeah, of course Yuri, man. Poland you said?'

'Ukraine, I think. He came over last month. He's only been with us a while.'

Zakis walked over to Harrison and spoke quietly now. 'And who actually knew he was here?'

'You mean his family? Or officials?'

'I mean both.'

'Well, he came in the usual way – I mean, the pick-up at Dover. He was stayin' in the usual place. Over at the hostel.'

Zakis smiled. 'You mean Zakis Towers?' Yuri, like so many of his new colleagues, had come over illegally and been secreted away into a large hostel that Zakis funded in east London. A grimy old sixties tower block into which the company packed dozens of illegal immigrant workers. Few questions were asked. Cash changed hands; money was sent home to families; everyone was happy. It was how the Zakis empire had been built.

'So no one in this country knews he was here, yeah?'

'That's right. Only the men he worked with.'

'And they all came over the same way?'

'Yeah.'

'And his family?'

'I asked the guys that last night,' said Harrison. 'They said they weren't sure, 'cos he was a quiet sort of bloke. Kept 'imself to 'imself. But they reckoned he just had a girlfriend in Ukraine. No kids. Dunno about his parents.'

'OK. That's good. His girl isn't gonna come looking if she knows he's not supposed to be here. Who's she gonna ask?'

'She might call us, sir.'

'Let her try. I've never heard of the man. Have you?'

Harrison looked out of the window and chewed his lip nervously. He knew where this was heading. Zakis was going to dispose of the body. Get rid of it. Pretend it had never happened. Carry on with the building. Back to normal.

Poor Yuri.

Zakis stared at Harrison. He was expecting an answer.

This was too much. Harrison had had enough. He could handle the work, the long hours, the lack of respect. He could even take the yelling and the threats, but now Zakis wanted him to bury a man without trace. As if he'd never existed. He turned round to face his boss.

'This is a *human*, sir. I mean a real person, like. He's not some piece of scrap metal we can bury in the ground. He's—'

Harrison never had the chance to finish his sentence. Zakis was on him. His fist thundered sharply into Harrison's stomach. He was winded. For a few seconds he had no breath. His face paled and he fell to the floor, clutching his chest.

Zakis kicked him in the back and said, 'I asked you a question. I said I've never heard of this Kozlosky, *have you?*'

In the split seconds he had, Harrison lay there on the metal floor of his cabin, thinking of his wife and children. His modest house, his car. The patio he was laying in the back garden, and the fancy BBQ he was saving up for. The extension they'd dreamed of. His home. His life. It was all too valuable to lose. If he didn't answer now, he'd surely follow Yuri into the ground, and his kids would be fatherless.

It just wasn't worth it.

'No, sir,' he whispered sheepishly. 'I've never heard of the man either.'

'OK,' said Zakis contentedly. 'Good boy. Now let me think.'

There was a noise outside. Someone was shouting. There was some kind of argument. Zakis made for the door. Harrison slowly rose to his feet and lurched towards the cabinet. With shaking hands he lifted out the bottle and glugged the whisky, at last.

'Harrison!' Zakis was yelling from outside. 'Get out here!'

He took another quick gulp, replaced the cap with trembling fingers and hid the bottle back in the cabinet. He ran outside.

It was the security guard, at the site gates. He was arguing with a delivery man who'd got out of his lorry and was shouting at him, pointing to the site and his truck. Zakis was returning to the cabin.

'Get rid of him!' he told Harrison, as he grabbed him and pushed him in the direction of the gates. Harrison stumbled over to the truck – a large, filthy cement mixer – and interrupted the security guard.

'Thanks, Frank, I'll deal with this.' He tried to sound calm. Then he turned to the driver. 'Should we have been expecting you today?'

'Yeah. What the hell's goin' on? Is it a bloody holiday or sumfin'? Where is everyone?'

'No, it's not a holiday.' Harrison tried to force a smile. 'It's just that we've had to close for the day as we've—'

Suddenly he felt a heavy grip on his shoulder. It was Zakis.

'Sorry, fella,' Zakis interrupted him, turning to the driver. 'It's been a long night, so I gave the boys a lie-in. Too soft, aren't I?' He grinned. 'Of course you can enter. Park over there. There's still a few men here, I'll go and get some help.'

Harrison looked at his boss with a bewildered expression.

'Sir?'

Zakis ignored him and marched back to the site office. Harrison followed quickly behind.

'What's going on, sir?' he said once they were inside.

'Business as usual. It's the cement for the foundations, isn't it?'

'Yeah. We were expecting it today, sir, but I thought you said—'

'Good. Then I suggest we get on and lay it,' said Zakis.

Harrison looked puzzled. 'But what about the men? And what about Kozlosky?' he said.

'I'll go and see the men. Tell a couple of them to get out there and help. Their silence will cost me, but it'll be worth it. Nothing that a nice bonus can't clear up. It's time we got back to work – we've got foundations to lay.'

Harrison still looked confused. 'But . . . but . . . what're we doin' about Kos—'

'Don't worry. We'll bury this story before it gets out,' said Zakis with a sinister grin. He picked up the phone.

Harrison felt sick. Reality dawned on him as the cement mixer began to grind ominously outside. A menacing rumble. The foundations were being prepared; Yuri would have his tomb.

CHAPTER 27

WEDNESDAY: 12.21 P.M.

ST THOMAS'S HOSPITAL

'You don't understand, Dad!'

'No, darling. You've been injured. Attacked. All I'm saying is this isn't what we expected. This agency business is more dangerous than we thought.' He glared at Bonati, who stood in the corner, trying to avoid his gaze. 'When your mum and I agreed to—'

'Dad! It's not always like this! I don't get coshed over the head every day, you know.'

'Look, I realise that, but I don't think—'

'Peter,' his wife interrupted him. 'Now is not the time to discuss this. Please. You can see Bex has had a shock.' She turned to smile at her daughter. 'What she needs is *rest*.'

De Verre continued. He was getting anxious. 'I know, I know, but Su, there's been too many fatalities. This isn't a game, you know. Bex could have been killed!'

Suyin De Verre put a handkerchief to her tired red eyes. She'd been crying since she'd taken the phone call from Detective Chief Inspector Khan. His words would remain printed indelibly on her mind for a long time yet. 'Your daughter's been injured.

I'm afraid she's been attacked, Mrs De Verre. I think you need to come down to London.'

The journey down from Oxford had been a blur. Peter De Verre had never wanted his daughter to go to the CRYPT in the first place; his wife, Suyin, had been surprisingly accepting of it – she knew how much it meant to Bex – so now Peter was blaming her. They'd hardly spoken in the car.

Bex was sat up in bed. She looked pale. Her hair was tied back and the bruise on her temple stood out against her fair skin. Tired and shaken, certainly, but she was OK. Since regaining consciousness, she'd been given the all-clear. There was no lasting damage detected. The tests and the CT scan had shown nothing untoward. She'd had a lucky escape, so they said. But Bex had failed to see what was remotely lucky about any of it.

'Have the police been yet, love?' asked her mother, as she wiped her brow for her.

'Get off, Mum! I'm fine,' snapped Bex, pushing her mother's hand away. 'And yes, they've already been and strutted their stuff. Khan seemed almost happy I'd be off the case.'

Bonati interrupted gently from the corner. 'The detective chief inspector was quite shocked, Bex. I promise you. He's most concerned.'

Bex acknowledged him with a reluctant nod. She was frustrated sat in the bed with everyone staring at her like she was some kind of exhibit.

'And you're sure you don't remember his face? The guy who did this? Nothing?' said her father impatiently.

'Look, I don't remember much at all, Dad. It all happened so fast. There was this figure. From the shadows. He came up behind me. I tried to scream, but there was this hand around my mouth.'

Her mother took a sharp intake of breath. The thought of it was too terrifying even to listen to.

Memories of the gaunt, skeletal hand suddenly appearing at her face sent a shiver down Bex's spine. Her headache returned once again: a pounding at the temples, and a steady throb beneath the bruise on her forehead. She touched her head again and grimaced in pain.

'I think that's enough for now, Peter,' said her mother. 'She's tired. Your head must still be very sore, love.'

Her father paced the floor. 'OK, Su, but I want to know who did this.' He turned to face Bonati. 'She may have recovered, Bonati . . . but it's not the last you'll hear from me.'

The professor remained calm. He nodded sympathetically and tried to understand their anguish.

'We'll do all we can to solve this mystery, Mr De Verre. I assure you we'll work closely with the police and find out who, or what, was responsible for your daughter's attack. I've got my best agents on it.'

Bex suddenly remembered – Jud! She was supposed to be meeting him for breakfast.

'Professor, what about Jud? I was meant to be seeing him this morning. We're supposed to be going through the evidence.' She was getting out of bed. 'I've got to go, I've got to—'

'Rebecca, you're going nowhere, young lady,' said her father, gently pushing her legs back into bed.

Bonati spoke calmly and warmly. 'It's OK, Bex. I've seen Jud. And I'll let him know you're all right as soon as I leave here. There's nothing to worry about.'

'Jud? Who is this Jud?' asked her father.

'Jud Lester,' said Bex proudly. 'He's the best agent we've got. Jud and I are working together. He's a good investigator.'

'Look!' her father snapped back. 'I've told you to stop this stupid nonsense! Investigating! Agents! This isn't a game, Rebecca, and it's got to stop.'

'But I wasn't *investigating* anything at the time, Dad. Don't you see? It could have happened to anyone. I was just out running.

If anything, living in the CRYPT makes me safer than most people in the city.'

Bex's father ignored her. He was thinking about the news bulletin he'd seen on the television. He'd caught the tail end of the report from Greyfriars. The fight. The angry mob of reporters.

Luckily for Bex – and for everyone else in the room – De Verre had missed any glimpse of his own daughter at the scene. He was unaware that she'd been involved in the fracas.

But Suyin had seen it all. She'd called Bex as soon as she'd seen her face on the news. 'You won't be able to keep this from your father for long,' she'd said on the phone. And she was right.

A nurse entered the room. 'I think your daughter has had enough conversation for now. You'll forgive me if I ask you to return a little later, after she's slept. She's still very weak.'

The parents left the room and Bonati followed them, but he turned to Bex as he moved past her bed. He looked genuinely shaken. His steel-blue eyes were fringed with dark shadows. He kept himself in good condition and his physical fitness usually belied his fifty years, but now he looked almost haggard, older.

'I really am sorry, Bex,' he said softly. 'Sorry for what happened.'

Bex grabbed his arm as he went. She held on to him and waited for her parents to disappear around the corner outside.

'It's not your fault, Professor. But you've got to speak to my dad. *Please*. You've gotta tell him I should stay. I can't leave the CRYPT. It's everything now.'

Tears were trickling down her cheeks. Bonati was saddened to see her this way. She'd been a tough, sassy girl since her arrival. Intelligent, resilient. He'd enjoyed seeing her give Jud a run for his money too. And he certainly hoped, as she did, that she would become a key member of the team.

The professor smiled warmly. 'They're your parents and they care about you, Bex. Very much, I'd say. This must have come as quite a shock. I'm sure, given time, they'll see things differently.'

Bex held his hand tightly. 'I hope so,' she said.

CHAPTER 28

WEDNESDAY: 3.01 P.M.

THE CRYPT

It was May. Nature's confetti was drifting from the cherry trees in the orchard. There was a smell of freshly cut grass in the air. Jamie was sprawled out on the lawn, staring up at the cotton-wool clouds above. The crenellated brickwork of the castle tower behind him cast shadows across his body.

His mother wandered from the kitchen, across the path and through the archway to join him. She was carrying a tray of Coke and biscuits, and smiling. His father was slumped lazily in a deckchair up on the terrace. He was talking to Bex; they were laughing and joking.

'Hey, son,' his father shouted over to him, 'do you know who this girl supports? Man City! Can you believe it!' Jamie watched them laughing together.

He stretched out on his back, pushed his feet to their limits and extended his arms out either side. Grassy tips tickled the backs of his arms. He felt the soft turf cushioning his body.

He closed his eyes and listened again to the symphony of birdsong and the soft breeze rustling the trees around him.

What a perfect day.

Gradually he became aware of a new sound penetrating into

the garden oasis, a new instrument accompanying the birdsong and the wind.

Traffic? It sounded almost like a lorry reversing. Its man-made electronic warning signal bullied its way into the air, shattering the natural peace. Why was it reversing into his garden? Who was this coming? And why had his parents not noticed? Was he the only one who could hear it?

The lorry's engine grew louder.

Soon it drowned out the birds, and the chink of the drinks, and the sound of his father's laughter.

Just the engine and the reversing signal, piercing his ears.

And then Jud woke up.

Above his basement window, out on the kerb, a lorry was making a delivery.

Jud sat bolt upright. Reality hit him like a blow to the stomach. He'd returned from his late breakfast, slouched sulkily on to his bed and promptly fallen asleep. A heavy, dream-laden sleep – long overdue. Images of the picture-perfect scene in the garden could only ever be a fantasy.

His mother was dead. He only spoke in code to his father most of the time.

And Jamie was gone.

Bex lay in a hospital bed. Jud was sure she'd be leaving the CRYPT. There was no way her parents would allow her to remain. Things had become so dangerous.

He slumped back on to the pillow and stared at the ceiling. Was it all worth it? The secrecy? The cloak-and-dagger stuff? The sleuthing? What had it achieved?

What had he *actually* achieved?

He stared upwards, eyes glazed. Deep in thought. A prisoner inside his cell. Sentenced to stay inside and research for Bonati. Memories of the secure room at the young offenders' institution still haunted him.

He felt alone. Acutely alone.

Return visits to the castle were rare now. And when he was there, all he and his father ever did was monitor for paranormal activity. Every type of equipment held in the CRYPT was duplicated and stored at the castle. Jud had measured the atmospheric conditions of that place countless times. He'd even spent many nights out on top of the tower, listening, watching, recording. But each time he'd found nothing.

The EMF meters and all the other gadgets had shown no abnormal readings since that fateful night. He'd heard, seen or felt nothing mysterious since then.

Whatever had caused his mother's death, whatever spirits he'd seen that tragic evening and heard countless times in the weeks that preceded it, they had now gone. The noises, the screams, the apparitions – it seemed like they'd all vanished. And with them, any hope of proving his innocence.

But one day. One day he'd catch whatever it was that had haunted his home and robbed him of his mother. One day he would hear something, feel something, set his equipment recording – and prove to the world that the castle really had been haunted all along.

Until then, whenever either he or his father was there, the old obsessions kicked in. They could never sit and relax, not when there was so much at stake. It was no longer a family home; its heart had been ripped out. It felt like a museum now, or a mausoleum.

But they could never sell the place. Not while there was a chance the ghosts would return. They had to keep it, and they had to keep revisiting.

So the CRYPT was Jud's only home. If you could call it that, with its harsh metallic corridors, cold tiled floors and hi-tech labs.

Was this really better than being locked up in the institution? Jud asked himself. Had it been worth losing his identity for? What was the difference? He was trapped inside, his movements were monitored and he was unable to make real friends with anyone, because that meant sharing secrets, and he knew he couldn't do that.

Lying on his bed, he closed his eyes again and tried hard to will himself to sleep, to return to the dream in the castle garden. If that was the only way he could construct the life he wanted, then so be it. He would live his life in dreams. He screwed his eyes tight.

But the traffic and the voices and the sterile air of the basement were all so far removed from the idyllic scene in the orchard. There was no way he could recreate it.

It was gone.

He opened his eyes again – saw his jacket flung over his chair; his wallet and the keys to his bike thrown on the desk; his helmet by the door; his boots.

He could go. Right now. Grab his keys and walk. The Fireblade was round the back. He'd be gone in minutes.

Was he *ever* going to be a success? Was Jud Lester ever going to last? If he ran now, he could soon be far away from London. In a few short hours he could be back at the castle. His father's helicopter would still be there. And his boat. He had a choice of escape routes. This time tomorrow he could be in France. Free. And the ghosts, and the skulls and the zombies, and the CRYPT would all be a thing of the past.

Jacket. Keys. Wallet. Helmet. Boots.

So easy.

He sat up. Looked out of the window. The grey clouds still hadn't shifted. There was an ominous feeling hanging in the air.

It wasn't the danger; it wasn't the fear; it wasn't even the bellman, who'd been haunting his thoughts since last night.

It was the loneliness. The isolation.

Ever since his arrival at the CRYPT, Bonati had been championing his cause. Telling everyone what a star they'd found in Jud Lester. How he was expecting big things from him.

Now, one year on, Bonati's boasting had not won Jud many friends. Jealousy. Resentment. Envy. These things followed him around like a stench. People were civil - most of the time. But deep down, the other skulls - and especially the guys - resented him being there. Getting all the best jobs. The biggest hauntings. The most dangerous missions. Showing them all how to do it.

Those who had managed to see beyond Bonati's claims about Jud had found him to be a cold, distant sort of character. They said he could never relax. Always obsessed with some investigation.

And now it had all come to this. Being told to stay indoors and stare at a computer screen. Unable to show his face in public for fear of being snapped by a photographer, or wound up by a reporter.

Keys. Wallet. Helmet.

Go.

Get away from the place. From the whole business of ghosts. Away from his life - and away from the blame game. The guilt that he carried round with him, for not being able to save his mother, and for not being able to save the people dying right now in the city at the hands of whatever was wreaking such havoc.

Go. Just escape.

He leapt up. Jacket on. Boots. He grabbed his things and, with one quick, sad glance over his shoulder at his cell, left the room. The door slammed.

Jud was leaving.

He'd no idea where he was going. He only knew he wasn't staying. There was no point now. The thought of Bex leaving - though he found it hard to admit it, even to himself - was eating him away inside. She'd been the only one since he'd left prison with whom he'd felt comfortable. Challenging, strong, cool. And now she was going too. Happened every time. Whenever someone tried to get close to him, they disappeared, deserted him.

His father was rarely here. Bonati was a strength for him, but Jud had always let him down, just like he'd done so far on this case. He would never be good enough for the professor. And now Bex was bound to leave. There was nothing left to stay for – his only company the policemen and MI5 officers who monitored him. And he knew he could outsmart them.

His bike was in the underground multistorey car park that backed on to Sector 3. He chose to avoid the lifts, too risky. Or the main staircase. Instead, he ran to the end of the corridor and pushed open the emergency exit. He rattled down the metal-tipped stairs, his boots echoing in the empty stairwell.

He was leaping flights at a time now, holding on to the banister, swinging round, and dropping with a thud on to each landing. Soon he was at Sector 3.

He pushed open the emergency entrance to the car park, his boots slamming against the metal skirting of the doors.

He was down. In the safety of the car park. Nearly there. The Fireblade was at the other end, past the lifts, near the exit ramp.

Jud ran. Just a few more seconds and he would be free. Free of the pressure. The expectations. The loneliness. If he was destined to be on his own, he'd rather be alone outside, out in the world, out where he could breathe, than in the claustrophobic subterranean lair of the CRYPT.

He was close to the lifts.

There was a ping as he approached.

The doors were opening.

Jud sped up. He had to make it past and get outside. *Now.*

The doors swung aside. He felt a hand on his shoulder. Another at his arm. Something was holding him back, gripping him tightly.

He turned.

'Going somewhere, Jud?' said Bonati.

CHAPTER 29

WEDNESDAY: 3.28 P.M.

FLEET SEWER, BELOW FLEET PASSAGE

The sewer engineers climbed down the drop-shaft into the labyrinth of tunnels below. The stench, so familiar to them now, penetrated through their masks as they climbed further down, deeper into the brick tunnel.

With an echoey splash, their heavy boots landed on the tunnel floor. The torches on their helmets flashed across the elaborate fungi plants that clung to the circular brick walls like gargoyles – one of few species that thrived in the godforsaken world far below Fleet Passage.

How times had changed. This was once a main tributary of the River Fleet, London's lost river, which had flowed southerly through the city down to the Thames. Over centuries the fresh, sparkling waters of the Fleet had declined to a stream, then a brook, then a ditch, until finally it became nothing more than a drain. Now an unromantic mid-level intercepting storm-relief sewer, an empty maze of hollow walkways, ladders and drop-shafts, it ran unnoticed from Hampstead Heath in the north down to Blackfriars Bridge, where it spewed out its unwanted contents into the Thames.

Doug, an experienced engineer, was here for his monthly inspection. And Matt had joined him on this stretch for the first time. The last few weeks had seen heavy and prolonged rain showers. Relief sewers like this one had taken a battering, and inspections were vital if they were to avoid future floods above ground.

They turned to face southwards and began the slow trudge down the pipe, checking brickwork and gates as they went. Far above them, the city's commuters walked on oblivious – leaving their extended lunch breaks and returning to their own more glamorous places of work up on Fleet Street and the Strand.

Matt walked ahead, swinging his hand-held torch across the right wall and above. Dough followed some way behind, checking the left side, pausing to kick rats through the muddy water whenever they scurried near his boots. It'd become a good sport.

On they marched, recording any visible damage with their cameras and quickly typing reference notes into their portable handsets. It was the job of other engineers to return to the same locations and conduct the necessary repair work.

Twenty minutes on. Still trudging southwards. Passing gates from interconnecting relief sewers. Past other drop-shafts. Booting rats in every direction.

Matt looked ahead. He stopped. What was that?

He shone his flashlight into the murky darkness. Soon Doug caught up. He removed his mask. 'What's up?'

Matt pointed ahead. Taking off his own mask he said, 'Up there. Can you see? What is it?'

Ahead, in the distance, their torches revealed something blocking the tunnel. It was difficult to make out what it was from this position – it was too far in the distance – but it looked solid enough. A discarded crate, or a large box? Some joker had obviously opened a manhole cover above and hurled something down into the sewer. It often happened. Litter, boxes, crates and bottles – dozens of bottles – were often found floating down the muddy stream. People often couldn't resist lifting the metal covers in the street and throwing something down to see how long it took to reach the bottom with an ominous splash in the murky depths below.

But this, whatever it was, seemed larger: too big to be thrown down a drop-shaft, surely.

The men kept moving towards the object. It was now fifty metres away, at the end of a straight stretch before the tunnel swept around to the left.

What *was* it?

The stench was unbearable. They were used to the rank smell of the usual detritus down here, but this was a different smell – like rotting flesh. Quickly they put their masks back on. As they did so, their helmet lamps momentarily lowered to the floor below. Rats, dazzled by the lights, sent frantic ripples across the tunnel.

The men looked up again, masks on.

And then they saw it. Their eyes registered, but their brains refused to accept. It couldn't be.

It just couldn't.

Up ahead, and getting closer by the second, was some sort of cart. Like the kind used back in the days when the Fleet flowed freely beneath open skies. There was something pulling it too. Towards them. And it wasn't a horse.

This was insane.

It looked like some sort of ox.

Trudging slowly through the muddy waters towards them, deep below ground, pulling a wooden cart.

The relief sewer opened out into the Thames not far up ahead, and the opening was large, wide enough for anything to come in, but an ox? A cart?

In here?

This was madness. The darkness was playing tricks on them. It had to be.

The men stopped and looked at each other. They both wore expressions of disbelief. But fear was slowly creeping into their faces too.

As the bizarre image became clearer, the shock hit the men like a knife between the eyes. Straight into their souls. Rattling around their bodies, bringing a deathly shiver and a pounding in their chests.

They turned and fled. Their large heavy boots were useless in the thick, syrupy water beneath them, but on they battled, yelling beneath their masks. Their steps were slow, awkward.

'Move!' shouted Matt. 'Get out!'

The cart was full of men. Or what had once been men, but no longer. They were empty shells of men – skeletal. A dozen of them at least, hanging over the sides of the wooden cart. Some started screaming now: great hollow groans that rattled down the brick tunnel towards the terrified engineers up ahead, who still tried to run on, too terrified to turn round. Fixed only on the shaft up ahead – their route to safety above.

Doug's foot caught on something in the water. It was a loose brick, fallen from the curved ceiling above. He went over on his ankle, shouting in agony. He grabbed something to try to break his fall. It was Matt's jacket. His partner went down with him.

His ankle throbbing with pain. Doug tried to get up. 'Matt! MATT!'

His friend was out cold. As Doug had brought him down into the water, Matt's head had struck the metal tip of a ladder fastened to the wall above them. It was a hefty blow, right to the back of his head. He'd fallen straight down on top of Doug.

'Matt! Get up. Wake up! What're you doin'?'

Silence.

Doug dared to look back, behind them. The wooden cart, its hideous load screaming and shouting, was getting nearer. It was now only a few metres away.

Desperately he freed himself from Matt's body, which was

slumped over his legs. He fumbled for his walkie-talkie inside his coat. He pressed the call button.

A mile and a half across the city, in an air-conditioned office, their employer heard the loud beep from the receiver on his desk.

'Jenkins here. Can I help you?'

'It's Doug.'

'Hi, how's it going? You and Matt still in there? You wanna get a move—'

'*Listen!* For God's sake listen to me!' yelled Doug.

'What?'

'We're in the south tunnel, under Fleet Passage. They're coming for—'

The line was breaking up. Reception was fading.

'Doug? What's going on? What's happened?' said Jenkins. 'Doug? Are you there?'

He heard him again – just fragments, but his voice sounded desperate.

'Quick!' Doug was yelling. 'They're comin'! Oh God! The cart. It's . . . coming! Help me! It's—'

'Doug? What's happened, man? What cart? What're you talking about?'

'They're comin'?'

'Who's coming?'

'They're getting off! Oh God. They're—'

The muffled voice became a scream, which burst out of the transmitter and rattled around the office. Jenkins went white. He got up and paced the floor, helpless. He felt sick.

'Doug! Doug!' he kept shouting into the transmitter. 'What's happening? Talk to me!'

A minute ago he'd been typing calmly at his screen, thinking about dinner. Listening to the traffic outside. Now he was caught up in a nightmare. Was this really happening?

Screams now filled his room.

His secretary ran in.

'Sir?'

Jenkins pointed to the receiver on his desk. 'I . . . I . . . dunno. Something's happened.'

The girl put her hand to her mouth and shrieked as the screams rang out from the receiver. The sound of Doug's desperate, agonising shouts was horrendous.

No words now. Only noises. Gruesome, horrifying cries from a grown man. A man now dying in a watery sewer below ground.

'Doug! Talk to me!' Jenkins yelled, one last time.

Nothing.

Doug was dead. Matt too. Trampled and beaten; stabbed and mauled. Their blood was already seeping into the river of rainwater inside the tunnel, creating a reddy-brown soup for the rats to feed on. The men lay face down in the stew.

The ox had trodden into flesh. The cart, with its hideous cargo, had driven over their bodies, deaf to Doug's pleas for mercy. Then the ghosts had leapt from the cart and attacked the men, stabbing them with skeletal limbs, finding flesh beneath their coats. Scratching, clawing, piercing. A frenzied attack, like a flock of vultures, but full of human revenge and hatred.

Breathless, Jenkins collapsed into his chair, staring at his frightened secretary across the room. Then he picked up the phone, and with trembling fingers pressed 999.

CHAPTER 30

WEDNESDAY: 3.55 P.M.

STARBUCKS, FLEET STREET

Bonati sipped his cappuccino. White froth rested on his top lip. He wiped it away with a freshly ironed handkerchief.

'You didn't have to run. You should've come to me. I told you. You don't have to face it on your own.'

Jud sat staring at the table. Stirring his coffee round and round. 'Face what?'

Bonati looked at him and said gently, 'Your new life.'

Jud kept staring down. He wasn't ready for this discussion. Just the opposite. He was ready to run away. He'd had enough discussions with the professor, and with all the police officers, therapists and psychologists, to last a lifetime.

He looked up and gazed at Bonati. Beneath the newly tinted brown eyes, Bonati could see he was still just a lost kid.

'I just wanna be free,' said Jud.

'I understand. After what happened at the castle, your father and I—'

'I never did it!' interrupted Jud.

'I know you didn't, Jud. We both know that.'

'So why? Why the secrecy, the new name. All this living in the shadows. I'm not a criminal . . . I never was.' Tears were surfacing at the edges of Jud's tired eyes.

Bonati felt for him. He always had. During the months of Jud's incarceration, it had been Bonati who'd visited him the most. More than his father, whose frantic schedule had continued to drag him away across the globe. But the professor had always been there. He'd believed in Jud. And he still did.

'Look, J,' he said kindly, 'I know how hard this must be for you. The temptation to run away must be huge. But you *have* got your freedom. You're a new person – and you mean a great deal to the CRYPT. You're its lifeblood. When the new recruits started, most of them said they wanted to be like Jud Lester.'

A rebel tear escaped the rim of Jud's eye and slowly trickled down his cheek.

'But *I don't*,' he said, his voice choking. 'I don't wanna be Jud any more. I wanna be me. Jamie,' he whispered. 'I want to start again . . . I had a dream today, sir.'

Bonati was finding it difficult to hold his own emotion back. Here was this kid, accused of the worst crime imaginable – a crime of which he was innocent – but with his new identity he wasn't even able to talk about it. Only to Bonati, and his father, who was always away. So instead it lay buried. The boy looked desperate.

'A dream?' Bonati said gently. 'What did you dream of, J?'

Jud sniffed back the tears and said, 'We were in the castle. Me and Mum and Dad. It was like a family.' He went silent for a second, thinking secretly how Bex had been in the dream too.

Bonati stared at Jud pensively.

This was madness, and they both knew it. The city was in turmoil. The world was expecting answers. And here they were, in a café, drinking coffee together and talking about dreams.

But it mattered. *Jud mattered.* Bonati could see it in his eyes when they were in the car park – he had no plan. He didn't know what he wanted. He just had to get out for a while. So

Bonati had persuaded him to come for a coffee and talk it through.

He said, 'Look, J. I can't imagine what it's like for you. Or for your father. God knows it's not a normal situation for either of you. But you have real talent. You have a bright future ahead of you. I wouldn't have gone along with it otherwise, would I?'

'What do you mean?'

'You know what I mean. The whole deal.' He spoke quietly now, bending closer over his coffee. 'When your father said he wanted you out of prison, here with us, I agreed straight away. And not just because we care about you – but because I knew you'd be the best agent we've got.'

'The best agent you *had*. I'm leaving, remember,' said Jud petulantly.

The professor was getting impatient now. 'OK,' he said. 'Leave. Go on. Right out of that door. But you better keep running. And don't even think of returning to the castle. It's the first place they'll look. The police will know you've gone. Even if I don't say anything. They'll know. And they'll be after you. And when they find you – you're on your own, J.'

Jud had stopped listening. Or tried to stop. He was staring down at the table, playing with his cold coffee.

'Listen to me,' said Bonati firmly. People at neighbouring tables looked up. 'Why can't you understand, J? If you disappear, if you escape, like some criminal on the run, it'll only confirm to the world that you're guilty. That you really did it that night at the castle.'

That was it. He shouldn't have said it. Jud stood up, jabbing the table into Bonati's stomach. The coffee cups wobbled and the loud chink rattled around the restaurant. Heads turned towards them.

'Sit down!' said Bonati.

Jud ignored him and began to push past, towards the door.

Bonati grabbed his arm and held on. A waitress was

approaching. He nodded to her and mouthed, 'It's OK.'

Jud turned to face him and saw Bonati's kind eyes imploring him to stay.

Grudgingly he slumped back on to the chair. He'd always respected Bonati; he was the only man he'd listen to. Not even his father had the same effect on him.

Bonati tried to speak more calmly. 'Look, I'm sorry. I know you don't like me mentioning your mother, Jud. God knows you must feel terrible about the whole affair, but it's the truth. You run out of the CRYPT, and you'll be locked up again. They'll be convinced you did it – I mean, why else would you be trying to jump ship now? Only it won't be the young offenders' institution this time; it'll be prison. And you'll be going there as an escaped convict. There'll be nothing we can do for you then. You need to wait it out until we can clear your name, officially. And we *will*, J.'

Jud couldn't face him. He felt trapped. Moving his spoon through the brown coffee rings on the glass top. Half listening; half switched off. Trying to visit the dream again. Trying to cling on to some fragment of that imaginary day. The garden. The laughter. The togetherness.

Gone.

It was never there in the first place.

A tear was struggling to break over his cheek again. He sniffed. And rubbed his eyes.

Don't let it out. Not here.

Keep it in. Don't be weak. Not here. Not with Bonati.

'Jud. Let it go. It's not your fault. You're worth something.'

The tears fell on to the table top and mixed with the coffee rings.

'We want you with us, Jud. We need your help – especially now.'

Jud looked up, and for a brief moment Bonati saw through the macho teenager to the boy inside.

'There's plenty of people in the CRYPT who feel differently, sir. Plenty of people who resent me.'

'They don't resent you,' said the professor. 'A bit jealous, probably, but no one resents you being there.'

'They do,' said Jud.

'Bex doesn't resent you. She was pleased to be paired up with you, that's what I heard.'

Bex. In all his wallowing in self-pity, he'd forgotten for a moment.

'How is she?'

'I thought you'd never ask!'

'Well? Is she awake?'

'Yes. She's recovering well. Her parents were with her when I visited.'

Jud's miserable expression returned. 'Getting ready to take her home, I suppose?'

The professor looked pensive again. 'Her father's pretty angry, as you can imagine. They're both very concerned about her. They don't think it's safe any more. The doctors were getting ready to discharge her when I left.'

'What? She's gone already?' said Jud.

'Why would she stay in hospital any longer than necessary?'

So that's it, thought Jud. The quickest friendship ever.

'I can't believe she's gone already.'

Bonati nodded. 'Yes. She was lucky they didn't want to keep her in for longer . . . Looking good, though.'

'What?'

'I said she looks good, you know, considering.' He was smiling now, and glancing over Jud's shoulder in the direction of the door.

Jud spun around.

It was Bex.

'What? How?' Jud said, looking confused.

'You got my text then, Bex?' said the professor, grinning, as she entered the restaurant and approached their table.

'Yeah, thanks. I talked to my parents – pleaded with them to give me one more chance. I think my mum must've spoken to my dad. She knows how much I want this. She's strong.'

She broke into a smile.

'A bit like me, I suppose,' she grinned. 'Hi, Jud. Sorry I missed breakfast.'

CHAPTER 31

WEDNESDAY: 4.32 P.M.

THE CRYPT

They took turns to stare into the retina recognition scanner.

'You first,' said Jud.

Soon the doors swung apart. Down the corridor. Into Sector 3. Another scanner, and they were finally in Jud's lab.

They sat down.

'You all right?' asked Bex.

'Yeah. Don't worry about me. You?'

'I'm fine.'

'You had us worried there, you know,' said Jud. 'What happened?'

Bex shook her head. The bruise was still clearly visible beneath her dark hair. 'I don't really know,' she said 'I mean, it all happened so quickly. I just remember this hand. It didn't seem human. There was something so skeletal about it. And the noise this thing made, as it grabbed me from behind. It wasn't a human noise. It was like some kind of clicking – like the bellman in the church, same kind of sound. It had to be one of the ghosts. I never saw its face, but I know it was. And so strong, too. Pulling me into the bushes.'

'Sounds terrifying,' said Jud.

'It was. But it was over so quickly. I don't know, maybe the ghost got scared or something. He threw me to the ground and must've fled. That's all I remember. I hit my head. Next thing I knew I was in hospital.' She felt the bruise on her forehead. 'Poor Grace,' she said. 'It was worse for her.'

'But is there nothing else you remember? I mean, didn't you see him? The ghost?'

Bex shook her head again. She didn't want an argument, but she was getting fed up of people asking that. 'No, Jud, I told you. Look, it happened so quickly. But I do remember being whisked around. Twirled, like. It sounds stupid, but . . . well . . . I dunno . . .'

'Go on,' said Jud, trying to sound more sympathetic.

'Well, I don't know if it's because I was dreaming when I was unconscious or something, but I swear I was . . . well, sort of dancing. Like being dragged around a dance floor by a stranger. You know, pushed and pulled.'

'Sounds like a dream to me,' said Jud.

'Like I said . . . stupid really.' Bex shrugged her shoulders and then, with a distant expression, said quietly, 'Bonati told me, you know.'

'Told you what?'

'About you leaving. Is that true?'

'I wasn't actually *going*. I was just . . . I dunno . . . getting some air.'

'Oh yeah?'

'Yeah. I don't like being cooped up like this. I like to get out now and again. You know, let off steam.'

'Yeah, of course. I know,' said Bex. But she was smiling now. 'And there was I thinking it was because you were sad that I might have been leaving.'

Jud flushed. Only slightly, but enough for Bex to notice. A faint redness creeping into his cheeks. He was flicking his hair, pulling his fringe back. He always did that when he was nervous, she'd noticed.

She continued cheekily, 'Couldn't survive without me, huh?'

He was doodling on a pad. Tracing the punched holes with his biro. Making elaborate spirals. Dodging her questions. He'd faced the kind of dangers that would've terrified people twice his age. He'd come close to death twice in twenty-four hours. But this. This was gruelling.

'Well?' said Bex.

'Yeah, whatever,' he said casually.

She was smiling. Grinning at him. This mysterious, courageous, complicated, secretive boy. Tough and yet so sensitive. Squirming with his feelings.

And then his mobile rang, shattering the atmosphere and offering Jud an escape route from this tortuous line of questioning.

He turned, pressed the receive button, held the phone to his ear and said, 'Jud Lester.'

Bex smiled. *Next time you won't be so lucky*, she thought.

'It's me,' Bonati said. His voice sounded tense. Something had happened. 'Are you plotting the locations on the map?'

'Yes, sir,' Jud lied. 'Why? What's happened?'

'Well I've got another one for you.'

'What?'

'Fleet Passage. Down in the sewer.'

'What's happened?'

'Two bodies were found. Engineers, I think.'

Bex saw Jud's face drop. 'What is it?' she whispered.

'Another one,' Jud said to her. 'How did it happen, sir?'

'Don't know exactly. It's still patchy. We've only got the account from the men's boss. He wasn't there.'

'How do you mean?'

'He was in his office. Apparently a message came in from one of the men working down in the sewer. Look, he's not making much sense at the moment, but Khan's on his way over to interview the man.'

'Do you want me to go, sir?' said Jud quickly.

'No, no. You stay and carry on with your research. I'll send another agent to join him. I want to know what's going on, and I don't want to learn it second-hand from Khan. But you need to get those locations plotted.'

'OK, sir.'

'Remember to add Fleet Passage now. The sewer underneath.'

'Will do.'

'And Jud . . .'

'Sir?'

'I'm glad you stayed. I'm glad you're still with us. But . . . well, for all our sakes, you better find a connection. And soon. This isn't over. MI5 said that Scotland Yard's going crazy. And I've got a horrible feeling this is only the beginning. If this one was caused by something paranormal as well, then they're all over the city. None of us are safe.'

'I'll do my best, sir.' Jud placed the phone back on the desk. He looked at Bex, who was pacing up and down the lab.

'Get the remote,' he said. 'We've gotta start. It's happened again. God knows there has to be a connection.'

She pressed the remote lying on the shelf, and the wall to their right began to revolve, revealing the giant screen. Jud quickly raised up a map of London on his laptop and the screen became a mass of streets and stations.

'OK,' he snapped quickly, 'let's get these locations plotted. Find out what's happening. There *has* to be a pattern.'

Bex flicked through the file of notes they'd brought in and began calling out the names across the room.

'Holborn station.'

'Who could forget it,' said Jud, and he highlighted the spot on the map. 'Next.'

'Kingsway.'

'Yeah, the abandoned bus. Those two guys. OK.'

'Greyfriars Garden, Newgate Street.'

Jud continued to highlight them on the screen. Large red circles appeared on the projected map.

'Then St Sepulchre's Church at Holborn Viaduct.'

'OK.'

'And the Old Bailey across the road. At Newgate.'

'Got it.'

'Then Hyde Park, where I was.'

'Right. And now Fleet Passage,' said Jud.

'So what happened there?' asked Bex, pulling up a chair alongside him to face the giant screen.

Jud shook his head. 'Dunno. Bonati didn't have much. It was down in the sewer, though.'

'Did you say *sewer*?'

'Yeah. We'll find out more, no doubt. Watch it on the bloody news tonight, I s'pose,' Jud said. Frustration was welling up inside him. He disliked reporters; hated photographers – how they leapt on a story before anyone had had time to even think. Anything to whip up the fear again. Get people chatting – and buying their newspapers. Playing out the drama like it was some film. He so wanted to be the first to find the connection. To solve what was causing these hauntings. Instead of reading about developments in the newspapers.

'Come on,' said Bex sharply, sensing that Jud was drifting off again. 'Do you see anything?'

They looked at the collection of red circles on the screen – the locations of the various hauntings.

Nothing.

Jud said, 'There is a link between St Sepulchre's and Newgate. That we know.'

'Yeah, the bellman,' said Bex.

'Exactly. He came for his execution bell. The plaque on the

wall said it was rung outside the prison the night before executions.'

'For the condemned prisoners in Newgate across the road. Make them repent.'

'Exactly. I could feel it too. In the church. There was this sense of foreboding. You know. Like the night before something bad,' said Jud.

'And that's where the Old Bailey is now?' said Bex.

'That's right,' said Jud.

'OK.' Bex was thinking. 'But why Holborn tube, or Kingsway?' she asked.

Jud was thinking. 'Eyewitnesses have all talked about the same kind of apparitions, haven't they?'

'Yeah,' said Bex. 'Claimed they looked like highwaymen or something.'

'Famous at the time, weren't they?' said Jud. 'I mean, notorious. Special kind of characters. Their hangings would've been public events. Like, big occasions.'

'S'pose so. Why?'

'I mean, they weren't like your average criminals, were they? More like celebrities at the time.'

'Celebrities?'

'Sure. People had a romantic view of them. Mysterious. Heroic in some way, I suppose. If they were arrested and found guilty, then everyone would know about it.'

'I guess so,' said Bex.

'Well, the place where they were hanged would've been famous too, wouldn't it?' said Jud.

'Yeah. Of course.'

'It would've been an important place – where maybe crowds would've gone.'

He quickly transferred the image to the small screen in front of him again, and Googled *Highwaymen hangings in London*.

Bex watched him and said, 'But none of this explains why

they should come back to haunt us now, does it? I felt real anger in that church. You said the bellman was radiating massive amounts of energy. Pure anger. I mean, what have we *done?*'

'Don't know . . . yet.' Jud was reading the text on the screen. 'That's what we've gotta find out . . . Hey, listen to this: "The hanging of highwaymen often became a great public spectacle. On the day of executions, thousands of people flocked to the gallows at Tyburn."'

Tyburn.

Where had he heard that name?

Tyburn.

He was sure it sounded familiar.

'Jud?'

'Just a minute.' He was thinking. Bex watched him closely. She saw his dark eyes flicking across the room, looking into space. Files inside his head were being hurriedly opened. Memories were being sifted through. *Tyburn.*

And then it came to him.

The new hotel. He'd been half asleep at the time, but the early-morning news had talked about plans for a new hotel complex. A Zakis hotel. The biggest and the best or something. He was sure they'd mentioned the word Tyburn.

The Tyburn Hotel.

Bex saw his face change. 'What? Tell me? Got something?'

'Dunno . . . er . . . maybe,' he said. He was quickly Googling *Plans for new Tyburn Hotel* into his laptop. A BBC report came up, first entry. They both read it on the large screen.

'Global chain Zakis Hotels plans its biggest project yet – a grand hotel complex at Marble Arch in central London. The Tyburn Hotel will be a state-of-the-art luxury resort right in the heart of the city.'

'But that's Marble Arch,' said Bex. 'Not Tyburn.'

'Same place,' said Jud. 'Look at this.' He'd found another website on hangings, and read: '"A plaque now commemorates the site of the Tyburn Gallows, at Marble Arch. The Tyburn Tree, as it was known, was a giant three-branched wooden structure, which could execute up to twenty-four people in one go."'

'Twenty-four people!' shouted Bex. 'Gruesome.'

'Yeah.'

'Twenty-four deaths together,' Bex said. 'Every week. Imagine that. And with twenty-four families all grieving . . . that place is steeped in emotion. And memories. The energy levels there would be immense.'

'Yeah, but listen to this,' said Jud as he read on. ' "It is estimated that from 1169, when the first recorded Tyburn execution took place, until 1793, when hangings were moved to Newgate prison, between forty thousand and sixty thousand criminals were executed there.'

'That's insane,' said Bex. 'Unbelievable. It's gotta be a highly active place for paranormal activity, after all those deaths. The energy levels would be off the scale.'

'I agree, it's a significant place,' said Jud. 'And I can see why there'd be activity there. Places where people actually die often record higher energy levels than the places where they end up buried. But we've forgotten one thing, Bex.'

'What?'

'There's been nothing reported at Tyburn, has there?' he said. 'No ghosts, I mean. No hauntings at all. *Nothing.*'

Bex's face fell. She stared at the screen full of text. He was right. Had their theory come to a halt?

And then she said, 'Nothing that we know of.'

'What do you mean, that we *know* of ?' said Jud, unconvinced. 'If paranormal activity – as hostile as the stuff we've seen so far – had been witnessed at Marble Arch, we'd know about it. The papers are full of this stuff. Any whiff of a haunting and they'd be on it like hounds.'

'True,' replied Bex. 'But what if it was hushed up? I mean, what if something has *already* happened but they've hushed it up?'

'Zakis, you mean?'

'Exactly,' said Bex.

'Possible,' said Jud. 'He's got a lot to lose if they condemn the site and stop his hotel plans. But it's unlikely.'

Bex shrugged and stared at him. 'What is likely or unlikely any more, Jud? What is normal? The city's gone mad. It's even happening in the sewers now.'

Jud returned to the web page on hangings and read on. ' "The journey from Newgate Gaol to Tyburn always followed the same path. It was customary that the condemned men would travel by ox cart from the prison. They'd stop along the way to collect flowers from St Sepulchre's Church."

'There you are,' he said. 'There's your link between Tyburn and St Sepulchre's. So not only did the bellman come from there, the prisoners themselves actually stopped there for sympathy on the way to the gallows. It explains the feelings I picked up. The atmosphere was so sad. Like something was going to happen and you couldn't stop it. I could sense it. All those men stopping there on the way to the gallows. They knew it was over by then.'

He looked at Bex. 'It's beginning to add up, isn't it?'

She grinned at him. 'Keep reading,' she said.

Jud returned to Google and clicked on another site displaying famous hangings.

' "The hanging of highwaymen always attracted a huge crowd. Perhaps the most famous of them all to die on the gallows at Tyburn was the notorious gentleman highwayman Claude Du Val.'

Bex breathed in sharply. She grabbed his arm.

'What? Bex? What's wrong?' He could see she'd gone pale.

She stared at the words on the screen, saying nothing at first. Jud could feel her shivering slightly next to him. He put his arm around her shoulder.

'What is it?' he said. 'Tell me.'

'It's that name.'

'Du Val?'

'Yes.'

'What about it?' said Jud.

'It's something Grace said, when she saw me in hospital.'

'I don't understand. Said what, Bex?'

'She came to see me before I checked out. She said she'd heard something. When she was waiting with me. In the bushes. I was out cold, but she said she heard a name.'

'Du Val?'

'Yeah. I'm sure it was.'

'Did you hear the name as well, Bex?'

She looked confused. Her head was beginning to throb again. She rubbed her temple.

'I just . . . I don't know. It's so unclear. But Grace said to me she was sure she'd heard a voice talk about dancing. Dancing with Duval, she said.

'And you said you thought you were dancing or something,' replied Jud quickly.

'I was. I swear I was. It was like being pushed around the floor.'

Jud quickly read on. ' "A gallant and courteous rogue, the legendary Du Val would hide on the heaths of London, where he would rob the rich noblemen and dance with their wives." '

'It's him! I've danced with Claude Du Val!' shouted Bex, half in fear, half boasting.

Jud said, 'There's just too much here to be coincidence. This has gotta be a connection. We must be on to something.'

'But the other hauntings,' said Bex. 'The other marks on the map. We've got to link those, haven't we? Holborn. Kingsway. That sewer near Fleet Street. What about those, Jud?'

He returned to the original page, which explained the journey taken by the condemned men, and read on: ' "After pausing at St

Sepulchre's, the cart of criminals would cross Fleet Ditch and then head back uphill to High Holborn, across Kingsway and down St Giles, stopping at the Bowl Inn for a last drink of ale, and then on to the old Tyburn Road (now named Oxford Street)."

'It's there,' said Jud. '*It's all there.*' He flicked back to the map and saw the red circles again. 'Every single haunting that's happened has been on the route.'

'Fleet Ditch? Is that the sewer?' said Bex.

Jud quickly Googled the words into his laptop and searched again.

'"Once a major river running through London, the Fleet is one of the city's lost waterways, shrinking to a stream, then a brook, then a ditch. It is now nothing but a storm relief sewer, running deep below Fleet Passage."'

They'd got it. Everything was slotting into place: the carnage; the hauntings; everything could be traced right back to the Tyburn site. The excavations that Zakis and his team were doing must have disturbed the souls of countless highwaymen who'd died there.

And now they were coming back.

For revenge.

CHAPTER 32

WEDNESDAY: 5.30 P.M.

SCOTLAND YARD

'Come in,' said Khan impatiently as he beckoned the group into his office. 'I've got thirty minutes. The Commissioner wants to see me at six. I hope you've got some answers.'

Bonati, Jud and Bex entered and sat down.

'So?' said the detective chief inspector. 'Talk.'

Jud and Bex had briefed Bonati in his office as soon as he'd come back from his interview with Jenkins. He'd listened, but had only been half convinced, until he'd heard Jud say the word 'cart', and that was it. Jenkins had told him that he remembered his sewer engineer screaming down the phone something about a cart coming towards him just before he'd died. Down in the sewer. It had to be the prisoners - on the road to Tyburn. It all added up.

What he had to do now was convince Khan. The inspector hadn't wanted to talk over the phone, so he'd told them to come straight to Scotland Yard. He'd sent a car for them. It would have been impossible to enter from the front - reporters and TV vans had been camped outside the station now for two days - so the police car had zoomed in through the back entrance and whisked the party up to Khan's sixth-floor office, without anyone seeing.

Now they sat across the table from him. And he didn't look like he was in the mood for hearing stories, however convincing they might have sounded back at the agency.

Jud began. He explained the whole theory, beginning with Newgate Gaol and the bellman at St Sepulchre's, and then all the hauntings along the road to Tyburn.

Khan sat and listened to him, without interrupting once. This was the kind of evidence he hated – circumstantial; theoretical; nothing conclusive. No prints. No DNA. No confessions either.

But what did he expect? These were ghosts. The living dead. What use were forensics now? But still he showed no emotion. His face was expressionless.

Jud reached the climax to his theory – the Zakis hotel. The excavations at Marble Arch – the site of the Tyburn Tree.

'Well?' said Bonati. 'It sounds plausible, don't you think, Detective Chief Inspector?'

'A great story,' said Khan eventually. 'It's got everything. History, drama, suspense. Just one thing missing.'

'What?' said Jud, anger stirring inside him.

'Proof! Nothing has happened at Tyburn. Or is that an inconvenient truth that you've chosen to omit from your little story, Lester?'

Jud stood up. 'Now hang on, Chief Inspect—'

'Sit down,' warned Bonati. Now was not the time for another one of Jud's petulant outbursts.

Bex interrupted. 'Nothing that we know of, sir.'

'What?' Khan now turned and glared at Bex.

'I said nothing's happened at Tyburn *that we know of.*'

'That we know of?' said Khan scornfully. 'Oh, I see. So the entire story is based on a hunch that something *might* have happened at Tyburn that my guys don't know about yet. You want me to go in there and ask Zakis, do you? A crime *might* have been committed, but we just haven't been told.'

'Well I don't think people who commit crimes are usually keen on telling the police, Inspector,' said Jud sarcastically.

'Or it hasn't happened *yet*,' said Bex.

'No!' shouted Khan impatiently. 'This is ridiculous! You could use that argument for any site in any part of the country! Crimes *might* happen anywhere, for God's sake. If we investigated places where crimes might be about to happen simply because of some hunch, then we'd be visiting every house in every town. And what would we be looking for? "Excuse me, Mr Zakis, we think a crime might be about to happen here. Any ideas? Only it would fit nicely with our theory, you see." Brilliant.'

Khan was pacing his office, towering over his seated guests. They could see he was tense. Beads of sweat trickled down his creased forehead. There was an almost imperceptible tremble to his hands.

'Crime *could* happen anywhere! It sounds boring, I know, Miss De Verre, but we have to wait for crimes to have taken place before we can solve them. Unless we have reliable information – a solid tip-off – that something's about to happen, in which case we act on it, see. But this isn't reliable! Where's your proof, huh? We need more than just your feelings.'

Bonati stepped in. Bex was one of his most promising agents. And she'd already been through enough over the last few days to last a lifetime. He wasn't going to tolerate this bullying, not from anyone. He stood up. His voice was calm but stern.

'I've heard enough, Detective Chief Inspector. You've asked us to investigate this on your behalf – because so far you've found no answers yourself. You've come up with nothing. My team have done everything I've asked of them, and more. We've found answers for you – answers that sound plausible to me. Strong evidence that links the sites of the hauntings across London. Every one of them. We've good reason to believe that the paranormal activity we've seen in recent days can be directly linked to the excavations and building work taking place at Tyburn. It is such a significant site for activity of this kind. It *has* to be that. If nothing has happened there yet, then I can assure you it will soon.'

Khan was standing at the other side of his desk now, trying to look like he was ignoring Bonati. Clutching his stomach beneath his jacket. Reflux from the acidic ulcer was rising up his throat. His heart was pounding. He turned to the window and looked out on the city. He saw the satellite dishes on the vans outside; the huddle of reporters; the cameras. And the crowds beyond them.

He pictured himself going before the masses with this kind of story. No forensics. No DNA. No confessions. Nothing but history lessons and hunches.

But Bonati was getting impatient.

'Detective Chief Inspector Khan! Ghosts don't leave fingerprints! This investigation is unlike any other. You *have* to trust us. The hotel plans *must* be stopped. Zakis must be moved on. Find somewhere else. We *must* let Tyburn rest in peace.' He sounded ominously serious now. 'Or I swear to you, the souls of those who hanged there will continue to haunt this city. Zakis has dug up something that should have stayed buried.'

The detective chief inspector turned round to face the group. The pain from his stomach kept jabbing into his frame like a knife, and the palpitations were gaining pace. He reached over to his desk drawer, grabbed the plastic bottle of pills and rattled some down his throat.

He stared pensively at the desk for a moment, and then said, 'I've no choice, have I? We've no other leads. We've no options.'

'None,' said Bonati.

'Right,' Khan said, glancing at his watch. 'I've got to see the Commissioner. Leave it with me, Bonati. You've already contacted MI5, I assume?'

'I rang them before we came over to you,' said Bonati. 'They're monitoring the situation. But they want answers.'

Khan knew he had to act. 'I'll deal with it,' he snapped.

Bonati led Jud and Bex out of the room. Khan returned to his desk. His face was pale and gaunt and his eyes were bloodshot. He knew he was cornered. He had to act. He had two minutes before he was due in front of the Commissioner.

There was just time.

Quickly he picked up the phone and dialled. A familiar voice answered.

'Silverman?' said Khan quietly. 'They're on to us. Tell Zakis. They're asking questions about Tyburn. They've made a link. Has anything happened there I should know about? For God's sake tell me the truth.'

CHAPTER 33

WEDNESDAY: 7.30 P.M.

PRESIDENTIAL SUITE, THE DORCHESTER HOTEL, PARK LANE

'Anyone see you arrive?' Zakis demanded.

'No,' said Silverman.

Zakis was pacing up and down the suite, a glass of vodka in his hand. His third. A dribble of spit clung to his stubbly chin. The whites of his eyes were yellow, and there were shadows beneath them. 'How the hell does anyone know about Kozlosky?' he shouted.

Silverman sank down on the giant leather sofa. His hands were trembling. Zakis's men sat at the table across the room in a cloud of cigarette smoke. They were watching him. Silverman could hear another man in the room next door shouting into a phone – Zakis's head of security. The whole suite hummed with tension.

Silverman said, 'I . . . er . . . well I don't think they actually know about him, sir.'

'What? But you said Khan was worried. "They're asking about Tyburn", you said.'

'Yes. But it's not about Kozlosky. No one's squealed. They

think something *might* have happened at Tyburn – or will happen.'

'What *are* you talkin' about?' Zakis was getting impatient.

'Well, they've made this link, see. Some superstitious story about hangings.'

Zakis stopped pacing and looked at Silverman. The word had triggered an image in his mind that he'd been trying to forget. The body of Yuri Kozlosky swinging from the steel frame on the building site. Hanging by his neck. Dead. And the stories from the construction workers. Their claims of shadowy ghosts coming up from the ground. Taking Yuri. Stringing him up. Harrison's pathetic whimpering about getting the police involved.

Had he squealed?

'It's Harrison, isn't it?' shouted Zakis. 'He'll be dead by tomorrow.' He glanced across at his henchmen. They grinned and patted the revolvers in their jackets.

'No! Wait, Mr Zakis, please – you're not listening,' pleaded Silverman. 'I've kept my mouth shut since you told me about it on the phone and no one else has squealed. I'm sure of it. Look if the police had been contacted by anyone, then Khan would have told me, wouldn't he? Or he'd have called you. But he doesn't know about it. Even *he* doesn't know. No one does.'

Zakis poured himself another vodka and said, 'Then why the hell are they interested in Tyburn? Why now?'

Silverman watched him take a gulp of his vodka. He too needed a stiff drink. His mouth was dry. 'Bonati's team have come up with some story about prisoners from Newgate Gaol being led to Tyburn Hill to be hanged,' he began.

Zakis started laughing. 'What is this? Huh? Some school play? These kids are somethin' else!'

Silverman interrupted; he didn't share the joke, 'But it *was* a gallows, wasn't it? I mean, that's where they were hanged – on our site.'

'Yeah, sure it was a gallows,' snapped Zakis. 'We all know that, and I don't need no history lesson, Silver. It was over two hundred years ago, for cryin' out loud. What's it got to do with anything now? How can they prove it's us?'

Silverman tried tentatively to explain. 'Khan said that these ghost hunters have plotted the locations of the hauntings across London and made a connection.'

'What *connection*?' shouted Zakis irritably. He was running out of patience. There was a slight tremble to his voice – which Silverman had never detected before. His men were getting edgy too.

'Well, you see, the condemned men – I mean the prisoners who were waiting in the gaol to be hanged – were taken from Newgate to Tyburn along a certain route. The same every time. They stopped on the way at various places.'

'So?'

'Well, these are the same places where the ghosts are now appearing.'

Silverman looked Zakis straight in the eye and said, 'They're the ghosts of men who were hanged at Tyburn, Mr Zakis. They say you've stirred up their souls. Reawakened them.'

Images of Kozlosky flashed into Zakis's mind again. He said nothing.

Silverman continued, 'This Bonati guy – head of this ghost agency – well, he told Khan that we must have caused the ghosts to come back, and so he has to investigate it. If he doesn't, Bonati will just take it higher. He's got friends, Bonati. Knows a lot of people. MI5 apparently. It's hard to know exactly what he is, but he's powerful. They'll come sniffing around.'

Silverman's pace had quickened. He was clearly panicking now. 'Even if they don't find ghosts, there's plenty of men around here who'll squeal if given the chance. I mean, about Kozlosky. If they come here asking questions, someone's bound to blow the whistle.'

Zakis downed his vodka and stared at the politician in thought.

'Sir,' pleaded Silverman, 'they said something might happen at Tyburn, and . . . well, we know it already has! What if their theories are right? What then?'

Zakis loathed this weasel. Pathetic, greedy man. No doubt he was after more money for his silence. He hated having people like this on his payroll. What had Silverman done to deserve the quarter of a million that would soon be rolling into his offshore account? Just bullied a few council officials, pulled a few strings, turned a blind eye. Sure, Zakis needed him, just like he needed all the other politicians whose loyalty he'd bought over the years, but Silverman still made him sick, with his pinstriped suit and his self-importance.

The grey-haired politician continued again; he *had* to make Zakis see what was happening. 'If they're right and we've stirred something up at Tyburn, the work will have to stop. You'll have to scrap the hotel. Find somewhere else.'

Zakis slammed his glass down on the marble table. 'Don't tell me what I might have to do, man!' He waved a stubby finger at him, 'Listen, Silver, this is how it's gonna be. Everyone – and I mean *everyone* – has some dirt on them, some secret they like to keep quiet, something they don't want you to know. And even if they don't, we can always make something up. Sleaze is easy to manufacture – you're a politician, for God's sake, you should know that! And when we have our story on this Bonati guy, we'll go to him. We'll do our bargaining.'

'You're talking about some secret agent guy – not even Khan knows much about him, sir.'

'Listen, no one is untouchable. Right? And you've got contacts, Silver. You've got Khan for a start. And all your Westminster cronies.' He paced the floor and stared out of the window, then turned back to Silverman again, 'Come on, Silver, you politicians run this city, along with the journalists.

218

You know all the gossip, and when there's none, you make it up.'

Silverman wasn't convinced, 'Sorry, sir, I just don't see how—'

Zakis interrupted him. 'No? You don't see? You don't get it, do you! I'm not asking you, Silver . . . I'm tellin' you!' He glanced over at his bodyguards, who got up from their chairs and approached the politician menacingly.

Silverman got the message before Zakis even spoke.

'OK, OK. I get it, sir.'

'You will.' He grinned at his men. 'You will, Silver. My men can be very imaginative in the way they dispose of corpses. I mean, we've even got the perfect burial ground for you . . . You could join the other Tyburn zombies!' and he gave a menacing laugh, as his bodyguards grinned and nodded obediently.

'So find out anything you can, Silver. I want to know everything there is to know about this Bonati guy, and all his little agents. I need bargaining power – you know how we work. I need some dirt. These kids who pose around the place pretending to be ghost hunters . . . I bet they're no angels. They'll have little misdemeanours we can remind them of. And if they don't, stick some mud on to one of them. Drugs or somethin'. Bring the place into shame. I wanna threaten it with closure. I want a story so big it'll frighten Bonati away.'

'And if it doesn't?'

Zakis stared back at Silverman with an expression devoid of emotion. 'If it doesn't? Well then my boys here will find other ways of silencing him. Look, Silver, this hotel is going ahead. You understand? I'm not gonna be stopped, especially by some Scooby Doo team of ghost hunters and their mad professor.'

Silverman stood up. Already fearful of what he'd got himself into, he now knew for certain that Zakis would stop at nothing to get what he wanted. And he knew that he was now so far in – so connected to Zakis – that he had no choice but to play ball. He belonged to Zakis now.

'Sit down!' Zakis bellowed. 'I haven't finished.' His guest sat down again promptly.

'Now,' he continued, 'I want you to speak to Khan again. Tell him he's gonna hold another press conference.'

'Press conference?'

'You heard me. Tomorrow. He's gonna tell the world that there's been new evidence, OK? I wanna stop this ghost nonsense. It's getting outta hand. People will believe anything now.'

Zakis was pacing the room again, thinking hard. Running his sweaty hands through his greasy black hair.

'You tell Khan to say they now suspect it's some violent group of protesters. Or a hi-tech group of vigilantes. Environmental warriors – I dunno, call them whatever you like. Say they're pulling these stunts around London, protesting against transport pollution. That's it. Some bunch of guys attacking trains and buses. Scaring us all into stayin' at home. And stop the planet warming up. You know, some crap like that.'

Silverman didn't look convinced. 'So you want him to say it was humans who did all this? All the hauntings? He'll never buy it, sir.'

'What? Khan has just as much to lose as you do if the hotel is stopped. He's in this as well. Up to his neck. But he doesn't know about Kozlosky. At least that secret's safe with us.' He glared straight at Silverman. 'Or it better be!'

'Of course.'

'So we say they've been using chemicals to make people hallucinate. And then putting on masks and stuff. Say they've got technical stuff to make images appear. It's all possible, you know it is. This isn't the dark ages, Silver.'

'I suppose it's just as believable as ghosts,' said Silverman, anxious to appease Zakis and get the hell out of there.

'Exactly.' Zakis smiled, walked to the door and opened it. 'Now get going, before Bonati and his kids turn up at the site.'

Silverman got up again and walked towards the door. 'Even if we close the place down, you know, I reckon he'll still keep nosing around. He won't give up. He's crazy, that kid.'

'Who, Bonati?' said Zakis.

'No. This Lester kid. You know, the one on TV. The one who lashed out at that reporter. He's like a little terrier. He won't stop if he gets a whiff of something.'

Zakis smiled across at his men, who were now standing. 'You leave the kid to us,' he said, grinning at them. 'We know what to do with him. It'll be a pleasure, won't it, boys?'

CHAPTER 34

WEDNESDAY: 9.01 P.M.

CHINA TOWN

Jud and Bex had found the evidence that linked all the hauntings together. Bonati had told them to start revisiting the sites along the route to Tyburn first thing tomorrow. Before then, if anything happened somewhere, he had other agents who could attend and take recordings. In a sudden attack of generosity - or perhaps because he knew they were too exhausted to be of any use tonight - he had given them the evening off.

Bex held tightly on to Jud as he wove the Fireblade in and out of the evening traffic like a needle and thread; bound for China Town. Since being told about the prisoners' route to the Tyburn Tree, and the link to Zakis's hotel plans, Bonati had sent his investigators to various sites almost immediately. And as Jud and Bex sped towards China Town, ready for some serious food, across the city their fellow agents were slumming it on dark shadowy street corners and hiding in buildings along the prisoners' route, ready to record paranormal activity with nothing but a sandwich and a can of Coke to keep them happy.

Jud accelerated across Trafalgar Square and up into Charing Cross Road. The traffic had died down now and he could let the Fireblade rip. Bex clutched tightly to his torso. She was fearless of speed – she'd pushed her own GSX to its limits many times before. And now, even though she wasn't in the driving seat, she trusted Jud and felt as relaxed as if she'd been steering the Honda herself. She rested her head on his shoulder, staring out at the buildings as they flashed past.

Jud stopped at the next set of traffic lights. Another biker had pulled up alongside them. There was a second on their right.

'This'll be fun,' he said into the microphone in his helmet. 'Who's your money on?'

'We'll win hands down,' said Bex. 'They're both Ninja ZXs. The Kawasaki's no match for the Fireblade.'

Bex's knowledge of bikes still surprised Jud. 'Let's have a go, then,' he said. 'Hold tight.'

The bikers stared at the red light, revving their engines. A sudden flash to amber, clutch in, pedal down, throttle back, and off. Within seconds Jud was ahead. But the Ninjas kept pace at equal distances behind him. It was almost as though they wanted to be trailing. They weren't trying to overtake. When Jud had to slow down to avoid a pedestrian, the two bikes slowed down too and stayed at the same distance behind him.

Were they following him?

He sped up again. Stepping through the gears, winding the throttle back. The Kawasakis kept pace but never overtook. The two riders were dressed identically, in the green and slate-grey leathers that matched the bikes.

Bex heard a crack behind her. Glancing over her shoulder, she saw some kind of weapon fixed to the side of the bike's fairing – it was like a miniature version of the guns on a military helicopter. Sleek and deadly.

Had they actually fired at her? Was that what the noise was?

'Oh God,' said Jud into his helmet. 'Look over there.' He was pointing up ahead, to the right.

Bex looked over his shoulder and saw a man lying on the ground. Two people had stopped to nurse him. That confirmed it for her. These guys were firing at them, and it didn't seem to worry them if an innocent bystander got hurt.

'Go faster, Jud. They're after us!' She shouted into his ear. 'I dunno who they are, but they're firing at us. Move it!'

Jud didn't argue. He pushed the Honda, and pushed again. Faster. The engine roared through the gears. He was riding in slalom style now, weaving left and right. They heard shots from behind. Both Ninjas were firing at them. Bex felt something ricochet past her helmet.

Jud darted into Newport Street and up into Gerrard Place. It was packed: people everywhere, spilling out of Chinese restaurants, carrying plastic bags from the late-night Chinese supermarkets. His foot caught a pile of spiky durian fruit, stacked up outside a shop. Some split into pieces that rolled around the pavement, sending a foul stench into the air. Pedestrians dived frantically for cover as the sound of the three bikes echoed across the narrow street. The Ninjas' gunshots sent them cowering into shop doorways and hiding beneath market stands.

Jud swerved into an alleyway. His headlights blinded the people coming his way. They leapt aside and clung to the dirty brick walls. The Kawasakis were closing in, flanking Jud's Fireblade.

'There!' shouted Bex, pointing left. 'In there. We'll lose them.'

Jud obeyed and accelerated towards a multistorey car park. The exit barrier on the other side had just lifted to allow a car out, and Jud quickly swung the Honda across the approach road and under the barrier before it lowered again.

Down the ramp. Deeper into the subterranean world. It was a mirror image of most car parks, like a reflection in a lake, each level leading further below ground. Jud sped down the ramps, sharp left, turn, down again. The sound of the engine catapulted around the walls, like a ball in a pinball machine, sending echoes slamming into concrete and bouncing off again at angles.

Bex felt dizzy. The bike was tossing and turning her and she struggled to cling on. She glanced over her shoulder.

Had they lost them?

Jud turned the bike again, down another ramp. Bex looked up through the gap in the walls to the floor above. She saw the wheels and bumpers of parked cars, and then the green flashes of the Ninjas. They were coming.

There was an almighty crash just behind them. One of the Ninja bikes had come shooting down the ramp on to the floor below and collided with a car reversing out of its space. The rider was tossed straight off the bike, bounced off the roof of the car and fell like a rag doll into the corner of a pillar. Slumped. Out cold.

The other Ninja rider stopped for a few seconds. He glanced at his mate folded and crumpled on the floor. Then he sped up and left him for dead. He *had* to catch this kid.

Zakis would have his guts if he didn't.

Jud had reached the end of the car park. No more floors. The only way was back up. He screeched towards the exit sign and began the ascent, climbing up through the floors. Bex saw the headlights of the Ninja behind; like demonic eyes they shone in the gloom of the cavernous building. Another crack. The rider behind had fired towards them again. Luckily Jud swerved to his right and disappeared up the next ramp just as the bullet sped past, lodging itself in the wing of a parked BMW, setting off the alarm.

Up they climbed. The Ninja was closing in and firing off shots like a machine gun. The rider was determined to take out these jokers before they reached the open city above, but there was still a floor between them.

As Jud reached ground level, his bike hit something slippery. It was a small patch of oil left there from a leaky engine. They felt the bike go beneath them. It skidded, swerved and went down.

The Honda was now resting on Bex's left leg. She was

225

screaming. Jud leapt off and began to yank the heavy bike upright. The Ninja was on the level just below them, its engine roaring like a beast approaching. The lights from its headlamps swung along the roof, illuminating the steel girders as the bike ascended the slope.

'Get it off!' cried Bex. 'It's crushing my ankle!'

But Jud left the bike. He sprinted down the car park in the direction of the exit ramp.

'Jud!' screamed Bex. 'Where are you going? Help me!'

'I'll be back!' he shouted behind him.

The Ninja was approaching directly below him now, about to climb the concrete slope. Within seconds the assassin would be on their floor, and he and Bex would be dead.

But as they'd hurtled up the ramp on the Fireblade moments earlier, Jud had noticed something in his peripheral vision. It was a fire extinguisher, attached to the side of a pillar at the top of the ramp.

He *had* to get to it.

Bex was still yelling in agony and trying desperately to release her leg from the bike.

The Ninja's headlamps flashed over the roof of their level as it swung sharply up the ramp.

Jud was waiting. Ready.

A second later, with an animalistic cry of anger, he launched the great metal fire extinguisher at the rider at the exact moment he passed. It met his helmet full on. The blow was strong enough to tip him off the bike just as it reached the top of the ramp. He skidded across the floor and ploughed into the back of a parked car, rapidly followed by the screaming Kawasaki, which pummelled into his frame like a giant bullet. The wheels of the bike still spun but the body of its rider lay motionless. Jud waited a few seconds to see him move, as a feeling of dread rose in his stomach. Had he killed someone?

'Come on!' he whispered, looking about him furtively.

Mercifully he saw the rider move a leg and heard him groan in agony. He was alive. Whether or not the other man had survived, he couldn't say. He decided he'd call anonymously for an ambulance as soon as he'd freed Bex.

He quickly ran back to her. He pulled the bike from her leg. 'I guess we're even,' he said.

CHAPTER 35

WEDNESDAY: 10.31 P.M.

SCOTLAND YARD

'Come on, Khan!' Silverman was demanding down the phone. 'You must have something you can give. A contact. A name. Who's pulling the strings?'

Khan was slouched in his office chair. His was one of the few offices on his floor that was still lit. He'd told the other members of his investigation team to go home, get some sleep and be in first thing in the morning – ready for another mad day.

He knew Silverman would be calling. He'd received a text already from him – telling him to expect a private call tonight. Khan knew what that meant. Another off-the-record conversation, presumably on behalf of their shared employer, Zakis. And now that the conversation had started, it was clear what they were after. Khan knew the way men like Zakis operated, and he could guess what Silverman wanted: access to any files on Bonati and his team. Some dirt. Anything they could use to discredit Bonati or one of his little agents. And stop the CRYPT from sniffing around at the Tyburn site.

Khan usually worked hard to close down bullies like this. Lock them up. Throw away the key. But Zakis had been different. The prizes he'd offered Khan, just like Silverman, for his loyalty had been too good to resist: the big cheque; the flat in France; and most tantalising of all, the job as his personal security adviser at The Tyburn – which meant he could leave the Met at last, before the stresses and strains of homicide investigations claimed his health once and for all.

He'd been approached by Zakis several months before, when the hotel plans were first dreamed up. His job, like so many of those on the Zakis payroll, was to turn a blind eye if things got rough. Silverman would see to the planning applications at the site, and Khan would ensure that Zakis had the protection of the police should there be any protesters or vigilante neighbours. The sites Zakis chose for his luxury hotels were often controversial, because they were always in such prime locations. There were always people who'd complain. But some took it too far. In the past, his men had been bribed at the site to pack up, or down tools; he'd received threatening letters through the post many times; and on several occasions he'd been assaulted himself. These protesters, especially the violent ones, needed silencing, and someone like Khan could look the other way when it happened.

Of course Zakis could take all the threats – he had skin like rhino hide – but he knew that unless they were nipped in the bud quickly, resentful protests often grew into something more difficult. Angry neighbours and interested parties, especially ones in central London, could always run to their precious lawyers and issue injunctions and preservation orders to block future building work. Owners of other hotels in the area would find reasons why he shouldn't build there. That was why Zakis had provided so many people with backhanders: lawyers, politicians, civil servants, and senior police officers. Khan was just one of many in a long line of people who could be bought.

But the problem was, Khan now found himself immersed far deeper in the sordid affair than he'd bargained for.

Supply a few beat officers to patrol the site now and again, that was what they'd agreed. Make sure any protesters were arrested and charged with breach of the peace (whether they were noisy or not). Supply the odd officer when Zakis was making a public appearance – no problem. And conveniently fail to find any evidence when Zakis chose to deal with angry protesters his own way. But now this – helping him to dig up some dirt on Bonati; if this was what Zakis wanted, it was beyond what they had agreed.

'What do you mean, "pulling the strings"?' Khan replied, trying to sound as naïve as possible.

'I mean who's running their operation from above? Who knows anything about them?'

'They're a secret organisation. They call themselves the CRYPT.'

'Which means?'

'Covert Response Youth Paranormal Team.'

Silverman was laughing. 'Did you say *youth*?'

'Yeah, I know. Crazy, isn't it. But it's impossible to find out anything about them. Why they have to be youths I've no idea. Sounds ridiculous to me. Very few people in Scotland Yard know anything about them. They're funded by Jason Goode, you know, the computer king.'

'OK,' said Silverman. 'So that's where the money's coming from. But they must have some connection to you guys. Why else would they be investigating? Where would they get their authority? Especially if they're bloody teenagers!'

'They're managed by MI5. Almost as a separate branch. I don't know how or why the deal was done, but Goode and MI5 set it up together.'

Silverman was thinking. 'This all sounds weird. I mean, why would MI5 work with anyone outside their agency? And why the hell would they work with kids?'

'God knows,' said Khan.

'And *paranormal*?' said Silverman incredulously. 'Do you mean *ghosts?* They actually investigate ghosts? Doesn't sound very MI5 to me.'

'Covert investigations? Running about in the shadows, hiding from the public? I'd say it's very MI5,' replied Khan, but it was late and he was getting impatient. This wasn't the time to have a lengthy debate about the range of interests of the security services.

'Listen, Silverman, I told you I don't know any more than that. What does Zakis want anyway?'

'I think you probably know that,' replied Silverman quickly.

'He wants some ammunition, I suppose. Some dirt he can take to Bonati and threaten him with. That's the way he usually works.'

'You got it,' said Silverman.

'Callous bastard.'

'Don't get all judgemental on me, Khan. You're in this up to your neck, just like all of us. He wants you to pull some strings, do some snooping, find out what you can about the professor and his CRYPT.'

Khan was shaking his head. 'And if I don't find any dirt?'

'Make some up! Come on, Khan. Don't be naïve! You know the way the world works. If we can find something on Bonati and threaten him with a scandal, he's bound to cooperate.'

'And leave Tyburn alone?'

'Exactly,' said Silverman. 'Now, that wasn't the only favour Zakis wanted.'

'What?' growled Khan. He'd had enough of this smug, slippery politician. He imagined himself interviewing him across a table for any number of crimes of dishonesty. He could have him locked up for years. The only problem, of course, was that he himself was now on the Zakis payroll, just like Silver. He too was being asked to pull strings, turn a blind eye and force things through, just so that he got his fat cheque.

He was one of them now.

'You mean there's something else? Bloody hell. Do you have any idea what kind of a day I've had?'

The politician ignored this pathetic response and continued with the second instruction from Zakis – the press conference.

Khan was filled in. He had his brief. And though he didn't like lying to the nation, telling them this crappy story about vigilantes and protesters with hi-tech equipment, he knew only too well that he was so deeply involved now, if he backed out he'd lose everything – including his life, probably. Zakis didn't like quitters. He had ways of disposing of them.

Khan agreed to the plan and Silverman rang off, saying, 'You're going to have a long night. I better let you get on with it.'

Khan was indeed going to have a busy few hours. As a senior investigating officer he had access to all files and documents. Or at least most of them; there were always some files only accessible via codes that were shared amongst a few people at the top. But Khan knew them. He'd been sure over the years to listen well, follow his nose and squirrel codes away. That was what made him a good copper. He'd never been able to switch off his detective button. When anything happened at Scotland Yard, he was always the first to know, because he spoke to more people than anyone else, listened better than anyone else and, unlike many of his colleagues, remembered everything he was told. His cluttered head was like a giant filing cabinet, rusty and squeaky, with some drawers difficult to open, but packed full of every detail he'd soaked up in his career at the Yard. He was a walking almanac.

Which was why this business with Bonati and his special team had always foxed him. It had been so covert from the outset. So few people had really known about it. He'd heard rumours – because he had good ears – that some police officers had been assigned to monitor the daily movements of the CRYPT, along with MI5, who ultimately steered the operation. But these officers were from the CPC – the Covert Policing Command – and Khan had rarely crossed paths with them.

But he knew that if he was going to make this nocturnal hunt for information as short as possible, it was better to start with the CPC than anywhere else.

After grabbing yet another coffee from the machine in the corridor, he returned to his desk and set to work on his computer. He'd cracked the codes that would give him access to the central files – including those of the CPC; all he had to do now was ask the right questions, search for the right names, and see what he could unearth – or make up.

Within a short while he'd located the Covert Policing case files and identified the branch within the CPC that had responsibility for tracing the movements of the CRYPT.

To his astonishment, the branch directly concerned was not the Covert Operations Group, as he'd suspected, but the PIU – the Prison Intelligence Unit.

And they weren't monitoring the movements of all the agents at the CRYPT at all.

They monitored just one of them.

Jud Lester.

Khan read on. This was getting interesting.

CHAPTER 36

THURSDAY: 8.29 A.M.

GOODE TOWER

The views from the thirty-eighth floor of the Goode Tower were breathtaking. The skyscraper soared above the traditional rectangular blocks like a space-age totem pole, its revolutionary curved mirrors and glass catching the sun's rays and sending them hurtling across the skyline in every direction. And from inside, here on the revolving top floor, you could see every landmark in turn: St Paul's, Canary Wharf, the giant gherkin, the Houses of Parliament, the London Eye.

But Bonati was disinclined to stop and take in the rotating vista. His head hurt from dehydration, his eyes stung from lack of sleep, and worst of all, he suffered from vertigo. A revolving floor, thirty-eight storeys up, was definitely not his cup of tea.

When the invitation had come to have breakfast with Jason Goode in his office, Bonati's acceptance had been reluctant. But he knew he needed to see him. Jason had flown back into the country from America in the small hours of the morning; he'd characteristically refused sleep and had texted his invitation to Bonati at 6 a.m. He'd been out of the country for less than a week, but the events that had unfolded in London over the last three days had meant him cutting short his business trip and flying back earlier than expected.

And now he wanted answers. What the hell had been going on, and more importantly, why were his agents not on top of it?

Bonati walked down the corridor, staying close to the left side – the right offering nothing but floor-to-ceiling windows, with a 150-metre drop beyond. Hard to believe he was on the same patch of earth as his office in the CRYPT – it seemed a whole street away, which effectively it was, only the street ran vertically instead of horizontally.

The double oak doors were shut, but they opened electronically before Bonati even had a chance to turn the great brass handles – a little trick that Jason had recently had installed. There were cameras hidden discreetly either side of the corridor just before the door. These were connected wirelessly to a monitor on Jason's desk, so he could welcome some visitors, force others to knock, and ignore some altogether. Provided he was in, of course, which he seldom was.

But he liked his toys.

As the doors swung shut behind him, Bonati strolled across the vast, minimalist office of shiny steel and black marble. The incongrous but welcoming smell of bacon sandwiches cut through the aroma of leather seats and potpourri.

'So, good trip, Jason?' he said, joining Goode at the smoked-glass table by the window, choosing the seat that faced inwards.

'Never mind the trip, Giles, what the hell's going on?' Jason said, ploughing into a giant bacon cob like a hungry schoolboy, grease dribbling down his chin.

'I know. I'm sorry. It's been mad, Jason. But we're on it.'

'What do you mean, "we're on it"? From the snippets of news I caught yesterday, and from what you told me on the phone, I'd say we're far from on it. I'd say we haven't got a bloody clue.'

Bonati shrugged. 'I said we're on it. We've come up with a

theory that connects all the hauntings. It was Jud who came up with it, actually.'

'How is he? I can't believe how lucky we've been. Does he understand how close he came to being identified? How awful would that have been, huh?'

Jason's fatherly concern was touching, but he'd wandered over to lean against the window, and the small but perceptible turning of the skyscraper was churning Bonati's stomach and making him feel even more nervous than he'd felt in the lift coming up. His knees tingled and he felt a compulsion to get off his chair and start hugging the floor.

'He's more than aware – this has been a real scare for him, Jason. But it's done with now. Let me tell you his theory about the hauntings. Come away from the bloody window, please!'

'OK. Sorry, I forgot about your vertigo, Giles! You really are a softie, aren't you!'

Bonati sniffed as Jason returned to the table.

Slowly the professor began to explain the theory that Jud and Bex had come up with. The locations, the connections to Newgate, the gallows at Tyburn, and the plans for the hotel.

Goode listened patiently, but before they could discuss it, Bonati's mobile rang.

'Yes?' he said quickly.

'Sir?'

'Jud?' Bonati flashed a look at Jason and smiled.

'I was just talking about you, J. How's it going. Any readings?'

'We haven't set off yet, we need to—'

'What do you mean, you haven't set off? Why not? I gave you the evening off yesterday, precisely so that you'd get an early start today.' He rolled his eyes in the direction of Jason.

'No, we need to speak to you first, sir. Didn't you hear about last night?'

'No. Jud, I don't know what you're talking about.'

'You mean Khan didn't tell you?'

'Tell me *what*? What happened last night?' The two men looked anxiously at one another. Neither could take yet more bad news. 'What, Jud?'

'Someone tried to kill us, sir.'

CHAPTER 37

THURSDAY: 9.07 A.M.

WESTMINSTER HOSPITAL

Lucien Zakis waited for the nurse to finish fussing over her patient and leave the cubicle again. He swung the curtains shut so there was no risk of being seen or heard, then he approached the bed and leaned over.

The man was lying on his back, a drip tube fixed to his nostrils and bandages around his head. The injuries he'd sustained in the car park had not been life-threatening – unlike those of his partner, who now lay in a mortuary across town, waiting for Zakis to dispose of him.

The patient could smell the stale stench of cigar smoke and vodka as Zakis bent over him. He spoke in a whisper. 'What the hell do you mean, they got away? They're just kids, d'ya hear me? Kids!'

The man in the bed tried to speak. The bandages restricted him, and his accent was heavy. 'But Mr Zakis, we tried—'

Zakis gripped the man's arm. His short, stubby fingers were pressing into his flesh. He rested his other hand on the man's broken leg and leaned downwards. The pain was excruciating. He pressed harder. The man writhed in agony but stayed silent. He knew that any form of protest now would see him losing his life when he finally got out of here. The new dose of morphine the nurse had just topped up was beginning to kick in, but the pain from his leg still soared around his whole body.

'You didn't try hard enough, did you?' whispered Zakis. 'And I don't like losers. You failed. D'ya hear me? D'ya understand? I said you *failed* me.'

'But please—'

Zakis moved a hand to cover the man's mouth. He leant his full weight on to his leg. The man spluttered and spat over Zakis's hand. He was gagging. The pain was too much. Had Zakis come to kill him?

Suddenly the curtain rustled and the rings scraped along the rail. Someone was entering. Quickly Zakis released his grip and turned to smile at the nurse as she came to the bed.

'Your time is over, I'm afraid. The doctors have said he really should be sleeping. You'll have to come back later.'

Zakis looked at the man now trembling in the bed. 'Oh, I will,' he said. 'I will, Nurse. Thank you.'

CHAPTER 38

THURSDAY: 9.14 A.M.

GOODE TOWER

Jud keyed in the number 38 and they both leaned back against the mirrored wall as the lift began its long ascent. As they watched the numbers climb, they reflected silently on the events of the night before.

The evening off had been such a welcome pleasure. They'd felt exhilarated as the Fireblade swept through the traffic towards China Town.

But it had ended so abruptly. So brutally.

They'd done the right thing and waited for the police to attend the scene. The statements had taken ages. Eyewitnesses were interviewed too, and CCTV recordings were handed over so that police could study them back at the station. Tragically, the first rider had not survived his brutal collision with the Range Rover, whose owner was in a state of shock, but the second – the one who'd met with the fire extinguisher – was going to be OK. Battered, bruised, and with several bones broken, but OK.

DCI Khan had not been at the scene himself, but Jud had spoken to him on the phone. He'd sounded particularly shocked to hear what had happened. Jud had detected a strange tone in his voice – almost one of disappointment, but he must have imagined that.

Khan had told the two of them to go straight home and sleep after they'd given their statements. He'd said he'd ring Bonati for them and tell him what had happened.

The night that followed had been filled with the two of them drinking too much coffee and eating a cold takeaway in a corner of the dining room back at the CRYPT, trying desperately to understand who the men on bikes were, and who had sent them.

It just hadn't made sense. If their suspicions were right, and the groundwork for The Tyburn Hotel had disturbed the souls of the highwaymen hanged there, then it was Zakis who was to blame for the atrocities that were now haunting London. And it was Zakis who'd have everything to lose if the story got out. His hotel would be scrapped before it was even built.

It had been hard during the small hours of the morning for either of them to think straight, but they'd both agreed before they went off to bed that the logical conclusion was that Zakis had somehow learned of their suspicions. He *must* have known, and sent his hired hit men to silence them once and for all. But how did he know? The only people who were aware of their theory were Bonati and Khan. To suggest that Bonati was in on the act and had tipped off Zakis about the plan was in the realms of fantasy, which just left DCI Khan.

But why would he have done it?

The morning alarms for each of them had brought a new dose of reality, and had quashed their questions, making their conspiracy theories feel like dreams.

But when they met for breakfast, they both agreed it was still worth sharing their thoughts with Bonati anyway, before they hit the streets and began following the route from Newgate to Tyburn as instructed. After all, he might have come up with a better theory of who the assassins were. And how Zakis had been tipped off, if he was behind the plot.

That was before Jud had telephoned Bonati and asked to see him. Now the whole thing seemed scarily possible.

'Bex. He didn't know!' Jud had said as he'd finished the quick call.

'What? What do you mean?'

'Bonati. He didn't know anything about last night.'

'What? But I thought they were telling him about it.'

'I know,' said Jud. 'And who was supposed to be telling him?'

Bex had put her hands to her face and breathed in sharply at the realisation that everything was adding up.

'Khan!' she said.

'Exactly,' said Jud.

Now the two of them found themselves being whisked to the top of the Goode Tower, wondering how on earth they were going to tell Bonati that the only possible explanation was that DCI Khan was working for Zakis.

It just *had* to be him.

The lift reached the top and delivered its visitors for the second time that morning.

Clutching the laptop he'd brought with him, Jud strolled out confidently. He'd guessed that the only reason they'd been invited to the penthouse must be because his father was back in the country. Otherwise Bonati would have met them in his own office, 150 metres below. He'd had no word yet to say that he was back, but that wasn't unusual. He began the walk down the long, shiny corridor.

Bex was more tentative behind him.

'Come on!' he said. 'What's wrong? Don't tell me you're scared of heights too! Bonati hates it up here.'

'No,' replied Bex, stepping out of the lift before the doors closed again. 'I'm not scared of heights! It's just I've never been up here before. I've never seen where Mr Goode works. I mean, it's a bit daunting, if you think about it.'

'Daunting?'

'Well, I mean, you know, he's so powerful and all that. So rich.'

Jud had never considered it like that. But then he wouldn't. He'd been up here many times. And to him, Jason was just his father anyway – albeit a frequently absent one, but still his own flesh and blood, and not the world-renowned billionaire that Bex and everyone else knew.

'Come on!' he said, half smiling. 'He's just a man! Yesterday you danced with the ghost of a three-hundred-year-old highwayman. I think you can cope with this.'

'OK, fair point,' she said.

She followed Jud, but clung to the left-hand side, away from the windows on the right, just as Bonati had done.

'Do you like the revolving bit?' said Jud. 'Cool, isn't it?'

'Oh yeah,' said Bex warily. 'Awesome.'

They approached the doors, which swung open automatically just as Jud started to turn the handle.

'Ah, young Master Lester and . . . let me see . . . don't tell me – Rebecca, isn't it? Rebecca De Verre?' Jason Goode was standing up to greet them warmly.

'Bex,' she said.

'Sorry, Bex! And you, Jud, how are you? It's been quite a few days, I hear.'

They were within feet of one another. Father and son. But they might as well have been strangers talking to each other from different worlds. The need for discretion and keeping things formal was painful sometimes. But secretly they could detect in each other's eyes the joy of seeing one another again.

'Er, fine. I'm well, Mr Goode – all things considered.'

'Yes, the professor here has told me what's been going on. You've had quite a time.'

They both nodded. Bonati invited them to sit at the table with him, while Goode called for some fresh coffee and more bacon rolls. Jud switched on his laptop in readiness for their explanations. He'd saved the map with the locations plotted on it, and all the web pages of research on Newgate and Tyburn.

'So,' said the professor, 'let's get down to it. I know you've got a great deal for us. I've already managed to fill Mr Goode in on the main points of your research thus far, and the theories rising from it, but I know he'd like you to start again, from the beginning.'

Jason Goode was nodding. He sneaked a subtle wink at Jud when Bex glanced out of the window.

Bonati continued quickly, 'But before you do, I think you need to begin by telling us again what happened last night. And tell us slowly; don't leave anything out. This is important.'

Bex began first. Together they explained the whole scene, from when they set off on the Fireblade, to the moment when the bikers flanked them and followed them into the car park. Then the scenes inside, which in the cold light of the morning seemed almost too violent to be true. The thought of the motorcyclist's body lying crumpled in the corner like a broken deckchair was a harsh reminder of the dangers of their own jobs.

Bonati and Goode listened patiently throughout. When the two agents had finished recounting the events, Bonati spoke first.

'Whoever they were, and whoever sent them, one thing's clear: they were after you two. They wanted to silence you both.'

The room was silent. This was getting serious. The enormity of the events of last night now appeared in sharp focus, like an alarm call for the group. Suddenly the secret headquarters of the CRYPT buried deep below them seemed less like a prison and more like a safe house. They felt relieved to be locked away from the world outside. Right now it was the safest place to be.

Jason Goode spoke up. 'We need to deal with this calmly and logically. The important thing is that you're both OK. Jud, I'm impressed with your quick thinking. Thank God you saw the fire extinguisher.

'But there must be a connection between the research you've done into the hauntings, and the threats against you last night. There has to be. We just haven't found it yet. But we *will*. Let's look at your research into this business at Tyburn again – and see where it gets us. OK?' He sat back in his chair and stared at Jud. 'But you'll have to convince me first. And remember, Jud, our reputation is already in the balance after Greyfriars.'

Jud and Bex went through their research again, referring to the map on the laptop where necessary – the connection to Newgate Gaol, the route the condemned prisoners took to the gallows, and the important fact that all the hauntings that had taken place so far had happened along the very same route to Tyburn. The road the condemned prisoners followed to their deaths.

Bex mentioned the connection to Du Val too – memories of the frightening event in the park still loomed large in her thoughts. She also reminded the two men that all the eyewitness statements had referred to similar-looking figures, dressed in seventeenth-century clothing. The deadly ghost on the train had even been brandishing a duelling pistol from the same era.

It seemed that Tyburn was at the centre of what was happening. It had to be Zakis, stirring up the souls who had died there. It just had to be. It was the only rational explanation for a series of events that were entirely irrational.

'OK,' said Goode. 'It's plausible. Hard to believe, but it kind of makes sense, if any of this does. But what it doesn't do is explain the events of last night. Where's the connection there? I said there must be one, remember, but I don't think you've found it yet. Why the assassins last night?'

'Zakis sent them,' said Jud. 'He must have done.'

'We don't know that,' his father replied. Jet lag was catching up with him. He rubbed his forehead and slumped back into his chair. 'We need proof, J. How did Zakis know about your theory? How did he know you were on to him?'

'Khan. He tipped him off. He's on the inside.'

Bonati interrupted, 'Now hang on, Jud. That's a big leap. We can't possibly say that for sure. He's a detective chief inspector, for heaven's sake! Do you realise what you're saying?'

'But no one else knew about our research, sir. Only you, Bex and me. And we took it to Khan.'

'But that's not proof, Jud.'

Bex came to Jud's defence. 'But last night, sir, on the phone, Khan told Jud he would tell you about the accident so we could just come home. He didn't tell you, sir, did he? You didn't know anything about it until we told you this morning.'

Bonati was shaking his head. 'True, but that means nothing. He could've forgotten, or been distracted. Something else could have come up. He's not a telephone message service.'

'So why did he offer to? We were going to come straight to you, but he insisted we go home to sleep instead,' said Jud quickly. 'He wanted to stall you. He knew you'd be on to him and Zakis as soon as you found out what had happened, so he wanted to buy some time. Give him a chance to talk to Zakis overnight and decide what to do next. He knew we'd tell you today – he just wanted more time.'

Bonati's mobile burst into beeps. A text had come through from Dr Vorzek: *Hi. Turn on tv. Khan doing press conf now. Kim*

'OK, we'll revisit this,' said the professor. 'It needs more talking through. Let's get the television on, quick, Khan's doing a press conference.'

'This'll be interesting,' said Jud.

The conversation was adjourned and they gathered around the large TV set in the opposite corner of the office. Goode found the channel and pressed RECORD on his remote.

They watched the screen as Khan shuffled into the room packed with noisy reporters and photographers.

'Thank you for coming again,' he began. 'We have more developments for you on the London raids.'

'Raids?' said Jud. 'I thought they were calling them hauntings now?'

'Quiet,' said Bonati.

Khan continued: 'Fresh evidence has come to light in the last twenty-four hours that strongly indicates that the raids we've been witnessing across the city are, after all, the work of violent protesters.'

'What?' Bex shouted at the screen. 'This is ridiculous!'

'We have reason to believe that those responsible are a group of extreme environmental protesters calling themselves Earth Warriors. They claim to have carried out these atrocities in the name of saving the planet. They believe that transport, in all its forms, will destroy the environment. So they've vowed to scare us all away from buses and trains. Make us stay at home.'

The room of reporters descended into chaos. People hurled questions at the detective chief inspector.

'How do you know?'

'Who tipped you off?'

'What evidence have you found?'

Khan raised his hands and tried to silence the crowd.

'Ladies and gentlemen, please! The call came in this morning from a member of the alleged gang. He claimed to be acting on behalf of the people of the world. He said they want their planet back. He warned that they'll continue to carry out further raids until their demands are met.'

'What demands?' someone shouted from the back.

'That all combustion engines be abolished and from now on transport should be powered by electrical means only.'

Again the room kicked off. People shouted. Some even laughed. Cameras were flashing. Reporters wanted more. This wasn't enough.

'But how did they *do* it, Chief Inspector?' a reporter shouted.

Khan answered quickly. 'It is unclear exactly how they carried out these atrocities, but it is believed they are highly skilled and are able to make use of hallucinogenic drugs, which may have caused the victims to hallucinate. It is suspected that this group also has access to sophisticated technical equipment that may have created the special effects seen. Holographic images and so on.'

'This is madness,' Jud muttered. 'Are they saying that what I saw in the church was a projected image? Or a man in a mask? Or I was hallucinating or something?' he added. 'You've gotta do something, sir.'

Bonati hadn't heard. He was staring at the screen. Saying nothing. He looked deep in thought.

'Sir?' said Bex. 'Sir! What have you seen?'

'I'm not sure,' said the professor. 'Can you live pause it for a second? Right – there, in the corner of the room, behind Khan. In the doorway. You see that man?'

'Yeah. Who is he?' said Jud.

'I don't know. But I've seen him before. And I think I know where.'

'Sir?'

Bonati ignored Jud and quickly rang Vorzek.

'Kim? It's Bonati.'

'Have you seen it, Giles? Can you believe what they're saying—'

'I know. We'll talk about it. We'll get everyone together later this morning, but first I want you to do something for me.'

'Go on.'

'We've been recording the news bulletins since the story broke on Monday, yes?'

'Of course. I've transferred them on to disc. It's in the lab.'

'Good. Can you bring it to Mr Goode's suite, right now?' He glanced at Jason, who nodded.

'Of course,' said Vorzek. 'Why? What's happened?'

'Just do it. I'll explain everything when you get here.'

'What's going on, Giles?' Jason said as soon as Bonati had finished his phone call.

'I've seen that man before. I'm sure I have, and if I'm right – then Jud and Bex might be on to something.'

'What?' said Jud. 'You mean you think Khan *is* in on the act?'

'Impossible to tell for sure – he's a senior policeman, and he's very good at covering his tracks if he is involved with Zakis. But he may have made a mistake.'

'Tell us!' said Bex.

'I'd rather wait. Because if I'm wrong, we'll be left with nothing. I'm not saying I'm definite. And I certainly don't want to raise your hopes. It's only a hunch. But as soon as Dr Vorzek's here, we'll know for sure.'

Within a few minutes there was a beep from the monitor on Goode's desk and he quickly opened the doors for Vorzek to enter, carrying the disc with the news footage on.

'Great, thank you, Kim.'

'Morning, everyone. Welcome back, Mr Goode,' Vorzek said politely.

Bonati continued, trying to hide his confidence, afraid of filling Jud and Bex with false expectations.

'Right. I need you to get us to Wednesday, between about seven thirty and eight a.m. – I think that's when it was on.'

'What was?' asked Jud. He was getting impatient.

'You'll see.'

Vorzek punched some buttons on the control for the DVD player. The news bulletins had been stored in a typically efficient and organised way. Bonati flicked through until he found the one he wanted.

They watched the 7.30 headlines.

'Now fast forward to about seven forty, please. I know it wasn't a headline story.' They watched the closing lines of a report from St Sepulchre's Church. Then the screen switched back to the newsreader in the studio.

'We'll bring you the latest on the London hauntings as we

receive it throughout this programme, but now, the rest of today's news . . .

'It will be the greatest hotel ever seen. A jewel in the crown. A haven in the heart of the metropolis. Such are the claims of Lucien Zakis, world-renowned hotelier. Plans for his new luxury hotel at Marble Arch are now well under way. Our reporter Giles Olson is at the site of the new Tyburn Hotel.'

They watched as the reporter began his piece. Jud remembered seeing this item the day before. In his sleepy state he'd switched it off and thought nothing of it – just another greedy fat cat getting even richer. But Bonati had watched it all. And remembered what he'd seen.

'Now, watch closely everyone,' he said.

The reporter was interviewing the man himself, Lucien Zakis, at the site of The Tyburn Hotel. He wasn't alone. There were two bodyguards with him. And in the background, viewers could just glimpse two other men.

'Quick,' said Bonati. 'Flick back to the press conference from just now.'

Jason picked up the remote and transferred to the new footage. Luckily his company had invested hugely in television technology, and one of the gimmicks his units offered was to be able to view pictures simultaneously on the same large screen. He froze the image of Zakis at the building site next to the press conference footage.

And they could all see it.

One of the men behind Zakis at the building site was also at the press conference with Khan. What the hell was he doing in both places? *Who was he?* And what was his interest in both stories?

He had to be the connection. The link to Zakis.

CHAPTER 39

THURSDAY: 12.01 P.M.

THE ANGEL, ST GILES HIGH STREET

'Well?' said Khan as he buried his face in his Guinness.

'A grand performance. Worthy of an Oscar,' said Silverman from across the small oak table. His lined face broke into a smile. In the dark shadows of the back room where they sat, he had a sinister air.

He always came here. It was his favourite pub; free from the thumping music, chrome rails and neon lights of so many bars in town. The Angel was a real inn, like they used to be. All oak panels and dark, shadowy corners. The deals Silverman had done in here, safely tucked away from the prying eyes of civil servants and inquisitive journalists. The small saloon bar at the rear had become like his second office.

'But will the public buy it? That's the question,' said Khan nervously. There was a faint tremble to his fingers as he placed the pint glass down and fiddled with a beer mat. Peeling layers of paper from it frantically. Rolling the fragments into balls.

'Of course,' said Silverman. 'Don't worry, Khan. It'll pass. These things always do. The incidents will stop eventually. The tabloids will move on. There'll be another crime somewhere else for the reporters to feast on. It'll pass.'

Khan snapped back at him, 'Don't you understand, man? I don't think it will. This is not a killer who'll move on somewhere else. Or get bored. It's something different this time.' He was looking around the dark room. Gazing up at the old oak beams and across at the tiny smoke-stained windows. He looked agitated. Nervous. As though someone, or something, was listening.

Silverman watched him. 'Oh come on,' he said. 'You don't actually believe in all this ghost rubbish, do you?'

Khan swigged his beer and signalled to the woman at the bar for another. 'Don't you?' he replied.

'No! Of course I don't!' Silverman lied. In truth there was every reason to believe it. If the gruesome story of how Kozlosky lost his life was true, then ghosts were indeed loose at Tyburn. They really had stirred something up in the dark earth. But Khan mustn't know. Covering up a murder, turning a blind eye to it – that would be too much for the inspector. Beyond the call of duty. Silverman and Zakis knew that Khan wouldn't stomach that. So they'd chosen not to share their little secret. Even when Khan had probed Silverman earlier for anything that might have happened at the site, the politician had remained dumb.

'My God, Khan, I thought you were a man of reason. Common sense an' all that. You're a police officer, for heaven's sake. Solid evidence. That's what you people look for. Surely you're not telling me you believe in all that fantasy stuff now?'

'I've just got a bad feeling about this,' Khan replied. 'And about the lies too. What I've said. The faces of those reporters. The cameras. All those people watching and wondering. What've we told them.' He was shaking his head and looking at the floor. His left hand trembled as the other clutched his pain-ridden stomach beneath the table.

'And then there's last night.'

'Last night?'

'Come off it,' said Khan. 'You know exactly what I'm talking about.'

Silverman just smiled behind his glass.

'It's the wrong way of doing things,' said Khan. 'Zakis is going to have to realise you can't send assassins after someone when you want them silenced.'

'Just be thankful it wasn't you they were chasing,' replied Silverman.

'Is that a threat?'

Silverman shook his head and shrugged his shoulders. 'Play the game and we'll all get what we want.'

Khan knew it was time to reveal what he'd discovered at Scotland Yard. But the evidence he'd found – the circumstances and the mystery that surrounded them – had affected him deeply and he hadn't slept at all when he'd finally returned home in the small hours.

What would happen if he revealed what he knew? Zakis and Silverman would use it to bury the entire CRYPT operation. There would be no paranormal investigators. The digging at Tyburn would continue. The hotel might even be erected, but would the ghosts stop haunting the city?

'I'm just not sure I wanna do this any more, Silverman. I wish I'd never gone in with Zakis.'

Silverman leant quickly across to him. His cool grey eyes looked straight into the yellowy spheres in Khan's face.

He whispered, 'Listen, Khan. *Listen to me!* You get an attack of guilt and decide to come clean – you die the same day. No one squeals on Zakis and survives. Hold it together. Do you hear? You do what we want, then you stay safe – and become very rich. Do you understand? *Very* rich. Very quickly.'

The young woman from the bar came over with the new drinks. Silverman quickly sat back in his chair again.

'Those look lonely, don't they, my friend! I think we'll have a couple of whisky chasers to go with them, if you please. We've got a lot to discuss.' The woman returned to the bar and fixed the extra drinks, before returning with them moments later.

'Now then, Khan. That's enough about the press conference. I've said you've done well, and you have. But what about the other part of the deal? Have you found anything on the CRYPT?'

Khan clutched his stomach again. His body was collapsing – slowly rotting with stress and the memories of all the murder investigations he'd worked on. It was too much for him now. He was in real danger of losing it. He didn't know if he would fail mentally or physically first; he only knew he would break soon.

And then he thought of the prizes: the cash; the flat in France; the big monthly cheque for the cushy job at the Tyburn; the free access to the best gym and health spa in the city.

He could get himself well again. He could find some sanity.

What was the alternative? Keep quiet about the information he had found; come clean about lying at the press conference; shop Zakis to the authorities.

He'd have no job, no money, no friends, no reputation, and, most likely, no breath in his lungs – Zakis's men would see to that.

He looked up at Silverman. The MP's grey eyes penetrated into his. Silver had already been through this dilemma – and come out clearly on the side that benefited him most.

'Life's not a rehearsal, Khan,' he said. 'You've gotta think about number one. Because no one else will. It's every man for himself.' He necked his whisky chaser. 'Now drink your drink and tell me what you've found.'

Khan picked up the whisky glass, threw the strong amber liquid down his throat and began, reluctantly but resolved.

'It was easier than I thought, Silver. You see, one of the agents at the CRYPT, Jud Lester – you know, the excitable one I've had so much trouble trying to discipline – well, it seems he has a reason to be on edge. He has a reason to feel nervous most of the time. No wonder he's got a temper. You see, Silver, Jud's not who we think he is.'

CHAPTER 40

THURSDAY: 12.20 P.M.

THE CRYPT

Bonati asked everyone in the meeting room to quieten down. News of Jud and Bex's narrow brush with death on the motorbike had come in. The skulls had been resentful of Jud's dominance over the case – and of his stupid actions in the garden at Greyfriars – but now they seemed more sympathetic. As Nik said, no one wanted biker assassins on their tail. Jud and Bex had been welcomed into the room and quizzed by zombies and skulls alike.

Other agents had also been gathering evidence from the various locations, as instructed by Bonati the night before.

There was no doubt whatsoever that the locations that were now plotted on the giant map behind Bonati – the same locations where the agents had held vigils overnight – were indeed filled with paranormal activity. Evidence was in abundance. Some had recorded extraordinarily high levels of electromagnetic energy on the new Tri-Axis 333s that Vorzek had bought. None as high as the levels Jud had recorded in the church, but still way above the usual 7 or 8mGs.

And many agents had also seen low temperatures on their thermocouple thermometers at the various locations. The four unlucky agents who'd been sent down the Fleet sewer to investigate – two experienced skulls and two nervous zombies – had recorded drops in temperature that had never been experienced at the CRYPT by anyone, not even Jud.

But no one had seen anything unusual on their thermal imagers. The ghosts had been there – the residual energy and temperature changes they'd left behind confirmed that, and of course the desperate accounts of the survivors involved – but they'd always moved on just as quickly.

Each agent had used their own gifts of perception to soak up the residual emotions left behind. And no one was in any doubt of the connection here – all the agents had described the same empathic feelings of sadness and abandonment. One – a talented new zombie named Luc – captured the mood well by saying he'd sensed that the spirits at the site felt forgotten about, and wanted revenge.

But the question on everyone's lips was: where would they strike next?

Bonati tried again to create calm. There was so much to discuss. So much to share. The case, though tragic and costly, and as frightening as any Bonati had experienced so far, was providing the CRYPT with valuable experiences from which the agents would learn much – far more than could ever be gained from a simulated case.

'I've gathered you together to share the evidence of last night's vigils, for which I thank you all deeply. Many of the places you visited are unpleasant at the best of times – special thanks to the four who braved the sewer, by the way – but at night time especially, and in the current climate of fear and panic, I think you've all done an excellent job.

'What is important now is that we learn from what you've recorded. Before you each give us your findings, Jud, load up the map and let's discuss the link between the locations and the evidence you all collected last night.'

Jud got up from his seat and began with a brief overview of the route the condemned prisoners took to the gallows at Tyburn, stopping at St Sepulchre's and the Bowl Inn.

The agents listened intently.

'Wait a minute,' said Grace, sitting near the back. 'Has anything happened at the pub yet?'

'The Bowl Inn?' said Jud. 'No, I don't think so. It isn't actually called the Bowl Inn any more. That was demolished years ago. It's now the Angel. Same site, but we've had no reports of any incidents there.'

Bonati interrupted. 'Yet. We'll need to get someone over there, though. We need to take readings. The levels there may still be high. Spiritually the place might still be active. We need to—'

The professor was interrupted by the ringing of Jud's mobile.

'Sorry, sir, should I take that?'

'Go ahead. There's lots for us to think about here. Look at the locations, everyone; see if you can get some inspiration.'

Jud quickly pressed the receive button, and put the phone to his ear.

The agents who were looking at him, rather than viewing the screens of evidence on the wall behind him, noticed a sudden change in his complexion. He'd paled.

The voice on the end of the line was slow, deliberate and clear.

'We know who you are.'

'Who is this?'

The stranger's voice – a middle-aged, well-spoken male – said calmly, 'That's not important. What is important is we know who *you* are, and we're going to tell the world about you . . . Jamie.'

'What's wrong, Jud?' Bonati could see that Jud had gone white. He was tottering on his feet, looking faint. Vorzek grabbed him before he fell. Bonati seized the phone and said, 'Bonati here. Who *is* this?'

The voice continued: 'Bring Jamie to Marble Arch tonight, ten p.m., and you'll find out. I have an acquaintance who'd like to meet you both. Someone who'd like to offer you an arrangement, Professor.'

CHAPTER 41

THURSDAY: 12.40 P.M.

THE ANGEL, ST GILES HIGH STREET

'You've done well, Khan. *Very* well. Zakis will be pleased. Jud Lester's a murderer, eh? You've hit the jackpot here. This is better than we ever dreamt. You realise we can close the whole damn thing now. Get rid of these kids for ever.'

Khan just glanced at his pint in quiet contemplation. The creamy froth sank slowly down the edges of the glass to mix with the dark liquid at the bottom.

'I'm due at the Dorchester to meet Lucien this afternoon,' Silverman continued. 'He wants an update. I'll be sure to give him your regards. I've no doubt he saw the press conference, and will be pleased with your performance, but when he hears about what you've unearthed on Lester, he'll be ecstatic . . . and *very* grateful, I've no doubt. You've done the right thing. You'll see.'

Silverman got up to settle his account at the bar before exiting into the sunlit, busy street. Back in the shadows of the saloon bar, Khan finished his last slurp of ale and staggered down the stone spiral staircase to the toilets hidden deep in the cellars.

He pushed open the door to the gents and stumbled into the small green-tiled room. A man finished washing his hands, flicked them under the heater and left. The door swung shut, thudding against its frame.

Khan visited the urinal and then went to the sink. He peered at himself in the metal mirror above. He looked tired and jaded. His eyes were glazed over and his teeth were stained with Guinness. He rubbed his face like a man just got out of bed. His hair was matted with sweat. His tie was loose at the collar. The years at the Met were taking their toll. And the events of the last few days had nearly finished him off. But soon it would be over. He thought again of the new car – a metallic blue Jaguar. Just what he'd always wanted. The head of security job at the hotel, and the French villa where he'd spend his summers. Walking to the patisserie every morning for warm croissants.

Soon. Keep going.

He looked down at the sink and splashed water over his face. He knew he needed to sober up – it was only mid-afternoon, and there was still much to do.

He glanced up again to the mirror.

His stomach lurched.

In the shadows of the dimly lit room there was a face behind Khan. He could see it reflected in the old, tarnished mirror. Staring at him from over his shoulder, its eyes glowing with an evil intensity.

Trick of the light. Too much ale. *It's your imagination. Don't lose it now*, he said to himself. He stooped again and splashed more water over his face. Then he looked again.

There it was, a glowing figure emerging before him. Like some illusion. Getting stronger, more vivid. A tall, imposing shape gradually becoming more visible. Great muscular cheekbones. Sunken eyes, ringed in shadow. Protruding from the square jaw was a kind of beard, made of maggots woven into the rotting skin. Writhing and feasting like parasites. The wide nose was broken and the cracked lips beneath it were beginning to shift and stretch apart.

Khan froze. He could feel the weight of the hulking figure pinning him to the sink. There was a hand around his neck. Holding him. He went to scream, but the hand moved round and grabbed his mouth. Muffled pleas of mercy were all he could manage.

The ghost grabbed him and turned him round to face him. Khan gagged on the rank stench of ammonia from the maggots.

It was the hangman.

Here to sell his rope, as he'd always done in mortal life. The Bowl Inn was his favourite place on execution days. He'd taunt the prisoners as they stopped for their last drink on their way to the gallows, then return after the executions to sell the same rope that had killed them.

The ghost spoke in deep whispers. 'What will you give me for this inch of rope? Six shillings? Used it this mornin' I did. Ten of 'em dropped at Tyburn. A good clean dispatch. No messin'. Strong rope, you see. That's the secret.'

Khan could only stare. The hangman had dropped his great muscular hand from Khan's mouth, but had pinned him against the wall. Now he thrust the rope at him, driving it into his neck. Khan's head was pushed backwards. He could feel the knots wedged into the sinews under his chin. His breath was fading.

'Come on!' the hangman screeched, before erupting into a coughing fit that sprayed maggots and phlegm across Khan's face. Through the retching and heaving he continued. 'Six shillings, mark you. It's a bargain and no mistake.'

The hangman towered over Khan. A giant of a man in life. Feared and respected. If the hangman offered you six shillings an inch, you paid up.

Khan coughed and choked. The rope was still pressed up against his neck and he was losing consciousness. This was it.

No more. He tightened his fists with what energy he had left, allowed his head to flop forward in submission, and braced himself. His heart was giving way. The pain was spreading through his chest like a leather belt tightening across him.

There was a sudden thud.

From outside.

Someone clattered the outer door to the toilets and opened it. A couple of steps and the internal door was now swinging slowly open. Someone was whistling.

Startled by the sounds, the hangman turned and launched at the man now entering, who went pale with fear and reached for the door again. He was too late. The hangman now had him by the throat. He pushed him against the wall with one hand, and with the other began to make a noose out of the gnarled old rope.

'Interrupt me would you?'

He turned to face Khan, who was slumped, cowering, in the corner beneath the sinks, clutching his chest.

'Wanna watch a hangin', sir?' whispered the ghost. 'I'll make it quick, see. Then you can buy the rope. It'll be worth more then.' Laughter fell out of his jaws.

'No!' yelled Khan as he struggled for breath. 'Leave him!'

The ghost dropped the rope.

'You dare to shout at the hangman?'

Khan staggered to his feet. His body was in pain; he was struggling to breathe; he was exhausted. But he wasn't about to sit by and witness a cold-blooded killing – paranormal or not.

The hangman swung around to face him. The man at the wall sank to the floor, scrambled to his feet and dived for the door. He made it out. There was a swing and a loud thud that rattled around the tiled room. He escaped upstairs into the bar, screaming.

The hangman was coiling up his rope again. He was going to enjoy this. His hands worked furiously as they bullied the old knotted rope into the shape of the noose. The anger within him was swelling up – like it was inflating him.

Now he was growing.

His great jaws were widening. His cheekbones were pulling and stretching beneath scarred grey skin. The maggots that clung to his chin were swelling too, now resembling worms, wriggling and writhing around. The great hulk of a body was gaining strength every second. His whole frame was glowing with electromagnetic energy. Khan cowered in the corner, unable to believe what his eyes were telling him. Waiting to awake from the nightmare.

The ghost now filled the room. Arms bursting out of the old shabby jacket he was wearing. Legs thickening. Anger, bitterness, jealousy – centuries of ill feeling were filling him with an electrical intensity that had become solid. And vast. A huge, evil presence in the room.

'You sadden the hangman,' he warned in a deep, ominous tone, 'and you swing from the rafters. That's the rule, sir.'

Khan prepared for death.

Suddenly there was a loud bang and the door to the toilet was flung open.

Two agents, dressed in black and carrying EM neutralisers, burst into the room.

It was Grace and Luc. Bonati had sent them straight to the pub after the briefing, to take readings and monitor the activity there. According to Jud's theory, it was likely that something would happen there soon. But he and Bex had been told to stay at the CRYPT. Jud had protested, but there was no way Bonati was going to let him out until they'd planned their response to the threatening phone call that had come in. There was too much at risk to let either of them out now, especially after the China Town incident.

On entering the pub, Grace and Luc had got more than they'd bargained for: a crowd of locals in the bar, all asking what the hell was going on downstairs. The man who'd entered the toilets and seen the ghost was now seated in a dark corner of the saloon bar, being comforted by a double whisky and an anxious-looking landlord. On hearing the man's screams, he'd called the police. They were on their way.

Without waiting for the police backup, Luc, tall and muscular with a reputation for reckless courage, pushed his way downstairs into the small room, followed by Grace. They began neutralising the energy levels in the atmosphere.

The hangman turned and faced them.

The neutralisers would have some effect, but they'd take time. Time they didn't have. They had to act now. They had to take him on.

Luc threw his neutraliser to Khan, now slumped in the corner of the room, and told him to keep pointing it in the direction of the ghost. He and Grace launched themselves at the hangman. The shock of their arrival, combined with the steady neutralising of his energy source, had visibly affected the ghost. He was shrinking; his face was altering, becoming greyer, his eyes were losing their intensity. But he still had strength. Summoning up the power left in him, he battled with the agents. Luc dived for his legs – just like in rugby training at school. He took him down, and Grace leapt at his great barrel chest. She pinned him to the floor.

Luc was tugging at the rope in the hangman's hands. As his power was leaving him, his iron grip was slipping. But he hadn't given up yet. He threw his great fists out in their direction. Grace was struck across the face, but she didn't go down. With a sharp kick she stabbed his arm with her boot and pinned it to the floor.

But the hangman's mouth began to widen. A great black, cavernous hole appeared in the centre of his face, as he roared in anger.

Grace and Luc knew what was about to happen. And so did

Khan. The eyewitness accounts had all talked of maggots and cockroaches being spewed forth from the ghosts' mouths.

But the force of the two neutralisers together was providing enough power to reduce the ghost's energy source. Nothing came forth. No cockroaches. Even the tiny maggots woven into his face were beginning to fade. The ghost's roar was thinning to become a scream, then a guttural kind of whisper.

'Tyburn,' he croaked. 'You'll swing at Tyburn . . . the tree will have you all . . .'

With one hand still holding the neutraliser, DCI Khan got up and helped Luc to swing the rope around the fading body of the ghost, pinning him to the floor. Grace continued to direct her own neutraliser straight into the face of the hangman, her heavy black boot still pinning his arm.

His great muscular legs were fading too. It seemed the ghost was departing. Becoming plasma. The levels of electromagnetism in his frame had reduced so much that his body was slipping away. Becoming less visible.

Soon Grace's foot was slipping towards the floor – passing through the ghost. His frame was now ionised plasma – visible but translucent, melding with the air around it.

Khan watched, dumbstruck. If the sight that had met his eyes in the mirror moments earlier had been too incredible to believe, then this was just fantasy. It couldn't be happening.

But it was. And the agents knew it. It was what they'd trained for. All those sessions, all the fake scenarios. This wasn't some hideous simulation dreamt up by Bonati and Goode. It was actually happening. Their adrenalin had carried them through.

Hit them hard, shock them and begin reducing their energy source, that was always the advice from Vorzek.

They watched as the hangman slowly continued to fade. The rope too. What had once been solid seemed to become transparent. Physical matter was passing over – as particles altered state. The ionised plasma that housed the hangman's spirit was fading too.

His frame, the outline of his great body, was less defined. Melding with the air.

And then it was over. The dark matter – his spirit – had left the room.

If Khan had been sceptical before, if he'd mocked the agents and their toys in the 'Crib', as he so loved to call it, and if he'd thought that ghosts were a figment of a teenage imagination, he'd changed his mind now.

He believed.

But if he thought his troubles were over, he was wrong. They were only just beginning.

Some locals had fled the Angel as soon as someone mentioned the word 'ghosts', but many had stayed to hear what the terrified witness had seen. The bar was alive with gossip and speculation about what was in there. Others had followed the agents to the toilets and waited outside, listening to the drama as it unfolded.

But now, as Luc opened the door of the toilet to leave, a wave of anxious customers pushed their way past the agents to see what the fuss was about. Luc and Grace knew exactly what to do. Get out of there as quickly as possible, just as Bonati had always told them to do.

Ignoring the shouts and questions, they pushed their way through the crowd, up the stone steps to the top. The saloon bar was heaving, but Grace noticed an emergency exit door to their right. They wouldn't have to leave through the bar.

'Quick,' she said. 'This way!'

And they were gone.

Downstairs in the cellar, the chief inspector was still trying to exit the toilet. But it was too late; the mass of bodies, all bursting in for a good look, blocked the doorway.

And then someone recognised him. All the interviews and the press conferences – they knew exactly who he was.

One of them shouted, 'Call yourself a copper! Protesters, you said? A gang? You need your 'ead seein' to, mate.'

Others joined in.

'Yeah, wake up! We're being attacked and *you* don't know any more than *we* do.'

'Why can't you sort this?'

'You're supposed to be protecting us. What kind of policeman are you?'

Tempers were spiralling out of control. Tension in the room was rising again, only this time the energy was from humans, and it couldn't be neutralised. Khan was going to get it with both barrels. More people crowded in. They wanted answers.

'I swear you better sort this out . . . or we'll all hang. Don't tell me these things aren't going to come back again, 'cos I know they will. Everyone knows it.'

'Yeah . . . apart from you, apparently.'

There was a sudden rattle of yet more footsteps on the stone stairs. It was the police. *Finally.* Backup was on its way, and it couldn't have been more needed. Quickly the officers broke up the crowd and sent them packing.

They saw their senior officer slumped in the corner of the gents. He looked physically, mentally and emotionally spent. Nothing left.

If he'd wanted real evidence of ghosts, then he'd just got it.

Though his nerves were shattered and his body was battered and bruised, his mind was resolved. He *had* to stop this. The protesters' story was never going to work. It was time to come clean, no matter what happened. The hangman's words rang in his ears: 'Tyburn . . . you'll swing at Tyburn.' The CRYPT was right.

Zakis had to be stopped.

CHAPTER 42

THURSDAY: 2.33 P.M.

THE CRYPT

DCI Khan looked terrible. Anyone could see that. Bonati and Jud noticed as soon as he entered the room; his clothes were dishevelled, his hair was unkempt and his face looked tired and worn.

Grace and Luc had filled them in on the Angel incident as soon as they'd reported back to the CRYPT. Jud knew it would only be a short while before this grasping little policeman would come crawling to them with a confession and a pathetic plea for help.

And now here he was. Confessing to everything. He'd filled them in on the whole Zakis affair.

But why had he got involved with Zakis in the first place? Was it simply that he was going through some sort of mid-life crisis? Was there an expensive divorce looming that he hadn't mentioned? Or was he just greedy?

They'd done all the speculating, trying to work out why some people chose to take the backhanders and become corrupt, and others didn't. All that lying at the press conference about protesters.

'But why—' Jud began.

Bonati cut him off. 'Jud. Not now.'

'No, sir. I'm sorry. I wanna know. *Why* did you do it?'

Khan shot a glance at Jud. 'Don't you think I've asked myself the same question? Huh? *Why?* Don't you realise that I've sat and agonised over it? That I hate myself already? Hate what I've done. What I've said—'

'It's OK, Chief Inspector,' said Bonati. 'No one's judging you. We're here to sort this out.' He glanced at Jud. 'We're not doing the blame game now. Not here. Leave it, Jud.'

The morning's press conference came back to Khan's mind once again. The lies. The deceit. On such a vast scale. The reporters hanging on to his every word – and the millions of people watching.

All deceived. And for what?

Greed. Money. An early ticket out of the Met.

Khan sat on the edge of the sofa in Bonati's office and held his head in his hands. He was finished, he knew that for sure, but at least he had now come clean. The narrow escape in the gents at the Angel had sent him running to the CRYPT. If he'd had doubts before about the purpose of the agency, he certainly didn't now. He'd offloaded the secrets that were eating him up so badly. He'd told them everything. And now it wasn't just his problem. It belonged to the CRYPT too.

'So?' said Jud.

'So what?'

'So? Was it you? The phone call.'

Khan sighed deeply and stared at the floor. 'I didn't call, no, but I found out who you really are, Jamie, yes. It wasn't difficult. There's dozens of files on you, if you know where to look.'

'But why now?'

'I think we know why, Jud,' said the professor. 'This was Zakis, wasn't it, Khan? He wanted you to find some dirt on us. Threaten to go public with it. Close us down. Am I right?'

Khan nodded. Now it was his turn to feel like a prisoner,

awaiting trial. He was at the mercy of someone else. His destiny, the rest of his life lay in the hands of others. The tables had turned. And it felt weird. Empty.

The professor was pacing up and down his office, exchanging anxious glances with Jud again.

'OK,' Bonati said confidently. 'Here's the deal. You can make amends tonight. You've still got time. We've been contacted. I assume it's Zakis we're supposed to meet?'

'It wasn't me that rang,' repeated Khan.

'Who was it? Zakis himself?'

'No. Silverman.'

Bonati stopped. 'The man at the press conference? The man in the suit who seems to pop up everywhere. Who *is* he?'

'John Silverman. He's a politician. A crooked one. He's on the Zakis payroll like me. He'll do anything to further his power and line his pocket. Greedy little—'

'Listen, Khan,' said the professor. 'You've got a chance here to do us all a favour. You can still convince Zakis – and this Silverman – to move on. You can meet him instead. You fix it tonight – you handle Zakis and Silverman, tell them the deal is off and they've got to move on – and then tomorrow you give us every bit of support we need to end this. To banish the ghosts.'

Khan sat up slowly.

Bonati continued, 'You do that, your secret's safe with us.'

Bonati shot a look at Jud. He could read his thoughts: *What? Let him go?* The man who was about to reveal Jud's true identity, and in so doing bring the whole CRYPT down? The man who was willing to let the ghosts continue to kill and maim across the city, provided he got his backhander? *You want to let him off?*

There was no way the CRYPT could continue operating if the public knew they were harbouring a killer – innocent or not, Jamie Goode had been charged with murder, and yet here he was serving as an agent. If the secret got out, the CRYPT would be forced to close, and Khan and his corrupt friends knew that.

Jud stood up. 'Sir,' he said, 'I really must speak with you. Outside.'

'No,' said Bonati, staring at him knowingly. 'Trust me. It's sorted.'

'But—'

'That's enough, J, really.' The professor spoke calmly. 'We're not in the business of revenge. We're here to save lives and put an end to the hauntings, as quickly and efficiently as possible.

'OK, the inspector here went too far in finding out about you. And he should have told me what happened last night. But it's Zakis we want. Our prime objective here is to get rid of whatever is haunting this city and allow the people to go about their daily lives in peace and safety. And how can we best achieve this? With Khan banged up behind bars? Think about it. He works with us. He supports us. And we support him. He's still a detective chief inspector with a lot of power. A *lot*.'

Khan remained still. It was as if he wasn't there. These people were talking about him, discussing his fate while he was still sat in the room. He had no view now. No opinion that mattered; he was an object. Just like the prisoners he'd banged up in cells over the years. Told to sit there and wait while he and his officers decided what they'd do with them.

Now he was in the same position. Guilty as charged.

'Well? Khan?' Bonati asked. 'Will you meet them?'

The detective chief inspector leaned back against the cushions. His stomach, his chest, his back, his head, everything ached.

'And say what? It's all over? You've got to scrap the hotel plans?'

'Yes!' Jud and Bonati chorused together.

'Then you're both madder than I am. Don't you know who this man is? Do you think he's the kind who'll say, "OK, then, Officer, I'll move along"? Huh? He'll kill me! And then he'll find another copper just as bent, and the whole plan will start again.'

271

Bonati was listening and watching this pathetic man. Here was a senior officer with the CID. A man with years of experience, cowering like a frightened schoolboy after being told to face up to the bully in the playground.

'You're forgetting something, Khan,' he said. 'You're a DCI. Take men with you. Arm yourselves. Plant snipers at every corner. Have whole gangs of marksmen waiting in the shadows if need be. And then if Zakis refuses to act and threatens you, then you come clean and tell him he's being watched. You arrest him!'

Now Khan stood up. 'You're more naïve than I thought! If I get him before he shoots me, and we arrest him, do you think he'll go down quietly? Do you think he'll say "fair cop" and take his punishment? He'll take me down with him! And Silver, too. He'll get some hotshot lawyer to reduce his sentence and paint us all with the same dirt. I'll go down for longer. Me and Silverman. We'll share the same bloody cell probably.'

Bonati stayed where he was. Jud flashed him an angry look, but he motioned with his hand to stay calm. He looked at Khan across the room and said coolly, 'That depends.'

'What d'you mean? *Depends?* On what?'

'It depends on what you choose to say about our friend Jud here.'

'What?' said Jud anxiously.

But Khan knew what Bonati meant. 'You mean will I spill the beans about young Jamie? But I'm not the only one who knows.'

Jud rose from his seat and moved towards the chief inspector. This was getting desperate.

'Sit down!' thundered Bonati. 'Let me finish, Jud.'

Jud sat down again, cracking his knuckles in his lap. He could feel the anger seeping through his veins.

'I know that,' said Bonati. 'But let's deal with you first, shall we? The others we'll handle. They'll be banged up anyway. No one will hear them from inside a prison cell. If Zakis cuts up rough, he'll go down for sure. And if he does that, he's bound to try to take you with him. But cooperate now and we could keep you out of court.'

Part of Khan was sickened at how Bonati knew everyone in authority. He had the kind of friends at MI5 and Scotland Yard that Khan could only dream of. But the other part of him shook at the prospect of being locked up. If keeping his mouth shut meant he could avoid prison, then why not? Why did it matter to him if the CRYPT kept going? If Jamie was allowed to stay? Who cared? After what had happened in the Angel, he'd realised how important the CRYPT really was.

And maybe, just maybe, this kid Jamie really hadn't killed his mother. Like he said, maybe the ghosts had done it. Khan had seen the violent force of ghosts with his own eyes now.

He chewed his lip and stared at the carpet, weighing up the options. There weren't any. And they all knew it.

'What do you want me to do?' he said finally.

'We want you to go to Tyburn with your men and end this,' said Bonati.

'Move him on, you mean?'

'Exactly. You can try.'

'And if he won't?' said Khan, looking desperate.

'You'll have every marksman in London trained on his face – he'll cooperate,' said Bonati coldly. 'You can threaten to expose him for corruption anyway. Tell him you've already confessed. The game's up. It's "move on and keep your mouth shut, or go down for a very long time". You're giving him a choice.'

'I have no option, do I?' Khan replied.

'I think you knew that when you came in here.'

CHAPTER 43

THURSDAY: 4.30 P.M.

THE CRYPT

'Where've you been?'

'Just with Bonati.'

Bex looked unconvinced. 'What do you mean, "just with Bonati"? What's happened now?'

'Something came up,' said Jud nonchalantly. 'But it's OK.'

'OK? You said you were going to meet me here in the labs. You were supposed to meet all of us.'

'I'm sorry.'

'What's wrong?'

'Nothing.'

'So what about the phone call? In the meeting room? Come on! We all saw your face, Jud. Who was it?'

'No one. It doesn't matter.'

Bex was incredulous. All the events they'd gone through together in the last few days. The way she'd saved his skin in the church. The researching together. The deadly chase on the bike. Just when she thought they were getting close, he was shutting her out.

'Look, you don't have to share it with me if you don't want to, but—'

'I won't, then.'

'But – I'm . . . well, I thought I was your friend. That's all. I'm concerned about you.'

Jud was about to lecture her. He was about to give the usual response of 'I don't need your concern'; how he didn't need anyone's concern or friendship for that matter; how he was tough enough to cope with life on his own, thank you very much. More than tough enough.

But he didn't.

He just looked at her sadly and said, 'Bex, all I'll say is, it's sorted, OK?'

'OK then.'

'Right, did you talk to the other guys? Did you see their evidence?'

'Some of it, but after the meeting was interrupted, and you and Bonati took off, some of them said there was no point. They'd wait until you came back. Meet you in the labs here.'

'I'm sorry, Bex, something came up.'

'Yeah, you said. So what's the plan now?'

'Business as usual,' he lied. 'We go through the evidence we've all gathered. We log it, then we send them out to other locations on the map that haven't been visited yet, other places where we'd expect the spirits to appear, and we try to communicate with them. You know the process, Bex.'

'So, do you want me to ask the skulls and zombies to come back again?'

'You better. We need the evidence logged and the agents out again soon. It's been a while since the last haunting and there's no evidence whatsoever that they're going to stop yet.'

'Right . . . And Khan?'

'What about him?'

'Jud! I know he's been here. Just now.'

Jud tried to ignore her. 'You heard about what happened at the Angel?'

'Yeah. Grace told me. Unbelievable.'

'Well, I think he believes our research now. And Mr Goode, too. They're all convinced. Let's leave it to them.'

Bex wasn't satisfied with this brush-off. 'Oh come on,' she said. 'I know he's been here.'

'What? Who has?'

'I'm not stupid, you know. None of us are. You've got a floor full of agents above us, all wanting some answers. Some of them saw DCI Khan enter the building. He was actually here, at the CRYPT. They said he looked dreadful. He was whisked away into Bonati's office, apparently.'

Jud said nothing.

'And you've just said you've come from Bonati's office. And you said that Khan believes us now. So you've obviously seen him. Now tell me, Jud Lester, what's going on? You can trust me.'

For a brief moment, she caught Jud's gaze. She could see that something had stirred him. He looked frightened. Different to before. Rattled. As though something was about to happen that threatened him.

Zombies were recruited into the CRYPT because of their powers of empathy and their extraordinary ability to perceive paranormal presences using ESP. But communicating with the emotions and thoughts of living humans was quite different. No one claimed to have powers of telepathy. But Bex came closer than anyone in the building. She knew something was troubling him.

'It's that phone call, isn't it?'

'What?'

'Come on, Jud,' she said more gently. 'We all saw your face. In the briefing room. You've changed since that call.'

Her dark oriental eyes were gazing straight into his. She looked so trustworthy. So serene.

This was dangerous, and Jud knew it. Too tempting. He was closer now to revealing his true identity than he'd been since his release from the young offenders' institution. It would be so easy to confide in her. Tell her everything and share this colossal weight that he'd carried round for so long.

He stayed silent, unwilling to take the risk of opening his mouth.

'OK. If you won't tell me what the phone call was about – and I respect that – why can't you tell me what happened with DCI Khan? Did Bonati confront him with our evidence. Did he question him?'

'Like you're interrogating me, you mean!'

'Jud! Give me something, anything!'

Jud finally relented and said, 'He didn't need to question Khan. That's why he came, Bex. He came to 'fess up.'

'But that's brilliant news, Jud! We were right. He tipped off Zakis about us making a connection to Tyburn, and Zakis thought he had too much to lose and sent the assassins to silence us and—'

'Yes! Slow down!' Jud interrupted her battery of words. 'We were right, Bex. Khan and Zakis *are* in cahoots. The man in the pictures was John Silverman – a corrupt Minister for Transport. A greedy little man who fixes things for Zakis in return for a nice big cheque. He pulls strings so that the millionaire can bulldoze his way into cities like London and build whatever he damn well likes.'

'OK . . . and . . . what else?'

Jud thought for a second. There was so much he wanted to tell her, but he knew he couldn't – how Khan was involved in the potential exposing of his real identity.

But he could tell her about the plan for Khan to meet Zakis tonight. There was no reason why she shouldn't know that.

'They're meeting tonight.'

'What?' she said quickly. 'Who are?'

'Zakis and Khan. Khan's going to tell Zakis to move on. That it's all over. That the building work must stop. The hotel will have to be relocated.'

'You're joking!' said Bex. 'There's no way Khan'll do that. Why should he? I know he was scared by the haunting at the pub – but surely he's got too much to lose. Zakis will never move on. He'll just kill him instead. Khan'll never be seen again.'

She suddenly gasped.

'But Zakis will know already about the haunting at the pub,' she continued. 'It'll have been on the news. He'll know Khan was involved and will have guessed that he's got scared and confessed to everything, surely?'

Jud shook his head. 'Khan and Bonati put blocks on the press. Police are at the scene. No one's allowed in or out of the pub. They're saying it was an attempted mugging. It might be on the evening news, but they're not saying it was connected to the hauntings. And there'll be no mention of Khan.'

'Why?'

'You just said it, Bex. Because we know Zakis will suspect something if he hears that Khan was attacked by a ghost. He'll expect him to blow the whistle for sure. Besides, we want to end it. Tonight. Khan's on our side now. Honest. He believes there's a connection – that Zakis must have stirred up the souls at Tyburn. And he's going to the site tonight to end it. One way or another.

'Now I've said too much, Bex. Don't ask me any more, please. Let's get the guys in here and start going through the evidence from last night.'

Bex was shocked. Not just by the revelations he'd shared with her, but because she'd had to bully them out of him.

'One more question,' she said. 'Are you going with him?'

'To Tyburn, you mean? It could be a bloodbath tonight.'

'You didn't answer the question,' said Bex.

'What do *you* think?'

'Your bike or mine?' she said, half smiling.

CHAPTER 44

THURSDAY: 6.01 P.M.

THE MINISTRY FOR TRANSPORT, WHITEHALL

They dressed in plain clothes, and arrived in two unmarked cars.

Through the window, the receptionist at the desk thought they were politicians and civil servants, arriving for a late meeting. DCI Khan had already flashed his card discreetly at the security officer in the porch and told him to keep silent.

'We're here to see Mr Silverman,' said Khan to the woman behind the desk. 'He's expecting us.'

'Second floor, office 209,' she said efficiently.

'Thank you.'

Khan had decided to make one more stop before seeing Zakis at the site. Silverman needed to know what Zakis had disturbed at that wretched place. Maybe if he heard what had happened to Khan at the Angel after he'd left, he'd help him get rid of Zakis for good. Together they'd find a way. It was worth a try. If Silverman didn't want to help, he'd arrest him before he could get to Zakis and tip him off. It was better to keep Silverman under lock and key right now, where he could see him. Besides, a spell in the clink might make him see things differently – make him cooperate.

Either way, Khan had had enough. He wanted out.

He'd briefed his men back at Scotland Yard. They were going in to question Silverman over some allegedly corrupt dealings with Lucien Zakis. Khan's evidence had been patchy – the constables and detectives accompanying him didn't need to know much at this stage, other than the fact that sensitivity was required because of the high-profile suspect. Khan would need to question him alone, but the officers would remain in close proximity if he cut up rough.

He positioned his men: two to remain in the foyer downstairs; one at the rear exit of the building; and two to wait in the corridor outside Silverman's office. All were instructed to have their walkie-talkies ready for Khan's command.

His officers out of sight, DCI Khan knocked on the door of 209. It was opened by a personal assistant – an insipid-looking man in his late twenties.

'Can I help you?'

'Yes, I'm here to see Mr Silverman.'

'Is he expecting you, Mr . . . ?'

'Tell him my name is Khan. He'll see me.'

The door was shut once again. Khan could here talking. Moments later it was opened by Silverman himself. He looked anxious.

'Ah, Mr Khan! What a pleasant surprise. Do come in!' He welcomed him into an anteroom, smiling through clenched teeth, and told his personal assistant he could pack up and finish for the day. He would see him tomorrow, bright and early.

Closing the door of his own large, oak-panelled office, Silverman faced Khan and said sternly, 'What the hell do you think you're doing waltzing in here? Who do you think you are? You can't just come here and—'

'Shut up!'

'I beg your pardon? I think you need to remember who—'

'I said *shut up*, Silverman!' Khan roared as he pushed him hard into a chair.

The politician fell back but immediately got to his feet again.

'Don't you *dare* barge in here and—'

'Sit down!' shouted Khan.

Silverman slowly sat down again. Whatever it was Khan wanted to say, he might as well get it off his chest, he thought. Then he'd have this grubby little bastard removed by security.

'Now listen to me, Silverman. After you left the pub this afternoon, do you know what happened?'

'Surprise me.'

'I was nearly killed.'

'Occupational hazard for a copper, surely.' Silverman was forcing an unsympathetic smile now, and wiping his brow with a large paisley handkerchief. He'd started sweating since Khan's arrival.

'Not by a suspect.'

'No? An aggrieved mistress, perhaps? Have you been a naughty boy?'

'Not by a human in fact,' said Khan ominously.

Silverman looked up. 'What're you talking about, man? Have you been on the bottle again?'

'I was almost suffocated by the ghost of an executioner, last seen working at Tyburn three hundred years ago.'

Silverman began smiling again. 'Oh dear,' he laughed. 'I reckon you stayed in the bar for a few more of those whisky chasers, Khan! Or were you on the magic tobacco? You want to stay off that stuff – very bad for you.'

Khan picked up Silverman by the scruff of the neck. He held his collar tight.

'Listen to me, ya smug bastard. I was attacked by a ghost. D'ya hear me? An apparition. A spectre. Whatever you wanna call it, it wasn't human. But it was real, d'ya understand? As real as you or me. As real as this fist, which is gonna crack you if you don't wake up and see what's going on in this city.

'And do you know who saved me? Huh? The babies from the Crib. That's who. They know what they're doin', those kids. I'm tellin' you.'

Silverman had pushed Khan away from him and moved swiftly to sit behind his large mahogany desk, where he felt safe and authoritative.

'Now wait a minute, Khan,' he said, trying to steady his heartbeat and sound calm. 'I don't accept this. You may have been frightened by a ghoul, poor you! But it doesn't change anything. What I said to you in the pub before you met your ghostly hangman was true: life is not a rehearsal. And neither is it a charity. No one has to carry passengers. We're here for ourselves. You look after number one in this world.'

'What the hell are you saying?' said Khan. 'That we should deliberately deceive the public and leave them to die at the hands of these violent spirits, just so that Zakis can have his hotel and we can get paid? Huh? This isn't going to stop here unless we do something about it! Unless we move on from Tyburn. It's cursed, man!'

'If you're stuck in your charitable "let's save the world" kind of mood, then think on this, Khan: the new hotel will create jobs for hundreds of people. And it will bring millions of pounds into London, from the tourists who stay there. Now how is that not helping the city?'

'Tourists? If this ghost thing spreads there'll be no bloody tourists! It'll be a ghost town. Literally. I tell you, Tyburn is evil. Something's buried there that should've stayed where it was.'

'Don't be ridiculous!' roared Silverman. 'You think you've seen a ghost and now suddenly you're writing the script for a new Scooby Doo movie. Get a grip, Khan! It was one bloody life!'

'What?'

'Huh?'

'What did you just say?'

Silverman's face had reddened. He'd said something he shouldn't have and Khan was on the scent.

'I said you should get a grip, man.'

'No. After that, you said "It was one bloody life." Now what did you mean? What're you talkin' about?'

Silverman shuffled uncomfortably in his chair. Zakis would kill him if he spilled the beans on Kozlosky. He'd swing too. He thought quickly and said, 'I meant that woman in the park. You know, the one that disappeared or something.'

'At Greyfriars?'

'Exactly. The woman at Greyfriars. Very sad, but we can't do anything about it now.'

Khan stared at Silverman across the desk. He was lying. Something was up. He knew he was not going to get anything else out of him. But he would. Eventually.

He cut to the chase.

'Listen, Silver. I know you rang Lester this afternoon.'

'What on earth are you rambling on about now? You know, you really should take some time off. I'm sure it's due you. You're not well, Khan. You're confused.'

'I know it was you! Cut the act. As soon as I said I'd go along with your sordid little plan, and I told you about Jud Lester, you got straight on to Zakis. I've no doubt you hatched out your plan to invite the kid to the site. Where, I assume, you intend to threaten him with going public on the Jamie Goode story unless he and Bonati agree to leave Tyburn alone. Am I right?'

Silverman was now at the drinks cupboard, pouring himself a much-needed Scotch and soda. He carefully spooned some crushed ice from a silver bucket.

'I won't dignify that rant with a decent answer, my good man. All I'll say is, if you're right, then it will be resolved tonight, the CRYPT will leave us alone and you and I will get what we've been promised. So I, for one, would be happy . . . if you were right, of course. But I'm afraid I couldn't possibly comment.'

Khan watched him sip the whisky. He was gagging for a drink but knew full well he was unlikely to be offered one. Not even a politician would offer a man a free drink moments after he'd assaulted him – even if the whisky was paid for by the taxpayer, and there were a dozen more bottles in the cabinet.

Khan had had enough.

'OK, Silver. Here's the deal. You're going to the site at the time arranged, with me. We're going to meet Zakis there and we're going to tell him the plan is off. He'll have to relocate. Or we'll turn him in.'

Now Silverman was chuckling and mumbling, 'Delusional, very sad' into his whisky tumbler. 'He's finally lost it.'

Khan continued regardless. 'You're comin' with me and we're gonna face him. And we won't be alone. I'll take the whole bloody force if I have to. I've already put in a request for marksmen, and plenty of backup. Logistics are briefing vanloads of officers as we speak.'

Silverman put down his glass. The joke had gone far enough. Khan might be delusional and intent on self-destruction, but there was no way he was going to go down with him.

'Look, you sad little man, you may not be able to work this out in that feeble, pedestrian brain of yours, but if Zakis is taken into custody, we're all finished. Either that or he'll instruct his henchmen to defend the site and we'll have a bloodbath on our hands. Except we won't – because we'll be *dead and buried*, you *moron!* Think about it. Zakis isn't a man who takes things lying down. Zakis isn't a man who'll say OK and just move on. And Zakis isn't – hey, what the hell do you think you're doing?'

Khan had moved straight for him and cuffed his hands behind his back.

'Get off! Get off me, you little shit. Let me go, you dumb bastard! Use your brains, man!'

Khan had heard enough, and they were running out of time. He'd guessed Silverman wasn't going to cooperate, so it was time for Plan B. Take him in. Shut him up.

Right now.

He radioed for immediate backup, and the officers stationed outside the room burst in and seized Silverman.

'This is *madness!*' he was now yelling. 'This is bloody insane! Khan!'

The politician was quickly bundled out of the room, down the back stairs and straight out of the fire exit, shouting all the way. The vehicles had been driven round to the rear entrance, as instructed, and he was hurled into one of them. Khan accompanied him on the short ride from the Ministry to Whitehall police station on Victoria Embankment.

He didn't exactly go quietly. Admittedly he'd stopped yelling by the time he'd reached the car; and he didn't throw one punch or kick.

But he cried like a baby.

CHAPTER 45

THURSDAY: 7.01 P.M.

THE CRYPT

They were sat around the cherrywood dining table in Bonati's office. He'd figured they'd all earned a good meal in the privacy of his room. The next twenty-four hours would be the most testing yet and they needed time to eat, think and plan. The professor always tried to give agents time in which they could discuss cases with him personally. It helped him – and ultimately MI5 whom he reported to – to keep on top of the CRYPT's work.

'So,' he began, 'did you see the evidence collected by your fellow agents, then?'

Jud and Bex nodded, while gorging on the sumptuous food.

'They've done well, sir,' said Jud when he'd finished his mouthful.

'OK. Well, there'll be plenty more to collate and discuss and learn from tomorrow – but tonight is going to be crucial.'

Bex suddenly looked awkward. Was she supposed to be here? She thought she wasn't supposed to even know about the plan, though she didn't know why.

Bonati caught her mood. 'Don't worry, Jud's already confessed to me that your powers of interrogation were too much for him.

You know about Khan coming to see me, I gather, and you know about his plans to face Zakis tonight?'

'Yes, sir. But why the secrecy? Why are you not telling—'

'You needn't start interrogating me now!' Bonati interrupted. 'You know everything you need to know – and more. Let's leave it at that.'

Bex returned to her food.

'What I've really asked you here for is to discuss the consequences of Zakis moving on. Let's say he gives up, or is evicted by Khan tonight. The site is cleared and any future hotel plans are blocked. Can we assume this will allow the ghosts to rest in peace? Jud? Thoughts?'

'If we're right about why they're here – and their souls have been troubled by the disturbances at Tyburn – then it stands to reason they'll leave us alone if we leave Tyburn alone. There have been other cases like it, sir. D'you remember the building works in Stockwell? The new flats on the site of that old warehouse? Where all those workers died in the fire. The spirits were really violent, remember, until the plans were relocated and the site was left alone. It happens. Spirits don't like being forgotten. They usually rest in peace when they've been acknowledged again. Treated properly, I mean.'

But Bonati looked troubled. 'Something's not right. It sounds too easy, J.'

'We could neutralise them, couldn't we?' said Bex.

Jud and Bonati both turned to her and smiled. They knew she was the bravest of the new recruits, and sassy too, and always up for facing any challenge without fear or trepidation, but she'd fallen into the trap of all new recruits, saying things before reasoning them through.

'There's too many, Bex,' said Jud. 'I mean, think about it. You could never neutralise them all – it would take hundreds of machines and weeks of running them. I know we were able to send the bellman packing up at St Sepulchre's, but that was partly because your grand entrance surprised him and caused him to drop the lantern, which was his main source of energy. To neutralise the whole area at Tyburn would take enough machines to destroy all the electrical devices down Oxford Street. You'd scramble every computer from Park Lane to Piccadilly.'

'OK. Maybe. But have you got a better idea?' she said, tucking into her steak.

'The ghosts should begin to leave anyway, once they know their site is protected,' said Jud. 'And that they're not forgotten.'

Bonati replied, 'I don't know. Ghosts are often quick to visit us but they sometimes take a long time to drift away once they're here. And in any case, how will they know the hotel plans have been dropped and they've got their site back?'

'The place will be cleared and the grass will grow again,' said Bex. 'We'll build a memorial. They'll see it for themselves. It'll be peaceful again.'

'It will, Bex, you're right – but that's going to take weeks. Months even,' said Bonati. 'And what do we do in the meantime? We can't risk losing more lives. I've already got agents stationed along the route to Tyburn as we speak, just in case something happens tonight. We're stretched as it is, Bex; we can't put agents out every night until the ghosts are gone. We need a quicker way of showing them they've got their Tyburn back, so they can rest in peace *now*. Besides, there are other cases that need our attention.'

Jud said, 'Simple, sir. We tell them.'

'How?' said Bex.

'I thought all agents communicated with ghosts, or am I the only one with ESP?' said Jud.

'No, we've all got it, Jud,' said Bex. 'What I meant was, how do we communicate on that kind of scale? I mean, we don't know how many are lurking around in the streets above us. There could be hundreds. How're you gonna speak to all of them?'

Bonati was listening. 'Bex is right, J. Zakis could have stirred up countless spirits – hordes of ghosts, all filled with revenge for what he's done to the memory of Tyburn. To communicate with so many on that scale . . .'

'I never said it would be easy,' said Jud calmly.

'Not least for the person doing the communicating,' said the professor. 'Surely you know the risks involved in acting as a medium for so many spirits? The EM levels alone could be dangerous.'

'The professor's right,' said Bex. 'Contacting spirits can be shattering for the psychic. We act as a voice. They channel their energy *through* us.'

'Spare me the lecture. I know, Bex. That's what *usually* happens,' said Jud. 'But sometimes the spirits operate separately. Just like in this case. They enter and exit this world freely. Charged with electromagnetic energy – which attracts plasma around it, which becomes visible to our eyes.'

'And in extreme cases the plasma becomes solid,' added Bex.

'OK,' said Bonati. 'So you've read the handbooks, both of you. Can we get to the plan, please?'

'Sorry, sir,' replied Jud, finishing his plateful. 'But you see, if I summoned them to Tyburn, they might choose to come freely – and then they won't use me directly as a medium and it'll be a safer seance.'

'Wait a minute,' said Bonati. 'You said "me". I haven't sanctioned any plan yet. I haven't said I'll allow you to carry out a seance on this kind of scale. God knows what could happen. It's against all CRYPT rules. Communicating with spirits requires strict procedure. We've never even simulated so many spirits in one place. We've no precedent for what might happen.'

'But Tyburn is the hub, sir, it has to be there – the place they either come from or travel to. It's the portal into our world. Beneath the foundations, right where the gallows stood,' said Bex.

'Yes, I know,' said the professor. 'And you're right. But it carries risks. Say we were able to summon them to Tyburn, even tell them that they could have their site back – who's to say they would come, or listen, or understand, or do anything other than what they've already done, which is kill and maim?'

Jud had gone quiet in thought.

'What if they were led by someone?' he said.

'What do you mean, Jud?' asked the professor.

'I mean what if we could summon up someone who would have influence over them. Someone they'd listen to.'

Bex had already guessed.

'Du Val,' she said.

'Exactly,' said Jud.

'And who is this Du Val?' asked Bonati.

They filled him in: Du Val's fame and notoriety; the respect and admiration felt for him at the time; and, of course, Bex's alleged encounter with the legend in Hyde Park.

'OK,' said the professor. 'So this Claude Du Val was a well-known celebrity at the time. This doesn't prove that they'll follow him. We're talking about hundreds of years ago. People didn't suffer from the same obsession with celebrity back then.'

'How do you know, sir?'

'Well . . . I mean, it's a symptom of the media age – television and all that. It's a recent phenomenon.'

'Is it?' said Jud. 'Or is it something deep inside us all – a human need to follow something? It's just the same as totem poles and tribes.'

'The need to worship something is a basic human instinct,' added Bex. She was already convinced the plan was going to work.

'Likening our love of celebrities to the worshipping of totemic symbols and gods by primitive tribes is simply ridiculous, but now is not the time to debate this – as much as I'd like to. We've got a case to solve!' said Bonati abruptly.

'I'm sure it'll work,' said Jud. 'I say we go to the site once Zakis has left, and summon up Claude Du Val. Then we communicate with him. We tell him he can have his site back. He will tell the spirits. They'll listen to him. Surely it's worth a try, Professor.'

'And do you think it will be enough, just to be told that they can have their site back? That they can rest in peace again?' asked Bonati, still testing their plan, scrutinising it, like he always did.

'If our research is correct, sir, yes,' said Jud. 'If so many people died at Tyburn, often in massive public executions, then surely Zakis *must* have caused these hauntings by stirring up the site and building on it. The souls who died there risk being forgotten. So many of them were hurled into a pit below the gallows, sir. It is their resting place after all.'

'Yeah,' said Bex. 'Jud's right. It's the fear of being forgotten that's causing this. You'd never contemplate removing all the gravestones in a graveyard and building on it, would you? These sites are there for ever – lasting memorials to past lives. No one builds on a grave.'

'OK, OK,' said Bonati. 'Enough. Tyburn is undoubtedly the place to do it. But let's test that kind of seance first. Right here in the labs. I want readings, possible scenarios. We'll simulate the conditions tomorrow. Create hundreds of energy sources and simulated spirits in a single place and then take readings. You've got no guarantee that this Du Val will come along and lead them. If the energy levels are dangerous, then the plan is scrapped. I won't let you do it.'

'The site has to be preserved, sir. It *has* to work. Du Val will do it. We have to summon him there first. Then the others.'

'Let's see,' said Bonati. 'If it's safe for you to be near so much paranormal activity, then we'll do it.'

'When?' said Bex, eagerly.

'Well, let's see what happens tonight first,' said the professor, trying to slow them down. 'Zakis is unlikely to go quietly, I fear. No matter what Khan thinks.'

Jud and Bex exchanged glances across the table. Jud spoke up. 'But time isn't on our side, sir – every day could mean more lives lost. Why are we waiting?'

'Because MI5 have asked us to stay away from the site tonight, to leave it to Khan and his officers. Let's face it, Zakis won't go down without a fight. It could be a real battle, Jud, and that's without the ghosts. I only hope it isn't, for Khan's sake.'

'So why aren't we going to help him?' said Bex.

'Because it's outside the CRYPT's jurisdiction. Way outside. We're not an armed force, Bex. This is one for the police. I admire your spirit, but this is very serious indeed. We have to give Khan time. He and his men have to get Zakis to move on, either voluntarily or by force if necessary. It's no place for us tonight.'

Jud remained quiet. *That's what you think, sir*, he thought.

CHAPTER 46

THURSDAY: 8.16 P.M.

WHITEHALL POLICE STATION

DCI Khan had delivered Silverman to Whitehall police station and tucked him up in the cells, ready for questioning. His sobs and protests and sad requests had fallen on deaf ears. Khan said he could sit and stew for a while.

His great yells of anger passed through the small hatch in his cell door and rang down the hollow corridors of the police station. The cold, austere surroundings of his new room contrasted with the plush offices back at the Ministry, the mahogany furniture replaced by a chipped metal table and a plastic chair, and the shag-pile carpet now substituted by hard stained tiles. No great oil paintings of the London landscape here; just bare walls and a fire regulations notice.

'I'll take you down with me!' Silverman had cried in desperation, claustrophobia already seeping into him like poison. 'There's no way you'll get away with it. If I'm going down, then you're comin' with me! *Khan!*'

'Drunken idiot,' Khan had said quietly to the station sergeant. 'Been on the bottle. Ignore his ramblings, Sergeant. He's deluded and drunk. Thinks everybody's crooked like he is. Mad.'

'He's in good company, then,' the sergeant replied. 'We're all mad in here.'

Silverman's threats to take the inspector down with him were meaningless to Khan. He'd already wrestled with the consequences of coming clean and facing up to his duty. He knew, as soon as he'd walked into the CRYPT and confessed to Bonati, that it would eventually lead to him being charged himself. The conversation with Bonati, and the possibility of avoiding prison if he kept silent over Jamie Goode, had been a bonus. How weird, he thought, that the illegal research he'd done at Scotland Yard might ultimately be the thing that kept him out of jail. Either way, Silverman could do nothing now.

There was a risk Khan would be charged – of course there was – but provided he kept his mouth shut, who knows, he might even get early retirement. All he had to do was keep Jamie's secret buried. It was worth it.

Besides, the alternatives were unimaginable. To allow Zakis to continue raking up the blackened earth at Tyburn, stained with the memories of the souls who had died by the rope, would bring untold danger to yet more people.

And who knows where it would stop? If the threat to go public with Lester's real identity had worked, then Bonati would have had no choice but to leave Zakis alone, and allow the violating of the lost souls to continue. How many more lives would have been sacrificed over Tyburn? Or would Jamie have turned himself in first? Either way there would have been losers.

Zakis had to be stopped. And the CRYPT had to be allowed to continue. The exact opposite of what Zakis wanted.

This was not going to be easy.

But it was time. Khan decided to go and give Silverman one more chance to cooperate. This time they'd use the interview room. A spell in the cell by himself and then a session in the formal interview room might help to break him down – show him who was boss.

Khan rose from his chair in the sergeant's office, where he'd been catching up on work and cramming a sandwich into his empty stomach. He instructed the sergeant to bring Silverman to Interview Room 1.

'Righto, sir.' The sergeant disappeared in the direction of the cells, and Khan made his way to the interview room to prepare.

He could hear Silverman's ramblings before he even entered the room. When he finally appeared at the door, Khan didn't stand up to welcome him. Why should he? Instead he just nodded to the sergeant to leave them alone and pointed to a chair opposite him for Silverman to sit in.

They were alone, seated across the small table, just as they'd been in the saloon bar of the Angel hours earlier, only this time the roles were reversed. Khan had the power. He was in the driving seat.

This was *his* interview.

'I've thought about your mindless actions over the last few hours,' Silverman began immediately, intent on shifting the balance of power from the start by leading the conversation. His feeble tears had gone and some semblance of his usual arrogance had returned.

'And I think that if you're insisting on going through with your self-destructive plan – a plan that will land both of us behind bars for a very long time, by the way – then I am forced to consider the only option available to me.'

'Which is?'

'To attend the site tonight, *before* the rest of you get there, and tell Zakis that the authorities have pulled the plug on his planning application.'

Khan smiled slightly. Perhaps the solitary confinement was working its magic. This was a change of tactic from Silverman. A mad plan, even stranger than Bonati's, but at least he was cooperating.

'I'll tell him it's not my fault,' continued Silverman. 'Orders from above. I'll say they've decided to overturn the planning consent. Deal's off.'

'After the foundations have been laid and the frame is going up – you're going to tell him his application's been turned down?' said Khan.

'Exactly,' said Silverman.

'You're madder than I am.'

'It's happened before, Khan. I've known it happen. Late objections come in, it takes a while for neighbours to get their appeals together. They file their lawsuits, injunctions are awarded, or maybe there's archaeological interest suddenly uncovered – all of which means that the decision to allow something to go through is overturned and the planning application is denied. The diggers have to stop, at least until the appeal is heard.'

Khan looked at the desperate man before him. His eyes were red, his shirt and tie were dishevelled and his hair was unkempt. Here was a man who had clearly just fallen a great height, from a luxurious ministerial office to an austere police cell. But he was still trying to keep his dignity. Hold the strings. Make the decisions.

Pathetic little man.

Khan felt no sympathy; no compulsion to support him, despite the fact that they were, technically, still in this together. But he was pleased to be shifting the responsibility from his own shoulders. If Silverman wanted to try out his hare-brained plan, let him. Khan had nothing to lose.

'Let me get this straight, Silver. You're gonna waltz in there tonight and tell Zakis to his face that the planning application you've already passed – the one he's effectively bought with his dirty money – is now in jeopardy and he must stop his building, maybe even withdraw completely to another site? Is that right?'

'Exactly. If planning officials were to say no, there'd be

nothing he could do. Nothing. He knows that. There are only so many people who can be bought off. He'll *have* to move on, even if my boys have to evict him. You can't argue with the Ministry. That's why he employed me in the first place – so that he has a door into an otherwise impenetrable place. But like I say, not everyone can be bought. There are powers higher than me who can't.'

'He'll just tell you to keep searching for someone else who can,' said Khan quickly. 'And get the decision overturned again.'

'Of course he'll try, I know. And he'll counter-appeal. But that takes time. If we're quick, we can get him out of there, close the site down and begin putting the earth back before he's even had time to recruit a new man on the inside.'

'Let me guess: the whole point of this is you get him to move on by blaming other people at the Ministry – none of this is your fault, so you don't lose your head. I suppose you'll say you've tried but they won't budge?'

'I'm not just saving *my* neck, Khan. You don't need to be implicated either. That's the whole point. The decision could have been made by people far higher up than you and me.'

Khan had decided. There was nothing to lose. Only Silverman's life, potentially, but that meant little to him now. If this desperate politician wanted to put his crazy scheme into action and risk facing the wrath of Zakis alone, then who was he to stop him?

'Right, I'll give you thirty minutes with him. You meet him there at nine forty-five. He'll be at the site. He was due to meet Lester and Bonati anyway, so he'll be waiting. Catch him early. But we'll be watching you, Silver. We'll all be following.'

'Who will? You going with Lester and Bonati, then?'

'No! What use are ghost-busters with a man like Zakis, huh? My marksmen will be primed and ready. If you haven't sorted it after half an hour, we do it my way.'

'But you'll take him out if he pulls a gun on me, right?'

'We'll try. But saving you isn't our prime objective, Silver, and you know it.'

'Great, thanks for caring,' Silverman said sarcastically.

'If Zakis decides to try and defend the place, though, he'll wish he'd never been born.'

CHAPTER 47

THURSDAY: 9.43 P.M.

MARBLE ARCH

Silverman stepped out of the taxi and quickly approached the large gates to the construction site. Rain was beginning to fall and the trees that flanked Marble Arch shook in the rising wind. The puddles on the pavements flickered from green to amber to red, reflecting the traffic lights that populated the busy intersection. The tarpaulin that wrapped around the scaffolding flapped and rattled, its chain cords clinking against metal poles.

The security guard in the hut opened the gates and allowed the politician to walk in. Silverman asked him to lead the way to the site office. Following the guard, he made sure the main gate was left slightly ajar, just as he'd been instructed to do by Khan. He could hear raised voices as he trod through the muddy puddles and approached the cabin. Behind him, several figures dressed in black, some of whom were armed, sneaked quickly through the gates and disappeared into the shadows of the building site.

Khan and his men.

The shouting inside the cabin was Zakis. Miles Harrison, the site manager, was getting both barrels for something.

Silverman felt his stomach lurch at the sound, and at the

prospect of telling Zakis to pack up the entire site and move on. It seemed like a suicidal plan, now that he was actually here.

'What d'ya mean, you've sent them home?' Zakis yelled at Harrison.

'Have you seen the rain, sir? Besides, we can't do much until tomorrow's delivery anyway.'

'Why do I pay you, Harrison? Huh? This isn't a holiday camp. I don't pay you to sit around waiting for the sun to come out. Zakis builders work night or day, rain or shine, d'you understand?'

'But,' Silverman could hear Harrison pleading, 'like I said, we're waiting on a delivery anyway. It was supposed to be here today, but there's been a problem with the suppliers.'

'OK, I'll sort it. But there's always plenty of other stuff to do!' shouted Zakis. 'I can't believe you've dismissed them! You'll pay for this in your wage packet, you can bet on that.'

Harrison was protesting feebly. 'Yeah, but the rain affects the foundations, boss. It's pointless laying the concrete at the moment.'

'Now listen, you pathetic little shit—'

The argument was interrupted by a loud knock on the window from the security guard. The shouting stopped.

'Yes?' snapped Zakis as he opened the door. 'Oh, it's you, Silver. Just when I thought my evening couldn't get any worse. You ready, huh? Have you seen this Lester kid yet? Are they here?'

'Not yet, sir. A few more minutes.' Silverman's face couldn't hide the tension he felt. He didn't even know how to begin. He waited until the guard had trudged away.

'Er . . . Mr Zakis. I need to . . . er . . . talk to you.'

He glanced over Zakis's shoulder to Harrison stood behind him. 'Er . . . alone, please?'

Harrison was glad of the chance to escape. 'You can have the office, sir. Don't worry, I'll come back.'

'No!' Zakis snapped. 'You're not going anywhere. I've not finished with you yet. You don't get out of it that easily. You can stay here. Have a whisky, I know how much you like it. And if anyone turns up asking for me, send them on into the site. We'll be waiting.'

'You expectin' someone, sir?'

'Just keep your trap shut and stay there, Harrison.'

He turned to Silverman. 'I fancy a cigar anyway. You like rain, Silver? Waitin' around makes me edgy. Let's walk. We'll keep an eye on the gate.'

'Well . . . er . . . OK, Mr Zakis.' Silverman had hoped to stay in the light. He glanced around. 'No bodyguards tonight?'

'They're not bodyguards,' laughed Zakis. 'Trust me, I can handle myself, Silver. Just associates. But they irritate me sometimes. Don't you find that, huh? Too many people hangin' around? Gettin' under your feet. Know what I mean?'

'I agree, sir, yes.'

'Especially when I'm doin' business, huh? And tonight we've got a little deal to make, right?' He grinned as he placed a fat cigar in his mouth. 'But first I wanna show you how the site's comin' along. Prepare to be inspired, my friend.'

The two men left the cabin and walked off in the direction of the site. Inside, Harrison breathed a sigh of relief, grabbed the usual bottle from the cabinet and went back to his newspaper.

The rain was lashing down in sheets. Muddy puddles ran into miniature channels that dissected the site like veins on the back of a hand. Silverman's polished shoes were soon clogged with clay and splashes were forming over his dark trousers.

Zakis marched on, in boastful mood, deeper into his kingdom, between the giant joists and the girders. Silverman noticed there had been progress since his last visit. The steel frame of the giant complex was now forming – a sprawling mass of metalwork.

'You can begin to see the size, uh?' said Zakis, proudly.

'Impressive, sir,' Silverman replied. *How am I gonna do this?* he thought desperately. *How do I start? Just bring it up?*

Zakis was pointing to his right.

'And that, my friend, will be where the Olympic-sized pool will be. The jewel in the crown of the leisure complex. An indoor sea surrounded by treatment rooms, jacuzzis, spas, saunas. Palm trees. You name it.'

Zakis puffed on his soggy cigar. Nothing would dampen his spirits when surrounded by his growing empire. This was yet another palace for him, right in the heart of London.

'You fancy a week here, Silver, you call me – any time. I'll give you good rates!' he laughed. 'Come on, let me show you where the gym's going. It'll be huge.'

Silverman stopped. 'Er . . . sir?'

'What?'

'Look, I don't know how to say this . . .'

Zakis returned to him. He was getting wet. And impatient. He'd already had to deal with one cowardly creep tonight – he didn't need another. 'Say what? What's the problem?'

Silverman paused, then decided that the only way to break something like this was to plunge straight in. Beneath his damp raincoat, his cold body shook with nerves.

'I, er, have some bad news.'

'Huh?'

'It's Highways, Mr Zakis. They've uncovered a problem, you see. The traffic island was to be repositioned, as you know. We had planned to push Cumberland Gate further into Hyde Park to give you more acreage.'

'I know! A favour for which you'll be rewarded handsomely. Wait a minute, what do you mean, *had* planned? What're you talkin' about?'

'Well . . . er . . . it's been blocked after all. The health and safety guys have got their hands on it. You know how it is. Red tape an' all that. They've now said it's not safe to reposition it there.'

Zakis stared straight at Silverman. Rain was trickling down his face. The smoke from the cigar in his mouth was swirling in the wind that circled his head. His eyes looked wild.

'What?' he thundered.

Silverman continued, though his voice was weakening by the second.

'And . . . er . . . the car park we promised you on Green Street? That's hit a snag too. Neighbours have appealed.'

Zakis stepped closer. He grabbed Silverman by the lapels and formed fists. His knuckles dug into the politician's chest.

'This is a joke, huh?' he said, deadly serious. 'A late April fool, yeah? Not even you would be stupid enough to try this for real.'

Silverman shook his head slightly. He was fumbling for words now. 'I . . . er . . . it's . . . er out of my hands. It's, er . . . well, I mean I've been trying all day to . . .'

Zakis released his grip and shoved Silverman backwards. 'You don't understand, Silver. Let me explain this again, very slowly. When Zakis starts something, he finishes it. That's why we're getting rid of these ghost hunter punks tonight.'

His right hand was fumbling inside his coat.

'When Zakis says he wants a hotel, Zakis gets a hotel. D'you understand?'

What was that in his pocket?

'If Zakis says jump, monkeys like you say "How high, sir?"'

It's not. It can't be, thought Silverman.

'And you're going to fix this. D'ya hear me?'

It was. Zakis had pulled out a revolver, which he now pointed directly at Silverman.

'D'ya know what I think?' he said, 'I think Silver's got cold feet. I think the little bastard is trying to wriggle away. Huh? Tryin' to back out all of a sudden. Gone yellow? Makin' up some cock-and-bull story. Am I right?'

Silverman said nothing, just shook his head. *Come on, Khan!* he pleaded silently. *If you're watching – let Zakis have it now!*

But nothing stirred.

Zakis continued. He began to jab the gun into Silverman's stomach.

'I think little Silver's lost his bottle.'

Silverman winced as the barrel of the revolver dug sharply into his gut.

And then he saw the shapes. Over Zakis's left shoulder.

He tried not to react. *Keep him talking.*

Don't let him know they're coming.

More dark shapes were moving in the shadows. *Not a minute too soon, Khan!* Silverman thought.

He allowed his eyes to flick momentarily to the ground behind Zakis's feet. It was hard to comprehend. There were shadowy figures approaching – but they were somehow rising upwards, from the muddy ground. Clambering up through the cracks in the dirt and the rubble. As if they were passing right *through* the stones.

Zakis was oblivious. He pressed the gun harder into Silverman and said, 'Am I right, man? Has Silver gone yellow?'

Silverman had to keep him talking. Whatever was emerging, whatever it was that was rising from the soil and taking shape, Zakis would get it first.

'There's no point in shooting me,' he pleaded. 'I'm . . . on your side. I'm more use to you alive than dead right now. I can try to fix it.'

'You misunderstand me, Silver. This gun isn't for you.'

'What?'

'Is your wife at home?'

Silverman shuddered. Zakis was scraping the gun around his stomach now, the hard metal bruising and scratching through his clothes. 'My *wife?*'

'You heard me. Shall I get my men to pay her a visit, huh?

They can be very persuasive with one of these.'

Silverman allowed his eyes to scan the ground behind Zakis once again. He hadn't imagined it. The shapes were rising still. Gathering behind him.

The souls of Tyburn's forgotten highwaymen had stirred again. Three, four, five . . . Silverman saw a mass of ghostly bodies bound up in dark cloaks. It seemed like they were gaining strength somehow. Cloudy images becoming stronger. Flecks of blue-grey bones and thinly stretched skin flashed beneath black, rain-soaked hats.

Anger intensified inside their hollow bodies, charging the plasma that formed around them. Dark matter was hardening into flesh.

Silverman wondered, had they come for him too? Should he run?

Why not? Zakis wouldn't kill him if he ran – not yet anyway. He just wanted to frighten him. He knew he'd be able to get to his wife before Zakis's men did.

But what about Khan? Would one of his trigger-happy officers take him out if he made a bolt for it? He knew their guns were trained on both of them, from their safe hideaways in the bushes.

He was trapped.

The ghosts were getting closer to Zakis now. Inches away. They made no sound. Silverman stared back at him.

Keep talking.

'OK, OK. Not my family. Please. I'm doing all I can, Mr Zakis. I'm sure we can sort this out. I'm sure we can—'

They had him.

The gun fell to the floor as Zakis felt a bony grip at his neck.

'What the—'

Now at his shoulders. He spun around and screamed. A loud, animal-like groan that rattled around the site like a wounded tiger caught in its own jungle. His arms were flailing. He was trying to fight them off.

'Help me, Silver! Help me!'

A horrified Silverman took a step back. The sight was sickening. They were at Zakis's throat, his face. They scratched and pierced. Ripped and crippled. Zakis was on the ground, the mass of dark shapes swarming over him. Amidst the desperate cries Silverman could hear a frantic clicking noise, like a plague of giant insects. Jaws rattling. Drawing in on the hotel tycoon, who flailed about helplessly, choking for breath.

'Get off me! Silver, get 'em off!'

But Silverman backed away, further still. He felt no sympathy. No compulsion to jump in, or dash for help. Nothing. This tyrant, this vicious, power-crazy entrepreneur had finally met his match. Zakis squirmed. His legs writhed in the muddy bath. Rubble and stones ricocheted out from beneath his shoes. Silverman caught a shower of dirty splashes as Zakis kicked on. Lashing, fumbling, screaming.

And then the ghosts began to drag him by his legs, backwards through the puddles. His body ripped over the jagged bricks. A terrified expression was etched on his face and he choked and spluttered uncontrollably. Rivers of mud poured into his mouth like a sickly gravy. Only gargled screams reached out to Silverman as he watched Zakis being pulled further into the shadows – away from the light. On, deeper into the dark, abandoned site.

Silverman stood frozen to the spot.

Seconds more and the ghosts had vanished around the corner of a giant steel post and off into the night.

They'd taken him. Taken their prize. They'd led his body to another dimension, a different time, a place without walls or solid earth. To wait in a fetid, ghostly hell, trapped between life and death, between the physical and spiritual worlds.

Until their real plans for him would begin.

They hadn't finished yet. It was necessary. And it would happen soon.

Silverman was incredulous. He *must* have imagined it. He must be sleeping. It was an irrational, stress-induced nightmare. That was all. A disjointed pattern of disturbing images in an alcohol-fuelled sleep. He was still inside his cell at the police station.

He'd wake up soon.

But he looked around him; felt the cold rain on his face. The wind flapped around his shivering body and rattled through his open coat. *It felt so real.*

He collected his thoughts. He pulled his mackintosh tightly to him and glanced around furtively for any sign of Khan or his men.

Slowly, looking dazed, several officers approached from behind huts and diggers and trucks. Khan himself appeared from the shadows and walked towards him. He looked shaken.

The sound of traffic faded back into Silverman's hearing and the tarpaulin around the site flapped loudly, shaking him into reality once again.

And then he saw the gun on the floor. He stooped and fumbled for it, and then brandished it towards the approaching men. He was panting. The enormity of what he'd just seen was penetrating into his mind. This was happening.

'Don't be stupid,' said Khan. 'Put the gun down.'

Silverman was shaking his head and rocking like some paranoid prisoner. He was darting about, looking around him wide-eyed, like some crazed madman. Shock had brought a desperation to his face and a feverish fear to his eyes.

'Get away from me! All of you! *Now!*'

Khan spoke slowly and deliberately.

'I said put the gun down, Silver. Look around. There are half a dozen guns trained on you. Now put it down. It's over. The ghosts have gone. They've taken their man. Put the gun down.'

307

'It's evil. I tell you. This place is evil. First Kozlosky. Now Zakis. They're coming for me. They're coming. Get away!'

But Khan stood firm and told his men to keep their guns trained on Silverman.

In a cool voice he said slowly, 'Who's Kozlosky?'

CHAPTER 48

THURSDAY: 10.06 P.M.

TYBURN SITE, MARBLE ARCH

Bex weaved in and out of the traffic, as Jud clung on. The Fireblade sped down Oxford Street.

As they approached Marble Arch, and the building site swung into view, they saw a man fleeing from the gates. He looked terror-stricken.

It was Miles Harrison. He'd seen it all. Watched it from his cabin window. The moonlight had illuminated the scene like some black-and-white horror movie. Only it hadn't been a film; it was real. And now his employer, global businessman and heir to the entire Zakis fortune, was gone. Taken by ghosts.

At first Harrison had been frozen to the spot by the window. He couldn't leave the cabin for fear of what might still be outside. But eventually he'd turned and fled from the gruesome scene, panting and twitching like some escaped convict.

Bex parked the Fireblade at the site entrance and they quickly disembarked on to the rain-soaked pavement.

'Did you see that?' said Bex. 'The man, I mean?'

'Yeah.' Jud's expression looked grave as he unpacked the equipment from the bike's panniers. 'See his face? Terrified, I'd say.'

'Yeah.'

'I swear that's not the kind of fear you get when you see police or guns. That man's seen something else. What's been going on here?'

The two agents gazed around silently and allowed their minds to soak up the atmosphere.

'There's a supernatural presence here,' said Jud. 'Do you feel it?'

Bex had gone pale. She was staring through the gates. 'Something's just happened,' she said. 'I can sense it. This site is alive with energy. The place is rotten, like an open wound that's been prodded and stabbed. It's rank.'

Loaded up with every form of equipment they'd been able to find in the labs – they were leaving nothing to chance – they moved through the open gate and edged slowly into the site. Jud held his EMF meter in his hand, ready to begin taking readings. He felt the weight of his neutraliser in his coat pocket. He wasn't going to lose it this time.

'That's why I told Bonati we should've all come. I knew something would happen tonight,' whispered Bex.

'Yeah, he should've believed us.'

Walking across the rain-soaked ground, they passed the abandoned site office on the right. The door had been flung open and the light was still on. Documents were swirling around inside in the draught that whistled through it. A half-drunk bottle of whisky was just visible on the desk.

What had gone on here?

Up ahead, narrow metal spires soared into the darkened sky like daggers: the struts for a hotel that was doomed from the beginning.

There was a clap of thunder not far away, which shook the disturbed earth beneath them, and a sudden gust of wind rattled the tarpaulin and the plastic sheeting, like sails on a ghostly ship.

As they walked deeper into the cursed site, they could see in the distance a group of men.

So there was life here still. The place had felt like a cemetery when they'd first entered.

The figures were encircling something; and pointing rifles at it.

'What the hell's been going on here?' said Jud, his voice battling against the growing wind.

And then they saw him. The man in the centre of the ring.

Silverman. They recognised his face from the television, though he looked dreadful – almost spectral. His clothes were splattered with mud. His coat was saturated and his grey hair looked thin and straggly in the rain. He was clutching a gun in his shaking hands. He was surrounded, and twitching violently, as though battling with some inner demons.

They moved closer. In the gloom, Jud accidentally stepped on a large piece of abandoned metal sheeting. It rattled on the stony ground and the crowd in front of them looked their way.

A marksman seized his opportunity and grabbed Silverman, bundling him to the ground.

Khan came over towards them.

'What the hell are you two doing here? Did Bonati send you?'

Their silence was telling.

'Oh? I see. Couldn't resist, eh? Well now that you're here, maybe you could tell us what all this means.'

'What the hell's happened?' said Jud.

'You better come with us into the office and I'll tell you. All I can say is I saw something, but it was difficult to make out in the darkness. I think they've got Zakis.'

'Who have?' said Bex.

'That's what I want you to tell me. We're going to interrogate Silverman now. He's making no sense at all. Look, I don't think this is the first time the ghosts have been here. I think something's already happened on the site. You need to hear what he's got to say and tell us what it means. And quickly, before they come back for us.'

They followed him towards the cabin. Officers threw Silverman in and remained outside. Khan and the two agents entered.

Silverman was shaking his head uncontrollably.

Khan grabbed the bottle of whisky abandoned on the desk and quickly offered it to him. He necked a huge glug and then sighed heavily. His shaking subsided a little as the Scotch brought a warmth to his throat. He sat down in Harrison's chair.

'Come on, Silverman!' said Khan. 'We saw some figures behind Zakis, but it was hard to make them out. Were they *ghosts*? What did they do with Zakis?'

Silverman drew another gulp from the bottle, breathed deeply to try to regulate his heartbeat and eventually spoke up. His voice was frail and wavering.

'I dunno. It seemed like they . . . well, like they came up out of the ground. Right up – through the rubble. There was nowhere else they could've come from, Khan, I swear. I saw them rise up behind Zakis.'

Bex interrupted. Her face showed no sympathy. 'What the hell have you started here?' she said. 'You and Zakis – you're both the same.'

Silverman continued his gruesome account of what he'd seen. Khan confirmed that it fitted with what he and his officers had managed to make out from where they'd been stationed.

Zakis really had been taken away.

'And you say it wasn't the first time, Chief Inspector?' said Jud.

Khan shook his head and turned expectantly to Silverman. 'Come on,' he said. 'Tell them what you told me about this . . . Kozlosky fella.'

Silverman took another swig from the soothing nectar, now beginning to work its magic, steadying his heartbeat, at least for now. He filled them in on what he'd learned from Zakis about the gruesome way Yuri Kozlosky had been dispatched.

'It was a hanging. A real hanging,' said Bex. 'Just like back then.'

She turned to Jud suddenly. 'Can you sense something?'

'Yeah. It's weird.'

'What?' said Khan quickly. 'What're you talking about now?'

'It's outside,' whispered Jud.

'What's going on?' said Silverman. His hands started to shake again with fear. He dropped the bottle. It smashed on the hard metal floor of the cabin, bringing an unwelcome jolt to everyone, and a waft of alcohol.

For a moment they looked silently at one another across the room. The portentous wind was whipping up again outside, shaking the sheeting and rattling the metal fixings across the site. Trees in the distance shook helplessly, and the rain slowly turned to hailstones, which beat a menacing rhythm on the roof of the cabin.

'Something's happening,' said Jud. 'Out there. The atmosphere's changed. It's foreboding. Come on.'

'Now wait a minute,' said Khan. 'No one's going anywhere until I've—'

But he was interrupted by another noise. From outside. Distant but clear. Everyone recognised it, but only Jud and Bex knew its significance, and they both shuddered.

It was the sound of a bell.

Jud's face wore an ominous look. 'It's the Execution Bell,' he whispered. 'They're coming.'

Fearful glances were exchanged across the tiny cabin.

There was a shout from one of Khan's men outside.

'Sir, I think you better come out here. Quick!'

Khan stood up and left the cabin, followed by the rest of them.

No one could've predicted the sight that met their eyes, even though the bell had tolled. Not even Jud had expected this.

Silverman collapsed to the floor. 'God help us!' he cried.

Khan staggered backwards, clutching his stomach, now filled with nervous acid.

'My God, it's happening all over again,' said Bex. 'History's repeating itself.'

The air was alive with activity. There were hundreds of them. Dark spirits, all mixing with the rotten earth, like broken scabs on a giant wound. Ghostly apparitions that mingled with the shadows. Hordes of dead souls, crowding around the construction they'd made. The site was buzzing with electromagnetism. Even the great metal struts in the distance fizzed and glowed with static energy.

'What the hell . . . ?' said Khan.

'Can you see them?' said Jud.

'What? Of course we can see them!' snapped Khan.

Jud turned to Bex and showed her the EMF meter. 'The levels of energy are mad. Never seen it like this,' he said. 'Off the scale. The ghosts must be as solid as you or me. Like in the church.'

Bex nodded, eyes still focused on the scene as it unfolded.

The ghosts had used timbers and metal poles that littered the site – anything they could find. All propped up in some makeshift reminder of the great structure that had once killed them. Jud recognised what it was meant to be. The Tyburn Tree – the three-sided ugly monstrosity he'd seen in so many drawings. Now dwarfed by the great steel joists that surrounded it, but recognisable.

And there, in the very centre, on a makeshift platform, stood the hangman. Khan felt a sickness in his stomach as his eyes caught him. He recognised that face. His heart was pounding in his chest as he steadied himself against Silverman. Would he make it through the next few moments? Or would his body finally pack up under the strain?

'This is it,' said Bex ominously. 'It's really happening.'

'They've been leading up to this,' said Jud. 'It's the only thing they know and so the only thing they could do when Zakis and his builders disturbed them. They're rebuilding Tyburn. Who knows how many more they're goin' to hang.'

They watched as the crowd of spectral bodies organised themselves around the tree. They were silent but highly charged, glowing with a ghostly aura. Each acting out their part in some master plan, like worker ants in a colony.

And then that sound again.

The bell.

Jud and the others turned to their right. Looming out of the shadows came a mob of ghostly highwaymen. Their dark coats flapped in the wind, revealing gaunt phantom faces. Leading them was the bellman, still ringing his bell, an ominous warning that death was close.

The ghosts behind him were carrying something between them.

A bundle? A sack?

It was hard to make out from where they were standing. But the next noise they heard revealed the awful truth.

A human scream.

They were carrying Zakis. To the gallows.

Through the crowds of ghosts, they could just make out his face in the distance. But his eyes. What had they done to his eyes? He must have been badly beaten, as both eye sockets had swollen up to an unimaginable size. And there was blood pouring from his lips. His dark hair, usually greased back, now fell over his forehead, matted with congealed blood.

His screams echoed ominously around the site, like a wounded animal.

Silverman placed his hands over his ears and shook his head violently.

Zakis was the condemned man. This was to be a real hanging. To the death.

315

Khan shouted, 'You've gotta do something!'

'I'm on it,' said Jud. And he burst from the group, towards the ghostly procession.

'What're you doing?' screamed Bex, running after him. 'There's nothing you can do for him now. Nothing!'

Jud paused, threw his EMF meter to the ground, fumbled for his neutraliser and hurled it towards Bex.

'Switch yours on too,' he shouted. 'It's better than nothing. And call for backup. We need everyone here. I'm going to help Zakis.'

'What?' yelled Bex. 'After everything he's done?'

'No one deserves to die like that. Not even Zakis. I've gotta do something. I've gotta find Du Val – try and plead with him to stop this. Now make that call . . . And don't follow me, Bex.'

He turned and sprinted off.

Bex spun round to watch Khan and the others. They hadn't budged. They were stood outside the cabin, helplessly gazing on. Some of the officers had their guns trained in the direction of the gallows. Pointless, but it gave them comfort.

'Why are you *stood there?*' yelled Bex. 'Why won't you help him?'

Khan shook his head. 'This isn't police business any more. We've done all we can.'

He looked afraid. *Actually* afraid. Even the marksmen wore faces of fear and hugged their rifles tightly.

Bex knew she was alone. She'd watched Jud disappear into the night, not knowing if she'd see him again. She felt the same fear and loneliness creeping up on her as she had in Hyde Park, moments before she'd been taken.

Du Val! She had to help Jud find him. But first she had to contact the CRYPT.

She threw her backpack on to the floor and fumbled frantically for her mobile. Finding it, she quickly keyed in the special code reserved for CRYPT emergencies.

A voice answered almost instantly.

'Name and number?'

'Bex De Verre, 214. Can you get me Bonati! I need to—'

'Location?'

'Marble Arch. Look, I need—'

'Incident report?'

The voice remained calm but purposeful. Bex should have known the drill. Emergency calls were rare, but when they happened, you had to keep to protocol. Facts only. And quickly.

She reported the scene to the CRYPT operator. The situation sounded unreal as she relayed it down the phone. Was this really happening? She put in a request for as many agents as they could muster. Now! Straight to the site.

'And Bonati!' she added. 'You've gotta get Bonati!'

'The clarion call will go to all staff and agents, and the GPS signal will locate you. Agents will be there soon. Stay safe.'

'OK,' said Bex. '214 out.'

'CRYPT out.'

She switched off the phone and threw it into her bag. *Stay safe?* If Jud was going in to save Zakis, there was no way he was doing it alone. They'd formed a bond in the last few days, strong enough to prevent Bex from standing by and watching while her partner faced danger.

She turned to Khan and his men, standing helplessly several feet away. They'd not even budged.

'Inspector!' she shouted.

'Yeah?'

'Agents are on their way. When they get here, tell them to set up their neutralisers as close as they can.'

'Their *what?*'

'Neutralisers!' Bex was getting impatient. 'They'll understand. Just *do* it!'

She swung the rucksack on to her back, picked up the two neutralisers and headed off into the darkness after Jud.

'Sir, surely we should go in after them?' said one of the officers to Khan.

He shook his head. 'There's nothing *we* can do. This is their job. It's what they're trained for.'

Khan knew, because Bonati had told him enough times, that his guns would be useless against the electrical plasma that made up ghosts. They might restructure the plasma momentarily – like throwing a stone into a pond and watching the ripples run – but they wouldn't kill them. They were dead already – just electrical impulses and highly charged plasma. Their hearts didn't beat, so their blood wouldn't pour.

There was nothing Khan could do now, except wait, and prevent Silverman from sloping off.

He turned to face him, cowering in the corner near the cabin. The politician was glugging from another whisky bottle he'd found inside.

Khan turned back towards the gallows. He saw that the hangman was preparing the scaffold. His body shuddered in remembrance of the encounter at the Angel.

He watched as the ghost placed a rope over the girder perched horizontally between two struts. He could just make out the chilling sight of the noose at one end. Was this really being prepared for Zakis?

And where was Jud? Khan's eyes tried to scan the semi-darkness for him, but it was impossible. And what about the girl? Had she gone in after him? You had to hand it to these kids, he thought. They had guts.

And then he saw the hangman remove another rope from his great shoulders and begin tying it to the girder a few feet from the first one. Was he preparing a second noose?

For whom?

The wind had picked up even more strongly and now rattled around the site. The tarpaulin, still clinging to the site's perimeter fencing, flapped furiously. With no men on site, Harrison had turned the floodlights off. It was a waste of energy. The only light spilling on to the muddy ground came from the silvery beams from the waxing crescent above, and the orange glow of the distant streetlamps of Oxford Street. To the south, the darkness of Hyde Park hung low. The intensity of the moon's rays fluctuated as the squally wind blew clouds across its path. At times, the whole site was plunged into darkness before relief came from the silvery light.

Jud was surrounded.

Bony fingers jabbed and scraped. Sinewy arms pushed him, working together, moving him in one direction. They'd seen him moments after his discussion with Bex and flocked towards him.

Now, gaze fixed on the ground so as not to be blinded by the piercing, demonic glow of the sets of eyes peering at him, he allowed his body to go limp. He knew from his encounter at St Sepulchre's that resistance was futile. There was no way he could compete with one highly charged ghost, let alone a crowd of them.

His only option was to allow them to carry him towards the gallows. He'd hoped this would happen. He wanted it to. Only from up on the scaffold could he scan the site for Du Val, call his name and beckon him to come forward. It would be his last chance. His final moments.

He closed his eyes and tried to shut out the noise of the clicking and ticking that rattled into his ears. But it was too loud. Too invasive.

Instead he found himself focusing even harder on the strange pattern of clicks that was emerging from the ghosts' mouths. There was a regular beat to it, which he'd not been aware of before.

The individual sounds were blending together. Forming patterns. Words even.

He strained to listen, using his sixth sense. He was connecting to them. He was listening; and they were communicating.

What *were* they saying?

Gradually the words formed themselves into some semblance of meaning. And the chilling truth revealed itself:

'*Hang 'im! Hang 'im! Hang 'im!*'

The procession pushed Jud onwards as the hangman finished tying the second noose.

Bex was running low, stooping close to the ground. Scrabbling in the dirt. As she drew nearer to the crowd of ghosts, she knelt on the floor and began crawling. She kept her distance and crawled past the edge of the angry mob, moving around them. She was headed in one direction only.

The gallows.

Like Khan, she too had seen the hangman preparing the second rope. And she'd guessed for whom it was intended. She'd heard the swell of noise after Jud had disappeared. Though she hadn't heard Jud himself – he would never scream – she knew that the rise in excitement could only mean one thing. They'd seized him.

There was a sudden growling noise in the distance, like a pack of wild cats. The roars ricocheting off buildings beyond the site.

Motorbikes?

Bex stopped. She looked back in the direction of the site entrance, the gates just visible in the gloom.

Then the halogen headlamps splattered silvery-blue rays across the fencing.

The agents were here.

Bex paused. Was there time to run all the way back to the gates and brief them? She looked quickly in the direction of the gallows.

There wasn't.

Her mind spinning into overdrive, she threw her rucksack to

the floor and opened it. A few seconds of frenetic fumbling and her hand stumbled over the hard cylindrical shape of the handheld laser flare. She grabbed it and gave it a sharp twist at the top. The patch of sky above her was lit up with a red glow.

The agents saw it. Staying on their bikes, seven of them sped off in her direction, sending great muddy splashes across the site and catching the boots and trousers of Khan and his marksmen as they passed.

Khan spun around.

'What the hell?'

'They're with me!' Bex shouted out over to them, the red shaft of light soaring from her hand into the night sky.

There was a screech of brakes as a muddy torrent engulfed Bex's rucksack.

Grace was the first to remove her helmet.

'What's happened, Bex? What *is* that?' She was pointing towards the makeshift gallows.

Quickly Bex filled Grace and the others in. Their faces were incredulous. It was unbelievable. But there was no time for debating it.

'Get out your neutralisers,' Bex ordered, 'Find somewhere out of sight and start reducing the ghosts' power. We've gotta weaken them.'

She started running off.

'Where are *you* going?' said Grace.

'I'm gonna distract him.'

'Who?'

'The hangman!'

And she was gone.

Grace was about to follow her – she didn't want a repeat of Hyde Park – but the others grabbed her.

'You heard what she said,' said Luc. 'Get your neutraliser out!'

* * *

Fumbling her way through the darkness – her eyes trying to adjust after she'd told the agents to turn their bike lights off to avoid unsettling the ghosts further – Bex finally reached the gallows. The great hulking figure of the hangman was about twenty feet away to her right. He was facing the audience of ghosts, all of whom were baying and screaming and clicking. She too had now sensed the meaning of their calls.

If Jud wanted to find Du Val, fine, but there was no way he could do that with a rope around his neck. She had to distract the executioner. Then sabotage the gallows. Break the rope.

She crouched behind the platform and peered over it.

Over to her left, she saw a figure on the wooden floor.

It was Zakis.

He was crouched down, his hands hugging his knees tightly to his chest, and rocking uncontrollably, like a crazed animal. His head was buried in his arms, as if to shut out the appalling horror that was enveloping him. His hair looked bedraggled and bloody, and his clothes were ripped and blackened.

Why wasn't he trying to escape? thought Bex.

Then she saw. He'd been tied up like some performing bear. Discarded cabling that littered the site had been wound around his feet, cutting into his ankles like a tourniquet, and tethering him to a giant girder. He was going nowhere.

She looked to her right.

A sinking feeling struck her stomach and made the blood drain from her veins.

It was Jud.

They were carrying him to his death like a pig on a stick. Only this pig wasn't dead; it was writhing and lashing about frantically. There was no way Jud was going without a fight.

His boots were crashing into the ghosts' skulls. But they just clung on to his limbs and shoulders. More ghosts came and held him tightly, pulling his limbs out, stretching him. He was held aloft, on his back, staring up at the dark sky, like a sacrificial animal being led to the altar. The bellman had now moved to Jud's procession and was ringing the bell as they brought the condemned man to the scaffold.

'Hang 'im! Hang 'im!'

He was being raised up on to the platform now, where the hangman stood ready and waiting.

Jud ceased his protests. His body was beaten. Strength had finally left him. He allowed the ghosts to heave him on to the stage. Slowly he staggered to his feet and opened his eyes.

The giant face of the hangman was staring into his.

'I reckon we got ourselves a second 'anging tonight.'

The noise from the spectral crowd rose to a deafening level and then gradually subsided.

A rank smell of rotting flesh wafted through Jud's nostrils.

The hangman went for him. Threw him to the floor, just a few feet away from Zakis. Jud landed on his injured shoulder and winced in pain. Zakis turned his bruised face and tried to open his battered eyes to see him.

The sight was horrific. Zakis's face seemed more ghost-like than human now – drained of colour, and swollen unrecognisably.

'It's over,' he choked.

But Jud shook his head. Then he turned to scan the site below him. Where was Du Val?

And where were the agents?

He'd seen the lights from the bikes plough in through the gates moments earlier, and had prayed it was them. But now there was darkness again. Where were they?

And were their neutralisers on? Were they working?

The hangman turned to finish preparing the ropes.

Jud scoured the site. Ghosts were cramming into every space around the stage. And they didn't seem to be weakening. There was no point in trying to run.

Besides, he *had* to end this. No one else would. Or could.

In the seconds he had left, he *had* to raise Du Val.

But would the crowd hear him? Or understand him?

He'd not realised how high the noise levels would rise once he was on the platform.

He slowly rose to his feet again, his legs scratched and bruised from the ghosts' handling.

The hangman was still at the gallows, teasing the crowd, as he often did in life. Showing them how difficult his job was. How much skill was required to prepare the nooses, getting the length of the rope just right so his guests would swing. Building up the suspense. He was an entertainer.

Jud seized his moment and moved to the front of the platform.

'Du Val!' he hollered. 'Claude Du Val. Show yourself!'

The ghostly figures below him – some thirty or forty of them now – chattered and clicked excitedly. Their mantra, 'Hang 'im, hang 'im!' rose further still.

'Du Val!' Jud bawled over the din. 'We ask you to show yourself.'

The hangman, hearing Jud's cries, made a move for him from behind. He'd intended to dispatch him second, but here he was volunteering to go first.

So be it.

He approached Jud.

And then the hangman fell.

His left leg had plunged right down through the makeshift floor of wooden planks and bits of metal. A gaping hole had appeared between the loose floorboards and he had stepped into it.

As he tied to stagger to his feet, another hole appeared in the floor and he sank down further, the jagged fringe of the hole jabbing into his chest. Both of his legs had disappeared right through the floor. He swivelled around angrily, looking for somewhere solid to press his hands down and pull himself up again, but everywhere he touched the planks were disappearing.

Bex scurried out from under the platform and returned to her hiding place at the back of the gallows. The planks she'd dislodged right across the stage were doing their job. Parting like gates. Falling like matchsticks. Beckoning their victim into the murky depths below.

It had been a risky strategy. She'd not known whether it was going to be the hangman or Jud or Zakis who would fall through, but someone would. She'd booby-trapped enough planks to cause something to happen.

As she watched, she saw the hangman struggle, lash out with his giant fists and then disappear. Right through the stage and down into the muddy sludge below.

Jud had his reprieve. But it wouldn't be for long, she knew that. The hangman would return, unless the neutralisers that she had stationed on the ground below the stage worked their magic. Only time would tell.

Jud quickly spun round at the shocking sound of the hangman's fall. His eyes scanned the scene, trying to understand what had just happened.

And then he saw Bex.

'Go on!' she said. 'Call for Du Val.'

He allowed a momentary smile to form on his cracked and blackened lips. He said, 'Thank you, Bex. Agents are here?'

'Yeah, they're neutralising now. But it's taking time.'

'Go and get them. Find a way through the crowd and bring them below the stage. We have to focus on the hangman. If he's gone, no one else will conduct the hangings. They never did back then and I don't believe they will now. Go!'

But Bex wasn't moving.

'You coming?' she said.

Jud shook his head. 'It's time to raise him.'

'Du Val?'

'Yeah. Now go! Before the hangman finds you.'

She ran off into the shadows.

The cries from the ghosts had faded slightly. They were no longer calling for a hanging. The disappearance of the hangman had left them dazed and confused. This was not what was meant to happen. Never at Tyburn. Like children they looked at one another, awaiting instruction. The hangman had been the ringmaster. The entertainer and executioner all in one.

Jud knew he didn't have long. He could hear the great hulk below him hurling planks of wood around and stumbling to his feet in the slippery sludge.

He shouted at the top of his voice once again:

'Du Val! *Du Val!* Show yourself to us! It's over now. This is your site. Your resting place. We've disturbed your earth and we are sorry.'

The ghosts on the ground below him were alive with energy again.

They'd seen him. Behind Jud.

He was climbing the scaffold.

The hangman was coming back. The neutralisers weren't working quickly enough.

Jud shouted once again in desperation: 'Du Val!'

In the shadows, Bex was rounding up agents.

'Come on!' she said.

When she had left them before, they'd run off to position themselves in a ring around the ghosts, each pointing their neutraliser into the crowd, waiting to see signs that they were weakening.

'Let's go. It's not working from here. You're too far away. We need to get to the centre. To the gallows. We need to get beneath it and focus the neutralisers up on to the stage. We'll neutralise the hangman. But we need everyone to do it. Follow me.'

She turned to face the gallows and saw that the hangman was back on his feet.

'Quick!' she yelled.

She led them back the way she'd come. Back into the shadows and on towards the splintered, muddy mess that stretched beneath the gallows.

Just like at the Angel, the hangman was swelling up again and radiating electrical energy at phenomenal levels. Anger and revenge ran through his body, hardening the plasma. Glowing like some demonic effigy.

Treading carefully to avoid the holes in the fractured stage, he picked up a large wooden pallet - several were strewn across the site from the forklift deliveries - and placed it beneath the two ropes.

The crowds were screeching again in triumph. They would get their hangings.

This was it.

Jud had had his chance. Du Val had not shown himself. He was on his own. The hangman seized his arm.

'It's your time,' he said.

His iron grip worked its way between the tendons and the muscles in Jud's arm. It was like being caught in a vice. The pain soared up his arm and added to the agony from his injured shoulder.

He tried to rip away. There was no way he was going to the gallows quietly.

He lashed and kicked like a salmon on the end of a line. Thrashing about. But the hangman's grip was too much. He'd never release him. Not this time.

As the hangman brought him nearer to the rope and placed it around his neck, still gripping tightly on to his arm, Jud felt the blood run from his veins. He'd paled to a sickly white.

The great rope felt heavy and sharp. Frayed ends dug into his neck like needles. The hangman tightened it. And kept tightening.

Was it to happen now?

Was this it? So sudden.

Jud closed his eyes and tried hard to picture the soft face of his mother. But the noise and the pain and the sharp sensations from the rope denied his brain the luxury of imagination. Her face wouldn't come.

He was alone.

Satisfied that the rope was tight enough to hold Jud in position, the hangman made for the condemned man slumped in the corner. He untied the cord holding him.

Zakis was pleading now. All the aggression, the greed, the power, it meant nothing here.

Just as he'd done with Jud, the hangman seized him and dragged him to the waiting rope. Zakis's last-ditch attempts at resistance were useless. Energy had left him anyway.

The cries from Zakis's bloodied lips penetrated into Jud's brain as the hangman strung him up. The fear in his voice ignited the same emotion in Jud – a rare sensation, but one so acute he felt like retching. Bile rose to his throat and he swallowed hard. His hands now shook and his heart felt like it was going to explode out of his chest.

His mouth went dry. He could feel his legs weakening.

Stay strong.

He gazed out at the scene. A savagely torn-up tract of land, with its forgotten souls leaking out like pus. A rancid place.

He saw the cabin in the distance and could just make out the outlines of people – Khan and his men, staring, motionless.

More headlamps lit up the far side of the site, near the entrance.

It didn't matter who it was. It was too late.

The hangman raised a giant boot to the wooden pallet they

were standing on, ready to kick it away and send the condemned men swinging.

Jud closed his eyes.

Their eyes fixed intently on the gallows, Khan and his men hadn't noticed the shadowy figure creeping away behind them.

Another few yards and he'd made it. The gates were already open, so it was easy.

Silverman made the dash running backwards, keeping his eye on Khan in the distance.

He didn't notice the car, approaching at speed from Oxford Street.

Bright, silvery halogen lights: a black Maserati.

Bonati and Goode.

When the clarion call had come through, Bonati was at the heliport, collecting Goode – he'd been away on a short business trip that afternoon, and the professor had chosen to collect him himself. That way he'd be able to fill him in on Khan's confession. But neither of them had expected the call they'd received on their way back to the CRYPT.

Instantly they'd headed over in Goode's own car – the fastest one they had. And they'd rallied Vorzek to find any more agents she could and head over too.

The Maserati screeched up to the site gates.

But Goode hadn't seen Silverman.

He hit him hard. He bounced off the black bonnet and dropped to the floor like a stone.

Goode got out and rolled him over.

'Silverman!' He recognised him from the video footage in his office.

He quickly checked he was breathing. Just.

Seeing the lights and hearing the arrival of the car, Khan now approached the open gates.

He saw Bonati and shouted, 'I think you better get inside!' Then he motioned to Silverman. 'Leave this rat to me.'

More headlamps lit up the roadside – Vorzek, in a black, long-wheel-based Land Rover, with more agents. They jumped out and Bonati told them all to follow him quickly through the gates. Vorzek instructed the agents to switch on their neutralisers. And to expect the unexpected.

An officer met them and pointed to where the gallows were, deeper into the site. They passed the abandoned cabin and the other officers.

'What the hell are you doing?' shouted Goode. 'Just watching? What are you? Spectators, huh?'

An officer spoke calmly. 'We were instructed to stay here, sir. We were told—'

Ignoring him, Bonati ran towards the crowd of figures in the distance and the strange construction they were gathered around. As he and Goode approached, followed by the others, the true significance of the scene hit them. The strange emergency call from Bex had been accurate.

This was a seventeenth-century hanging.

The moon reappeared from behind the clouds, casting silver rays across the gallows, unveiling the identities of the men condemned to hang.

Zakis and Jud.

'Oh no,' cried Goode. 'Please, *no*!'

Bex and her team were just arriving at the platform. It had taken an age to reach it, dashing in and out of shadows, giving the crowd a wide berth so as not to arouse yet more attention. Bex had said they didn't want any more agents carted off to the scaffold.

They reached the space beneath the stage, a foul swamp of mud and filth and broken planks of wood. The moon's wash penetrated through the gaps in the floor above them, giving the hollow space a chilling feel. Above them and all around they could hear the cries of the crowd. There wasn't one agent in the group who needed to ask for a translation. The noise – just clicks and rattles and cries to the adults at the site – rang through their senses and morphed into that familiar call.

They placed their neutralisers on wooden planks and struts and anywhere they could find a good footing. Then, under Bex's instructions, they set about dismantling the stage.

Suddenly Grace shrieked.

'Wait! I can see Jud.' She was peering up through a gap. 'He's at the bloody scaffold! Oh God, oh no! It's too late. The rope's on him!'

The others came and crowded around her, staring through the space above them.

She was right. In the time Bex had spent searching for the agents, Jud had been strung up, along with Zakis.

'We can't dislodge the stage,' cried Bex desperately, her voice cracking with fear now. 'If we collapse the floor beneath him, he'll . . .' She couldn't say the words. But they all knew it. Gravity would take its victims.

They *had* to keep the floor intact.

Goode ran towards the crowd, tears in eyes and a tremble in his body. His boy was up there. He *had* to save him.

'*No*, Jason!' shouted Bonati, chasing after him.

'I've gotta do something. I gotta—'

Bonati caught him and held him. Goode struggled in desperation.

The professor tried to stay calm, though the situation, and the sight of his old friend in pieces like this, brought a lump to his throat.

'You can't!' he said. 'Don't you see? Jason, listen to me! *Please!* If we go in there now and disturb them, they'll get frightened and carry out the hanging even quicker. We'll lose him, Jason! *Jason!*'

The other agents joined him, with Vorzek, and together they held Goode back. He was roaring like an animal now. This was not going to be how he would lose his son. Not now. Not here.

'Get off me! Get off! *Now!*'

'He's right, Jason,' Vorzek pleaded over the top of his cries. 'If we dash in and shock them they'll do it even quicker. We have to approach them slowly.'

'Where the hell are Bex and the other agents?' demanded Bonati, holding Jason and staring at Vorzek. 'I thought some were dispatched immediately? Where are they?'

'I don't know, Giles,' said Vorzek. 'But we have to trust them. They'll be there. They'll save him.'

Jud could feel the rope burning red tracks into his neck. The rain had not ceased and his body was like a damp rag. But he sniffed away fear. He would face this with the same courage he'd always shown. He gritted his teeth and clenched his jaws.

The hangman was distracted by the lights that had spanned the sky across the site near the gates. His face was confused. The circular halogen headlamps of the Maserati, and the Land Rover that had followed, had seemed animal-like to him.

But as quickly as the strange beasts had entered his vision, their illuminated eyes had vanished. Darkness had returned, and the crowd below him were getting impatient.

With a grin he swung his giant boot back once again, ready to kick the crate away.

Jud and Zakis breathed a final breath.

There was a thunderous shot.

The hangman turned.

It was a deafening crack that silenced the crowd.

Slowly Jud opened his eyes. In the distance he could see the crowd of police officers, still frozen with fear and desperation. Had the shot come from them? The ghosts below him were in a frenzy.

There was another ear-splitting crack. Even closer now.

Across the site, the armed marksmen readied their guns and looked in every direction. No one had fired.

Up on the gallows the hangman caught the butt end of a giant pistol clean in the face. The force pushed his huge frame backwards and he fell off the back of the weakened stage. Fragments of wood and metal collapsed over him. The agents beneath the platform saw the great body land.

'He's fading!' shouted Grace. It was true. The combined force of the neutralisers was working. The hangman's body was weakening.

But giant splinters of wood were dropping from the stage fast.

'We've gotta get out!' shouted Luc. 'It's going to collapse.'

'No!' shouted Bex. 'What about Jud! If the floor gives way, that's it!'

'Come on!' Grace said. 'We're no good to him trapped underneath it. We've gotta get out there. Quick!'

They ran out into the shadows, behind the crumbling scaffold.

Jud tried to look to his left, to see who'd made the shot, as the rope dug further into his skin. He perched precariously on the crate beneath him, praying it wouldn't give way just yet. It had lurched to the left and he was now standing on tiptoes to keep the rope slack.

He saw a tall, dark figure. It spun round. A handsome, striking face, even in death. Defined jaw, piercing eyes, framed in black curls.

Claude Du Val stepped up and faced the crowd.

His presence swept across the mob like a cult leader. They knew him. They loved him. In death, just as in life, the crowds jostled and fought for a clear glimpse of the most famous highwayman of them all. The stories, the legends. The games played by the urchins who'd grown up with tales of their hero. And now, spanning centuries, the mythical figure had come. Like a king of Tyburn. This was his throne.

'Enough!' Jud heard him cry in a deep, throaty voice. 'We have our Tyburn! This is our right. Our grave. And now we have it back.'

They were listening, in obedience.

Just metres away, Bonati and the others had stopped. They too were listening.

'Who's that?'

'What's happening?'

'What's going on?'

The adults had failed to glean any words from the mass of clicking and ferocious insect-like noises that rang across the site. But the agents with them could understand everything.

Nik, who'd joined Vorzek on the second wave, said, 'Whoever he is, he's telling them to leave. Saying they've got their site back.'

Du Val continued his speech. 'There shall be no more killing! No more hangings. This is *our* site.' He turned to face Jud at the rope.

'You heard what this boy said. They're leaving Tyburn and so must we. There shall be peace within us, at last. We shall be remembered now . . . It is *over!*'

Peering over the back of the platform, Bex and the others couldn't believe what their senses were telling them. They could hear the crowds repeating 'Over, over!'

'Did he just tell them to leave?' said Bex, needing reassurance that she wasn't dreaming.

'Yes,' said Grace, looking incredulously at the sight. 'I can hear him too. He's telling them to go.'

'She's right,' said Luc. 'He's telling them they've got their site back. They know it's over. Bex . . . Bex?'

But she'd already gone. The stage was still dismantling. The crate was wobbling. But Jud was going nowhere. She'd climbed the scaffold and grabbed his legs. Luc followed her and began loosening the great rope around his neck, while the others saw to Zakis.

'Now you owe me again,' Bex said, panting for breath.

They both turned and stared into the distance.

'They're going!' Grace shouted.

Du Val stood tall at the edge of the crumbling platform. Though he was a shadow of what he'd been in life, he still commanded respect. Adoration even. Jud and Zakis both stared at him, speechless, helpless. Exhausted.

Was it really over?

Du Val slowly stepped down from the platform, his pistol still raised to the sky, and disappeared into the crowd of adoring onlookers. They parted as he moved through them. They clambered to see him. Touch him. Watch him. The clicking sounds were fading steadily.

'My God!' said Jason Goode, staring across the site with the others. 'He's calmed them.'

'They're at peace,' said Vorzek, smiling through her tears.

The noises dissipated. The solid bodies that had housed the dark spirits were beginning to fade too, reducing to plasma one by one. Melding with the air. At peace.

The translucent shapes were dancing. Swirling in the wind.

Then they followed Du Val into the shadows.

And beyond.

CHAPTER 49

THREE MONTHS LATER

TYBURN SITE, MARBLE ARCH

Bex raised her face to the sun and closed her eyes. The steady hum of daytime traffic blended with the singing of the birds in the trees and the clacking heels of the busy shoppers heading for Oxford Street. At the other end of the bench, Jud glanced across at the traffic through the black railings. The sunshine brightened and he cupped a hand over his eyes. The great white arch above them cast a shadow over the ground.

'Ironic, isn't it?' said Bex.

'What is?'

'Zakis and his gang.'

'What about them?'

'Well, him and Silverman, and Khan, I mean they're all still awaiting trial, aren't they?'

'I think so,' said Jud.

'And they didn't get bail, did they?'

'You're joking. In custody, the lot of them.' He knew well that deals were being struck. Zakis, just like the others, would be offered a much shorter sentence in return for his silence.

'And the trial's going to be at the Old Bailey, isn't it?'

'Yeah, bound to be. At least for Silverman and Zakis. I think

Khan's going to be dealt with more quietly. Bonati wants to keep him on side. He might be useful.'

'So it's ironic,' said Bex, smiling. 'Zakis and his friends will be sat in the cells below the Old Bailey.'

'Don't tell me,' said Jud. 'On the site of Newgate prison. Brilliant. That's justice for you.'

Bex gazed up at the cottonwool clouds as they floated serenely across the sky.

'Hard to imagine it now,' she said.

'Yeah.'

'I mean, it doesn't seem real. Like it never happened.'

'It's often like that,' said Jud. 'As the days and weeks pass, you find yourself questioning whether it ever actually happened at all.'

'Exactly.' Bex looked across at the commuters leaving the gloom of the tube station and squinting in the brightness outside. 'But those poor people,' she said, 'I mean the ones we lost. The innocent ones who died.'

Jud gazed at her. 'I know,' he said gently. 'It seems so wrong.'

A gentle wind rustled through the trees above their heads and Bex looked over towards Hyde Park. A prickly shiver began in the base of her neck and ran down her spine. She wasn't sure if it was a mood she was sensing on the wind, or a memory of something inside.

'It could've been me,' she said.

'I know.'

'It just seems such a waste. Those lives. The victims had nothing to do with him. With Zakis and his greed.'

Jud thought for a moment. 'If we've learned anything from Tyburn, it's that you can't ignore the past when you're building for the future. I mean, you can't just bulldoze your way through life. Land has *memories*. You have to respect it. Wherever it is.'

Bex giggled. 'Very profound, Professor.'

'Yes. I thought so too.' He nodded.

They both laughed, then sat in silent thought for a while. Jud rose from the bench and beckoned for Bex to follow him. They strolled beneath Marble Arch as the traffic of Oxford Street droned steadily behind them.

Up ahead, the Tyburn Memorial sent shadows across the ground beneath it. The twenty-foot-high bronze gallows soared above newly clipped turf.

Bex approached it and read the plaque once again.

This memorial is to the thousands of people who were hanged here at Tyburn. Some may have been guilty of their crimes; others were not. May their souls rest in peace for ever.

Read a sneak preview of

CRYPT
COVERT RESPONSE YOUTH PARANORMAL TEAM

TRAITOR'S REVENGE

Out March 2012

WEDNESDAY: 3RD NOVEMBER

HOUSES OF PARLIAMENT, WESTMINSTER, 7.01 P.M.

'So what's the problem?'

'I saw someone down in the basement.'

'There's nothin' unusual in that, Kev,' said Mike. 'There's always someone down there. Probably working on the pipes. You know what the heating's like in this place.'

'I've checked the record,' said Kev. 'There was no one scheduled to do work in that area today. Look, just wait will you? Watch this. You'll see.'

'See *what*?' Mike was getting impatient. He'd just started his shift and was waiting for Kevin to sign off and leave him in peace. He'd got his coffee, his new magazine and his iPod. He was hoping for a quiet night.

The two men were squeezed into one of several security cabins flanking the rear gates to Westminster. Kevin looked tired and jaded from staring at the bank of screens all day. He was glad Mike had arrived to take over the shift, and was looking forward to getting home, but he had to show someone what he'd just seen. He needed a second opinion. It had been so strange after all. Had the job finally got to him – was he now seeing things?

The work was monotonous but well paid. And he'd been there fifteen years this year, though the place was unrecognizable compared with back then. Since the global threat of terrorism had engulfed the country, the dark security buildings surrounding the Houses of Parliament had been constantly added to so that the complex now resembled a village in silhouette, surrounded by a maze of black, concrete barriers. And at the centre of it all, still untouched, the gothic masterpiece – the vision of architect Charles Barry. The home of democracy.

'Come on, Kev, what're you tryin' to show me?'

'You'll see.'

Kev released his finger from the skip button and the action returned to normal pace. There was definitely someone there. Down in the basement, below Central Lobby.

'Big deal,' said Mike. 'So someone's down there. How long have you been working here, Kev? Honestly, sometimes it seems like I'm the experienced one and *you're* the new guy.'

Kevin just smiled to himself. He knew what was coming.

'Just wait,' he said.

They stared at the screen as the digital seconds flashed by in the corner. The images became pixilated at times and the screen flickered occasionally. There seemed to be some elecrical disturbance down there. But they could both see the shape of a man moving about. He had his back to the camera. It was hard to make out but it wasn't a particularly unusual sight. The flickering seemed strange but nothing alarming.

'Like I said, Kev, probably just inspecting the pipes or somethin'.'

'But—'

'Yeah, don't tell me,' said Mike. 'You said there's no record of it in the work book, but he probably just thought he'd inspect that area while he was down there. I can't see his face from this angle but I bet it's one of the regular guys. And his equipment's probably interfering with the CCTV. So what? Look, Kev, if you don't mind I really wannt get set up for tonight. You can clock off now. There's a programme on the radio about to start and I—'

Mike stopped. And stared at the screen.

'Holy shit,' he said. 'How did he do that?'

WEDNESDAY: 3RD NOVEMBER

ALL SAINT'S CHURCH, YORK, 7.58 P.M.

The icy wind was whipping up again and Fiona pulled her coat tight around her chest. Her damp hair was blowing across her face and a droplet of water was forming on the end of her nose. She watched her steps carefully. The old pavements were uneven at the best of times, but with a light covering of snow on them, slowly freezing now in the night air, they were especially hazardous. Her work shoes didn't help, but her boots would have looked stupid with the skirt she'd chosen for work that morning. Vanity won over safety, every time.

Coppergate was quiet tonight. Maybe it was the weather, thought Fiona. It really was bitterly cold. Everyone would be safely tucked up at home by now, in front of their TV sets, mugs of cocoa in their hands (or a gin and tonic in Fiona's case). But it had been a chaotic day, with back-to-back clients all morning and then a case in court in the afternoon, which meant she hadn't even started to catch up on her correspondence until teatime. No wonder she was running late.

She walked on against the wind, in the direction of the car park down on Stonebow.

Just time for one quick fag.

She stopped to fish for her cigarettes in the trendy but oversized tote bag which went everywhere with her.

Rooting through its random contents, trying to ind her lighter too, she dropped her phone on the floor. Thank goodness she'd just bought that fancy case for it – the one her kids had teased her about. She knew it was worth having.

She stooped to pick it up.

Cigarettes located, she placed one to her lips and tried to

light it on the move. The wind kept extinguishing the flame within seconds. She stopped, and cupped her hands around the lighter, cradling the bright flame.

She sucked on the cigarette, inhaled her first lungful of smoke for the day, and pocketed the lighter again.

Her eyes were blinded momentarily by the brightness of the flame. But then, as they readjusted to the light, Fiona saw something which made her stop.

And scream.

The handbag fell from her hands, spewing its contents across the floor as it dropped. A lipstick rolled into the road.

For a second Fiona stood there incredulous. Frozen to the spot. Then she regained her survival instinct and turned to run. But her ankle slid out from under her on the slippery curb and she dropped like a stone onto her back. Her head struck the edge of the curbside as she fell.

She was out cold.

A few steps ahead, outside the church of All Saint's Pavement, there was a figure.

It wasn't walking purposefully. It was staggering aimlessly around the small garden, bumping into the solid oak door and crashing into the stone porch.

But it wasn't the reckless behaviour of the figure that had frightened Fiona.

It was the fact that it was headless.

WEDNESDAY: 3RD NOVEMBER

WESTMINSTER, 8.16 P.M.

The evening traffic was heavy down Victoria Embankment. Jud wove the Fireblade around the taxis and cars like a slalom.

He felt impatient, as usual. Bonati rarely gave much information away when he sent agents to a haunting. He liked them to arrive with an open mind and let their ESP work its magic free of influence and speculation.

All Bonati had said was: 'Get down to the Houses of Parliament, Jud. I want you to go and watch some TV.'

Jud had replied facetiously that watching television was precisely what he'd been doing at the time, along with Luc. And what was so special about the televisions at Westminster anyway? But the professor hadn't appreciated this humour. The film would have to wait.

But the patchy details he'd been given about this sighting in the basement amounted to no more than a security guard not doing his job properly – at least it seemes that way to Jud. Of course, he knew there'd be more to it than that. Bonati was no fool.

The halogen headlights swung across the base of Big Ben and on towards Parliament Square. A sharp left into Katherine Street and soon Jud could see the long lines of concrete barriers leading to Victoria Tower, the tallest part of Westminster Palace. Strange that a building with towers over three hundred feet tall can be protected by a four foot wall, thought Jud, as he pulled the Fireblade slowly up to the security office and dismounted.

A senior officer from the Palace of Westminster Division of the Met' took Jud into the nearest security cabin, where Kevin and Mike were still staring at the screens.

'This is Mr Lester' said the officer. 'He's here to ask you some questions.'

Looks about twelve, thought Kevin. 'Oh, right,' he said, trying to hide his surprise. 'And why is he—'

'We don't need questions from you, Kevin. We need answers. Just show him the tape, please.'

Jud could sense there'd been an argument in the room already. He guessed this wasn't the first time voice had been raised tonight. An intruder in the basement at Westminster represented a serious breach of security and someone would pay.

'You'll be touring the basement with us shortly,' said the officer, 'But first you need to watch this.'

Kevin had already prepared the CCTV footage. He pressed play once again and Jud watched the screen. It looked like any other basement in a large complex of offices: pipes and elecrical wiring; generators and boilers; air conditioning units with giant metal pipes feeding from them and disappearing down the long corridor in the centre of the screen.

And then Jud saw the figure come into view.

It was obviously a man, his back to the camera, shuffling around.

'So this is it?' he said.

'Yeah. That's him.'

'Ok,' said Jud, becoming impatient. 'So you've had an intruder. And you've already checked and there shouldn't have been an engineer in that area today. So you don't know who he is. It's a serious breach, I can see that, but I don't—'

'Sorry,' the officer interrupted. 'I think you should wait a moment. You haven't seen what he does next.'

Jud sighed and stared back at the screen. He slumped in the chair and wished he was back at the CRYPT with Luc, finishing the action film they'd started.

And then suddenly he sat upright. He'd seen it. The reason why the CRYPT had been called. The reason why this was no ordinary breach of security.

The dark figure shuffling around the basement had stopped momentarily, turned, and then passed right through the wall.